THE TYCOON'S TEMPORARY BRIDE

BILLIONAIRE BRIDES OF GRANITE FALLS

ANA E ROSS

CEDAR TREES PUBLISHERS

THE TYCOON'S TEMPORARY BRIDE

Copyright © 2012 by Ana E Ross
ISBN: 9780988367975
Cedar Trees Publishers

All rights reserved. Except for brief quotes used in reviews, no portion of this story may be used or reproduced in any form by any electronic, mechanical, or any other device now known or invented hereafter without the written permission of the author. These forms include, but are not limited to xerography, photocopying, scanning, recording, distributing via Internet means, informational storage or retrieval system.

This story is a work of fiction. All names, characters, places, and incidents are the products of the author's imagination and are used fictitiously. Similarities to actual events, locales, business establishments, or persons living or dead, are purely coincidental.

Edited by Crazy Diamond Editing
Cover Design by Najla Qamber Designs

ISBN: 9780988367975
ISBN-13: 978-0-9883679-7-5

www.anacross.com

ALSO BY ANA E ROSS

Billionaire Brides of Granite Falls Series

The Doctor's Secret Bride

The Mogul's Reluctant Bride

The Playboy's Fugitive Bride

The Tycoon's Temporary Bride

With These Four Rings: Wedding Bonus

Beyond Granite Falls Series

Loving Yasmine

Desire's Chase

Pleasing Mindy

Billionaire Island Brides Series

Seduced by Passion (2022)

To my lovely daughter, Nicoya, who tells me she's proud of me more often than I deserve.

CHAPTER ONE

Tashi Holland took a deep breath of the summer air as she exited one of her favorite shops at Stone Crest Shopping Mall Outlets. Bags in hand, she strolled along the walkway, wheeling her way through the throng of residents and tourists who frequented this delightful small town nestled in the foothills of the White Mountain National Forest of New Hampshire.

She headed for one of the many gazebos in the plaza and, setting her bags on a stone bench, she pulled her camera from her backpack and began clicking away at the breathtaking views of the shimmering waters of Crystal Lake and the green majestic mountains in the background.

Granite Falls was a long way from New York City, the place she'd gone to study photography, and even farther from Ohio—the place where she was born and raised, but never felt any real connection to. Granite Falls wasn't a bad town for settling down and starting over, but it was remote and lonely. Lonelier, because she hadn't made any friends and had spent the last few months trying to make sense of the events that had changed her life a year and a half ago.

Sometimes it felt like yesterday, and other times it felt like a lifetime. And then there were times when it felt as if it never even happened. She'd listened to the news and searched the Internet day and night for weeks, then months, trying to find evidence that her nightmares weren't just some figment of her imagination.

But there was nothing. Never anything—except for one fact.

Tashi sighed and, putting her camera away, she sat on the bench and folded her arms across the stone tabletop and indulged in her favorite pastime. Watching people mulling about and speculating about their lives had helped to keep her mind off her own lifeless existence.

Who was she, anyway? She was a girl with a name, and only a name. One she couldn't use. She couldn't open a bank account or use her credit cards. Her driver's license was useless since she couldn't rent or purchase a car, or even book a hotel room for a night.

She had the cell phone the FBI agent who'd rescued her had given her—her only communication to the world beyond Granite Falls' border—but she had no one to call, except the closest pizza parlor and Mountainview Café for occasional deliveries during the past cold winter nights. She kept her phone charged and protected like it was an infant, hoping and praying each day would be the one she would receive *that* one call she lived for—the call that would give her back her life.

Maybe she would never get her life back. Maybe they thought she'd died during the shootout in that house in New York City, fifteen months ago.

But then again, who were *they*?

She had no family. She'd never met her father. Her mother died when she was four, and then her uncle who'd raised her suddenly and unexpectedly lost his life to pancreatic cancer almost two years ago. She'd been alone and scared in the craziest city in the world until Scottie showed up. He'd seemed real and charming and had treated her like a princess until…

Tashi covered her face with her hands as visions of that night stormed into the forefront of her mind. Those visions never surfaced gently. They always came at her like a silent freight train speeding around a bend. She only knew it was there after it hit her.

What if Scottie was real, but the man who'd claimed he'd come to rescue her along with the others who were posing as guards and parents were just actors his real parents had hired to get rid of her? After all, she was a nobody, and Scottie was the heir to some multi-million-dollar corporation. Maybe they thought she wasn't good enough for their son. Tashi had watched enough movies to know that rich people could get away with almost anything. What if they were all fakes? Except…

She wrapped her arms around her middle as the pain seared through her. The one thing about that night that wasn't fake was the fact that she'd killed a man. She'd climbed undetected into the back seat, pointed a gun at the back of his head and pulled the trigger. *Twice.* Then she'd watched, numb from head to toe, as he slumped against the steering wheel. It was the blare of the horn that had propelled her into action. She'd pushed the dead man out of the car, and driven off.

His death was the only event that had made the news. It was described as a drug deal gone wrong. He'd left behind a wife and three young children. There were no suspects and last she'd read, the case had been closed.

What if killing the driver was the only real event about that night? What if Scottie's parents were using that incriminating fact as a means to keep her away from him? If the man who'd claimed to be an FBI agent had made it out alive, where was he?

He'd promised to find her and explain everything to her. What was 'everything'? What did he need to explain?

Tashi didn't know what to believe anymore. And here she was in a strange town where the agent had sent her in search of a man who was supposed to protect her. A man without a face and a name. Tashi scanned the crowds as she'd done countless times in the past months, hoping beyond hope that her *savior* would see her, recognize her, and help her.

He could be anybody, even that giant of a man with his arm around the petite woman as they pushed a set of twins in a double stroller. He reminded her of the FBI agent—large, dark, and handsome. The couple nodded and smiled at her as they walked past.

Tashi smiled back. She felt as if she's seen them somewhere before, but then she quickly averted her eyes as the woman said something to the man, and he turned and gave her another smile.

"She said you're very beautiful, and I agreed," the man said over his shoulder.

"Thank you. And so is she." Tashi's smile deepened, as the couple disappeared into the crowd.

One thing she could say about this town was that the majority of people were nice and friendly. They probably didn't think the same of her since she never made any attempts to engage in conversation, nor did she respond to personal questions about herself—legitimate questions people ask when they were interested in someone.

Not knowing whom she could trust, she trusted no one, not even Mindy, her garrulous neighbor, whose kids she'd babysat on a few occasions.

Tashi gathered her bags and left the gazebo. It was laundry day, and she didn't have a washer and dryer in her one-bedroom apartment—an apartment in the not-so-nice side of town. But it was the only place where the landlord would allow her to pay cash—no questions asked.

The FBI agent had given her a bag of cash and she'd carved out a hole in the back wall of her bedroom closet and hidden the bag inside it. It wasn't like she could take the money down to the local bank and make a deposit. Her closet was the safest place she could think of to hide it. She'd bought a piece of plywood, painted it white and leaned it up against the wall to hide the hole. Every time she left her apartment, Tashi worried about someone breaking in. But so far so good.

The car she'd driven to Granite Falls, and the gun with which she'd killed the man had become real estate for fish in the deepest parts of the Hudson and Aiken Rivers, respectively. She had enough money to last her a decade, if she spent it wisely. Hopefully, before it ran out, she'd have some answers to her past and be able to live a normal life.

Her stomach rumbled, reminding her that she'd had a light breakfast. Tashi smiled at the idea of enjoying a juicy, smoked ham sandwich from Mountainview Café, just two blocks over from the outlets. She would grocery shop tomorrow after her kickboxing class. On that thought, Tashi headed for the café.

Having no job, and no people to visit, she'd learned to spread out her outdoor excursions over several days, just to have a reason to leave her apartment, and keep herself from going crazy. It had been hard during the cold long winter months. Sometimes she didn't know which was worse—sitting in her apartment reading, or watching TV and snow fall through her window, or braving the freezing temperatures and trekking through snow banks to do her laundry and groceries. On milder days, she'd walk six blocks to the public library, curl up in front of a warm fire, and read. A few times, she'd even fallen asleep in one of the oversized comfortable chairs, only to wake up to face the long walk back and the destitution and isolation of her apartment.

Tashi prayed that something would change before winter came around again. She didn't think she could survive another six months of cold in this lonely town. She'd thought of leaving, but that promise from the FBI agent to find her and explain everything had kept her grounded. She didn't want to miss him when and if he ever came looking for her.

An hour later, Tashi placed some money next to her empty plate and grabbed her bags from the floor. As she stood up and spun around, she collided, head-on with a solid wall of hard muscle. She immediately felt strong arms close around her.

"Whoa…"

Was that thunder? Was this an earthquake?

Tashi stiffened as a flicker of fear rushed through her. Her face was pressed tightly against a hard expanse of human flesh that smelled so good. A man was holding her. A strange man.

You're a witness. They'll be looking for you. Don't trust anyone.

She panicked, her heart thundering as she fought against him. "No! No! Let me go!"

"Hey, take it easy. I was only trying to catch you before you fell flat on your pretty little face."

The man abruptly released her. Then he bent down and retrieved her bags that had fallen to the floor. He straightened up and handed them to her.

So it wasn't thunder. Tashi tilted her head back to gaze into a pair of the bluest, most intimate eyes she had ever seen.

Her heart did a double take and something hot sizzled through her stomach. More adrenaline rushed through her as she took a good look at him—from his waist-length wavy black hair to the tips of his black leather shoes. He wore designer jeans and a gray shirt. Or maybe they wore his tall, hard, sexy frame.

The food stains on the front of his shirt caused Tashi to look behind him where he'd parked a baby stroller. A little girl, who looked about two years old, was fast asleep inside it. Tashi took a long, deep breath as her panic subdued. He couldn't be one of the mob's men. He didn't look the type. They wouldn't be running around after her with a baby in tow. And how would they have found her, anyway?

"I'm—I'm sorry," she stuttered. "I really should look where I'm going."

"Don't apologize," he said in a deep, rumbling voice. "I'm the one who sneaked up on you. I hope I didn't hurt you." He gave her body a bold raking gaze, then his soft blue eyes came back to her face, and that something hot sizzled through the core of Tashi's body again. It was nothing like she'd experienced before.

Their eyes locked for tense moments as if they were both waiting for the other to make the next move.

"No. I'm fine." Tashi licked her lips that had suddenly become parched. She tugged her eyes from his, only to stare at his wide and generous mouth with lips that reminded her of blooming rosebuds. They were so pink and succulent.

She studied his face. It was passionate, beautiful, and irresistible, down to the narrow, hollow grove etched into the taut skin under his straight nose. His features were sculptured so perfectly, so symmetrically, that he was almost too beautiful for a man. *Italian? Greek?* Tashi took another look at the adorable baby-girl sleeping in the carriage.

He's married! Not that it really mattered. She wasn't looking for a husband. Heck, she wasn't even looking for a man. Well, she was, but she didn't know who that man was. She didn't know if he was supposed to be black or white, old or young, rich or poor... All she knew was that he should be single and his name began with an *A*. She didn't even know if the *A* stood for a first or last name.

"I—I have to go," she said in an awkward, tremulous voice.

He opened his mouth as if he were about to say something, but instead, he gave her a sensuous stare that made her heart turn over in response. Close Encounter of the Magnetic Kind, Tashi thought on a raspy breath as she hurried away. What a man! God, she didn't realize they made them like that. His appeal was extremely unsettling. She'd never been this affected by a man before. It was scary and exciting at the same time.

When she reached the sidewalk, Tashi looked back at the café to find him standing at the wall of glass in the front, looking at her. He smiled, and waved. She smiled, and waved back. His smile turned to a charming grin and it was then that Tashi felt as if she'd seen him before. It was the second time today that she'd run into slightly familiar faces.

For some reason, she didn't feel threatened by the man who was now watching her, especially when Miss Felicia, one of the owners of the café, came up and hugged him before bending over to pay attention to the child sleeping in the stroller. She was probably his mother-in-law, Tashi thought, since Miss Felicia was black, the man was white, and the baby had olive-toned skin, an indication that she was biracial or multiracial.

No, Tashi thought walking away, this man wasn't after her. Nevertheless, she decided not to head home, just in case he was tempted to follow her. She crossed the street and entered the supermarket. She'd do her laundry tomorrow. She didn't have her list, so it took longer than expected to get her shopping done.

With two bags filled with groceries, and two filled with additions to her new wardrobe, she exited the automatic sliding doors of the supermarket and froze. The tall handsome man was standing near the entrance, talking on his cell, his back to her. He must have heard her gasp, because he turned around and immediately ended his conversation. His dark shades obscured his eyes, hiding his expression from her. For all she knew, he could have been talking to the men who were after her, letting his boss know that he'd found her.

Real fear gripped Tashi this time. Scottie had been charming and sweet, just like this man, but according to the FBI agent, he'd been hired to befriend her and trap her.

Her bags slid from her hands. She heard glass crunching, and then red liquid leaked around her sandals. *Blood. Blood splattered on the windshield, on the dashboard, and ran down the back of his fat neck, staining the collar of his white shirt.*

Tashi's heart thundered and her stomach clenched tightly. *Dear God. No.* She started to run, but didn't get far. Her eyes closed in defeat as he caught her and spun her around. "How did you find me?"

"Who are you running from? Why are you so paranoid?"

She opened her eyes and stared at him. He'd removed his shades and his blue eyes pierced through her as if he were trying to read her soul. "Why are you following me?"

"I'm not following you. I swear I'm not following you. I wouldn't do that. Stalking is illegal in this town." He smiled, and the afternoon sun illuminated his soft blue eyes. "I came to the market to get some pull-ups for Tiffany. Her mother didn't pack enough this morning."

Tashi's breath came out hard and rapid. Of course. He wasn't one of them. He was married. He had a little girl.

She felt so weak. She was so tired. Tired of hiding. Tired of the unknown. She just wanted a life. She wanted to feel safe and secure, just for one moment. Tashi gave in to the overwhelming emotions that had been building up for fifteen months. She was only human, after all. She fell weakly against the strong, hard chest. The hot tears ran in torrents down her cheeks, dampening his shirt. She felt his arms close around her. His fingers tangled in her hair as he pressed her face into his chest.

"Hey, it's okay," he whispered gently in a deep voice as he

held her, his hands soothing and comforting as he caressed her back and shoulders. "It's gonna be okay…"

They stood holding onto each other in the parking lot with curious people watching and the warm July sun beating down on them.

After a while, he put his hand under her chin and lifted her face to his. "It's gonna be okay," he reiterated, gazing into her eyes. He backtracked a few steps with her, bent down, picked up her backpack and shopping bags, and handed them to her. "Your groceries are ruined." He bent down and began to scoop up as much as he could of the mess of food from the ground.

Tashi slid one strap of her backpack over her arm and bent down to help him. As they carried the soggy paper bags with ruined groceries over to the trashcan and deposited them inside, Tashi felt an unexpected warmth from his tenderness. His genuine concern for her—a stranger—was touching.

"If you come inside with me, I'll replace your groceries," he said.

"You don't have to do that." She could have salvaged most of the items and washed off the spaghetti sauce once she got home, but she was too tired to bother. "It's my fault for being paranoid."

"Why do you take on so much blame?" he asked. "In the café, you blamed yourself and now… I snuck up on you there, and I scared you just now. It's not all your fault, you know."

A heaviness settled in Tashi's stomach. But it was. *If I hadn't been so naïve that nice FBI agent would be alive today, and that driver too—even though he was a bad man.* It was her fault.

"At least let me reimburse you." He pulled his wallet from his back pocket.

"No. It wasn't that much. I'm fine." She hoped her camera was fine. It was expensive and she didn't want to have to replace it. At least her phone was tucked safely inside the pocket of her dress. She would die if it was ever lost, damaged, or stolen.

The man's eyes continued to bore into hers as he replaced his wallet. "Are you in some kind of trouble?" His voice was deep and rich, and it made her feel safe.

Tashi needed that voice at night as she lay in bed trembling and frightened, whispering that everything would be all right. She needed that voice to bring her out of the nightmares that continually plagued her sleep. She swallowed and shook her head, then pressed her hands against her temples. "No. I'm just tired. It's been a long day."

"It's only noon," he pointed out in a patient tone.

She tried to smile, but the corners of her mouth just trembled. "Where's your little girl—Tif—Tiffany, right?" she asked, noticing what she supposed was green dried baby food in the tresses of his long black hair. She envied the woman who had this gentle, loving man to comfort and protect her. She wished she had someone like him to lean on. To trust.

"She's with her grandmother," he answered, offering her a smile that made her knees weak, not from fear or heartache this time, but attraction. "Come back to the café with me. Have a smoothie and some apple pie. It'll calm your nerves, make you feel better. I promise."

Tashi shook her head. "The apple pie is delicious. I usually have it for desert." *Usually*, she thought in wonder. She hadn't ordered it today, and if she had, she would still have been sitting at her table when this stranger walked in. She would not have stood up and bumped into him. "I just ate and I'm really full."

"Maybe another time then?" he asked, on a warm smile.

"I'm sorry for crying all over you," Tashi said, willing herself not to fall victim to his charm. The lingering smell of green beans and applesauce on his shirt made him even more irresistible. He was somebody's dad—the one thing she never had growing up.

"Why did you cry all over me?"

She hesitated before responding. "It's just that, when I saw you standing there talking on the phone, and then when you turned around, I panicked. I thought you were—" She stopped, and dropped her gaze.

"You thought I was someone else. The person you are running away from?"

"I'm not running from anyone." Tashi's defenses instantly returned. She didn't know this man. He was nice, but he had his own family to take care of. If she were his wife, she wouldn't appreciate him paying so much attention to another woman—especially one who in spite of the mental brakes she was trying to apply found herself highly attracted to him. She stepped back and glanced up at him. "I have to go." She hooked the other strap of her backpack over her shoulder.

"Where? Where do you have to go?" he asked, the beginning of a new smile tipping the corners of his sexy mouth.

"Bye." She turned and walked away, clutching her two garment bags in her hand.

"I'm Adam. Do you live around here?" he called after her.

Tashi stopped in her tracks. *Adam. His name was Adam. His name began with an A...*

Her mind rewound fifteen months to the night in New York and the split second just before the first round of shots blasted around her: *"When you get to Granite Falls, look for A—"* and just before that, *"I'll send word to my friend. He is to give you the protection of his name and family by making you his temporary bride."*

Tashi did not dare turn around. It was too good to be true. He couldn't be *that friend*. The agent hadn't said anything about him having a child, and she was certain that if Adam was already married, the agent would not have asked that he marry her. What if he'd gotten married in the fifteen months she'd been wasting away in this town? Well, if he was *that man*, he could still give her protection, just not as his wife. "Yes," she said in a voice squeaky with hope. "I live around here."

"What's your name?"

"Tashi. Tashi—" She hesitated, then decided to go for it. "Tashi Holland."

She waited for some indication of recognition. A "My goodness, I've been looking for you for months," or something along those lines. When none came, Tashi continued on her way.

Tashi.

"Tashi Holland." Adam whispered her name as he watched her walk through the parking lot, her long jean dress flapping loosely around her ankles. When she exited the lot, Adam realized that she didn't own a car. The thought that she couldn't afford a car upset him. How many other basic necessities of life —things people like him took for granted—did she live without?

He was tempted to follow her, even though he'd told her he hadn't been following her. That was then. This was now—now that he knew she was afraid of something or someone, the urge to run after her and hold her again mounted by the second. Twice in one day, within the hour, he'd held her against him, pressed her cheek close to his heart—his heart that was now beating madly out of control.

Adam pressed his palm into his chest where her cheek had lain. His shirt was damp from her tears. His skin tingled from her heat. He fisted his hand as if he could capture her sadness and make it his own.

"What frightens you, Tashi? Who scares you? An obsessive boyfriend? An abusive husband?" he asked out loud as he watched her cross the street and walk west on Beacon Avenue, pass Mountainview Café, toward Union Street.

Soon she would be out of sight, but positively not out of

mind, he thought as he recalled her eyes—wide sapphire pools of mystery and magic, bright open windows to her timid soul. His pulse quickened as he remembered the rich golden glow and enthusing aroma of ginger scenting her soft auburn curls, and the sensuous bouquet of jasmine and vanilla emanating from her smooth silky skin.

Exotic. Sweet. Enticing. *Lei era la spezia e il sapore al suo stufato* —yes, the spice and the flavor to his stew, indeed. The kind of woman a man wished he could bump into again and again—all pun intended.

Adam's excitement waned when she made a right turn onto Union Street—the low-income part of town, littered with rundown multi-family houses where people existed from paycheck to paycheck. His heart squeezed mercilessly. A woman like Tashi didn't belong in that kind of neighborhood. She belonged in a palace surrounded by servants eager to grant her simplest request.

As her diminishing figure disappeared from his view, Adam walked into the supermarket. His concern for the girl sprouted wings and his protective instincts toward any damsel in distress bulldozed through the barrier he'd erected several years ago. It ripped through him like a fist smashing through the surge of a waterfall.

Tashi was in trouble. Not the kind that went away with a threatening phone call or a letter from an attorney. She was in deep. The girl was a bundle of nerves, and seemingly as defenseless as an alley cat trapped with its back against the wall.

Much like Claire, sans the entourage of negative vibes.

As he pulled the box of disposable diapers from the shelf and headed to the checkout, Adam tried to put all thoughts of Tashi Holland out of his mind. He told himself that she was not his concern. He berated himself for asking her name and if she lived in the vicinity. Why couldn't he have left well enough alone?

It wasn't that he was opposed to helping damsels in distress. It was just that damsels in distress were his weakness.

He'd discovered his Achilles' heel at age twenty-one when he'd rescued Claire, a damsel in distress from an abusive relationship. A practicing yogi and meditation guru since the age of twelve, he should have known that a woman with that kind of baggage and high levels of toxins circling her orbit would tip his Libra scales way out of equilibrium.

Perhaps the challenge of teaching her to trust again, to show her that not all men were cruel, and most emphatically the fact that she was the first woman he'd made love with had clouded his mind, made him think he was in love with her, and pushed him to propose. It could also have been his father's frequent referral to the fact that since Adam was his only heir, it was his duty to carry on the Andreas bloodline.

Or perhaps it was that longing in his heart to share his life with someone special, to create his own home with a wife and children that was filled with joy, happiness, laughter, and respect —much like the one he'd grown up in. Whatever it was that had pushed him to ask, Claire had accepted his proposal, and had seemed excited about marrying him in the months they'd spent planning the elaborate wedding of the decade.

Then she'd broken his heart.

Eventually, his heart had healed and had forgotten the ache of rejection. A true believer in love and Happy Ever After, he'd opened up to another damsel in distress. He never got as far as the altar with Denise, and he couldn't say that his heart had been broken the second time around—just a little hurt and somewhat disappointed at failing again.

That kind of consecutive rejection could wreak havoc on a man's confidence, not to mention his ego—even if that man practiced yoga and meditation on a daily basis. While yoga and meditation were efficient in helping him regain and maintain balance in his inner universe, they, however, were ineffective when it came to matters of the heart and soul.

The heart and soul, he'd discovered, were restless teammates —forever on perpetual journeys to find their one true love—the ultimate mate to complete them. Twice burned, Adam had learned that the best way to deal with his heart and soul was not to engage them, to keep them away from things that affected them most.

For him, that *thing* was a woman in distress, since the moment he thought he had to rescue a woman was the moment he began falling for her.

After his emotional disasters with Claire and Denise, he'd made a conscious effort to only pursue independent women who didn't need to be rescued, women who wanted a career more than they wanted love and a family, those who bowed out as graciously as they bowed into their affairs with him. To be fair, he was always mindful to let them know right up front that there was no permanency in a relationship with him. Consequently, he was known as "Temporary Adam" to some, and "The Temporary Tycoon" to others.

Adam had been initially surprised that there were actual women out there who didn't see marriage and children as the prime reason for their existence, that it wasn't a goal they needed to attain to feel complete and valued by the opposite sex, or by society. What many women *really* wanted had changed in recent decades. Some of them just wanted to have fun.

Adam appreciated their contemporary philosophies, and while the opposite was true for him, *temporary* was working out just fine. The heart couldn't always get what it wanted, and since he'd conditioned his not to fall in love, it seemed to have ceased its endless quest.

The safest way to keep *temporary* permanent was to stay away from damsels in distress. That meant no opening of Pandora's box—well, in this case, Tashi's box—for a quick and curious peek inside.

By the time he walked back to Mountainview Café and handed the box of diapers to Felicia, Adam had succeeded in putting all thoughts of Tashi Holland out of his mind.

At least that's what he thought.

CHAPTER TWO

Once inside her apartment, Tashi turned the dead bolts and dropped her bags on the floor. She leaned against the door and took deep breaths of the stifling hot air into her lungs. She felt as if she'd been holding her breath ever since she'd collided with that incredible man in the café.

"Adam." She finally allowed herself to say the name that had been bouncing around in her head during her fifteen-minute walk home—the longest and most difficult she'd ever taken. Ever since she took the first step away from him, her legs had been wobbly and stiff—a contrasting combination she didn't know was possible. It was a miracle she hadn't collapsed on the sidewalk.

"Adam," she said again as if repeating it would somehow ease the constriction in her lungs, the quaking in her belly. As the sound of his name bounced off the walls of her apartment, the image of his gentle blue eyes, the lingering feel of his arms wrapped around her, the warmth from his hard strong body made Tashi flush all over. Even now in the delicious aftermath of their brief physical encounter, she felt as if her skin was on fire.

But that fire quickly waned as Tashi remembered the little girl in the stroller. *He was married.* He had a child, maybe more than one. Ms. Felicia was his mother-in-law. Maybe that's where she'd seen him before—at the café. She shook her head. No. If she'd seen this man in person before, she would have remembered. He was not the kind of man a woman forgot meeting.

He was kind, and gentle, and considerate. Okay, yes, and sexy and appealing too. He'd offered to replace her groceries even though it was her own paranoia that had caused her to drop her bags. And he'd invited her back to the café for dessert—to help calm her nerves he'd said. Why hadn't she accepted? Because he was married, and if she were his wife, she wouldn't appreciate him sharing anything with another woman, no matter how innocent it looked. That was how illicit affairs began —innocently.

He could be divorced. Separated. Widowed, her lonely heart debated. Could be, she thought, squinting her eyes, trying to remember if she'd seen a ring on his finger.

Tashi slid her backpack off her shoulders and made her way into the living room, where she placed it carefully on the glass-top coffee table.

In an effort to bring down her body heat, she flipped the switch to the air conditioning unit in one of the two living room windows. As the room vibrated from the ruckus of the cooling unit, Tashi plopped down on her posh leather sofa, picked up her laptop from the coffee table, and opened up her browser. There were a lot of men with Adam for a first name living in Granite Falls, but Tashi knew without a doubt that the first name on the first page belonged to the man she'd collided with today.

Adamo Alessandro Andreas. Triple A's for *first, second, and last names.* He seemed like a man who would be first, at the top of his game, at the top of everything, including a list of website pages. He was *A* all the way. *Adam*, the first man God created. Tashi's heart pounded furiously at the realization that she'd been nicknamed

"Little Eve" after her mother, Evelyn, because she looked so much like her.

Expelling a ragged breath, she clicked on the Wikipedia link. Several images of Adam popped onto the screen and his intense blue eyes seemed to pierce through her like they'd done in person earlier. With curiosity burning a hole in her belly, Tashi leaned back into the sofa and began to devour as much information as she could about Adam Andreas.

He was thirty-two years old, the only child of Alessandro and Arabella Andreas, and sole heir to Andreas International—an exclusive chain of restaurants and hotels situated all over the globe. Tashi remembered walking past both Hotel Andreas and Ristorante Andreas last summer when she'd decided to extend her walking parameters as far as Lake Crystal at the eastern border of town. It was a long walk from her apartment, but well worth the effort. She'd photographed some interesting sights on the way, and once there, she'd people-watched from the boardwalk, and enjoyed both a delicious seafood lunch and a dinner at two of the local restaurants.

Having nothing and no one to go home to, she'd stayed all day, and had even dipped her feet in the cool crystal water while the town residents and visitors frolicked around her, and mini yachts docked and undocked all day long, picking up and dropping off rich-looking men, women and children in a noisy melee of fun and excitement.

It was nightfall by the time she'd finished her dinner, and although the crime rate in Granite Falls was less than a quarter percent compared to the rest of the state and the country, she'd decided to take a taxi back to her apartment.

Tashi clasped a hand to her mouth. That's where she'd seen Adam Andreas before. She'd picked up a copy of *Granite Falls People News* magazine from the back seat of the cab, and had been absentmindedly leafing through it during the latter part of her ride. She'd turned a page and just as her eyes landed on a photo of four men all dressed in business attire, her taxi ride had ended.

Tashi clicked on the *Granite Falls People News* link and began to read the first article. The four men she'd glimpsed in the magazine that night were featured together. They were all very close friends, and they were all billionaires. Dr. Erik LaCrosse was a world-renowned OB/GYN who often visited third-world countries to attend to war-torn and natural disaster victims and refugees. Bryce Fontaine was owner and CEO of Fontaine Enterprises—an international conglomeration that comprised of a vast variety of businesses. He was the man she'd seen at the outlets with the woman and twins today. His face was also featured in the Fountain Towers TV ads. That's why he'd seemed familiar to her. The glass skyscraper of his Fontaine Enterprises headquarters towered over the town. Many buildings bore the Fontaine name. *Wow.* And Massimo Andretti, Adam's cousin, was heir to Andretti Industries—the largest textile manufacturer in the world. They were all powerful men, and they were all married, with children, except Adam.

Except for Adam. He wasn't married. A leisurely smile spread Tashi's lips as that realization sunk into her brain and her heart.

The article described Adam as the Temporary Tycoon and the last available billionaire in Granite Falls to be snatched from the eligible bachelors' shelf. He was nicknamed the Temporary Tycoon because he always warned his lovers up front that the relationship was temporary. At least he wasn't giving anybody any false hopes. "And I shouldn't be having any either," Tashi vocally schooled herself. The FBI agent had said she was to be married temporarily, not that she was to marry the temporary tycoon, even though his name began with an *A*.

So his little girl, Tiffany, must have been born out of wedlock. Lots of unmarried couples shared children these days. She herself was illegitimate, but unlike Tiffany, whose father seemed to be a presence in her life, Tashi had never met hers.

She had no idea who he was, or if he was dead or alive. Her mother died before she was old enough to ask questions, and when Tashi had asked her overprotective Uncle Victor about her father, he'd said that he didn't know him, had never met him. The one thing Tashi knew about her father was that he was black. Her light-brown complexion attested to that fact.

Tashi clicked on some more links but found nothing about Tiffany or her mother. She wondered if Adam was still involved with the woman who'd given birth to his beautiful little girl. She smiled as she recalled the food stains on his shirt and the dried baby food in his hair that spoke volumes about him as a devoted father. Tiffany Andreas was a very lucky little girl.

Feeling as if her head would explode with the overload of information, Tashi closed her laptop and set it back on the coffee table, but some unseen force made her open it up again. She pulled her phone from her pocket and added the phone number for Hotel Andreas to her list of three other contacts—Mindy, Mountainview Café, and her favorite pizza parlor next to the camera shop on Oak Street. Before shutting off her phone, she made Hotel Andreas her number one favorite.

Tashi closed her laptop again as she tried to analyze her spontaneous behavior. It wasn't like she was going to call his hotel looking for him. He'd probably not even remember her. What would she say, anyway? "Hey, Adam, remember me, the girl you met at Mountainview Café the other day?" Nope, she thought with a twist of her lips, calling Adam would be tacky, and could be construed as stalking—the very thing she'd accused him of when she'd seen him at the grocery store. There was no explanation for saving his number to her phone, except that it gave her a connection to him, made her feel close to him—in an odd sort of way.

The apartment was a lot cooler than it had been when she first arrived home, but still her skin felt as flushed as when she'd collided with Adam Andreas. He'd left a lasting impression on her.

Well, at least she could rule one thing out, she mused as she got up from the sofa: a wealthy, powerful man like Adam Andreas was definitely not the one the FBI agent had sent her looking for. It was highly unlikely that a New York City FBI agent would know a man like that, be friends with a man like Adam Andreas.

And she needed to stop thinking about him, she scolded herself as her heart began to race with the memories of being crushed against his body. He was definitely out of her league. Way, way out—like a billion light years away.

Nope, Adam's knee-jerk reaction to her today was merely hormones—a normal reaction to a man meeting a woman he found attractive. He was probably over it by now. And if he knew she'd killed a man in cold blood, and was a fugitive from the law, his attraction would turn to disdain. He might even turn her in. Nope, it was best she stayed away from him. She needed to occupy her mind with something else.

As she walked into her bedroom and began to separate her laundry into two laundry bags, a knot formed in Tashi's stomach. Her *savior* was still a mystery. He might forever be a mystery since she had to face the harsh reality that the agent may not have made it out of that house alive.

Maybe it was time she gave up on him and began planning a life on her own. She was so tired of not being able to enjoy the basic human things ordinary people enjoyed on a daily basis. Like owning a car, having a job to go to, making friends, and even—maybe even trying her luck at romance again.

She would do a background check on any potential boyfriends this time—no more Scotties pulling the wool over her eyes. Her uncle was right, there were a lot of bad people in the world, but there were some good ones too, she had to admit. That FBI agent who had saved her life was one of them.

As the loud music from her upstairs neighbor's stereo blasted through the ceiling, Tashi knew that it was time she got out of this hellhole. Winters wouldn't be so bad if she lived in a nicer area of town. With the money she still had left, and a salary from a job, she knew she could afford one of the luxurious studio or one-bedroom apartments at Fontaine Towers that overlooked the Aiken River.

She wasn't born into a wealthy family, but she'd never lived in such a destitute place either. She'd lived with her mother and her uncle in an upper middle class neighborhood, and after her mother died, her uncle had moved them into a similar neighborhood far away from the previous one.

As a child, she never got everything she wanted, but she'd never wanted for anything. Her maternal grandparents had set up a decent trust fund for her mother and her uncle, but they'd never touched it. That money had supported Tashi through, and beyond college. She had no student loans to pay back, and she'd been able to rent a nice studio apartment close to her university in New York City. There was still a lot of money left, but she couldn't take the risk of withdrawing it, not that she needed it with all that the agent had given her, anyway.

As she swung her bags of dirty laundry over her shoulder and left her apartment, Tashi wondered how difficult it would be to assume a new identity. She had no idea where to begin or if attempting to change her name would trigger cyber waves that might reach her enemies, and alert them to her whereabouts.

One thing was certain, she could not continue living like this.

Adam couldn't sleep. Not since he'd collided with Tashi Holland, three days ago. No matter how hard he tried, he could not get her out of his head, and his other head kept standing at attention and drooling at the prospect of making her acquaintance.

He wasn't presently involved with anyone, so starting something with Tashi wasn't a problem—maybe just a quick fling to get her out of his system might be all he needed. His most recent relationship had lasted two weeks, perhaps because he'd found the woman boring compared to his previous lover, Sadie, a fifty-something-year-old with a penchant for younger lovers. Their relationship had lasted about a year. It was the first time he'd been involved with an older woman, and like the others before her, Sadie had known it wasn't permanent, even though it had begun to feel comfortable for both of them. So when her company offered her a promotion and transfer to Austin, Texas, she'd immediately jumped on it, and four months ago, she'd spent one last passionate night with him then bid him farewell the next morning.

She hadn't called since she left, and he'd found himself missing her for a host of reasons. Sadie had never been married, had no children, was well traveled, well educated, and spoke several languages. She had the body of a twenty-year-old athlete, and was the best lover he'd ever had. She'd even taught him a few tricks she swore would drive any woman out of her mind. Tricks he hadn't had the chance to try out on anyone else, yet.

Yes, he missed her—their deep meaningful conversations, especially—but not badly enough to call her.

Rules were rules, and he was sticking by his.

Well, that was until he'd bumped into Tashi Holland.

After the first sleepless night and waking up the next morning with a rock-hard cock that refused to go away, even after he gave it some attention, Adam had boarded his jet and flown to Austin. He just needed to forget Tashi. Forget her big emerald eyes, her sexy mouth, her curly auburn hair, and the soft feel of her delicate little body in his arms. Forget that she might be a damsel in distress. Sadie could help him forget.

But Sadie wasn't having him. It was over. She'd moved on with another lover who was even younger than Adam, but she'd treated him to lunch. When she'd asked about the real reason he'd flown to Texas, he'd told her about Tashi and the pull she had on him. He'd admitted that he was afraid he might start something he might not have the power to end. And since ending was his thing...

Sadie had had a good laugh, and then she'd said, "You should have known the day would come when a woman would challenge your commitment to your temporary rule, Adam Andreas. You can't stay balanced for the rest of your life. There's no excitement there. It's the imbalance, the chaos that provide us the opportunity to learn and grow, that make us want to take risks to tip the scales in our favor again."

"You, more than anyone know how to keep me balanced."

"No, sweetness," she'd said, resting her hand on his. "This Tashi girl tipped your scale. You and she are on this seesaw together. You have to work with her to tip it back. The fact that you broke your rule and came to see me tells me that *you* know that *your* heart knows something you're not ready to admit."

"My heart has been wrong before."

"Was it your heart that was wrong, or was it you, Adam?"

His heart had skipped a beat as if agreeing with her.

"Don't fight the pull, darling. Explore the possibilities before this opportunity moves on to someone else."

"What if it doesn't work out?" he'd asked, trying desperately to refute her wisdom.

"What if it does? Sometimes we just have to live the questions, Adam," she'd admonished, giving him a lingering kiss on the lips for old times' sake before sending him back to Granite Falls and his impending fate.

Adam tossed the sheet off his naked body and got out of bed. It was a little past two, but he knew the restless hour and a half of sleep was all he was going to get tonight. *All*, he thought, gazing down at his cock pressed tight against his belly with drool easing out of it. It was literally becoming a pain to wake up horny with only one way to relieve the tension—well two, but he hated cold showers.

Adam grabbed an elastic hair band from the nightstand and secured his mane into a ponytail as he left the bedroom of his third floor master suite. He crossed the hall, and walked through the dining and living rooms to the kitchen. There he busied himself making a pot of coffee. What he would enjoy more was a strong espresso, but he was out of his favorite beans, and since his mind had been flooded with nothing but thoughts of Tashi Holland lately, he'd forgotten to restock. Coffee would have to do for tonight.

As he waited for the java to brew, he walked to the wall of French doors on the other side of the kitchen and gazed out into the darkness of the night.

Upon his return from Austin, he'd gone straight to the café where he'd met Tashi Holland, hoping beyond hope that she'd be there. Mountainview Café and Hair Salon was jointly owned by Lillian Fontaine and Felicia LaCrosse, the mothers of two of his best friends— Bryce Fontaine, and Erik LaCrosse who was the father of Adam's goddaughter, Tiffany.

Adam, Erik, Bryce, and Adam's cousin Massimo Andretti had been best friends since high school. They were closer than best friends. They were brothers who'd sworn a blood oath to always be there for each other.

His brothers were all married with growing families. Massimo had taken a wife just last year and had already produced an heir to the Andretti fortune. Married life had put a damper on their "guy bonding" time, and when they did manage to get together, his married friends did nothing but swap pictures and stories about their children, and talk about silly spats with their wives. Adam, of late, was feeling more and more displaced around them, having no stories of his own to share.

It was ironic that he was the only one of the group still not married when he was the one who'd had the most interest in starting a family years ago—way back when his man-whore cousin, Massimo, had taken an oath never to marry just to spite his philandering father who'd picked out a suitable wife for him. On the contrary, Adam had caved under his own father's pressures to expand the Andreas bloodline, and had thus proposed. He'd wanted to make his old man happy even it meant making himself miserable.

Within a year after their breakup, Claire had married some web design entrepreneur, but four years later when his company went bankrupt and he was unable to support her lavish lifestyle, she divorced him. She'd tried to rekindle whatever she thought they'd had, claiming that Adam's deep spirituality and journeys into his inner universe, and the pressure from his father to immediately start a family had scared her. She'd said she'd made a mistake by leaving him at the altar. He'd told her she hadn't made a mistake and that he was over her completely. Lady Fate had been kind to him, and he wasn't about to throw her gift back into her face.

Ten years had passed, and he hadn't even been mildly tempted to go that route again. But his desire to contribute to the filial conversations had prompted him to begin taking Tiffany out —once in a while. Being with Tiffany reminded him of the void in his life, but he nonetheless enjoyed spending time with her, and then reporting on the unexpected things she said and did. He also appreciated the added bonus she provided after Sadie left.

Seems like a single man with a baby was the ultimate female magnet. He'd procured several dates because of Tiffany's cute little smiles and darling antics, even her whining on cranky days.

But three days ago, Tiffany ate, pooped, and slept at the park and at the petting zoo where he'd taken her on their morning date. It was a hot day and he guessed she wasn't feeling up to impressing him or attracting ladies, so he'd taken her back to her grandmother earlier than planned. And if he hadn't, he would not have run into Tashi.

He'd questioned Felicia about the scared little rabbit who'd cried in his arms. How long had she been coming to the café? Did she have a pattern, a specific time when she came in? Was she ever with anyone? A man specifically. Had she ever ordered out? What was her address? Felicia answered all his questions, but the last.

As fond as she was of him, she refused to give up a customer's address, just as he would never give up a room number of a guest in his hotel. And so Adam had stuck around for a good portion of the day, and the next, hoping that Tashi would make an appearance, but he got nothing.

Nothing seemed to be all he was getting these days, he thought, glancing down at his now flaccid shaft. With no playmate available, it had gone back to sleep. Too bad *he* too couldn't enjoy the luxury of slumber.

At the chime from the coffee maker indicating his brew was ready, Adam made his way toward it. He picked up the coffee pot and a mug and walked back to his bedroom. He pulled on his robe, then made his way down the hall toward his home office. It was midmorning in Europe, a good time to check in with his hotel managers on the other side of the pond. He'd barely sat down at his desk and taken a sip from his mug when his landline rang. He glanced at the display. It was the general manager at Hotel Andreas-Granite Falls.

Now, for what possible reason would his general manager be calling him at two thirty in the morning? A disgruntled guest or an employee, perhaps? What would anyone have to complain about while staying in one of the most luxurious hotels in the world? As to his employees, they knew they would never find better employment anywhere in the hotel industry.

He picked up the receiver. "Yes, Oscar."

"I'm sorry for calling at such an odd hour, Mr. Andreas, but a young woman called here looking for you a little while ago."

He frowned. Why would a woman be calling his hotel and not his cell? And why in the middle of the night except for a booty call? The fact that he wasn't currently involved didn't stop his cock from stirring at the very thought of playing a game of hide and go seek. "Well, did she leave a name?" he asked with a touch of restiveness.

"She said her name was Tashi, sir."

CHAPTER THREE

Adam's heart flew to his throat and his back became ramrod straight. "Did—did you say Tashi?" He could hardly get the words out as he pushed to his feet.

"Yes. She sounded a bit hysterical."

"What do you mean, hysterical?"

"She was crying, Mr. Andreas."

Adam felt like a ton of lead had been slammed into his gut. He pulled on his ponytail in an effort to keep his mind from going numb as his body was threatening to do. "Did she leave a message?" He paced the floor, forcing his blood to circulate.

"She left her number and her address. She said she needed you, sir. I forwarded the information to your cell, but I know you turn on the DND feature after midnight."

"Thanks, Oscar." Adam dropped the phone on his desk and sprinted back to his bedroom.

Tashi needed him.

He grabbed his cell from the nightstand and searched for Oscar's message as he shrugged out of his robe. He memorized the address then dialed the number Oscar had forwarded while he reached for the pair of shorts he'd draped over the footboard not too long ago.

Tashi's number just kept ringing, and as the seconds ticked by, the sound of Adam's racing heart beating against his chest grew louder and louder and his breath seemed to solidify in his throat.

Tashi was in trouble. What if whomever she was running from had found her? What if he was too late? Refusing to entertain the horrific possibility, he pulled his shirt from the foot of his bed and raced downstairs like a pack of wolves was after him.

He made the thirty-minute drive to the not-so-nice section of town in less than fifteen. He brought his Aston Martin to a stop in front of 85 Temple Street and got out. The multi-family house was shrouded in darkness, as was the neighborhood with many of the street lamps burned out. Adam flew up the short flight of steps, made a right on the rickety porch, and passed an old ragged sofa, a three-legged coffee table jammed against the wall, and a half-worn-down broom. He knocked on the door with the number four.

"Tashi," he called. The only response to his call in the night was the bark from a neighbor's dog. "Tashi," he said again, trying the door. Of course it was locked.

A prickly feeling crept along Adam's back as his mind raced ahead of him. Suppose the people she was running from were holding her at gunpoint inside the apartment? Or worse, suppose they'd done what they'd come to do and had already left, leaving her lifeless body to be discovered by a neighbor?

Adrenaline pumped through Adam's veins. He had no idea what was waiting for him behind that locked door. He could be walking into a trap for all he knew. He thought about kicking the door in, but realized that if her captors were still in there, he might startle them into shooting blindly at him. Then he would be of no use to her. He thought of calling the police, but immediately decided against it since he didn't know the nature of Tashi's trouble. Involving the authorities might…

"Adam."

He cocked his ears as he heard the faint whisper of his name through a crack in the window on his right. He moved toward it. "Tashi?" His voice trembled on those two syllables.

He heard a low moan, then, "In here." It was barely a whisper.

"Are you alone?"

"Yes. I'm sick." She whimpered again. "I'm so sick."

Sick. She was sick. He let out his breath, and on his intake, the stench of seasoned vomit and other putrefied odors he didn't care to identify wafted up his nostrils. Why hadn't she called 911 instead of him? Sliding a finger under the crack, and finding no screen, he pushed the curtain aside and peeked inside. It was still too dark to make out anything in the room. "Can you open the door?"

"I can't move. I can't walk."

The panic, the pain, in her voice brought tears to Adam's eyes. "Okay, baby. I'm gonna climb through the window then," he said, sliding his hands beneath the splintered wood on the bottom of the sill.

Her response was another heart-wrenching groan.

It was a small window, but he was a man, and since men always delighted in the challenge of squeezing big objects through tight openings, Adam welcomed the scrapes and cuts on his arms and legs and the splinters piercing his flesh as he forced his frame through the window.

He landed on a pile of clothes on the floor and stood to adjust his eyes to the darkness, even as he forced himself to ignore the stench in the air. Another moan gave away her location and Adam made his way toward her, bumping into what felt like a trashcan at the side of the bed. He swallowed the bile that rose to his throat.

"Tashi," he called, making his way to the head of the bed. He switched on the bedside lamp and almost fainted at what he saw. Tashi was rolled up in a ball on the bed. Her long auburn hair—encrusted with only God knew what—was spread out above her head, and the pink nightgown she was wearing was stained with human excrement, and *blood*.

Adam's heart dropped to the pit of his stomach. "Tashi." Without a moment's hesitation, he dropped down on the mattress and gathered her into his arms. She was burning up with fever. "Tashi." He pushed her hair out of her face and cradled her head in the crook of his arm. "*Cara*, why are you bleeding? Did someone hurt you?"

"No. No. I—I have my—my period."

Adam let out his breath, relieved that he didn't have to go out and commit murder. "Is it always this bad?"

"No. It's not because of that. I didn't know my fridge had died and I ate some leftover chicken."

"When? How long have you been sick?"

"Since the day I met you. I had the chicken for dinner that night and I woke up with a bellyache." She sank her nails into the fresh cuts on his arms and screamed as cramps apparently ripped through her stomach.

Her breath smelled horrible, but Adam pressed her face against his. He spoke softly and soothingly to her, and rubbed her belly lightly as he waited for her cramps to subdue. When they finally did, and she relaxed her hold on him, he gazed down into her eyes. They were hollow, almost transparent like her ashen skin. The vibrant colors he'd seen in her complexion and her eyes three days ago were gone. It was as if he was gazing into the face of a completely different woman—her apparition.

"I have to get you to the hospital," he said, easing off the bed with her in his arms.

"No. No. No hospital."

No hospital? The girl was dying from food poisoning and she didn't want to go to the hospital. "Why, Tashi? Why don't you want to go to the hospital?"

She started to cry, her lithe body shaking from her sobs. "If I use my name, they—they could find me. They—they'll kill—they'll kill me. I have to stay below the radar."

"Who? The people you're running from?" he asked, caressing her arms and her back in an effort to calm her down.

She nodded as more tears poured out of her eyes, ran down her cheeks, and into the fresh cuts on Adam's arms. He steeled himself against the stinging of his raw flesh from her salty tears.

Dear God, his suspicions were correct. She *was* a damsel in distress. The worst kind, if she was too afraid to seek medical help even though she was one hairsbreadth away from death. People wanted to kill her. Who? Why?

"Okay," he said. "I won't take you to the hospital, but I have a friend who's a doctor and I'm going to call him. I can trust him. He wouldn't tell anyone about you. Is that okay?"

She nodded.

He reached into his pocket for his phone only to realize that he'd left it in the car. He picked up hers from the nightstand. It was dead. Her charger was nowhere in sight. That's why she hadn't answered his calls earlier. He was grateful she was able to make the last call to his hotel before the device went completely dead.

He glanced around the chaotic room, hardly able to breathe in the foul air. Soiled clothes, used tissues, and dishes with leftover food were strewn everywhere, but he noticed the two empty gallon water containers on the floor. At least she'd been drinking water to ward off dehydration. It was probably the reason she was still alive.

She'd been sick for three days. Sick, alone, and scared to seek medical help. That's why she hadn't been back to the café. Felicia had said that she came in at least three or four times a week, and always on Thursdays for the special lunch buffet. Yesterday was Thursday and Tashi hadn't shown because she was sick.

Adam's gaze landed on the trashcan he'd bumped into in the dark. Now he could see the gross contents inside it. She'd started using it because she'd become too weak to walk to the bathroom. He shivered as a small black rodent scurried from one corner of the room to the next and disappeared behind the radiator.

Adam shook his head with disgust. He couldn't ask Erik to come here. He didn't want his friend to see Tashi in this condition, in this place, this neighborhood. He glanced down at her again. She needed a bath, and so did he now that he too was covered in her waste.

"Tashi. I'm taking you to my home. No one else is there. It will just be the two of us," he said, just then deciding that his entire household staff would be enjoying a nice paid vacation for however long it took to nurse Tashi back to health. "Is that okay?"

She nodded, then closed her eyes and groaned as another cramp apparently ripped through her. As he held and caressed her through it, the heat from her body seemed to burn off Adam's clothes and flesh.

When she went limp again, he eased her back down on the mattress and stood to his feet. She curled up into a ball, trembling. He hated to leave her side, but he had to get going. He took the trashcan into the bathroom and flushed its contents down the toilet.

"I'm going to clean you up a bit and change your clothes before we leave," he said, returning to her bedside. She needed a good soak, but he didn't want to spend any more time than necessary in this dump. A quick wipe-down would have to suffice for now.

He walked to a bureau on the other side of the room and quickly scanned the contents of the top drawer—a neatly folded colorful pile of silk and lace thongs on the left side, and a pile of practical cotton panties on the right. He grabbed the first item from the right pile—a pair of pink boy shorts with white polka dots and the word "Angel" printed on the front.

Two side steps brought him to her tiny closet—more like a hole in the wall. He pulled a lime green dress from its hanger, and a clean bed sheet from the shelf. He set them on the nightstand, next to a box of sanitary napkins, then walked into the bathroom. He took a washcloth from the shower curtain rod, lifted a plastic tub from the floor and half filled it with cool water. Grabbing a bar of soap, he returned to the bedroom, took off her nightgown—the only piece of clothing she wore—and gave her a hasty bird bath.

"Hold me tight," he said, picking her up. While she wound her arms about his neck and her legs around his waist, he cradled her naked body with one arm while he stripped the bed of the soiled sheets and tossed them on the floor. He arranged a clean sheet on one half of the mattress, eased her back down on it, and dressed her.

"Thank you," she said, her voice cracking as she gazed up at him with liquid emerald eyes.

Adam smiled down at her, then reaching out, he traced a knuckle along one cheek, wiping at the tear that had slid from the corner of her eye. Her skin was soft and silky. She had lost weight since the last time he'd seen her. She looked so small, frail, helpless, and alone. "I'm glad you called me."

Their eyes locked. He'd seen her naked and had bathed the most intimate parts of her body, taken care of her woman's monthly business, yet it seemed to Adam that there wasn't an ounce of embarrassment on her side, and definitely not a shred of lust on his. It were as if they were old acquainted souls who already knew each other's secrets, wants, and needs in every possible form, who'd witnessed the best and worst of each other, and were still…

A sharp pain pierced Adam's heart and a lump lodged in his throat.

He was paralyzed for a moment, then he turned away abruptly, shaking off that invisible seize on his heart. He took the tub to the bathroom, flushed her bathwater down the toilet, and then soaped and washed his hands thoroughly. He took a clean face towel from a shelf over the toilet and soaked it with cold water. "This will help with the fever," he said, placing it on her forehead. "Where're your keys?"

"Living… Uh…Uh….room…"

Adam's heart twisted with pain as he watched her writhe in his arms. It was all he could do to hold back the tears from his eyes. He'd never witnessed anything like this before, and quite frankly, it scared the hell out of him.

"Here we go," he said when she lay shivering in his arms. He scooped her up inside the sheet, and pushed to his feet. She was so light, he felt like he was carrying a young child in his arms.

On his way to the front door, he grabbed her keys from the coffee table, and lingered when he saw her opened backpack on a corner of the sofa. A laptop, a camera, and her wallet were inside it. Remembering that he'd seen her carrying it the day they met, he figured she used it in place of a purse. He zippered it with one hand and slung it over his shoulder.

He locked her dead bolts and descended the porch stairs as quickly and carefully as he could. He laid her on the backseat of his Aston Martin and tucked the sheet around her. He'd love to put her up front beside him, but knew she'd be more comfortable in the back where she could stretch out. He buckled her in and then got behind the wheel. If he hurried, he'd have enough time to give her a quick bath before Erik got there.

"You'll be feeling better soon, Tashi," he said, as she groaned in pain again. He called Erik and asked him to meet him at the Andreas estate, equipped to treat a young woman with a fever and a severe case of food poisoning—perhaps salmonella.

He couldn't answer Erik's litany of questions about the identity and family history of the young woman. He knew nothing about Tashi, except for the fact that she needed him tonight.

As Adam sped along Route 80 and made his way northwest toward Mount Reservoir, he wondered who Tashi would have called if they hadn't bumped into each other at Mountainview Café, three days ago. Didn't she have a job, coworkers, friends, family, or a neighbor she could have called? A boyfriend? Girls her age usually had boyfriends.

Why was she so alone in this world that she had to call a total stranger whose private phone number she didn't even have?

There are no coincidences in life, his now deceased friend, Michael Rogers, used to say. The prophetic truth in those words had rung true in the professional areas of Adam's life. In the past few years since his parents moved back to Italy and gave him absolute control of the family business, he'd been able to expand Andreas International at an alarming rate because of the people and connections he'd made along the way.

But never had the divine power in those words affected the personal aspect of his life until now, Adam realized. He was supposed to have taken Tiffany two days before, but her Uncle Robert had made an unexpected visit to Granite Falls to spend some time with her and her siblings, thus changing Adam's date day with his goddaughter. Then if Tiffany had been her usual perky self instead of sleeping the morning away, he would not have cut their date short and taken her to the café and her grandmother so early on that fated day. They would still have been at the petting zoo, and he and Tashi's paths would never have crossed.

It was as if the blueprint for every single event of that day had been carved in stone eons ago, and then set in motion two years ago when Lillian and Felicia had discussed buying out Mountainview Café with their sons. Neither Bryce nor Erik had thought it a good idea. It was too close to the wrong part of town. They didn't see the financial benefits of owning it. And they were worried about their mothers' safety on a daily basis. The café had been held up four times in the past two years—the main reason the previous owner had put it on the market.

But Lillian and Felicia were determined to own a café and beauty salon together. They had purchased it, along with the adjoining pawnshop, torn down the buildings and erected a beautiful structure—one half café and the other half beauty salon. To ease their sons' fears, they'd hired a team of 24/7 security guards. Two were always on the premises during hours of operation. Mountainview Café and Hair Salon had become a flourishing business where the once-divided social classes of Granite Falls now mingled.

The prices were just right for the poor, and the delicious delicacies from the bakery, along with the remarkable hairstyles Lillian whipped together were just right for the rich.

It was the perfect place for a billionaire to literally run into a poor damsel in distress.

No coincidences. Everyone is simply following the path they've been predestined to travel. If Felicia and Lillian hadn't followed their dreams, and if Robert hadn't made a surprise visit to Granite Falls when he did, he and Tashi might never have met, and she would not have called his hotel tonight looking for him.

Every person we meet comes into our lives for mutual and specific reasons and benefits—another of Michael's profound truisms. Tonight, he was saving Tashi's life—*his* specific reason for meeting her, *her* benefit for meeting him. What was *her* specific reason for meeting him, *his* benefit for meeting her? What would, *could* she ever do for him?

As he pulled his car to a stop in the courtyard of his home, Adam realized that he might never know the answers to those questions since he was planning on setting Tashi Holland loose the moment she was feeling better.

This serendipitous liaison between them, this intimate, yet nonsexual relationship was as temporary as his sexual ones. And speaking of sex, or the lack thereof, it was time he began looking for another temporary playmate, one he knew without a doubt he'd have no trouble walking away from once the relationship had run its course. He needed someone to help put distance between him and Tashi Holland before his heart and soul became engaged.

Sadie was right. Balance was safe, and imbalance torment. His scale wasn't tipped to the point of toppling over yet, and at this stage, he'd rather be safe than relive the pain Claire and Denise had caused him.

Happily Ever After wasn't for him. Temporary was working just fine.

CHAPTER FOUR

They were in a tub of cool water, yet the heat from his body was so intense it seemed to scorch her skin from her bones. Or was it her skin that was generating the flames that seemed to fuse their naked bodies together in the scented bubbly liquid?

The water was all the way up to her chin, but she had no fear of drowning because the man sitting behind her, cradling her between his muscular thighs had a secure grip on her lower body.

He was scooping water up with a container and pouring it over her head, then he was massaging her scalp, running his fingers through her hair while he spoke to her in a soothing voice, telling her that everything would be all right, that she was safe, and that he wouldn't let anyone hurt her.

He washed her tenderly like a mother washes her newborn infant, passing a soft washcloth across her back, up along her neck and throat, over the mounds of her breasts, then beneath them. His fingers and the cloth trailed across her chest and her stomach, lower and lower he washed until the cloth brushed between her thighs sending shock waves rushing through her.

"You've been sold to an Arabian Sheikh. They're shipping you out tonight. You've been sold... Sold... Sold... Sheik.... Sold... S..."

"No. No." She struggled against him, fighting to disconnect her body *from his.* "Let me go. Please let me go." *She tried to stand up, to get out of the tub.*

"It's okay, Tashi. It's okay. It's me, Adam. You're safe, dear one. I'm just giving you a bath. Relax, baby. Just relax..."

His voice was like a cascading waterfall, deep and soothing, bringing her back, or pushing her forward—she didn't know. She closed her eyes and settled back down, allowing her body to relax into his.

"There, there," *he murmured.* "It'll all be over soon."

The distant sound of a deep male voice brought Tashi awake. She lay still, her heart racing in her chest as she tried to get a perspective on her surroundings. Turning over onto her back, she opened her eyes and took a panoramic look around.

The room was enormous and everything was white—the walls, the chandeliers extending on silken cords from a vaulted, white tray ceiling that seemed as far away as the sky, the floor-to-ceiling drapes that had been drawn to shade the room, the sofas and chairs scattered about on a white carpet, and the white marble fireplace on a far wall.

Frowning, she narrowed her range of vision. She was lying on a soft mattress covered with white sheets. The padded headboard and footboard of the bed were upholstered with a white silky material that matched the intricate designs of the fluffy white comforter spread over her. Lifting the comforter, Tashi noted that she was wearing a white satin nightgown and panties—items of clothing she'd never seen before.

Was she in heaven? Had she died and gone to heaven?

"No," she whispered as the desire to pee, and a dull ache on the backs of her hands alerted her to the fact that she was still mortal. Her uncle used to take her to church, and according to the minister, there was no pain or peeing in heaven. Well, he didn't actually say that one didn't pee, but she'd gotten the gist of his account of what it meant to be an immortal soul living in heaven.

She glanced toward the left side of the room where a wide archway opened up onto a white marble floor and walls. *Bathroom.* Throwing back the covers, Tashi tried to raise herself up, but immediately fell back against the pillows. The room seemed to spin around her. She let out a soft moan and was trying to gather her strength for a second attempt when she heard a noise like a chair being pushed along the floor. She cocked her ears. The voice she'd heard earlier had stopped, but the sound of heavy footsteps approaching made her pulse quicken.

Burrowing down, Tashi pulled the covers up to her chin and lay very still as the footsteps grew closer, then stopped. Peering through one eye, she glanced at the door on the right side of the room. When she recognized the magnificent figure of the man standing in the doorway, it all came back to her.

She'd been sick for three days. She'd called Adam. He'd come to her aid and brought her back to his home. His friend, Dr. LaCrosse, had examined her while asking her a bunch of questions about what she'd eaten before and since she got sick. He'd asked her about her medical history: how much she normally weighed, if she had any allergies, were there any chronic diseases in her family history, could she be pregnant, and so on. He'd checked her temperature, and then he'd set up an intravenous line. He'd said it was to help her sleep, ease her cramps, bring down her fever, build up her strength, and keep her hydrated.

He'd worked very swiftly, giving Adam orders on how to help. After she was hooked up, the doctor and Adam had left the room talking in hushed voices. Tashi had lain in bed, watching the liquid drip from the sacks hanging on a metal hook at the side of the bed. Soon the medicine was coursing through her veins, working its magic on her. Her cramps had stopped, or maybe she just couldn't feel them, and as she'd drifted off to sleep, Tashi remembered Adam lying next to her, his comforting arms holding her tight through the night.

She mildly remembered him waking her up several times to carry her to the bathroom, rolling the metal hook with her bags of sustenance beside him. She'd gone back to sleep each time, and then he was waking her again. The needles in the backs of her hands were gone and so were her bags. More than once, Adam had propped her up against the comfy headboard and spoon-fed her something warm and tasty then encouraged her to sip something sweet from a glass, and a lot of water. He'd brushed her teeth after each meal.

As she watched him now, standing in the doorway, his handsome face kindled with a sort of passionate beauty, something fluttered around in Tashi's belly. It wasn't hunger. It wasn't cramps. It was the same sensation she'd experienced when she'd bumped into him in the café. Her body had come alive, as it was now…curious about him and confused about the way he made it feel.

As that curiosity intensified, Tashi realized that the vision she'd had a few minutes ago wasn't a dream after all. They were memories. Memories of Adam sitting behind her in the tub, bathing her before Dr. LaCrosse saw her. He'd lifted her from the tub, dried her off in a big fluffy towel, then taken her to the bed and dressed her in the white nightgown and panties. He'd repeated those actions several times during the time she'd been sick. Every time she awoke, it seemed like he was there—as if he'd never left her side.

How long ago was that? How long had she been in his home, in his bed?

Anxiety cooled Tashi's heated thoughts. Where was her bag of cash? Her cell phone? Her eyes darted frantically around. She had to get back to her apartment. If she lost that bag and her phone, she would…

Tashi held her breath as Adam pushed away from the door

and began walking across the gigantic room toward the bed, her anxiety over the whereabouts of her possessions giving way to a different kind of apprehension. He was irresistible in a pair of khaki cargo shorts and a light blue shirt. His lustrous black hair flowed down the sides of his face and bounced against his chest, the tapered ends brushing his narrow waistline as he walked.

As he got closer, Tashi could make out the corded muscles of his arms and legs with the mat of dark hair sprinkled along his olive-toned skin. His humongous bare feet sank noiselessly into the fluffy white carpet. He looked god-like, as if he was above everything on this mundane planet, yet Tashi knew better. He wasn't above it. He'd embraced it—the most elementary part of it—and without hesitation.

Suddenly, all the embarrassment Tashi thought she should have been feeling since Adam Andreas crawled through her bedroom window in the middle of the night, now crashed over her like a tidal wave.

How could she ever face him now? How could she look into those enigmatic blue eyes knowing that he'd seen her in the most disgusting condition of her life, that he'd breathed her stench, washed her filth from her body, seen and touched parts of her anatomy that no other man had ever seen or touched.

And still they were strangers. *Intimate strangers.* Tashi closed her eyes and tried to relax her face muscles and breathe normally as he came within a few yards of the bed. Maybe he'd go away if he thought she was sleeping.

"I know you're awake, Tashi," he said in a low husky voice. "And if you're not, then perhaps a kiss would do the trick."

Tashi's eyes flew open to see a smile playing at the corners of his sexy mouth. A dark stubble shadowed the lower region of his face. He probably hadn't shaved since she'd last seen him. "I'm awake," she said when he attempted to bend over as if he was going to carry out his threat to kiss her.

His smile widened, revealing the even whiteness of his teeth. Tashi had never admired a man's teeth before. She didn't know that a woman might fantasize about a man's teeth, about the way her nipple might look caught between them before his lips closed around her breast.

Tashi felt a curious swooping pull in the area just below her bellybutton. She forced her gaze from Adam's mouth to his eyes. They were soft and gentle as he gazed down at her. They seemed full of knowledge—knowledge about her. No one had ever looked at Tashi that way before—like he knew her, but was still seeing her for the very first time. It made her uncomfortable and excited in the same breath.

"Hi, there," he said.

"Hi." She could feel her dry lips trembling.

"Feeling better?" He perched on the side of the bed as if it was the most natural thing in the world to do, like they'd known each other for a lifetime and were accustomed to sharing these unplanned moments of harmony.

Her need to pee resurfaced, but she still felt lightheaded. He'd done so much for her already, she hated to ask for more of his help. It wouldn't be good for her to become anymore dependent on him. "Yes," she said, licking her lips that were consistently growing drier.

"You must be thirsty. The doctor said to keep you hydrated." Reaching out, he picked up a crystal pitcher from the nightstand and began pouring water into a glass.

"I need to go to the bathroom. Really badly," she said as the sound of water trickling into the glass made her want to pee more. It would be a lot more embarrassing if she wet his nice white bed. "Can you help me up, please? I'm still a little weak."

"Of course." He flashed his even whites at her, and before she could wink, he pulled down the comforter, slid one powerful arm under her upper body and the other under the backs of her knees and picked her up. "Hold on tight," he said, as he'd said the night he'd crawled through her window and picked her up out of her own filth.

Tashi rested her head on his shoulder and wrapped her arms around his neck as he carried her effortlessly across the floor. He smelled nice, like sandalwood and spice. His soft mane and his facial stubble tickled her cheek causing a series of quivers to surge through her veins.

If she weren't certain before, Tashi now knew that she was well on her way to a full recovery. Her body was becoming aware of and responding to Adam in a way it couldn't have while she was writhing around in pain, drugged, and half conscious.

He strolled down a passageway, passing two closed doors on each side. Then they were in a spacious circular-shaped bathroom with wraparound marble counters, a large, open shower stall, and an equally large Jacuzzi under a wall of windows—the only wall in the en suite that wasn't mirrored. Tashi trembled as she recalled sitting naked on Adam's lap submerged in water.

When he set her down in front of the door that opened up to the commode, she was astonished that her legs supported her. "Thank you," she said, glancing at him through lowered lids.

"You're welcome." He gazed down on her, his galvanizing look stirring that army of butterflies in her stomach again.

He was seeing her differently too, Tashi thought in dismay as his gaze slowly traveled down the length of her. She wasn't his sick helpless patient anymore. She was a woman, a young beautiful woman with hot blood running through her veins. A woman whose naked body he'd seen, and bathed, and touched. She was a woman he now desired.

Those primal feelings, those natural cravings for that ultimate physical union between a man and a woman were making their way to the surface of both their minds. Tashi shuddered outwardly

He took a step toward her. "If you need more help, I'll—"

Goodness no. She jumped back and collided with the closed door. "No. I—I can manage." It was one thing for him to hike up her nightgown, pull down her panties, and sit her on the toilet when she was half conscious, but no way now while she was fully awake would she allow him to treat her like a toddler. It was probably second nature to him, seeing he had a two-year-old daughter. But he'd gone even further than merely helping her to the bathroom. He'd seen her through her period that was now thankfully over—changing her pads and taking care of her like nobody in the entire universe had ever done.

To keep her embarrassment hidden from him, Tashi stepped inside the private space and closed the door. She squinted at the sunlight streaming through the window. It wasn't nighttime anymore. The sun had broken through—literally and figuratively. They were no longer shrouded in darkness, and she was no longer delirious with fever and pain—just with desire.

His blue eyes had been laced with as many questions about her as they were with desire for her. He had questions she couldn't answer. She didn't want him getting any further involved in her life. It was too dangerous for him, and his daughter. She would never forgive herself if she caused harm to come to that innocent little girl. The people who were after her wouldn't think twice about killing a child if she got in their way. They were in the business of selling children, some as young as five, into sexual slavery. They killed those who crossed their paths. They'd killed that FBI agent. She was certain that's why she hadn't heard from him. And they would kill Adam, too, if he got in their way.

She'd already said too much when she told Adam that *they* might find her and kill her if she went to the hospital.

Why, oh why had she told him that? Tashi wondered as she

washed her hands and splashed cold water on her face. Why hadn't she just told him that she couldn't go to the emergency room because she didn't have medical coverage? That was the truth. Ever since she'd been on the lam, she'd made it her priority to take care of herself—eat healthily, exercise, dress warmly in the winter, and stay out of the rain in the summer. She'd never been sick once.

Tashi sat down in a nearby chair and dropped her face in her hands. The FBI agent had told her not to trust anyone, not even the police—no one but the man whose name began with *A*. Why hadn't he given her the name when she'd first walked into the house that night, before he gave her all the other instructions on how to escape from the house, the city, about what to do once she got to Granite Falls?

He'd even questioned her about whether or not she'd slept with Scottie—a strange question she'd thought at first, and one she'd refused to answer until he'd asked her quite adamantly again. When she'd responded negatively, he'd let out his breath and the tight line around his mouth had relaxed.

Why was that information more important to him than first giving her his friend's name? The name that had been swallowed up in the first round of gunshots that rang out into the air that night. The agent hadn't even given her his own name. So she couldn't drop it in the hopes that some man here in Granite Falls whose name began with *A* would recognize it, say he was the agent's friend and that…

"Tashi. Are you okay? Do you need help?"

Raising her head, Tashi pulled herself together. There was no lock on the door. "I'm—I'm fine, Adam. I'll be out in a second," she called, hoping to keep him on the other side of the door.

Standing, she stared at her reflection in the mirrored wall above the sink. God, she looked horrible. Dry, tangled hair that was sticking out every which way, puffy eyes, hollow cheeks, and cracked lips made her look like a wasted scarecrow. Yet, just a few minutes ago, Adam had lusted after her. The man was impossible. Too good to be true.

Giving no thought to invading Adam's privacy, Tashi rummaged through the drawers on both sides of the sink until she found a pack of hair elastics. She pulled her hair back from her face and secured it in a ponytail. She pinched her cheeks trying to bring some color back to her complexion. That would have to do until she got back to her apartment. The sooner the better. But she didn't know how to tell Adam she was leaving without seeming ungrateful.

After all, he'd just spent… She had no idea what day it was. Taking a deep breath, she opened the door. Adam was standing on the other side like a sentry on duty, ready to pick her up again if she just said the word.

"What day is it?" she asked, walking ahead of him toward the bedroom. Her legs were still unsteady, but at least she could walk, and without pain at that.

"It's Monday. Afternoon. Four thirty to be exact."

Monday? She faltered in her step.

Immediately his arms went about her. "Whoa. Take it easy."

She leaned back into his support for a few wildly exciting moments and curled her toes into the white carpet that was so silky and fluffy, she felt as if she were standing on air. The heat from their entwined bodies and the distinct bulge pressing into the small of her back reminded Tashi that she was scantily clad and alone in a huge house with an irresistible man. Prying his arms from around her, she continued toward the bedroom, and reached for a robe lying at the foot of the bed. It matched the nightgown she was wearing. She slid it on and tied the satin belt around her waist.

"Adam, whose clothes am I wearing?" she asked. Borrowing a

nightgown wasn't such a big deal, but the thought that the undergarments might belong to one of his lovers made her nauseous.

"My mother's. You're both the same size. Petite and slender."

His mother's? That was worse.

"Don't worry. They've never been worn. You can keep them if you want."

"I thought you said you lived alone." Tashi turned and perched on the edge of the mattress as the effects of being on her feet for too long began to take a toll on the little strength she had. "You said no one else but Dr. LaCrosse would know I'm here."

"I do live alone. My parents live in Como, Italy, but they visit often."

Another reason for her to get out of here fast, Tashi thought as she encountered a certain watchfulness in his gaze. His questions and suspicions were evident and valid. He'd brought a total stranger into his home and nursed her back to health. A stranger who'd told him that people were trying to kill her. He'd done his Good Samaritan deed. She would do him a favor and relieve him of his duties.

She glanced around the room again, and breathed a sigh of relief when she saw her backpack on the floor near the door with a green dress she recognized draped over it. How thoughtful of him to have grabbed her backpack on his way out the night he brought her here. She wished she'd been lucid enough to ask him to get her duffel bag from its hiding place. But that would have led to questions about its contents.

If he knew what was in that bag, he might get the wrong idea. He might think she robbed a bank or something, or that she was a drug dealer, or perhaps had associated with or stolen from one. He might think that a drug-dealing organization was the "they" she was hiding from. Then whatever little respect and sympathy he had for her would be gone. Even though they might never see each other again, Tashi didn't want any thoughts Adam might have about her to be bad. Months, maybe years from now, she wanted to be able to look back on their time together with a smile of gratitude and the thud of excitement in her heart. She wanted to believe that his thoughts of her were pleasant.

The fact that her stuff was stacked near the door meant he was ready for her to leave. He probably had a lot of work to catch up on, work he'd set aside to take care of her. And then there was the matter of his daughter. She could be taking up precious time he should be spending with his child.

She brought her gaze back to his face and offered him a warm smile even as the thought of leaving his tender loving care, of perhaps never seeing him again caused a dull ache inside her. "Thank you, Adam. Thank you for coming when I called, and for taking care of me for these past three days. But I'm feeling a lot better now, so—"

"Well, that was the idea. Getting you better."

His voice was as soft and tender as his eyes. They seemed to massage the hurt, desolate places inside of Tashi—places the human eye couldn't see—just as effectively as his hands had massaged her aching body throughout the past three nights.

"Yes," she said. "That was the idea, and now it's time for me to return to my apartment so you can get on with your life. I know I can never repay you, monetarily—" Well, she could, but he'd want to know where she got the money. "But if there's ever anything I can do to reciprocate your kindness, just say the word. I can babysit for you." She tossed out the lie easily, knowing that the first chance she got, she was leaving Granite Falls. She'd finally come to terms with the possibility that the FBI agent who'd helped her escape that night was dead. He was never coming to explain anything to her. There was no reason for her to stick around and put Adam's, his daughter's, and his parents' lives in jeopardy.

His brows furrowed. "Babysit? And whom would you babysit for me, Tashi?"

"Your daughter. Tiffany."

He threw back his head and laughed.

Tashi swallowed the cry of humiliation that rose to her throat. "You probably have a long list of professional nannies, huh? Why would you trust a stranger with your daughter?"

"No. It's not that," he said, his laughter fading to an arresting chuckle. He crouched down in front of her and held her hands in his. "Tiffany isn't my daughter. She's my goddaughter. I was spending quality time with her that day you and I ran into each other. Dr. LaCrosse—Erik is her father. I don't have any children, Tashi—not yet, anyway, nor do I have a wife," he added as if it was important for her to know that.

"I feel so foolish. I thought..." Her voice trailed off. She'd known that he wasn't married, but it was a relief to know he didn't have any children either. She didn't know why she felt that way, but there it was, a scintilla of elation that he hadn't reproduced with any other woman. But was he involved with anyone? The article she'd read on the Internet hadn't specified about his private life, and she'd been too sick to dig any further into his background.

"You'd really do anything to return my kindness?" he asked softly, rubbing the pads of his thumbs across the insides of her wrists, sending sparks shooting through her blood.

"Anything." Her voice shook.

"Stay."

"What?"

"Stay. Stay here with me. You may be feeling better, but you still don't have your full strength back. Erik said it would take at least a good week or two before you're feeling yourself again.

And that's with you eating three healthy meals a day and staying off your feet. You need someone to take care of you, Tashi. The fact that you called my hotel looking for me that night tells me that you have no one else. Am I right?"

Tashi tugged her hands from his and wrapped them around her middle. The invitation was tempting, but the repercussions could be deadly for Adam. "Why? Why are you being so kind to me?"

"It's the right thing to do."

"Meaning you would do the same for a stray dog."

He tilted his head to one side and gazed at her. "Where's this sudden hostility coming from, Tashi?"

It seems like the only way to get you out of my life. "I have to get back to my apartment," she said, attempting to rise from the bed.

He placed his hands on her shoulders and pressed her gently back down. "You can't go back to your apartment. Not yet."

Panic rioted inside her. "Why? What happened?"

"Nothing. It needs to be cleaned and fumigated. There were rodents running about the night I took you out of there. And you need a new refrigerator. Remember how you got sick?"

She dropped her gaze to the floor. Tashi had never felt so ashamed of where she lived before, of the image of her in that place branded in Adam's mind. She'd been too sick to think or care about it, but sitting now on Adam's white bed, in his white palatial bedroom, in his mother's white satin clothes, she felt the heat of humiliation creeping through her.

"I'll talk to your landlord and have him replace the fridge," Adam said, obviously unaware of her dilemma.

Her head shot up. "No. You can't talk to my landlord."

"Why not?"

"It's not his responsibility. The previous tenant left it there. It's my responsibility to replace it."

His eyes narrowed. "Can you afford to replace it? Do you even have a job, Tashi? How do you survive?"

Alarm and anger rippled along Tashi's spine conquering the spaces where humiliation had occupied seconds ago. She hadn't even realized what she'd done until she was halfway to the door.

"Tashi."

She glanced over her shoulders to see Adam sprawled on the floor where she'd pushed him in her haste to escape, a stunned look on his face. "I'm sorry, Adam. I don't mean to seem ungrateful, but I have to go."

She gave no thought to taking off her clothes in front of him. It didn't matter. He'd already seen all of her that was to be seen. She dropped the robe and the nightgown on the floor and pulled her dress over her head.

"Tashi, I'm sorry if my questions upset you, but you can't leave like this."

Tashi felt miserable for treating him so unkindly after all he'd done for her, but it was the only way to keep him safe. She turned as he came up beside her. "I'm sorry, Adam, but I need to go. I have to go, and I can't tell you why. Just—just let me go."

"Okay," he said, raising his hands in treaty. "I'll take you back to your apartment, but only after you eat something. You haven't eaten since breakfast. You slept through lunch so I know you must be starving. I made you a chicken casserole. It's warming in the oven."

Tashi's stomach growled at the mention of food. She was hungry, and there was nothing at her apartment to eat. Since she didn't have a fridge, she would have to live on takeout until she figured out her next move—what state, what town she was moving to, and how to go about obtaining a new identity. She would love to leave the country, but using her name to obtain a passport would definitely raise a lot of red flags. Maybe after she assumed a new identity...

Tashi never thought her life could have gotten any more complicated after that night in New York City. Fifteen months ago, she'd gone into hiding after killing a man who intended to hurt her. And since then, she'd been living with guilt about the one who'd died to save her. Now here she was, running again to save another who wanted to help her.

An inner torment gnawed at Tashi as she faced the harsh realities of a life of loneliness. Until she knew what happened in that house after she escaped, until she knew who was after her, she could never have friends, or a…

As her fears mounted, she had an overwhelming need to rest her head on Adam's chest and feel his arms about her one last time. Until the day she'd bumped into him, it had been months since anybody had hugged her, so long since she'd felt the warmth of human contact. She longed to be close to him again, kiss him even. But she throttled back those feelings for his sake. If she showed any weakness now, he would be more adamant about keeping her around.

"Tashi? Will you eat something first?"

His gentle voice pulled Tashi out of the cocoon of anguish wrapping around her. "Yes. Okay. I'll—I'll eat. Then you'll take me to my apartment?"

"Yes."

"No more questions?"

"No more questions."

CHAPTER FIVE

Adam watched relief settle into her features at his promise to cease questioning her. He knew she was pushing him away because she was afraid for him. She was alone in the world, but when the one person she'd reached out to in her hour of dire need offered to help her, she panicked.

"Come." Taking her hand, he led her out of the bedroom, across the hall, through the living room and into the dining area. Her hand felt almost as small as Tiffany's clasped within his. She was so frail, a strong gust of wind would send her toppling to the ground.

He seated her at the table that was already set for two. He brought the casserole from the oven and served her a good portion, then he got the pitcher of vegetable and fruit he'd juiced while she was in the bathroom and filled up their glasses.

"Thank you," she said, attempting to give him a smile. "It smells delicious."

"Too bad you don't have a refrigerator to take some home for later. When do you think you'll have one? I can bring some food around for you."

She dropped her head, picked up her fork, and immediately began eating.

Was she trying to shut him up or was she that hungry? Maybe a little of both. Adam smiled inside at her subtle wit as he lowered his weight into the chair across from her and picked up his fork.

They ate in tacit silence, and he kept filling her dish and her water and juice glasses while questions she'd asked him not to ask swam around in his head. Questions like who were the 'they' she'd mentioned the other night? Why did 'they' want her dead? Was she afraid to be around him because 'they' had hurt or killed someone she loved?

Adam tensed as he recalled Tashi's reaction when he'd tried to bathe between her thighs the other night. She'd been weak and feverish one moment, then the next had suddenly become violent, jabbing her elbows into his ribs and fighting to get out of the tub. Had someone sexually molested her? His stomach crunched at the thought, and a need for revenge he never knew was in him sizzled through Adam.

Her attempt to shield him from danger wired his resolve to find whoever had hurt her and make them pay. She was a damsel in distress, but a fighting, independent, strong-willed one, totally different from those in his past who'd expected him to fight their battles and save them from their plights.

Tashi was trying to save him by pushing him away. But if he granted her wish, Adam knew that he would regret it for the rest of his life. Strange, since he knew nothing about her—but there it was anyway—that nagging feeling in his gut, that *knowing* in his heart that his cousin and his friends said they'd gotten when they first met their wives.

He'd never felt that with Claire, or Denise, or any other woman he'd ever dated.

"What's in this drink?" she asked, breaking into his thoughts.

He looked up to see her twirling the juice around in her glass. He smiled. "Um, let me think... Uh—cucumber, broccoli, squash, kale, carrots, celery, ginger..." He furrowed his brows. "An apple, an orange, a banana, and yes, a couple slices of lemon. Do you like it?"

She nodded. "It's tasty. I never knew fruits and raw vegetables could taste this good blended together." She gave him a bright smile, making his heart flip over in his chest. "This is what you've been feeding me for three days? Along with warm broth?"

Adam finished his juice and set his glass noiselessly down on the black placemat. "Yes. It's a great way to get your vitamins and other nutrients without the fiber. And fiber you did not need. The natural sugars and salt provide electrolytes that help to balance the water and pH level in your blood and strengthen your muscle function. You lost a lot of electrolytes. That's why you were still feeling a little achy and lightheaded earlier. How do you feel now?" He placed his elbows on the table and leaned in a little toward her.

"A lot better. Thanks." She rubbed her tummy and flashed him another demure smile that made his heart skip another beat. "You know a lot about treating salmonella poisoning," she added over the rim of her water glass.

"Well, I'm in the food industry, so..." He spread his hands. "And Erik gave me instructions on how to take care of you. He called this morning to see how you were. He's been calling everyday, actually. He'd like to see you again to give you a good bill of health."

She shook her head. "No, I'm fine. Please, thank him for me."

Meaning: *I won't be around much longer.* The thought caused a dull ache in his gut.

Her lips parted slightly. "You're a good man to take me in

and care for me, Adam Andreas. Nobody but my uncle has ever been this kind to me."

Through the glass-topped table, he watched her hands fold and unfold on her lap. "Where's your uncle?" he asked as casually as he could. *Why hadn't she called him?*

She averted her gaze for a brief moment by looking out the wall of glass overlooking Mount Washington and the Presidential Range. She turned back to him. "He's dead."

Sadness dulled her voice and the glimmer of light that had returned to her emerald eyes. "How did he die?"

"He had pancreatic cancer. It's been almost two years."

Adam let out the breath he'd been holding since she mentioned her uncle. He'd expected her to say that he'd died at the hands of whoever was after her. "I'm sorry. It sounds like you were very close."

"He raised me since I was four years old."

"Really? Where were your parents?"

She shivered as if someone had poured a bucket of ice-cold water over her. "It's getting late. I should help you clean up before I leave." She picked up her empty plate and silverware from the table.

"No. No. Leave them. You're to stay off your feet. Doctor's orders." Adam tried to force some humor into his voice even as he battled his frustration over her determination to leave the safety and comfort of his home, to refuse the tender loving care he was extending toward her. "Would you like some dessert?" he asked, desperately seeking a way to keep her around a little bit longer. "I have some leftover blueberry tart."

"Thanks, but no. I'm quite full. Everything was delicious, Adam. You are an amazing cook."

"I'll be happy to cook for you every day, Tashi."

Bypassing his bait, she pushed back her chair.

Adam dropped his napkin on the table and hurried around to

help her up. He placed his hands on her shoulders and turned her around to face him. "Tashi, please stay, if only for the night. I'll take you home first thing tomorrow morning." It was killing him to think of her being in that dump, much less being there alone when she wasn't fully recovered.

"I—I—can't. There are things I need to do." She pulled out of his grasp and began making her way back toward the bedroom.

"What kind of things?" he asked, following behind her. There was a distinct spring in her steps now that she'd eaten. He was happy he could do that for her. "What do you have to do that can't wait until tomorrow, Tashi?"

She continued walking without even as much as a turn of her head to acknowledge that she'd heard him. Her silence intensified his curiosity, but remembering how she'd withdrawn into her shell when he'd asked about her parents a few minutes ago, he decided not to push any further.

"Thanks for bringing my backpack," she said, picking it up from the bedroom floor and setting it on the chair.

"It was open, and I noticed your camera, laptop, and wallet inside it. I didn't want to leave it at your apartment—just in case—"

"I know. It's not a safe neighborhood. There're a lot of break-ins."

"Someone broke into your place before?"

"No. I keep my windows and doors locked all the time. You did lock up, right?" she asked looking up at him with panicky eyes.

"I did." As he stared at her, Adam had the feeling that her concern went a lot deeper than someone breaking in to steal her clothes, furniture, and the few personal items she might have.

She searched through the compartments of the backpack. "You didn't happen to grab my cell phone, too, did you?"

He shook his head. "I'm sorry. I didn't think…"

She bit her lower lip as if that bit of bad news was particularly distressing.

"I'm sure it's fine, and if not, I'll buy you another one. I'd be happy to replace your fridge, too. You can't live without—"

"It doesn't matter. He's never going to call anyway," she said, staring across the room as if she'd just lost her last bit of hope.

"Who? Who's not going to call, Tashi?"

"Nobody. I'm ready to leave." She glanced down at her bare feet. "Do I have shoes?"

"No. I carried you out of your apartment that night and didn't think of grabbing those either. I wasn't thinking of anything that night but bringing you here so Erik could examine you. I'm sure I can find a pair of my mother's you can borrow, or I could just carry you again," he added on a smile.

Adam was taken aback when she took a step forward and wrapped her arms about his waist and rested her cheek against his chest. He hesitated for a split second before his arms went about her. Her hair was dry and stiff like straw. A good shampoo and deep conditioning in his downstairs spa would rejuvenate the soft, silky curls he'd felt almost a week ago. But he knew she wouldn't stick around for that lavish treatment. So for now, he took what she offered and held her as tightly as he dared in her delicate condition. Yet, her fragility didn't stop his body from responding to her like a man responds to a woman's touch.

Tashi was beautifully housed, exquisite, and the image of her lovely naked hourglass body, the firmness of her high-perched breasts, the silky texture of her skin, the soft curves of her hips, the erotic feel of her buttocks pressed against his morning erection were stamped in his brain for all eternity. All the emotions and sexual tensions Adam had been suppressing while he'd been taking care of a sick Tashi were now demanding acknowledgement.

His body was on fire. He wanted to kiss her. God, how he'd love to taste her lips, but he knew it would be a terrible mistake to even attempt to satisfy his yearning. She might be feeling better, but she was still weak. Besides, the memory of her fighting him in the tub warned him that any kind of sexual advances toward her would be a mistake.

Tashi Holland was a woman he dared not pursue in a sexual way. He had to stand down and wait patiently for her to make the first move. He hoped she would learn to trust him enough to open up about her past so he could help and protect her. It was impossible to help and protect someone when you didn't know what kind of help they needed and from what or whom you were providing protection.

Adam rubbed his hands along the curve of her back and basked in the blessing of having her in his arms on her own volition.

"We should go," she said, pulling away and bringing his euphoria to an end, much too soon.

No, we shouldn't. Three days ago, he'd vowed to set her loose the moment she was feeling better. So why was he having such a hard time of it, especially when she wanted to leave? Why was he finding it difficult to keep his own law: no damsels in distress?

"If you don't mind, I'd appreciate it if we could stop at the grocery store on the way to my apartment," she said, picking up her backpack and looping her arms through the strap.

"I don't mind. Whatever you need."

Two hours later, Adam parked his Aston Martin on the curb across from Tashi's apartment building. He glanced out his tinted side window. A balding, potbellied man, wearing nothing but a pair of plaid boxers sat on the porch steps, smoking a cigarette. The man glanced briefly at his car as if he sensed he was being watched before moving on, completely uninterested and unimpressed.

A skinny young blond woman in a tank top and cutoff jean shorts was reclined on the old couch jammed against the wall. Her bare feet with soles black with dirt were slung over the wooden railing of the porch. She was texting away on her cell phone and paying no attention to the two toddlers who were splashing water on each other from a kiddie pool that was too close to the road. A brown lab, perhaps the one that had barked the night he'd come to rescue Tashi, was asleep on the floor behind a screen door situated about four feet away from Tashi's.

Adam's gaze shifted to the park across the street where four teenage shirtless boys were shooting hoops into a tattered basket. An old rusted fridge lay on its side against the side of the broken-down fence that once surrounded the park. A washing machine in similar shape was stacked on top of it. The appliances had been there so long that grass and shrubbery had grown up around them.

Adam's jaw flinched at the scene that was synonymous with poor neighborhoods. It had taken all his willpower not to turn his car around and head for the hills the instant he entered the depressing zone. He didn't think these people were beneath him in any way. He just felt sorry for them, and even sorrier that he was bringing someone he'd cared for, and was now definitely beginning to care about, to the neighborhood.

"I guess this where we say goodbye."

Adam turned his head at the sound of Tashi's voice. *Goodbye? No.* Seated beside him, she clutched her backpack as if it held everything dear she had in this world. "Tashi. I don't feel right leaving you here."

"It's fine, Adam. I've been living here for a year and a half and nobody has ever bothered me." Her faint smile held a touch of sadness, even though her tone rang with tenacity.

Where did you live before that? "There's always a first for everything."

"Just because these people are poor doesn't mean they're bad, Adam. Most of them work hard to provide for their families—sometimes two and three jobs just to survive."

He noted that she hadn't included herself in the equation of nice poor people. She was living among them, but the way she carried herself, her very appearance and the fact that she owned a very expensive camera and laptop, and had nice furniture in her run-down apartment, said a lot about her upbringing, her past. She was used to nice things, perhaps not as luxurious as he was, but nice.

He would guess that the uncle who'd raised her lived in a middleclass neighborhood—nothing like this place. So what was she doing here, two years after he died from pancreatic cancer? Did the treatment for his illness deplete all his financial resources, leaving him bankrupt, and Tashi without any means of support? And again, the question about the whereabouts of her parents surfaced.

Adam sighed inwardly as the mystery of Tashi Holland thickened. "That's true, Tashi, and I wasn't suggesting that—"

"Sometimes the privileged are the worst people out there. They act nice at first to get you to trust them then they prey on the poor and the naïve to satisfy their own selfish needs."

Adam wondered at the vehemence in her tone. What privileged jackass had hurt this girl? What had "they" done to make her so afraid, so paranoid, so distrustful, so hostile? "Tashi—"

"Thanks for the ride, and for everything else." Her hand went to the door handle.

"Wait." Adam unbuckled his seat belt and exited the car. Was the fact that he was privileged the reason she was becoming wary of him? It was one thing to call him in the middle of the night when she thought she was dying. That was a matter of survival. But now that she was feeling better and could think clearly in the light of day, she was seeing him differently. He was no longer her *savior*. He had become a threat, a reminder of something bad in her past.

And here he was, thinking that Tashi Holland wanted to protect him, when what she *really* wanted was to get the hell away from him as fast as possible. He almost laughed at himself for thinking that she needed him. She didn't need him. She probably despised him, merely because he was privileged.

Adam opened her door and took her backpack. A zap of electricity coursed through him as he held her hand to help her out of the car. He swallowed the dizzying effect her touch had on him. He watched her eyes widen and darken as she inhaled quickly before pulling away, dropping her gaze to his chest where his heart was making an awful ruckus inside his ribcage. Yep. She'd felt that too. She was becoming aware of him as a man, a man she perceived as a dangerous attraction, and perhaps even a threat to her life.

Forcing the nauseating thought aside, he handed her her backpack and opened the back door of the car to retrieve her two bags of groceries—peanut butter, raspberry preserves, bread, some cans of soup and tuna fish, a small assortment of fruits and vegetables that didn't need to be refrigerated and some Gatorade he'd suggested she purchase.

"I'll see you inside," he said, closing the door and straightening up to his full six feet, three and a half inches.

She tried to pry the bags from his hand. "I can manage from here."

"Tashi, I'm seeing you inside."

"There's no need, Adam. You've done enough already." The line of her mouth tightened a fraction.

"I'm either seeing you safely inside your apartment or I'll put you back into my car and take you back home with me. It's your choice, Tashi." He made no attempt to suppress his steadfastness. Did she think she was the only one who could be headstrong?

Her green eyes flashed defiance before she turned and took an agitated step off the curb, and into the street.

He grabbed her arm and pulled her back up on the sidewalk as a black Mazda sped around the corner and zapped past them with its stereo blasting at top level. A few yards down, tires screeched as it swerved and braked, barely missing a child riding his bike across the street.

"Stupid punk!" the man on the steps shouted. "He's gonna kill somebody one day."

The dog was barking up a storm from behind the safety of the screen door. As dogs were wont to do, a couple more from nearby houses joined the canine chorus, until the texting young woman who was now on her feet yelled, "Shut up, Bacon!"

Bacon growled and shut up, and soon all was quiet in the neighborhood again—well except for the clamorous humming of the window air conditioning units.

Adam felt as if a year of his life had been shaved off in those few frightful moments. He couldn't tell if time had stood still or if it had sped up since the car, now long gone, had come careening around the corner.

As the thought that Tashi could have been killed registered in his brain, Adam glanced down at her flushed cheeks and wide frightened eyes. "See, you do need me."

"Thanks for saving my life. Again." Her hand was pressed against her heaving chest and her breath was coming out in gasps.

"Is this normal around here?"

"Why, isn't it normal in your neighborhood? No rich young punks live in your neck of the woods, Mr. Andreas?" She stared blankly back at him.

Her flippant attitude reminded Adam that he was the outsider here, and when she tried to tug away from his hold, he also remembered that she didn't trust him, even though he'd just saved her life for the second time in less than a week. Or was she deliberately trying to make him not like her? Well, she might as well…

"Hey man, sweet ride."

Adam looked up as the boys who'd been shooting hoops walked toward them. The speeding car, the barking dogs, and the yelling neighbors must have drawn their attention to him. Downwind of them, he almost choked on his next breath. They smelled like young men who'd been sweating profusely on a hot and humid summer evening.

"Is it hot?" one of them asked as he walked around the Aston Martin inspecting it closely, but respectfully not touching it.

"No, it's very cold," Adam replied, tightening his hold on Tashi's arm.

"Did you win it in a game or something?" another asked.

"Wanna play us for it?"

"Perhaps another time," Adam said with a smile as he addressed the dark-haired one who was dribbling the basketball on the sidewalk. The boy reminded him of himself when he was that age. Always ready for a competition. He and Massimo had challenged each other over a host of things when they were younger, even girls. He was about to lead Tashi across the street when he stopped. "What's your name?" he asked the boy who'd dared him.

"Joshua Cain McCall," he said, tucking the basketball under his arm. "Some of my friends call me Josh, and some call me Cain. My mom goes to church."

"She lives there," one of his friends piped in, drawing chuckles from the rest.

"Hey, don't talk about my momma." Josh playfully shoved his friend.

Adam watched them, enjoying the camaraderie between them. It reminded him so much of the Granite Falls Bachelors Club that he, Bryce, Erik, and Massimo had formed in high school. He felt a little blue that he was the only remaining member of that club. "Do you know where Granite Falls Country Club is, Josh?" Adam asked as a thought materialized in his mind.

"Yeah. It's off Country Club Road on the other side of town near the highway."

Adam nodded. "They have a great court and if you're still up to the challenge, my friends and I will be happy to play you and your friends. Four on four."

"Yeah, we're up to it," his friends said in unison.

Josh's jaw dropped. "Seriously?"

"Seriously. You have nothing to lose and this baby to win." He jutted his chin at his car.

"Okay, dude. You're on." Josh dug into the pocket of his shorts. "Here's my C.I."

Deciding not to release his hold on Tashi who'd been subtly trying to pry loose during his exchange with the boys, Adam set the bags of groceries on the hood of his car and took the card Josh held out to him. He glanced at the company name: McCall & Co. Computer Services. "You're a computer geek?"

"Yeah. I started MCCCS as a little side business. I fix computers, build websites, and offer Internet advice, et cetera, to help out my mom. I'm the oldest of five. My dad split when my sister was a baby." He shrugged. "But we doin' fine. We still here. When they saw how lucrative the business is—" He waved at his friends. "My boys came on board. We work out of my mom's basement for now and we're all trying to get into MIT next year when we graduate. But you know how it is. Fierce competition and lack of tuition funds."

Adam had no idea how it was to want something and not be able to have it. Well, until now, he thought shifting his gaze to Tashi. Her trust was something he had to earn.

"I need to go," she said, her emerald eyes flashing the annoyance she felt at being forced to stay and listen to a conversation that didn't concern or interest her one bit.

Josh's gaze followed his to Tashi. "Wow, she's hot. She your girl?" he asked.

"No. I'm not his *girl*."

Adam stifled a laugh as Josh and his friends jumped back, their eyes wide as if a snake had hissed at them. He slipped the card into his shirt pocket. "I'll call you with the time of our tournament, Josh."

"Okay. I'm looking forward to it."

The boys filed back toward the park, debating who would hold the keys to the Aston when they swept the court with the old dude and his friends. One suggested selling it for tuition money for all of them. The others agreed that was a good idea, and that once they finished college and their computer business was thriving, they could each buy an Aston Martin of their own.

Impressed with their confidence in winning, and their long-term goal planning, Adam picked up the bags of groceries and glanced both ways before escorting Tashi across the street.

"Would you really give them your car, just like that?" she asked gazing up at him.

"Of course, if they win."

"Right."

Adam smiled at her "I'll believe it when I see it" roll of her eyes. She probably thought he had an ulterior motive for accepting the young men's challenge, that he was cooking up some devious plot to *get them*. Well, he would just have to change her mind about him.

"Would you like to play me for it or another of your choice?" he asked. "I notice you don't have a car. Is it because you can't afford one? Do you have a job? Do you even have a driver's license?" The answer to at least one of those questions would give him an idea of where she was from, where she'd lived before moving to this godforsaken neighborhood. He was going to have a talk with the town planning board. This was just unacceptable.

"You're asking questions, Adam."

"How else am I supposed to get to know you?"

"You don't need to get to know me."

Too late, I've already seen you naked.

"Hi, Kyle. Hi, Britt," she called to the toddlers as she passed the kiddie pool.

"Tashi, Tashi," the little boy said, giving her a huge grin. The little girl just smiled.

They were really cute kids. Adam killed the desire to pull the kiddie pool away from the road and farther into the yard that would have been a lawn if someone had taken the time to plant and maintain the grass. He could understand how a well-kept lawn would be the furthest thing from these residents' minds, especially when they worked two and three jobs to make ends meet.

"Hi, Billy," Tashi said, as they ascended the steps.

Billy grunted, took the last drag on his cigarette, and crushed it out on the step. He paid no attention to Adam, got up, and walked down the stairs toward the kids as if he was deliberately trying to avoid small talk. He needn't have bothered, Adam thought as he watched Billy gather the kids and walk them to the back of the house. He'd had no plans to engage him.

"Hey, Tashi," the young woman said as they walked across

the porch toward Tashi's apartment. "Where you been, girl?" She leaned against the railing, ready for an earful.

"Hey, Mindy," was Tashi's only response as she stopped in front of her door.

So, it wasn't just him, Adam thought. She was closed-mouthed with everyone.

While Tashi dug into her backpack for her keys, Mindy smiled at him, her brown eyes running slowly up and down the length of him while she smacked away on a piece of gum.

She wasn't bad looking, Adam thought. A good scrub and some decent clothes would significantly enhance her appearance and chances. He'd seen the improvement in several Granite Falls residents whom he'd help transition to the better side of town by way of scholarships, apprenticeships, and good-paying jobs.

His, Erik, and Massimo's fathers had taught them that it was their civic duty to help those less fortunate than themselves, especially the citizens of their immediate communities. A town was only as affluent as its people. It was up to the wealthy to keep the scales tipped in their favor. Adam felt a sense of duty as he glanced across the street at Joshua Cain McCall and his friends. The balance would be tipped a little bit more in his favor.

"This your new boyfriend, Tashi?" Mindy asked, her eyes never wavering from Adam. "He's hot."

"No," Tashi replied, as she began to slide her keys into the locks, one at a time. "He's just a friend."

Oh, so he *was* a friend. He would never have guessed.

"You left your bedroom window opened, so I closed it," Mindy said.

Adam watched Tashi's body go stiff.

"What? When?"

"Yesterday. The bottom part was wide open. I know how you are about keeping your windows closed especially when you're out. I called out for you, but you didn't answer, so I thought you forgot to close it. That's what good neighbors do for each other. You babysit for me and wouldn't let me pay you, so I thought I'd return the favor."

Adam hadn't even realized that Tashi was no longer on the porch until he heard the blood-curdling scream from inside her apartment.

He dropped her bags of groceries and raced inside. "Tashi!"

CHAPTER SIX

Tashi swung her hands frantically back and forth inside the gaping hole in the back wall of her bedroom closet. Maybe she'd missed it the first time she looked. She swallowed in desperation, but as her hand moved noiselessly through the black empty space, the harsh reality registered in her brain.

Her duffel bag with all her money was gone. *Gone.* And so was her cell phone.

Tashi screamed her anger into the air, and as an avalanche of utter despair and hopelessness descended on her, she collapsed to the floor and buried her face in her hands. Hard sobs erupted from her throat as a numb ache settled in her belly then quickly spread to the rest of her body.

How was she going to survive without that money? She couldn't buy food or pay her utilities. She couldn't leave town. She couldn't work. *She couldn't do anything.* She was trapped. *Trapped, broke, and alone.* And in two weeks, she would be homeless since she had no money to pay her rent. She may as well be dead. Her eyes stung from the hot tears that poured out of them.

"Tashi. Sweetheart."

Tashi was barely aware of Adam's voice, or his body dropping down beside her, cradling her against him.

"*Tesora, ciò che è sbagliato?*"

"It's gone. It's gone. They took it. They took it all!"

"What's gone? What did they take?"

"My money. All of my money. They took all of it. It's all I had in this world." Her hands fell listlessly to the floor and her head slopped down on Adam's chest as she gave in to the agonizing maelstrom inside her.

"*Cara.* I'm sorry. I'm so sorry. It's my fault. It's all my fault. I forgot to close the window."

"I can't…. I can't do this anymore. I can't live like this… I can't…" She wrapped her hands about Adam's waist as her body shook from her misery and defeat. "They took…they took my cell and…and now he…he can't call me. He can't call me…."

Adam's heart was ripping apart for the woman weeping hysterically in his arms as she clutched him as if he were her only hope in the universe. He wanted so much to ask her about the "he" who couldn't call her, about how much money was stolen from her, and what she meant by she couldn't live this way anymore.

Now he understood the frantic look in her eyes earlier today when she'd asked if he'd locked up the apartment and if he'd happened to grab her phone the night he'd taken her to his home. Her money and her cell phone were the reasons she'd been anxious to get back to her apartment, only to find them gone. He felt horrible for failing to close the damn window after he'd crawled through it, for creating more havoc in her already tumultuous life.

God, he wished he knew what was going on with her. What kind of trouble she was in.

"What's wrong, Tashi? Why you crying, girl?"

Adam looked up to see Mindy standing near the bedroom door, staring at him and Tashi on the floor.

Tashi's sobs ceased and she stiffened in his arms, but she didn't try to lift her head or respond to Mindy? In fact, her arms tightened around him as if silently begging him to shield her from the rest of the world, to never leave her alone, to never let her go.

In that instant, Adam vowed in his heart that he would die protecting her if it came to that. Whoever was after her would have to go through him first, and then his three trusted friends before they got to her.

"Someone broke into her apartment," he said to Mindy. "They stole her money and her phone, and maybe more." He shrugged. "I don't know, yet. Did you see anyone strange hanging around in the past three days?"

Mindy shook her head. "No. We weren't home since Friday. Me and Billy and the kids went to visit my mom in Evergreen. But I can ask the kid two doors down. He came by to feed and walk Bacon. My mom doesn't like dogs. They must have come through there." She jutted her chin at the window. "That's why it was open. You want me to call the cops?" She held up her cell.

"No. No cops." Tashi pushed out of his arms, and stared at Mindy.

Just like no hospital the other night, he thought, watching her closely. Was she hiding from the law? God, he hoped not.

Mindy gave her a strange look. "You sure? 'Cause they caught the guys who broke into Mrs. Shane's house last week. They got back most of her jewelry and stuff. How much money we talking about, anyway?" She advanced farther into the room. "You got some nice furniture, Tashi," she remarked, glancing around. "That leather couch, and plasma TV... How you afford this stuff? You don't even work." She ran her hand along the glossy cherry surface of Tashi's bureau that matched her nightstands, and the head and footboards of her bed.

Tashi looked at him with a hesitant plea in her eyes.

Mindy's curiosity mirrored his, but Adam was not about to let her questions upset Tashi any further. The girl had been through enough, and whether or not she wanted him to, he was taking her back to his home, and he was keeping her there until she told him her story. All of it.

She owed him the truth, and her trust.

He helped her to her feet, and leading her over to the bed, he sat her on the edge of the unmade mattress. "Just sit here, *cara*. I'll take care of everything."

Too weak, too numb, and too distraught to protest, she leaned against the footboard and stared across the room as if she didn't recognize where she was. Or perhaps she just didn't care. Someone had invaded her private space and stolen her most treasured possessions—possessions that were obviously linked to her survival, and to someone important in her past.

Adam closed his eyes briefly, hoping that the "he" she'd mentioned wasn't a man she was in love with and who was in love with her. The thought of her with another man was...

"You sure he's not your boyfriend, Tashi? 'Cause he sure treating you like he is. Girl, you should make him your boyfriend. If a guy treated me like that, I'd be——"

"Mindy, can you do me a favor?" Adam walked over to the window and opened it to let some air in. The smell wasn't as horrible as the night he'd climbed through it to save Tashi, perhaps because it had been ajar for two days, but it was stuffy in the room, nonetheless.

Mindy gave him a provocative smile as she smacked away on her gum. "Sure. What?"

"I'll need some large trash bags. Can you check the kitchen?"

"Sure." She looked a bit disappointed, but immediately left to do his bidding.

She was a pleaser, Adam thought as he began emptying the contents of the bureau drawers and the closet on the bed.

Tashi didn't have much, so by the time Mindy returned with a box of thirty-gallon trash bags, all of Tashi's clothes were in a small pile on the bed.

He gave a bag to Mindy. "Can you gather her personal things from the bathroom and put them in this? No cleaners or laundry soaps or anything like that. Just necessities you think a woman would want to take if she were going on a long vacation."

"Sure. Okay. You taking her with you?"

She'd thankfully discarded her gum. The clicking sound was getting on his nerves. "Yes." He began to stuff handful of clothes into a trash bag, hangers and all. He just wanted to get the hell out of this place as soon as possible, even more so than he had the other night.

"Can you take me, too? Me and my kids?" Mindy asked from the bathroom.

"What about Billy?"

"What about him?"

"You'd just leave him like that?"

"He'd be happy if I left. He's always complaining that my kids are noisy and annoying. But he puts up with us."

"Really? He puts up with you?" Adam's lips twisted into a hard line as he tied the drawstring of the first bag, set it on the floor, and pulled another bag from the box. *Two bags.* All Tashi's clothes fit into two trash bags—well, one and a half bags, since the pile on the bed was a lot smaller now.

"Wait a minute," Mindy yelled from the bathroom. "You think Billy is my…" She chuckled.

"Billy's her brother."

Adam turned and glanced at Tashi. She still had a blank look on her face as she watched him stuff her belongings into the bag. He hesitated, waiting for her to stop him. She didn't, and instead turned her head and gazed out of the window, as if she were at peace with the fact that someone was making decisions for her.

Mindy emerged from the bathroom. Her bag hardly had anything in it. "My mom had me late in life. She said I was an even bigger mistake than Billy. She was good to us and looked after us when we were kids, but she wasn't overly joyful at having us." She opened the drawer of the nightstand and began to toss the contents into the bag. "She didn't even put any effort into naming us. Just, Billy and Mindy. They aren't short for anything, and we don't have middle names." She shrugged dismissively. "I got pregnant with Kyle when I was seventeen, and she threw me out. I moved in with his father and two of his friends, then we had Brittany."

Adam set the other bag on the floor. It was hard to believe Mindy was basically the same age as he suspected Tashi was, yet she looked a lot older. A hard-knock life did age a person. Billy was probably ten years younger than he looked, and if Tashi stayed here, she'd be aging fast, too. "Where's the kids' father?" he asked Mindy.

Mindy sat down on the mattress. "He died in a motorcycle accident when Brittany was two months. I've been living with Billy ever since."

"I didn't know that, Mindy. I'm sorry," Tashi said, joining the conversation.

Dear Lord, this place was chock-full of sorrow and disappointment. Grabbing another bag from the box, Adam walked to the closet to get the few pairs of shoes she owned, and to make sure he hadn't left anything but the neatly folded sheets and towels on the shelf. He grabbed one more bag and scooped up the soiled bed sheets and her nightgown that he'd tossed on the floor three nights ago and dumped them inside. He tied the bag securely and dropped it in a corner.

"Thanks for all your help, Mindy," Tashi said.

"Hey." Mindy scooted down to sit next to Tashi. "I'll miss you, and not just because you babysit for me for free once in a while when I have to work late, and you keep to yourself a lot, and don't socialize, but I'm sure you have your reasons. Even though I can't say we're friends, I'll miss you. I'll miss not having you next door."

Adam's heart did a jig when he saw the slight hint of a smile on Tashi's face. While the women talked, he went and washed his hands in the bathroom, then walked into the living room and the kitchen to check for important items Tashi might want to take. There was nothing of sentimental value as far as he could tell.

There were no pictures on her walls, no little trinkets or other personal items, no photographs—none of the little odds and ends people collected over the years and displayed to express their uniqueness and make a house a home. There was nothing to show that Tashi Holland had a past, nor where that past was located. That lack of "stuff" only meant one thing: she'd left her previous home in haste. All she'd brought with her to this new location was a bag of money and a cell phone, and now they were gone.

She had nothing tying her to this neighborhood. *She has nothing tying her to this town either.* The perturbing point sent him back into the direction of the bedroom where the women were talking quietly and holding hands like longtime girlfriends, even though their earlier conversation indicated that they hardly knew each other.

"Where do you work, Mindy?" he asked, strolling over to them.

"At the convenience store on the corner. I don't have a car so I had to take something in walking distance."

"Do you like it there?"

She snorted. "Like I like sandals in winter. They keep my feet off the snow, but they don't keep them warm."

Adam was impressed at her analogy. The girl had a brain. She'd just made some wrong decisions at too early an age, and was now stuck with raising two children on her own. He understood all about making wrong decisions—he'd almost made two horrific ones, and he was educated and privileged. Mindy could have sat at home and collected government assistance, like many unwed mothers were doing, but she'd chosen to work for a meager wage to provide for her children.

"Billy doesn't charge me rent, and he pays all the utilities. I just can't ask him for anything for me or the kids and I can't bring any guys home. Like I would." She puffed out air through her lips as she flipped her blond hair over her shoulders. "Plus, when guys find out I have two kids, they run the other way." She sighed. "My neighbor watches them when I'm at work and she doesn't charge me that much, so..." She shrugged her thin shoulders and looked off with a hint of embarrassment on her face. "I'm doing the best I can."

Yes, she was. And Lord, she was a talker, but she had nothing to be ashamed of. All she needed was a chance. She was a fighter, a survivor, just like Tashi. The only difference was that Tashi was all alone—well that, and Tashi didn't talk. She had people hunting her and no support system, which made her a lot more vulnerable than Mindy who had family and friends nearby. Mindy had been kind to Tashi, and for that reason alone, she deserved her chance—one that he could offer. "Do you know who I am, Mindy?" he asked.

"Besides the fact that you're hot and sexy, maybe rich on

account of the car you drove up in, and *not* Tashi's boyfriend?" She butted her shoulder playfully against Tashi's. "No."

"My name is Adam. Adam Andreas."

Her mouth dropped opened and her eyes popped wide. "Like in Andreas hotels and restaurants? You related to them?"

"Yes, that Andreas," Tashi chimed in. "He's CEO of Andreas International. He's one of the wealthiest men in Granite Falls. Maybe in the world," she added, sending him a tangled look he couldn't decipher. "Not only is he hot and sexy, he's filthy rich, too."

"Oh my God." Mindy's hand flew to her mouth. "Tashi, you sure know how to pick them, girl. Or not." She leered at Adam.

Adam gazed at Tashi, a smile tickling the corners of his mouth. Was she becoming jealous of the ease with which Mindy had taken to him, was engaging him in conversation, had told him her life story just minutes after meeting him, when she'd spent three days with him and told him nothing about herself? Well, in all fairness, she was in no position to engage in small talk for two of those three days, but....

"Mindy Marshall." Mindy held out her hand.

He shook it. "A pleasure."

She glanced at Tashi. "Since Tashi doesn't want you as a boyfriend, Adam, I—"

"I would like to offer you a better paying job with full family medical benefits in one of my establishments," Adam said, cutting her off. Although he liked her bubbly temperament, he had no interest in starting a liaison with her. "You can move out of Billy's apartment and into something of your own in a nicer part of town. Would you like that?"

"Would I? Yes. Yes." She jumped off the bed and threw her arms around him, quite indecorously. "Thank you, Adam. Thank you so much."

"You're very welcome." He tried to pry her arms from around him. He was too conscious of her breasts crushed against his chest. He would lie if he said he wasn't somewhat aroused. Heck, he hadn't been with a woman in months, and here was one clinging to him, offering him a temporary fix—the kind of fixes he liked, yet he squelched that physical reaction in an instant. He wanted more, something deeper and more meaningful.

And the woman with whom he wanted that deeper and more meaningful connection was staring at him questioningly. *The rich prey on the poor and naïve and use them for their own selfish needs.*

"So, how do we do this? Over dinner or something like that?" Mindy asked.

Adam pushed her at arm's length and stepped back. "No, Miss Marshall. We wouldn't be meeting. You can call Hotel Andreas tomorrow and ask for Mrs. Templeton in H.R. I'll let her know you'll be calling. You'll be interviewed to determine your skills and figure out where you best fit in. You'll have all the on-the-job training you need, and we offer full scholarships to our employees who wish to attend college."

She'd gotten the message and dropped her gaze and her attempt at seduction. "I'd love to go to college to get a degree in accounting," she said, her voice taking on a more professional tone. "I barely finished high school. I'll work hard. I won't let you down, Mr. Andreas."

"I don't expect you to." He spoke to Mindy, but his eyes bore into Tashi in an attempt to eradicate any misconceptions she might have about him fraternizing with his employees. He wondered if a male superior had sexually harassed her at her former workplace. Had she been threatened when she complained? Was the money that was stolen hush money? If it were, why would "they" still be after her? His head was about to explode with the unanswered questions.

"I can't wait to tell Billy I'm moving out." Mindy's voice

broke the invisible thread of tension that was spinning between Tashi and him. She gave Tashi a hug and a kiss on the cheek. "We'll stay in touch, right?"

"You bet. And Mindy, you can take the furniture or whatever else you want. But you have to move it before my lease runs out in two weeks. The keys are on the kitchen counter. Give them to Mr. Yoder when he comes around. Tell him I say thanks." She paused. "I'm really happy for you, Mindy. I'm glad you're getting out—moving up," she added on a smile. "Good luck, and take care of those babies."

"I will, and thanks, Tashi. I really mean it, 'cause if it wasn't for you, I would never have crossed paths with this man." She chuckled. "It's not like we run in the same circles. Thank you, Mr. Andreas. I'll call the hotel tomorrow."

"Miss Marshall," Adam called as she reached the door. "Can you keep all this to yourself? Don't say anything about the theft, or about my taking Tashi to my home, not even to your brother. Can I count on your silence?"

Her blond head bobbed up and down. "Yes, Mr. Andreas. This never happened. I don't know where Tashi is going." She winked at Tashi and left.

Alone at last, Adam gave his full attention to Tashi. "Is there anything else besides your clothes and the stuff from your bathroom that you want to take with you?"

"Nothing," she simply replied, staring at him as if she'd just discovered he was made of gold or some other precious metal.

He hadn't discussed moving her in with him, but the look on her face told him that she would not fight him on it. She'd just given away her furniture as if it meant nothing to her, as if she was used to leaving things behind. What else could she do? She had no money and no job to maintain any type of lifestyle, not even one in a run-down neighborhood like this one. Because of her association with him, a neighbor who wasn't even a real friend was on her way to a better life and gaining independence when she'd just lost all of hers, yet she was happy for Mindy.

The fact that she was thinking and talking coherently, making decisions, expressing joy for a potential friend and wishing her luck, meant she was bouncing back from the shock and devastation of losing her money and her phone—well, that's the way it seemed outwardly.

Adam wished he knew what was going on inside her head, behind those incredibly appealing emerald eyes of hers.

He pulled back his hair that had become loose and secured it at the back of his head. "Tashi, I don't sleep with my employees. And I don't tolerate sexual harassment among my employees either." He just felt as if he needed to make that clear to her.

She smiled. "Okay."

He tilted his head. "Okay. Just okay?"

"Okay, I believe you."

She believed him. And she'd said he was hot and sexy. His heart fluttered, and as he absorbed the sensation, Adam realized that it was different from any he'd ever had. It was deep and filling, yet made him yearn for more.

"I need a job. But you'll have to pay me under the table," Tashi said, obviously unaware of the effect she was having on him. "Then I wouldn't be a burden on you. I can stay here." She swept her hand around in the air. "For now, until I figure out what to do next. You've done enough for me. I don't want to cause anymore interruptions to your life."

"You're not a burden nor an interruption, Tashi." If she knew that his household staff was on hiatus waiting for his orders to return to the estate, she'd definitely refuse to go along with him. "You don't have a fridge, and you just gave away your furniture," he said for the sake of argument. "Besides, do you have the heart to disappoint Mindy by telling her she can't have the furniture after all?"

"I wouldn't do that. I can live without furniture for a while. I'll buy a fridge later, or better still see if this one can be repaired."

"Tashi." She was still trying to be a brave, self-reliant soldier, and he admired her need for autonomy, but... "No."

She shot him a disparaging look. "Why not? You offered Mindy a job and you've known her all of fifteen minutes. Why not me? I can work. I have skills," she said with a stubborn jut of her chin.

Something told him that the kind of skills she had were still very much untapped, and it would be illegal for him to pay her to exhibit them in the state of New Hampshire—maybe if they were in Vegas...

"I'm sure you have lots of excellent skills, Miss Holland, but I can never hire you." Deciding to express just what he meant, Adam took a step forward, bringing him so far inside her personal space, her breath fanned his shirt, and the heat from her body wrapped around him like sparkling sunshine. He glanced down at her hands clasped tightly together on her lap as if she were forbidding them from reaching out to him.

"I'm not going to hurt you," he whispered, brushing his knuckles along her cheekbones—very slowly and lightly until heat and color illuminated the surface of her smooth tawny skin. God, she was lovely, far lovelier than any woman he'd ever met.

She gasped on a quiver that resonated throughout the very core of him. Her breathing grew shallow and heavy and her eyes darkened with uncertainty and heightened expectations, but she didn't pull away from him, not like she had in the tub the other night. Her violent reaction then must have been a by-product of her fever and disorientation, he thought. Something had happened to her, but she wasn't damaged to the point where she would shy away from intimacy with a man—with him.

Their eyes locked as the tension between them grew hot and

strong, saturated with immanent passion, wistful memories, and intrepid curiosity. It felt as if they were nowhere, yet everywhere, floating together in a timeless atmosphere. When a soft moan escaped her parted lips, Adam dropped his hands to his sides and stepped back from her. He was becoming too aroused and this was definitely not the place to indulge in those kinds of fantasies.

She pressed a hand to her chest and took a series of quick shallow breaths, reinforcing his suspicions that she was still innocent, unaccustomed to the awakening of her own sexual power and needs. She'd escaped before "they" could harm her, and "he" was not her lover.

He cleared the passion from his throat. "This is the reason you can never work for me, Tashi Holland. As I said, I don't fraternize with my employees, and you and I have been fraternizing for three days and three nights. We're way beyond that, and we can't go back."

She didn't refute his statement, but as her gaze traveled down his body, he could feel the heat from her eyes, especially when they centered on the evidence of his arousal. As he watched her swallow and lick her lips, Adam's own lips burned at the thought of kissing her for the first time, and then moving beyond that. She was definitely not a talker, but she was old enough, and now, *well* enough to know that if she moved into his Garden of Eden, at some point down the road, he would be tempted to pluck her forbidden fruit and enjoy it to his heart's content.

His erection throbbed, and ignoring it, he bent down and hoisted the four bags with her personal items over his shoulders. "I'm taking these out to the car. You think you'll be ready to leave when I return?"

"It's only temporary. My staying with you," she added in a flat voice, as if her declaration needed clarifying.

"Of course. Temporary, it is." Adam was beginning to dislike the sound of that word.

She rose from the bed and walked unsteadily across the room to retrieve her backpack from the floor. She walked out of the bedroom and the apartment without a backward glance.

Adam followed her, carrying the weight of her life on his shoulders.

She wasn't heavy. She wasn't heavy at all.

CHAPTER SEVEN

Tashi was growing stronger with each passing day, and along with that strength came a deluge of confidence, togetherness, and happiness she hadn't experienced in a long time—not since before Uncle Victor died.

She'd gained back the pounds she'd lost during her bout with salmonella poisoning, and perhaps gained a few more, she thought testing the waistband of her jeans. She no longer looked like a broomstick belted upside down inside a flour sack, like she had for the past two weeks. Her skin was subtle and glowing and her hair had regained its shine and bounce. She felt like a person, almost like a desirable woman again.

And she owed it all to Adam Andreas.

Setting her e-reader down on the mauve marble table next to the mauve leather sofa she was curled up on, Tashi glanced out the wall of glass encasing the second-floor sunroom that overlooked the valley of Granite Falls and the surrounding towns. It was a fifteen to twenty-minute drive to the center of town, but from the mountaintop, it seemed much farther away.

Up here, she felt far removed from reality. A reality she knew she'd have to return to soon. She couldn't pretend she was Rapunzel locked up in a castle tower forever. At some point, she would have to face her fears and the world, and strike out on her own again. But for now... She reached for her glass and took a sip of the freshly squeezed orange juice Adam had prepared for breakfast.

Tomorrow would make a week since she'd moved into his hillside mansion and slept in his humongous white bed. Alone. He'd been taking excellent care of her, and had been treating her like a princess every second that they were together, that even long after he left her, she still felt the effects of his presence, the warmth of his smile, the deep thrilling hum of his voice, and the affection in his eyes and accidental touches.

He'd been conducting Andreas International business from his third-floor home office instead of going to the hotel. Even though she'd insisted that she'd be okay, he'd refused to leave her alone. He'd given her a tour of the house and a partial tour of the grounds on the first day, and had presented her with a map of the grounds—which she clearly needed to navigate around the five-hundred-plus-acre estate.

He'd also given her a cell phone with numbers to his cell, the house, and another private number—that only she and his parents had access to—already saved in the first three Favorite spots. Even though she had no one else but Adam to call, the anxiety she'd had over the stolen one was gone. She didn't sit around watching it, willing it to ring so she could pick it up to hear the voice of the FBI agent on the other end.

That short phase of her life was over. The only way she'd ever find out if the agent was alive would be if he made a personal appearance in Granite Falls to visit his friend. And even then, he might not find her since she hadn't found that friend, and had been staying off all radars since she moved here. Plus, she had already made up her mind to leave Granite Falls as soon as she had the opportunity. She couldn't expect Adam to take care of her forever.

Tashi glanced at her camera bag lying on the other end of the sofa. Besides her laptop, her camera was the only valuable possession she had. She would hate to part with it, but if push came to shove and she couldn't find any other means of buying a bus ticket out of Granite Falls, she'd have to sell it. She knew she would only get a fraction of what she paid for it, and that she might never be able to replace one of its worth, but she couldn't melt it down and eat it.

She'd already searched a few electronic e-stores to see what a used camera like hers would bring in, and if she was really frugal —ate two measly meals a day—she might be able to feed herself for a few weeks until she could do better. Where she would sleep and bathe on a daily basis was a different matter. Maybe she should start checking out homeless shelters in the southeast part of the country. It was too cold in the north to be homeless. Florida would be a good choice. It was warm and farther away from New York City and the people who wanted her dead. California would be even better, but she doubted she'd have enough money to get that far. Maybe later.

Adam hadn't questioned her about her past or the money and cell phone that were stolen from her, and she never brought it up during their daily conversations. She listened as he did most of the talking. At first it was about Andreas International projects in the works. He'd recently purchased an old hotel in Japan and was remodeling it into the newest Hotel Andreas. He was working on plans to purchase a vineyard in California, and he was opening a restaurant in Boston next year. Andreas International was expanding in leaps and bounds.

He'd filled her in on Mindy and her new position as a clerk in one of the boutique at Hotel Andreas. Tashi had felt happiness for her friend, and wished she could see her, but then had decided it was best she didn't form a deeper bond with her since she'd be leaving eventually. She had to protect Mindy and her children just as she had to protect Adam.

When she'd asked him about the basketball playoff with the boys from her neighborhood, he'd informed her that since he suspected they would have sold his Aston Martin for college tuition, he and his friends had agreed to split their tuition costs between them. In return the boys would intern at Fontaine Enterprises and Andretti Industries during their school breaks and that they would all return to Granite Falls to give back to their community once they graduated from college.

Tashi had been awed by the deal. It didn't get any better than that.

Last night, during dinner, Adam had gotten a little more personal and talked about his childhood growing up with Erik, and his cousin, Massimo, and later in high school when Bryce Fontaine came to town. Adam was the youngest of the four men, and he'd expressed his frustration at always seemingly walking in their shadows. Yet he loved them to death—they, their wives and kids—and would do anything for them.

"Even my cousin who had a notorious reputation when it came to women, and who'd sworn never to get married, is now enjoying matrimonial bliss when I haven't been with a woman in months."

Months?

Was he fattening her up so he could be with her? Tashi had dropped her gaze to her plate and toyed with her green salad. So he was currently unattached. Surely, if he were involved, he'd be having sex regularly. Plus, his girlfriend would probably have already made an appearance demanding to know why he was spending so much time caring for another woman. That's what she would have done if her boyfriend had been cooped up alone in a mansion with another woman—sick or not.

"Do you want to get married?" Why the heck had she asked him that?

He'd paused for a long time while he slowly chewed on a mouthful of pasta. Tashi had watched him, only then realizing the sensuousness with which he ate. He never hurried through his meals like most men did, but seemed to take his time to savor every single molecule of whatever was in his mouth. The awareness had made her nipples tingle, and to her dismay, she'd felt them straining against the silky lace of her bra. Mortified at the prospect of drawing his attention to her breasts, she hadn't even glanced down to check if her nipples were poking out against her blouse. Yeah, he'd seen her naked, and had cupped her breasts in the palms of his hands, but she'd been half-conscious and delirious at the time. This was different. She was extremely conscious of his effect on her, even from across the table.

He'd taken a sip of wine then passed the tip of his tongue across the rim of his glass to capture a wayward drop trailing down the side. Tashi had felt a horrendous convulsion inside the walls of her lady parts. It had been all she could do to keep from moaning out loud. She'd never in her life experienced anything remotely similar. It was as if she were experiencing an internal earthquake.

With a subtle smile on his lips, as if he knew exactly what was happening inside her, he'd said, "Marriage was something I used to want when I was younger, but—" He'd paused and shrugged. "Maybe it's just not in the cards for me. They don't call me the temporary tycoon for nothing."

As he tried to mask his loneliness with his last statement, Tashi had detected a faint glint of sadness or regret in his eyes and voice as if some woman had hurt him. Was his temporary law a way to protect his heart? And what woman in her right mind wouldn't want to be married to a man like Adam Andreas?

If her circumstance were different, she'd… Tashi had silenced her wishful thinking. "Maybe you just haven't met the right woman, yet."

"You sound like my friends. They say I'll know her when I meet her, when I first gaze into her eyes." His eyes, shining bright in the fading light of the setting sun, had looked like blue diamonds—assessing, alluring, daring Tashi to prove or disprove that she might be that woman.

"Did you tell them about me, that I'm here with you?" She'd changed the subject as the quivering inside her increased under his sensual gaze.

"Well, Erik knows you're back. I had to let someone on the outside know what was going on, and since he already knew you were here the first time, I clued him in. He doesn't know anything about you being robbed, just that you're staying with me for a while. I asked for his silence. He wouldn't discuss you with Bryce or Massimo."

"What about his wife?" she'd asked, taking a bite of the blackened swordfish Adam had grilled for dinner.

"He wouldn't say anything to Michelle, either. You have nothing to worry about, Tashi. I promised you privacy and secrecy, and that's what you have," he'd added, placing a spear of asparagus drizzled with hollandaise sauce into his mouth.

"Erik seemed nice," she'd said. "Is Tiffany his and Michelle's only child?"

"Oh no. She's the youngest of three. They have an eleven-year-old daughter named Precious and an almost three-year old —Erik, Jr. We call him Little Erik. In fact he has a birthday coming up in a few days."

"What about Bryce and Massimo? How many do they have?" she'd asked. Knowing Adam meant knowing his friends.

He'd taken a sip of wine before answering. "Massimo and

Shaina have a daughter. Aria. She's six months and already a heartbreaker."

Tashi had felt his affection for his little cousin.

"Bryce and Kaya have a set of twins of their own," he'd continued after another sip of wine. "Eli and Elyse. They're also raising Kaya's sister's three children. Jason is twelve. Alyssa is six, and Anastasia is—" He'd twisted his mouth thoughtfully. "She's two and a few months, I think."

"Wow, that's a lot of kids. What happened to her sister?"

A dark shadow had crossed his face and he'd adjusted his weight on the chair. "Lauren and her husband, Michael, were killed in a car crash a couple years ago."

"I'm sorry," Tashi had said at the pain that was still evident in Adam's eyes. She did a quick calculation and realized that when she'd lost her mother, she was the same age Alyssa was when she lost both her parents. Thank God for loving aunts and uncles who picked up the parenting baton when parents died, and absentee fathers were nowhere to be found. "Those poor kids, to lose both parents at the same time."

"It was rough for the first year, but with the love and devotion from Bryce and Kaya they're on their way to total recovery. It helps that we're all very close. The kids have a huge support system."

As they'd entered an interlude of silence, Tashi had felt a deep sense of relief at the bond of trust between the men. Even though they probably shared the most private details of their lives with each other, they nonetheless, kept one another's secrets, even from each other. What she wouldn't give for a friend like that, a sibling, or a cousin to confide in.

She'd had friends growing up in Ohio, but no one close enough to form a lifetime bond like Adam and his friends—partly because of her over-protective uncle who watched her every move and limited her social interactions. He'd tried to talk her out of moving to New York to attend college. New York was too big, too far away, and filled with bad people who could lead her astray. Tashi had told him that she was going with or without his approval. He'd stared at her as if he'd seen a ghost, like he'd been trapped in a moment of *déjà-vu*.

It was the first time she'd ever challenged his authority, or even shown a hint of rebellion against his principles, and it had felt good, a little wicked, actually. They'd argued long and hard and she'd told him that since she was eighteen, he couldn't legally stop her. At that, he'd conceded and given her his blessings, with warnings to be wary of strangers and not to trust people too easily and quickly. They'd parted on the best of terms and had spoken to each other every single day until he died.

Tashi had thought her uncle weird when she was a child, but as she'd gotten older, she'd begun to suspect that his paranoia was a direct result of the ambiguous circumstances surrounding her mother's drowning death. They'd ruled it a suicide, but her uncle always told her that her mother had loved her more than life and would not have taken her own life, leaving her little baby girl motherless.

He'd lost his only sibling, and his niece was the only relative he had left. He'd felt it his duty to protect her. He never displayed any bitterness or anger, just caution and mistrust when dealing with strangers, and sometimes with people they knew.

During her college years in New York, Tashi had made a few friends, but still no one close enough to form a lifetime relationship. Then her uncle had died unexpectedly, casting her into a state of even greater loneliness. He hadn't told her he was sick. In the letter she'd received after the fact, he'd explained that he hadn't wanted her to worry about him, to give up her life to care for him. She would have gone to him in an instant.

Tashi had bit back the sob that almost escaped from her throat. Scottie had come along shortly after her uncle's death.

Her vulnerability and her need for human contact had weakened her defenses and left her wide open to his trickery. If it weren't for that agent who'd died saving her, only God knew where she'd be right now.

Her uncle had been right all alone. It was best not to trust people, yet, she'd thought, glancing across the table at Adam, here was a man who'd proven he could be trusted. "It's hard for me to trust people," she'd said to Adam as the prospect of her impending isolated future had settled in her belly. The thought of being out there alone again scared her. She doubted she'd ever meet another Adam.

"I sense that," he'd replied, smiling. "But trust comes with time, Tashi. It took Erik, Bryce, Massimo, and me years to form the level of confidence we have in and with each other. Especially Massimo," he'd added with a chuckle. "We fought constantly when we were children. Our fathers were best friends and were always pitting us against each other, always pushing us to challenge each other and ourselves. Up to this day, my father still compares me to him."

"How are you and Massimo related?" She'd intended to continue her background reading on him, but then she'd gotten sick, and since he'd been taking care of her, Tashi had felt as if she would be invading his privacy if she continued to snoop into his life.

"Our mothers were sisters," he'd responded.

Tashi had detected a catch in his voice. "What are the odds that two sisters would marry two best friends and settle down in the same town? I know of some siblings who can't stand being in the same state, much less live next door to each other."

"My mom was only thirteen months older than Aunt Giuliana, so their sibling bond was formed from an early age. They attended the same fashion design university and worked in marketing in the same fashion house in Milan. Even though it's been twenty odd years since Aunt Giuli died, my mom still misses her. I believe it's one of the reasons she moved back to Italy where the happiest memories of their lives were spent." A melancholy frown had flittered across his features as he swirled the wine around in his glass, watching the white liquid undulate against the clear glass as if he were predicting its movement in response to his motions.

"So who met whom first?" she'd asked to lighten the mood.

He'd set the glass down and captured her gaze again. "They all met at a moonlit night festival while on a Safari in Kenya." His voice had regained some of its vigor. "Mom had won a trip for two in a lottery, and quite naturally—"

"She took her sister and best friend with her."

"Yes. It so happened that Dad and Uncle Luciano were also there on their annual safari." He'd stopped talking for a while and allowed his gaze to wander off over the tops of the green tree line. "Fate had placed them in the right place at the right time."

"It reminds me of Shakespeare's Midsummer Night's Dream. Was there a mischievous Puck to get them all confused before they figured out who really loved whom?"

"Oh no, *cara*. There was no Midsummer Night's Dream mix-up. Each person had fallen instantly in love with the right mate, and six months later, they exchanged vows in a double wedding ceremony."

"That's romantic." Tashi had never believed in love at first sight. How could she when she'd been programmed to distrust at first sight. Her paranoid heart was never opened to the possibilities of any close relationship. It was desperation, not love or friendship that sent her into Scottie's arms. And although she'd been awestruck when she'd first met Adam, and since then had begun to develop affectionate feelings for him, she had to remember that it was also desperation that had brought her to his home. What she was feeling could be a strong dose of gratitude.

But perhaps love at first sight was real for those who'd experienced it.

"Do you believe in fate, Tashi?" Adam had asked, watching her closely, his enigmatic blue eyes glittering in the afterglow of the radiant sunset illuminating the terrace on the west side of the mansion overlooking a deep green ravine with the rushing sound of what sounded like a waterfall in the far distance.

"I don't know," Tashi had responded on a shrug. "I think things just happen."

"Do you really believe things just happen after the way we met at Mountainview Café, then at the grocery store? When did you Google me?"

"How do you know I Googled you?"

He'd smiled. "I only gave you my first name. So you must have looked me up on the Internet to find out that I was the Adam Andreas of Andreas International. Otherwise you wouldn't have known to call me three days later when you were in need."

"Okay," Tashi had admitted grudgingly. "I looked you up as soon as I got to my apartment. I was curious." She'd averted her gaze for an instant as her mind wheeled back to the moment when she'd added his hotel's number to her phone. It's a good thing she had because she would have been too sick to look him up the night she'd needed him.

As she'd sat there, subjected to his surveying eyes, Tashi had begun to feel lightheaded at the realization that Adam might be right about fate having a hand in her being in his home. He was sent to help her in her hour of need. But why Adam, specifically, and not someone else, some other man?

"I'm happy you decided to feed your curiosity," he'd said

breaking into her thoughts. "But what if we'd never met that day, what would you have done?"

"I guess I would have called someone else." She'd still been trying to deny the truth, the evidence of destiny playing a role in their meeting, their lives.

"Like who?"

"Mindy." Why hadn't she called Mindy? It would have made more sense since she lived next door.

"She wasn't home. Remember she told us she was gone all weekend? But you didn't know that because you hadn't even attempted to call her, which tells me a lot."

Could it really be fate that made her call Adam? "Then I guess I would have died," she'd stated defensively as a chill had washed over her. No one would have missed her. No one would have known she was dead until her body had begun to decompose and stink up the place.

Tashi flinched now at the thought. She was too young to come to such an end. She'd read about these end-of-life scenarios happening to lonely old women with lots of cats, never a young vibrant woman who hadn't yet experienced life.

"Well, I for one am most thankful that didn't happen, Tashi," Adam had said with a gentle softness in his voice. "I've only known you for two weeks, but I can't imagine my life without ever knowing you. I've enjoyed taking care of you, watching you get stronger, watching the spark return to you beautiful emerald eyes, hearing the confidence in your voice."

As Tashi had gazed across the table at him, she'd been tempted to tell him something, give him a little piece of the woman he'd nursed back to health, but she knew that the less Adam Andreas knew about her, the less danger he'd be in if her nemesis ever made it to Granite Falls.

Adam clearly believed fate had brought them together. Maybe

they would have met again after that initial collision and the run-in at the grocery store—she didn't know. But there was some merit to his thinking: she did get sick, she did call him, he did bring her to his home and nursed her back to health, and just when she was planning to leave town and him behind, her money was stolen, forcing her back to his home and his care. What was the meaning, the purpose of it all since her association with Adam could bring him harm in the future? Was he fated to die because of her?

Guilt, and some other emotion she didn't recognize had pushed Tashi out of her chair. They'd cleared the table and stacked the dishes into the terrace dishwasher then she'd excused herself and escaped to the master suite for the rest of the night where more guilt over occupying his personal quarters had assailed her.

It was those precarious moments when they'd stood on the edge of something astronomical, when some epiphany was about to be revealed that scared her most. She tried to avoid them as much as possible, especially because she'd come to sense a deep spirituality in Adam.

He seemed to be at peace with himself and one with everything around him, and he smiled a lot. Warmth flowed through Tashi's being as she thought of Adam's smile that exuded balance and confidence, a smile that always made her feel safe, like she was home, in a place where nothing and no one bad could harm her.

If she took away nothing else from her brief encounter with Adam Andreas, Tashi knew she would take the visions of his smiles with her. When she felt doubtful and afraid in the future, she would think of him. He'd renewed her belief that there were genuinely kind, decent, and good men in the world. Men like her uncle, the nameless FBI agent, and Adam. Those three men had one thing in common—they'd all cared for her. She would make them proud.

Tashi took another sip of her orange juice as the grandfather clock across the hall chimed out the mid-morning hour.

This morning, like every other morning, Adam had awakened her with a kiss on her forehead, and then escorted her to the bathroom where a bath was waiting for her. As she soaked in the scented bubbly Jacuzzi, he made breakfast and set it on the balcony off the master bedroom, where they'd eat while enjoying the view of the majestic green mountains and interlocking lakes in the distance.

They'd settled into a routine where Adam would disappear after breakfast while she cleaned up the kitchen, made their beds, and twice she'd done their laundry. Having no other chores to occupy her time, Tashi read a lot, just like she used to do when she was living on the other side of town. She couldn't say she missed the town's library since Andreas Estates was equipped with a well-stocked one that housed both hardcopy and digital books. All she had to do was download to her eReader for borrow.

She was never big on TV, so when she was tired of reading, she swam laps in the first-floor Olympic-sized indoor swimming pool, worked out and practiced her kickboxing in the fully equipped gym next to it, soaked in the hot tub, perspired in the sauna or the steam room—depending on her mood—and a couple days she'd just lazed around and watched old classic movies in the ultramodern home theatre.

That was the daily life of Princess Tashi of Andreas Estate for the past week.

Adam had never joined her on any of her indoor excursions, and the mansion was so big, she never ran into him. But during their daily meals, he always asked about her use of the numerous amenities and if she were enjoying her exploration of the house. A few days ago, when he'd been late starting dinner, she'd mentioned that he didn't have to cook every day, nor did he have to join her for every meal.

"They're not just meals, Tashi," he'd responded. "They're dates."

"Dates?" she'd asked, frowning at him. "We're dating?"

"Yes. I'm getting to know you as I hope you're getting to know me."

"But I haven't told you anything about me."

He'd chuckled, folded his arms across the tabletop, and leaned toward her, his body, his presence eating up the small space between them. "Quite the contrary, Miss Holland. I'm learning a lot about you, even though you don't talk."

"How?" She'd wanted to move back, give herself breathing room, but she was transfixed, immobilized by his electric eyes.

"My preparing your meals every day, waking you up with a kiss every morning, and running your bath is equivalent to driving to your home to pick you up. Sometimes I stand and watch you sleep, anticipate the moment when you open your eyes and smile at me. Those are the most fulfilling and exciting moments of my day."

"I didn't know that," Tashi had responded as her heart began to race at a thousand beats per second. "And how are these dates going for you, Adam?" As soon as she'd asked that question, Tashi knew she was ready to engage in the subtle games of truth and dare, subdue and conquer, that men and women played with each other. She couldn't remember ever being that audacious with anyone, much less a man.

Paradoxically, it was Adam's calm demeanor that seemed to coax out the naïve, yet wantonly curious girl who'd been hiding in the shadows her overprotective uncle had cast over her. She felt safe playing with Adam, like if she broke her doll, he'd mend it, or if she sent a ball flying through the neighbor's window, he'd take the blame for her. She felt like she had a pal who'd be there for her, no matter what.

His smile conveyed his enthusiasm in sharing his thoughts with her. "Meals for me aren't merely about eating, or satisfying a hunger, Tashi. It's a very intimate and pleasurable event. I love to watch you enjoy my dishes, just as much as I enjoy preparing them for you. My heart flutters when your eyes pop wide as you place something tasty into your mouth. I love to watch the way your lips curl around your fork or your spoon, the subtle motions of your mouth while you chew, and the ripples of muscles in your throat when you swallow. Your goodnight kiss to me is when your little pink tongue emerges from your mouth and slides across your lips to capture remnants of your meals."

CHAPTER EIGHT

Tashi had had trouble breathing as Adam's sensuous words hummed inside her. He hadn't touched her, yet she'd never felt so aroused, so feminine in her entire life. She'd quivered deep inside and expelled a soft sigh as something hot and burning erupted inside her. To her dismay, she'd felt moisture settling inside her panties.

"The way a person eats is indicative of what kind of lover he or she will be," he'd continued, smiling as if he knew exactly what was happening to her. "You, my little Tashi, would be shy and uncertain at first. Your irises would widen at each new sensation, and your pupils would lighten with curiosity, then darken with desire as you test the level of pleasure each touch brings you. Then as you gain confidence and satisfaction, you'll abandon your inhibitions and let the pleasure wash over you."

Later that night, with her skin flushed and her body aching, Tashi had lain awake in the darkness of Adam's white bedroom and imagined what it would be like to make love with him. He would be gentle and patient at first, nibble on her body slowly and sensuously, then as her passion grew, he'd relax his control and lick and lap at her indelicately…

Pushing the sensuous thoughts aside, Tashi rose from the sofa and walked over to the glass wall. It was a beautiful day. The sky was a deep blue with wispy clouds scattered across it. The sun was high and she could almost feel the rays melting into her skin as she gazed down on the colorful flower garden surrounded by trimmed shrubbery and walking paths below her.

She glanced back at her camera bag. She'd taken lots of shots from various angles inside the mansion, but she'd never ventured out to inspect the grounds. Perhaps it was time to extend her exploration and enjoy the grounds as much as she'd been enjoying the interior of Andreas Estates before she made her departure.

With her camera bag in hand, Tashi left the sunroom and made her way down to the first-floor compartmentalized shoe closet where all shoes were kept. The room was bigger than her multi-family apartment building. Adam allowed no one to wear shoes past the first floor. He'd told her it was because he didn't have a housekeeper, but Tashi believed it had a lot to do with his spiritual personality.

He was always barefoot, but who needed slippers in a house with radiant heating and climate controlled rooms that automatically adjusted when one walked in? She'd noticed one wall in the library stacked with literature on living the minimalistic lifestyle, yoga, meditation, and other types of mind-channeling material, some of which she'd never heard of before.

The mansion had been remodeled into a minimalistic, neutral-colored heaven of uncluttered space that offered an abundance of serenity and harmony. Instead of numerous little trinkets most people filled their homes with, Adam's home was simply, yet elegantly decorated with furniture of the highest quality. Except for the portraits of his parents in the first-floor foyer, there were no other family pictures gracing the few walls of the house. Who needed pictures when the architecture was so stunning and the walls of glass offered uninterrupted views of the natural beauty surrounding the house?

His décor was comprised mainly of priceless life-size effigies of mythical African, Egyptian, Greek, and Roman deities, and numerous oddly shaped sculptured objects that only the rich could afford. Some were made of glass, some of marble, granite, pearl, and precious metals. They were so strategically and perfectly placed throughout the house, Tashi felt that moving one just a fraction would cause imbalance and disorder, not only to the room, but to Adam's demeanor as well.

He must have felt like a fish out of water in her apartment, Tashi thought. He did not belong to that world, any more than she belonged to this.

He'd done his disappearing act after breakfast, but she knew he'd reappear for lunch. She would offer to cook him something for a change, but the kitchen was one place she didn't know her way around. She and Uncle Victor had eaten out a lot, and when they did eat in, it was frozen, canned, and boxed processed, readymade meals. In the summers, Uncle Victor used to grill hot dogs and pre-seasoned hamburger patties—stuff that Adam Andreas would never have in his kitchen.

Other than slicing them up, Tashi wouldn't know what to do with the vegetables in his fridge or the canisters of brown rice, quinoa, beans, and other whole grain staples in his cupboard.

In the past week, she'd never had the same main dish twice for any meal, not even breakfast, and everything was always fresh and delicious and tasted as if it had just been pulled from the ocean or off a tree branch, lifted from the butcher's slab, or dug out of the ground. Every night, he cooked her a four-course dinner, and everything was always so beautifully presented that sometimes Tashi thought it was a sin to mess up the dishes. Adam Andreas was a master of culinary skills. He wasn't just in the restaurant business, he was a connoisseur of food—from the way he prepared it to the way he consumed it.

Her sneakers laced, Tashi made her way along a corridor that ran the perimeter of the first floor. Its translucent glass walls created a surreal image of continuity between the interior beauty of the house and the meticulously furnished, landscaped back courtyard with its evergreen shrubs, wide green lawn separated into squares by copper-colored marble borders, and protective railings of stone and steel that extended as far as the eye could see. She squinted as the sun shimmered off the roofs and steel panels of several other buildings scattered across the estate.

Tashi descended a short flight of stone-cut stairs and lifted her face to the sunlight peeking through the line of evergreen trees. She was dressed in an aqua, long-sleeved, button-down shirt and jeans—suitable attire to protect her arms and legs during her hike. She took her camera from its case and without giving it any real thought, she followed the nearest path of several leading away from the courtyard. She hadn't brought her map with her, but she had her cell phone in her pocket. If she got lost, she would just call Adam.

A chorus of chirping birds serenaded her as she made her way through the evergreen timberland. She welcomed the kiss of the light breeze on her skin and reveled in the smell of pine, birch, maple, rich dark soil, and an occasional whiff of the colorful mountain flora bobbing gracefully from the moist forest floor. She stopped here and there for a candid snap of squirrels and chipmunks scurrying through the woodland searching for nuts and pinecones, or chasing one another in the catch and release game males and females of all species played with each other.

Coming upon a cluster of maple trees lining the sides of the path, Tashi stopped to admire a male cardinal enjoying the maple sap dripping from a hole in the trunk of one of the trees.

She managed to get a few shots before he spread his red wings and flew out of sight. Higher up in the branches a female—probably his mate of the season, or several seasons—fed seeds to their fledglings. She only got two shots before the momma bird spread its brown wings as if to protect her young from view.

Tashi smiled. It felt great to be outdoors again, to experience this simple, yet extraordinary slice of nature. Tashi wished she could stay here forever and forget about the world beyond Andreas Estates, where people wanted her dead. But that was wishful thinking.

Encountering a fork in the winding road, Tashi pushed her somber thoughts aside as she contemplated which one to take. Frost's poem, "The Road Not Taken" popped into her head. They seemed equally traveled to her, and realizing that it really didn't matter, she took the one on the left. In a few yards, it opened up into a meadow with a crystal blue lake surrounded by clusters of pine and a variety of other flowering trees she couldn't identify. A range of gently sloping hills on the other side created the perfect backdrop.

Tashi stood in the middle of the dirt road that ran the perimeter of the lake and admired the natural scenery around her. Never in a million years would she have imagined a lake nestled inside a mountain. This was a treat any serious photographer would die for. Searching through her camera bag, she fished out her 20mm wide-angle lens and switched it for the 45mm micro she'd been using while traipsing through the forest. As she followed the road around the lake, Tashi took her time compiling a collage of the breathtaking, colorful landscape from every angle possible.

She'd gone about a quarter of a mile, passing stone-cut picnic tables and benches, when the sound of rushing water caught her attention. Guessing that it was the waterfall she'd heard from the house a few nights ago, Tashi took the narrow path that led from the road into another wooded area. She passed a flagpole with a white flag in the lowered position, and followed her ears toward the gushing sound. As she traveled deeper in, the air became crisp and fresh and charged with electricity—similar to the way it felt right after a heavy rainstorm.

Rounding a bend, Tashi stopped suddenly as two white limestone square structures situated in the middle of a green lawn with garden beds bursting with blooming flowers and herbs lining its perimeter. Marble effigies of Greek and Roman mythical goddesses scattered about seemed to keep watch over the private refuge. Rolling lush hills, ancient sprawling trees, and an abundance of foaming waterfalls gushing from a rocky hill into a gigantic whirlpool completed the background.

The structures, separated by a white stone canopy, each exhibited three oblong windows with golden panes that cast off an iridescent glow against the midmorning sunlight. But the serendipitous discovery of the picturesque sanctuary-like structure in the middle of a modern day Garden of Eden—minus the Tree of Life—wasn't what made Tashi gasp.

It was the naked, motionless man coiled into a yoga pose that only a seasoned yogi or a very advanced practitioner would dare to attempt. His knees and shinbones were flat against a white floor, and his body was curved backwards with his stomach and chest stretching toward the sky. His forearms were flat against the mat—perpendicular to his legs. His hands gripped his ankles while his forehead rested between them with his face upside down and facing away from his body. His long black mane was pooled around his arms and legs creating a stunning contrast to his muscled tanned body fashioned into a graceful human triangle.

Inevitably, Tashi's eyes zeroed in on his erection extending like a bronze flagpole from the thatch of curly black hair at his groin. She'd never imagined a man's penis could be that big, especially from a few yard's distance. She was very naïve when it came to human anatomy. She'd attended all-girls' parochial schools all her life where pictures and drawings of naked men and women were prohibited in biology classes and where even the first violation of that rule brought immediate expulsion. With the church's philosophies and her uncle's strict rules, it was a wonder she hadn't turned into a frigid maiden, incapable of any type of sexual sensations.

Sensations that were frighteningly powerful and foreign, she realized as saliva gathered inside her mouth and her skin began to burn with curious excitement. Her nipples tingled and hardened and pressed painfully against the cotton material of her shirt, but most poignantly she felt an incessant throbbing deep inside the core of her womanhood as moisture poured into her panties. She felt as if someone had turned on a faucet inside her and then broken off the handle so there was no way to stop the flood once it started. The sight and sounds of the gushing waterfalls in the background and the subtle blend of jasmine, mint, oregano, and other herbs floating on the gentle breeze toward her only seemed to intensify her arousal.

"Adam."

His name slipped from her mouth, unwittingly. It was a tiny whisper, but when Tashi detected a slight tremor in Adam's body, she knew he'd heard her above the roar of the waterfall. She should leave, she thought, but her feet seemed to be rooted to the ground and her eyes glued open to the irresistible specimen of male flesh in front of her.

Her heart fluttered when he began to unfold like a graceful ballerina. Walking his hands away from his feet, he brought his head and torso upward with slow controlled movements. Coming into a kneeling position with his shins flat against the mat, he bent forward and rested his torso on his thighs, his forehead on the mat, and his forearms extended backward along the sides of his body. He stayed in that position for about thirty seconds before he brought himself to a kneeling position again. This time he extended his arms out on either side, his palms raised toward the sky, his thick black hair falling down his back, past his waist to rest gently against the firm hills of his buttocks. He clasped his hands together and bowed in reverence, twice.

Tashi had never seen anything so magnificent, so arousing in her life.

She held her breath as he turned his head and gazed at her, finally acknowledging her presence. Tashi's body felt heavy and warm as he pushed to his feet. Again, she wanted to leave, to apologize for wandering into his private sanctuary, but neither her limbs nor her tongue would obey her.

He glanced at a white robe lying on the floor next to the mat, but instead of picking it up, he walked to the edge of the podium and down a flight of wide steps toward the lawn. He seemed to cover the short distance between them in slow motion, his eyes never leaving her face as he drew closer to where she stood next to a granite table and cushioned chairs under the shade of a sprawling willow tree with branches so low, they kissed the grass.

He stopped a couple feet in front of her and held his hand out to her like a guru welcoming the newest member of his shrine into the fold. "Come, Tashi," he said, ever so gently.

His smile was devastatingly sensuous, and his invitation was a passionate challenge, hard to resist. Tashi's heart began to pound in her chest and her stomach began to heave like an ocean wave battered by the force of hurricane gale winds. What in heaven's name had she wandered into?

"Come," he repeated. "I've been waiting for you."

. . .

Adam's pulse pounded at finally admitting to himself that Tashi Holland was *the* perfect woman for him—his heart and soul mate. He'd known it the moment he first gazed into her eyes and felt the heat and light of her soul connecting with his, saw the glorious sunrise and the golden sunset of his future illuminated within their emerald depth, felt the fusing of their spirits in that sharp bolt of electricity when they first touched.

As he gazed into the emerald pools of her eyes, Adam felt himself falling, tumbling into space where little boys and girls with auburn and black hair, green and blue eyes floated around him and Tashi. He'd often dreamed about the children he'd have one day, but never had he seen them so clearly—as if they already existed, were already inducted into the circle of life.

Adam had never felt this mystic connection to any other woman. He hadn't felt this way about Claire, not after investing months of time and energy into their relationship, not when he'd gotten down on his knees in front of his family and friends and asked her to marry him.

Tashi Holland had revealed nothing about herself in the two weeks they'd spent together, yet Adam felt as if they'd known each other all their lives, and even before then in a former life. Time and circumstance had separated them, but the instant they'd collided, their souls and hearts had rejoiced at meeting again. Well, that's how he'd felt about her. How she felt about him was another mystery in itself.

It was no coincidence that they'd collided in Mountainview Café, two weeks ago. If he'd come through the door, or if she had gotten up from her table one second earlier or later, they would have missed each other. Fate had placed them both in the right place at the precise time. But due to his past experiences with her kind—damsels in distress who'd kicked his world off its axis—he'd fought the magnetism. He just couldn't trust his heart.

Fate had been kind enough to give them a second chance

meeting outside the grocery store. Again, he would have let her walk out of his life, perhaps forever, when something had propelled him to shout out his name to her—his name that she'd been curious enough about to look up on the Internet. His name had saved her life.

And now here she was standing in his most private, most cherished place on earth—a place where he came when he wanted to connect with his inner universe. Since he'd built it, Adam hadn't invited anyone to his sacred sanctuary, and no one had come. He hadn't invited Tashi either, but here she was—being everything to him that her name signified: blessings and good luck, prosperity, and connection to the divine.

"Hello, Tashi," he said, breaking the electrifying silence.

"I'm—I'm sorry." She took a step back from him, but kept her eyes locked with his. "I didn't mean to disturb you." With one hand, she gripped the strap of her camera case hanging from her shoulder while her other hand was balled into a fist at her stomach.

Adam noted the mixture of curiosity and awakening desire in her eyes, the convulsing of her body as she tried to cope with the magnitude of sexual tension running rampant through her. She looked so innocent and inexperienced, so way out of her element, it was almost sinful to stand before her in all his naked glory while she was still fully clothed.

Adam cleared his throat. "You didn't disturb me, Tashi. Come," he said for the third time, holding his hand out to her, willing her to trust him, to take his hand and let him lead her into their future, show her how safe and protected she'd be with him.

She shook her head and crossed her arms over her stomach. "I should go. You were clearly in the middle of something deep."

"I was, but it's okay. Perhaps we can get into something deep together."

Her forehead crinkled. "I've never done yoga."

"Would you like to try it? I can teach you. We'll begin with the basics, of course."

"Now?" Her eyes flittered down his body and lingered briefly on his erection that had begun to lose some of its rigidity. It came instantly back to life as if she'd caressed him with her gaze. She looked away. "You're naked. Do you usually do yoga naked?"

Adam smiled. "When the weather permits, I try to make the most of it. It's a beautiful day, so… Does it bother you that I'm naked, Tashi?"

A blush appeared in her cheeks. "I've never seen a naked man before."

Relief flooded Adam as he ruled out sexual abuse and assault as the reasons for her violent reaction to him in the tub. It was perhaps the strange novelty of having a man touch her so intimately that had scared her. "But you've seen pictures, I'm sure. I don't think there's a girl out there past the age of fifteen who hasn't at least taken a peek at naked men on the Internet." The truth in his words distressed him.

The ease with which children could access adult material was a disturbing by-product of the digital age. Kids were growing up much too fast for his liking these days. Innocence seemed to have flown in the face of the sexual revolution epidemic sweeping the globe. It wouldn't be so bad if they had adult supervision while viewing that material to explain exactly what was going on. Then their perception of human sexuality wouldn't be so warped and depraved.

"You're looking at one, and I'll be twenty-three in December," Tashi said, her voice dropping in volume. "There was some nudity in my textbooks in college." She shrugged. "I studied photography, and we did a chapter on nudes, but other than that, no. I've never seen a live naked man, nor have I ever peeked at them on the Internet. I've never even been kissed."

Adam was floored. "Never been kissed? Where did you grow up, in a convent?"

That brought soft chuckles from her, and she cupped her hand over her mouth to stifle her merriment. The sound of her laughter and the light of humor in her eyes were priceless. Adam wished for more of this side of her. She was breaking out of her silent shell.

"Something like that," she finally said, catching her bottom lip between her teeth. "I attended parochial school all my life, and my uncle…" She paused. "Uncle Victor was very strict. He didn't allow too much socializing, and boyfriends were out of the question."

Uncle Victor. She'd given up his name, albeit with a little hesitation. It was a small step forward, but every step she took toward him was progress. *Bravo to her Uncle Victor*, Adam thought. He'd probably lock up his daughters, too, ban computers from the estate until they reached the age of consent. "So you have no idea what goes on between a man and a woman."

"Well, I'm not stupid." Exasperation edged her voice. "We were taught about the birds and the bees, but we were forbidden to indulge in self-stimulation and carnal debauchery, as they called it."

Adam couldn't suppress the laugh that rose to his throat. "Carnal debauchery?" That was taking it to the extreme. "Did your teachers commute from the Middle Ages in time machines?"

"It felt like it." She chuckled. "And sometimes they dressed like it too with their ankle-length skirts and long-sleeved blouses."

The fact that she could laugh at her cloistered upbringing was a healthy sign. "You were never tempted to peek?" he asked.

She shook her head. "Some girls peeked. Those who were caught were expelled. Although," she added with a touch of compunction, "when I look back on it now, I realize that expulsion was probably the best thing that could have happened to those girls. They were free to experiment and explore while I was still stuck in an archaic institution."

"Why didn't you peek?"

"I was afraid."

"Of being expelled?"

"Of burning in everlasting fire. I was afraid of even touching myself, except to bathe, and…" Her voice trailed off as her gaze returned almost spontaneously to the area of his groin.

Adam's gaze followed hers to the junction of his thighs where his cock stood proud and tall, strutting its vigor and power like a royal ambassador. It seemed to be applauding her for finally relinquishing her fears, challenging her to take the next step and dance with him in the flames of passion until they both incinerated into ashes. "How does it make you feel to look at a naked man, Tashi? To look at me, specifically?" he asked.

She shifted from one foot to the other and moved her camera case from her left to right shoulder as if its weight had suddenly become too much for her to bear. "It makes me feel funny."

Adam cleared the croak from his throat. Standing here talking to innocent Tashi about sex and nudity was the biggest turn-on he'd ever experienced. His cock had never been so hard. The way it was palpitating against his stomach like a restless serpent ready to strike should scare her, but she seemed rather fascinated with it.

From what he could remember from his Sunday School lessons, Eve hadn't been scared of the serpent in the Garden of Eden, either. She'd been enthralled by it. "Funny how?" he asked in a throaty voice. "Can you describe how you feel?"

She licked her lips and folded her arms around her stomach as a shudder shook her slender frame. "Warm and tingly," she said, her gaze moving slowly up his body to his eyes. "Maybe hot, and jittery. My breasts feel swollen, my nipples are hard and achy, and I—" She licked her lips again. "I feel thirsty and empty, yet full, and I have this ache, this throbbing deep inside me like an earthquake is happening in the very core of my being. "And…" She dropped her gaze to his bare feet nestled in the green grass.

Adam's throat tightened as he watched her chest heave. "And what?" He could hardly speak.

"My panties are wet. I've never felt like this before—before I met you."

A sharp pang ripped through Adam's gut. *Did she have to be so honest, so forthright with her feelings?* He inhaled deeply and sharply, fisted his hands at his sides, and closed his eyes to control the yearning rolling through him. When his breathing steadied, he opened his eyes to see her staring up at him with curious wonder in her emerald eyes.

"Do you want to take off your panties, Tashi? I mean since they're wet and all." *Why did that sound so perverted to him?* Dear God, she was a virgin, and he shouldn't, but seeing that she was his soul mate, it was only natural that they begin exploring the intimate aspects of their relationship.

"I don't think that's a good idea."

"I've seen you naked, Tashi. I've bathed you. I've touched you on more than one occasion." He wanted to touch her again. Intimately. Not as a caregiver, nursing her back to health, but as a lover, teaching her about the joys and passions of lovemaking, helping her explore the depths of her own desires, alleviating the aches, the throbs, the tingles and heat she'd just described to him.

She trembled on a sigh. "This is different, though. You might want to do things, things I might not be ready for."

She was ready, physically, at least. She just didn't know it, and wouldn't know it until her mind, her heart, and her soul caught up with the longings in her body. Every aspect of her being had to be in total harmony before she could experience maximum and ultimate pleasure and fulfillment. Tashi was as chaste as an angel. An angel that had fallen from heaven and into his arms—literally. Because of her innocence, he would have to tread carefully with her. Too much, too soon and she could be turned off forever.

"We'll only do what you want, what you're comfortable with. Nothing else," he said. "We've had sixteen dates in the past week. Most people are in bed by their third date. This is just the next phase in our emerging relationship."

She stiffened at the words "emerging relationship" and her lips quivered as she gazed at him, wide-eyes. In the past week that he'd been studying her, Adam had learned to decipher sudden changes in her mood. The tension in her body, the dread in her eyes suggested that she was scared, not of him, but for him.

The imminent danger of her circumstances suddenly flooded Adam's being, reminding him that she was running and hiding from some bad people who wanted to harm her. People who were prepared to kill anyone who stood in the way of what they wanted: her.

He could tell her that she need not be afraid, but he knew those words would be meaningless to her. He had to show her that she could trust him in all areas of their relationship. She'd trusted him as a caregiver, and now she must learn to trust him as a friend—a friend with whom she need not project pretense, caution, or hesitation. They had to learn and grow together as one unit, and the only way they'd know the true essence of their souls was if they bared themselves, emotionally, psychologically, and physically to each other.

There should be no secrets between them, but there should be explicit consent. Tashi had grown up with philosophies about the human body that were vastly different from his. Adam had no desire to convert or steer her away from those teachings, but if she wanted to explore the wellspring of her sexuality, he would be delighted to be her guide.

"Do you want to get naked with me, Tashi?" His gaze held hers, willing her to take the first step into the unknown, feed her curiosity and explore another realm of the complexity that comprised Tashi Holland. Her name wasn't Eve, but the vision they would create couldn't be more allegorical—Adam and his woman, completely naked, and one with nature in their own Garden of Eden.

Her lips parted as if she wanted to say something, but no words came out.

"Do you trust me, Tashi?"

She shifted her weight again, her irises a kaleidoscope of bluish-green hues as she fought the war between submission to the yearnings in her body and subservience to her past.

Finally she nodded. "Okay. Yes, I—I trust you, and I—I want to get naked with you."

Heat whipped through Adam as she caught her bottom lip between her teeth. His skin tingled as he imagined her nibbling on his flesh, ever so daintily. "I promise to go only as far as you wish. You can stop me at any time. Okay?"

She gave him a demure smile—half consent, half trepidation.

Finally, he'd have the honor and the pleasure to enjoy the sight of Tashi's exquisite body as she peeled each layer of clothing away. He'd still have to wait—he hoped not too long—to caress the silkiness of her skin, mold the delectable curves he'd recently noticed developing under her clothes, revel in visions of her lying in his arms—sated, damp, and quivering after they'd ridden the high tide of desire together, over and over again.

When he'd undressed her before, she'd been half-conscious with no desire or strength to stop him. Today, he wanted her to undress herself, to be fully aware of what she was doing, even if she wasn't certain of why she was doing it. Even though he'd seen her naked before, it felt to Adam like it would be the first time.

To aid her introduction into his uninhibited world of nudity and intimacy, Adam reached out and slid her camera case off her shoulders and set it down on the slab of granite. "Take off your clothes, Tashi."

She glanced around the perimeter of the garden, spanning the trees as if she expected her uncle or her educators to float down from the branches and reprimand her for being naughty, prurient, for being charmed by the serpent.

"There's no one here but us. It's just you and me. I promise not to touch you until you're completely naked. Then, and only then, will I know that you're ready to explore these feelings of desire you've been experiencing."

Adam's heart began to beat wildly and furiously against his chest as Tashi's hands crept up her body toward her throat where her pulse vibrated violently against her skin. He sucked air into his lungs when her slender fingers closed over the top button of her shirt.

CHAPTER NINE

What are you doing? Have you lost your mind? Your uncle is turning over in his grave to see what you've become.

Quieting the censoring voices that had been governing her thoughts, crowding her mind, suppressing her desires to explore the sexual titillations she'd been experiencing since she hit puberty, Tashi kept her gaze locked with Adam's as she undid the first, second, and then third buttons of her shirt.

She could almost feel the doors of her soul bursting open, freeing the sheltered girl who had been locked away in a prison of proselytization for most of her life. That naïve girl, cloaked in decadence seemed starved for her first taste of forbidden pleasure. She could see her unfolding before her eyes, rising from the darkness, pushing to her feet, and reaching her fingers upward toward the light of her inner universe—becoming a woman with needs and expectations.

Tashi couldn't say that she resented her uncle for the way he'd raised her. In fact, she appreciated that he'd shielded her, and that he'd sent her to schools that demanded chastity and celibacy. With a less strict upbringing, she might have ended up like Mindy—teenage and pregnant, or she could have become an unwed mother like her own mother, struggling to take care of a young child, alone. Perhaps that's what her uncle had been afraid of most—that she would become her mother. That's why he'd stopped calling her Little Eve.

What Tashi wished was that her educators had been a little more open-minded and forthright about a young girl's developing body, about the hormones running wild inside her, instead of teaching her that her awakening arousal was bad, even evil to a point. Teach her instead that her desires were normal, and that one day she would meet a man—that one special man—with whom she would want to explore those feelings and find fulfillment of the most delicate form.

That special man for Tashi was Adam, the man who'd save her life, and in whose presence Little Eve felt safe and treasured enough to emerge from the shadows where her uncle had shoved her, eighteen years ago.

Little Eve loved the sight of the man before her—his elegantly chiseled cheekbones and straight nose, his rosy lips forever curled on the edge of laughter, and his sharp chin that spoke of distinction and dominance. Little Eve loved the wispy mat of hair on his chest and stomach that extended into a thicker thatch at his groin, then thinned out again on his thighs and legs.

The last button undone, Tashi slid the shirt off her shoulders, down her arms, and let it slither to the grass behind her. She inhaled sharply as the cool summer breeze—charged with the electricity from the force of the waterfalls—caressed the skin of her arms, her chest, and quivering stomach. It whispered of the wanton thrills awaiting her.

You'll burn, Tashi. You'll burn...

Tashi tossed her head in defiance and sighed deeply as her long curls brushed against her shoulders and across the curve of her back—tickling her. Extending her arms out at her sides and throwing her head back, she closed her eyes and rotated her neck from side to side ever so slowly, and welcomed the nascent sensations nursing her arousal.

Never had she imagined that something as simple as her own hair brushing against her skin could send jitters up and down her spine. Perhaps she'd been aware all along but because she'd been programmed not to respond to anything slightly sexual, she'd ignored the elusive stimulation. If her own hair could induce such titillation, she could just imagine the fire Adam's silky mane trailing up and down her naked body could evoke in her.

She hoped to burn until the thirst and the hunger inside her were assuaged, until there was nothing but ashes left of her. Her head began to sway as if to its own music—a secret melody her soul had composed eons ago. Picking up the tempo, her body began to rock from side to side, undulating on a weightless wave.

"Tashi."

The whisper of her name brought Tashi floating back to shore. Her lids fluttered open to find Adam staring at her. His eyes were ablaze with a sensuous flame, his sexy mouth pulsing with the promise of the passion that could be hers if she dared to reach out and ask for it.

She wanted it. Her gaze slid across his aristocratic face, brimming with gentleness, kindness, and strength. It was a face she hadn't known she'd been searching for her entire life. It said nothing, yet everything she'd ever want to hear. For the first time since they'd met, Tashi didn't feel shy about openly admiring Adam, gazing unabashed into his eyes, feeling the magic pulling her down into the enchanting chasm of the blue oasis of his soul. In the past week, she'd stolen glances at him while they ate their meals together, but each time he'd met her gaze, she'd averted hers, but not before she'd caught his smile that seemed to say, *Don't look away. I enjoy your furtive glances.*

Today, Tashi felt different, reborn, like everything she'd known about herself up to this point in her life had been false.

She felt as if she was meeting the real Tashi Evelyn Holland for the first time. She liked her—this serenely wild, slightly adventurous young girl who was eager to enter the new and unfamiliar cosmos unfolding before her eyes.

Little Eve had found her Adam, her light, her guide, the man who could teach her how to dance and play, laugh and revel in this numinous place where no one or nothing could hurt her.

Anxious to shed the remnants of her clothes as quickly as she felt the restrictive teaching of her past dissolving around her, Tashi reached behind her and unsnapped the clasp of her bra. Keeping her eyes locked with Adam's, she slid the straps off her shoulders and let the lacy garment fall noiselessly to the ground on top of her shirt. Her nipples hardened and tingled when Adam's gaze and the cool breeze seemed to simultaneously brush them in an invisible kiss.

"Your home is beautiful, Tashi. More lovely than any I've ever seen," he said, his voice husky with emotion.

Tashi thought it strange that he hadn't said she was beautiful, but then she remembered that he was a yogi. He would regard the human body as a house for the human spirit—the true *you*. He hadn't really met her yet. *She* hadn't met her.

"Your home is beautiful too, Adam." There, she'd said them, spoken the words that had been echoing inside her since she first collided with him in the café. He'd been naked in her presence before when he'd first brought her to his home. Although she'd been faintly aware of his strength and virility, she'd been in no condition to evaluate and appreciate him. She was well now, and definitely appreciating him.

Tashi felt a rush of wickedness as her gaze slid from his face to his neck where his pulse seemed to beat in time with hers. She admired the way his broad and muscular chest and shoulders tapered off into a flat, corded stomach, narrow waist, and slim hips. She'd often admired his physique under his clothes, but she was salivating now as her eyes drew lower to where his engorged penis protruded like a pillar of bronze muscle from the thatch of dark hair at his groin. It was far more intimidating, yet captivating up close. She wondered about the texture of the thin skin that ran the length and girth of him—from the root to the glittering tip with a wide opening that looked like a small mouth.

Tashi licked her lips as muscles pulsed deep inside her body.

"Go on, Tashi. Take it all off," Adam coaxed, reminding her of his promise not to touch her until she was completely naked.

Incited by his words and impatience, Tashi toed off her sneakers and heeled them behind her. She then unsnapped the clasp of her jeans and pulled the zipper down. When her fingers slid beneath the waist of her jeans and her panties, Adam groaned. Capturing his gaze again, she began to push them off her hips, slowly and provocatively, wiggling her hips and buttocks to fight the restriction. Down, down, she eased until she felt the breeze ripple through the auburn carpet covering her Venus mound.

Adam groaned again. The sound knocked her off balance and finding herself pitching forward, she put her hand out to break her fall. Of all the places her hand could have landed on Adam's anatomy, it chose to land on the area of his groin. A shot of adrenaline, mixed with fear and excitement coursed through Tashi's system. The naked hardness of his body excited her.

Curiosity got the better of her, and she moved her hand just an inch to the right and fisted her fingers around the column of flesh—not completely circling it. It felt like smooth velvet, hot and hard, and it pulsed in her palm as if it had a life of its own. The inner walls of her vagina began to respond to the stimulus, contracting and throbbing and spewing hot juices from between her thighs.

She felt Adam's hands on her arms steadying her, applying slight pressure as he seemed to combat his rising desires, but her eyes remained glued to her hand that was full of him. Of its own volition, her hand began to move up and down, pushing the thin smooth skin back and forth, watching the red glittering tip appear and disappear within the folds. She was fascinated by the way the muscles of his stomach convulsed like a wave rolling across the ocean, and the harsh sounds of his breath rumbling through the garden.

So this was what it was like to caress a man. Liking the power it afforded her, she continued to arouse Adam's passion, stroking him harder and faster as he grew hotter and stronger, until a slippery, clear liquid oozed out of the opening and crowned the tip.

Adam released her, and fisted his hands at his sides. His body began to spasm as if sporadic bolts of current were passing through him. She knew what happened during sex, what went into what. What baffled her now was how the deed would be accomplished. How could this enormous column of flesh enter her body without causing her excruciating pain? Could a woman's body really stretch that wide?

"Tashi."

Tashi stopped in mid-stroke to gaze up at him. His eyes were a deep, deep blue, like the ocean after a quick storm, his lips moist and swollen as if they'd been beaten by passion. She wanted to please him, show him that she wasn't shy or afraid. Tashi had no idea what kind of lascivious imp had inhabited her body, infected her blood, but as she stood there in the shade of the willow tree, half-naked with her jeans and panties halfway down her thighs, and her hand clasped around Adam's private part, she felt bold and empowered.

"Tashi, stop," he commanded in a choked voice, jerking his body backward and away from her. "Release me."

Tashi released him and frowned in confusion as she

straightened up to her full five-foot four-inch frame. "I'm not afraid, Adam. I want to be with you."

"And I with you, but you're not ready for that, *cara*," he said, even as his head began a lazy descent toward hers.

Her heart began to thump at the anticipation of introducing her lips to his. For the two weeks they'd been sharing a roof, neither one of them had made any sexual advances toward the other—except for that brief moment in her apartment when he'd trailed his fingertip along her cheek to show her why she couldn't work for him. Yet every day since they'd met, they'd been exchanging the mutual essence of their passion through bathing, dining, and gazing—preludes to their first kiss.

His lips inched so close to her forehead, she could feel the blood pulsing through them, the tension and the electricity in the small space between them. Lower he edged, across her temples, her cheeks, to the sides of her trembling mouth, sniffing, heating her skin with his breath—so close, teasing without touching.

Tashi had never smelled passion, didn't even know that it had an odor, but she was certain that that's what she smelled pouring out of Adam. It was heady, raunchy, musky, intoxicating and she wanted to bathe in it. She leaned closer seeking contact with him, but he drew back.

"Finish undressing," he whispered, his hot breath searing the sides of her mouth.

Anxious to be free, Tashi resumed her task and pushed her jeans and panties down her thighs and legs while Adam stood there and watched her. When her clothes were a tangled mess around her ankles, he dropped to his knees in front of her. His long hair tumbled over his shoulders and brushed her legs, tickling her. His face was in perfect alignment with the junction of her thighs. She could feel his breath stirring the hairs on her Venus mound and the heat from his gaze warming the flesh beneath.

"Finish," he coaxed again.

His words seemed to strike a physical blow to Tashi's womanhood, and as they reverberated deep inside her, she swooned. Adam's hand on her hips kept her from falling right onto his face. She imagined his lips kissing her, his tongue parting her, seeking entrance. Unable to control the spark of excitement at the prospect of Adam feasting on her, Tashi opened her mouth and expelled the moan that had been choking her.

Adam lifted his head and gazed up at her. "You're almost there. Use me."

Understanding his offer, Tashi braced her hands against his shoulders. She tried to ignore the silky feel of his mane and the rippling muscles of his shoulders under her palms as she raised one leg at a time and pulled off her jeans, panties, and socks. She kicked them behind her and dropped her hands to her sides. There, she'd done the unthinkable—stripped herself naked in the presence of a man.

"Stand still," Adam said. Starting from her toes, he took his time inspecting every inch of her body. Tashi's skin tingled as he moved up her legs, her thighs, her groin area where he lingered as if he were trying to decipher the secrets to her femininity.

She let out a long harsh breath as he continued his languid scrutiny, unfolding his body in slow motion in the same way he'd done from his yoga pose. Her belly rippled, her breasts grew full and heavy, and her nipples tightened as he caressed them with his eyes. The pulse at her neck throbbed, her mouth quivered, and her eyelids fluttered under his watchful gaze.

Moving behind her, he gave her backside the same leisurely survey before coming to stand in front of her again. Their gazes met and held and in those breathless moments, Tashi found a deeper significance to their visual exchange than any words she'd ever heard uttered.

"Come." He turned and began walking toward the structure.

Leaving everything she'd brought behind her, Tashi followed him.

He stopped at the steps leading up to the podium and turned to catch her gaze. "How are you, Tashi?" he asked.

"Excited, tingly, flushed—"

"No." He shook his head. "Those are physical reactions to the fact that we are both standing here in our birthday suits. You're filled with anticipation about making love with me. I want to know how *you* are. Inside."

"Free," Tashi said without hesitation. "I'm free, Adam."

"No shame at baring yourself in front of a man, in front of me? No guilt for going against what you've been taught? No resentment toward me for daring you to challenge your upbringing?"

"No, none of the above. I feel—" She stopped and searched her mind for a word to describe what was happening inside her. "Natural. Looking at you naked, and then taking off my clothes felt natural." And strangely, all the anxiety and sexual tension she'd felt just a few moments ago had evaporated. "I feel like the person I thought I was all these years has become a stranger to me," she continued. "The moment I began taking off my clothes was the moment I really saw me for the first time."

"You've found *you*, Tashi—the goddess, the little girl who'd been buried alive."

"Little Eve." The words slipped out even before they materialized in Tashi's mind.

Adam's forehead crinkled into a frown. "Little Eve?"

"My middle name is Evelyn, after my mother. She was Eve for short. I look so much like her, down to my red hair and green eyes, that when I was a child people called me Little Eve. She died when I was four, then my uncle started calling me Tashi." Tashi provided the information as if it were the most natural thing in the world to do. And he hadn't even asked.

He stared at her for a long moment as if he were digesting what she'd told him—that her name was Eve, and that her mother had died when she was four. She'd told him more about herself in those few seconds than she'd revealed in the two weeks they'd been together.

"Fate was unkind to you, Tashi," he said. "You were robbed of the most important person in your life way too early."

Tashi shrugged. "I hardly remember her, but I remember her smell," she said, her heart quickening on the memories.

"It is said that when it comes to memory, smell is the most faithful of all the senses. So I'm not surprised. Your mother's smell was the most significant to you as a child. You still carry it inside you. What did she smell like?" he asked.

"A combination of ginger—"

"Jasmine and vanilla," Adam finished her sentence. "I love those fragrances on you, Tashi. They're very natural, subtle, and appealing."

Tashi smiled as heat generated under her skin. "When I was old enough, I began using her line of hair and skin products. It was my way of honoring her, keeping her memory alive in my mind and my heart."

She glanced off to where a bird chirped in one of the nearby trees. She was quickly losing the image of her mom's face. Most of the pictures of her mother were in a storage unit in Sebring, Ohio where her uncle had stored them before he died. She'd taken a few to New York, but only God knew where those were now. She might never see them again. "I wish I could remember what she looked like," she said, bringing her gaze back to Adam's.

"All you have to do is look in the mirror."

She'd never thought of that. She didn't need pictures of her mother. She was a living image of her. She was certain she'd inherited her wild, curious, carefree spirit, too—the spirit she'd just exposed, the one her uncle and her educators had "buried alive" according to Adam.

"Are you ready to learn more about Little Eve, Tashi?" Adam's deep mellow voice drew her back to the present.

"Yes. I want to get to know her."

"Well, this is the perfect place for new discoveries. This is where I come for deeper connection to my inner universe, and for healing, and inspiration. I leave everything behind when I come here, even my clothes. So I want you to forget everything you've been taught, everything you think you know about yourself, and begin with a clean canvas where Little Eve can begin painting her own story."

He took her hand and led her up the black marble steps. On the second to the last step that was much wider than the others and seemed more like a small foyer, Tashi noticed a chrome basket containing the clothes Adam had worn at breakfast that morning. He wasn't kidding when he said he left everything outside of his sanctuary.

One more step and a soft white floor gave way under her feet. Tashi gazed out the other side of the platform to the blue pool bubbling with white foam from the force of the waterfalls feeding it. "It's a lovely place, Adam. Serene and magical." She had no doubt that the ambiance played a huge role in emboldening her. "How long has it been here?"

"I built it five years ago when my parents moved back to Italy," he replied, his eyes following hers. "I come here as often as my role as CEO of Andreas International allows. When the weather is favorable, I spend the night." He pointed at a closed door on his left. "That's a bedroom suite, and—" He pointed to the right. "Kitchen, living, and dining area. I spend more time here when my parents visit."

"Do you always come alone?" she asked, taking a swift glance at a slab of granite on one wall that served as a table. A pitcher of water with what looked liked mint leaves floating inside it, and two glasses were situated on one end of it, and a black leather toiletry case on the other.

"The only other people who come here are the landscapers, and they stay away when the flag is up."

"So that's what the flag is for."

"Yes. And for additional security and privacy, I had retractable, one-way, mirrored walls installed on each side of this platform to protect against the elements of Mother Nature, scurrying animals, and uninvited guests. The front part has two panels—one for the foyer—" He pointed to the wide step, "and one for the platform. They are remotely controlled and when in use, I can see out, but no one can see in. You're the first person I'm sharing my sanctuary with, Tashi Evelyn Holland."

Tashi quivered from the indulgence in his voice when he spoke her full name.

"I've been waiting for the right partner to join me, to share this special place with me. And now here she is."

"How do you I'm the right partner?"

"How do you know you're not?" A faint light twinkled in the depths of his blue eyes, like a prelude of voltage to a lightning storm about to break. "Sometimes we should just let the questions lead us into the answers, naturally."

Tashi's heart took a perilous leap. If he only knew her—that she'd killed a man, taken the life of another human being, he might ban her from his special place.

"Tashi." His eyes searched her face as if reading her thoughts. "You won't be able to explore the complexities of your soul if you harbor negative thoughts. You must let everything go if you intend to find the true and secret knowledge of *you*. Let Little Eve be your guide, your compass as you discover a different way of thinking, breathing, reacting to situations and stimuli in your life. Just trust her. You think you can do that?"

"Yes. I can. I want to."

"Good." He looked her over. "We need to secure your hair so it doesn't get in your way." He walked over to the granite pillar.

As he rummaged through the toiletry bag, Tashi couldn't stop herself from admiring the twin hillocks of his buttocks projecting from the strong columns of his thighs, and the slight flexing of the muscles beneath the taut olive-toned skin. It was sexy and provocative and she wondered how his skin and his muscles would feel under her palms.

He turned suddenly, and her gaze once again landed on his groin. His erection had lost some of its vigor, although it seemed to retain much of its girth and length. She dropped her gaze when he began walking back to her.

"It's okay to admire me, Tashi," he said in a low silky voice. "I can take the attention." He held out his hand.

Tashi took the hair elastic from him. He could take her attention, but could she take his, she wondered when his gaze zeroed in on the lift of her breasts as she raised her hands to pull her hair into a ponytail.

"Ready?" he asked, giving her a flashing smile.

She cleared her throat. "Ready." Anything to shift her focus.

"The first thing I want you to do is stand straight with your feet together and your hands clasped, like in prayer." He demonstrated the posture.

"Say the word *Namaste* three times as you bow toward me. We'll do it together."

Tashi wanted to ask him what the word meant, but thought it would break the spiritual aura already twirling around them. So she tucked her questions away, clasped her hands against her heart, and on Adam's cue, she bowed toward him and repeated *Namaste* in unison with him.

"Now," he said on an impressive smile, "drop your hands to

your sides and your head forward and just let it hang there, like a robe on a hook."

Tashi mimicked him.

"Close your eyes. Good," he said when her eyelids fluttered shut. "Now allow your body to relax and melt into the space around you. You are the air you breathe, the light you feel, the wind that bathes your skin. Breathe in that light and that air slowly through your nostrils while simultaneously raising your head, and then exhale through your mouth while bringing your head back down. Release the toxins that have been building inside you over the years to the wind. Again. Breathe in. Deeply. Slowly... Out... In... Out... Inhale... Release..."

Tashi was so caught up in learning to breathe, and relax, and ridding herself of toxins, that she didn't even realize Adam had moved until she felt him standing directly behind her, so close she could feel the heat from his body bridging the tight gap between them, his musky odor scenting her space. A gust of wind picked up a few strands of his hair and whipped them over her shoulder. They landed on her chest and danced across her left breast as they swayed to the motion of the wind. Tashi trembled, and her heart began to thump.

"Keep breathing," Adam whispered. "Don't break the rhythm. Control the sensations. Breathe them in, make them flow through you, send them to every fissure of your body, command them to assuage your aches for as long as you desire, and then release them into the ethers when you've had enough. In... Out..."

Tashi did as he instructed, and soon her heart settled into a steady pace, and the tingling sensations of Adam's hair brushing against her breasts and nipples, his voice and his smell transitioned into wellsprings inside her spewing streams of impalpable warmth throughout her inner being. It was magical, like desire alleviating yet amplifying desire. It satisfied her, yet drained her... Unable to stand the contrasting delight, Tashi opened her mouth and sent it into the ethers.

Her heart was pounding, her limbs were languid, and she felt dizzy, like she was spinning in space. Her knees buckled.

Adam's arms circling her kept her from falling. "Good girl. You're a quick study. No, no," he added softly when she tensed from the warmth of his skin on hers, the hairs of his chest and torso tickling her, the feel of his smooth hardness pressing into her back. "Don't tighten your body. Don't fight. I promised that we won't do anything you're not ready for. You can trust me, Tashi. Just relax into my embrace and think of me as a vessel channeling you calmly to shore on the waves of your sensations. Use me."

Soothed by his gentle voice and tender touch, Tashi relaxed into the rhythm of the waves and soon her heart was calm and beating against her chest in a steady rhythm again.

Adam unfolded his arms from around her, and drawing his body away from her, he placed his palms to the backs of her hands and laced his fingers through hers.

The simple contact seemed even more intimate than when his body was pressed against hers. She swallowed a lump in her throat.

"Bring your head up, and take a deep breath," he said as he raised her arms slowly away from her body and up above her head. "Hold that breath," he said, touching her palms together before releasing her and stepping back. "Now turn your palms facing outward and bring your arms very slowly back down to your sides as you release your breath. Don't forget to lower your head to your chin on exhale."

Tashi exhaled on a smile, amazed at the equanimity that controlled breathing brought her. No wonder Adam seemed so balanced and serene all the time.

"Good," Adam said coming to stand in front of her. "Now try it again, at your own pace this time."

After a few more breathing exercises, Adam began to demonstrate a series of yoga poses for beginners. First it was The Mountain, then The Tree, The Warrior, The Seated Twist, The Cobra...

As she transitioned from one position to the next, Tashi's body felt limp, relaxed, and light as a feather, like she was looking at an apparition of herself floating through time. Her mind was free, empty. He was one with the wind, the light, and the air surrounding her. She heard nothing but the deep sound of Adam's coaching voice. She felt nothing but his strong warm hands on her body as he helped her perfect one pose after the next.

Tashi even forgot that they were both naked.

Finally, they sat facing each other in the Crossed Leg pose.

"Rest your arms along your thighs with your wrists on your knees, your palms facing upward. Drop your shoulders and your head. Close your eyes. Relax your body and breathe normally. Invite your spirit and your soul back home. Stay like this for as long as you need, and when you're ready raise your head, and open your eyes."

Silence wrapped around them, then Tashi became aware of the physical environment—the leaves rustling in the wind, birds chirping. She was certain that she could hear the buzz of a bee above the gushing waterfall. Raising her head, she opened her eyes to find Adam watching her.

"Now, for the grand finale," he said with a smile. "Clasp your hands together like you did in the beginning. Keep holding my gaze as we say *Namaste* three times while bowing to each other."

And so they ended their session as they'd begun.

"You did excellently, Tashi."

"You're an awesome teacher, Adam."

"I should warn you that you'll have some aches and pain tomorrow morning. You've used muscles you've never used before."

She would probably have aches and pain after their first lovemaking session, too. She was certain that he would be just as awesome as he introduced her to the ecstasies of lovemaking. Involuntarily, her eyes were drawn to his midsection. Sometime during their yoga session, his erection had returned. She swallowed as she felt the heat of his gaze traveling slowly down her body. He stopped at the place between her thighs where the breeze cooled the warm moisture seeping from inside her.

Their gazes collided and held. Tashi's stomach lurched at the flicker of passion she detected in his eyes. She wanted to be with him—be one with him. How could something that felt so beautiful, so right, be forbidden? If she lay back on his soft floor and invited him to fit himself to her, would he, or would her innocence deter him? "Adam—"

He shook his head as if he knew where her thoughts had gone. He uncrossed his legs, pushed to his feet, and reached down to help her up. "You're a very desirable woman, Tashi Holland, and I've been thinking about making love to you since the day we met, but your physical condition kept me in check. And now that I'm aware of the way you were brought up, I'm wise enough and experienced enough to know that you're not emotionally or psychologically ready for such a life-changing experience."

Tashi knew he spoke the truth, and she appreciated the control he'd exhibited on her behalf. But her time with him was temporary, limited. "How will I know when I'm ready?" she asked him.

"When you stop questioning yourself. We will both know when that moment arrives, and our union will be pure and sweet and wholesome. I'll wait for you, Tashi. I'm not going anywhere."

But I am. Pain squeezed her heart.

He stepped to the side, picked up his robe from the floor, and slipped it on. He then opened a built-in drawer on a wall and lifting out a folded matching robe, he held it open for her. "This is brand new. It's been waiting for you, I suppose."

Tashi slid her arms into the sleeves and wrapped the silky material around her body, securing it at her waist with the belt. He seemed to keep a lot of brand new items of clothing around that fitted her...

"Perfect fit," he said, smiling at her with his electric blue eyes that seemed to pull her a little further into their unfathomable depth every time she looked at him. He turned and picked up the pitcher of water she'd seen earlier and filled two glasses. He handed one to her. "Would you like to do this again sometime?"

"Yes. Definitely. I enjoyed it."

"I enjoy you, Tashi," he said, his lips curling into a sensuous smile as he raised his glass for a long sip.

He spoke of enjoying her in the present as if it was continuous, with no beginning and no end. Tashi gulped down the cool minty water, willing it to moisten and soothe the dryness in her throat, cool the heat in her body. "What does *Namaste* mean?" she asked when he set his empty glass on the pillar.

"It's a word the Hindu use when they meet and part from each other."

"Kind of like *Aloha* in Hawaii?"

"Kind of, but with a deeper, more significant meaning. When you say *Namaste* to someone, you're saying: 'I honor the place within you in which the entire universe dwells. I honor the place within you, which is of Love, of Truth, of Light, and of Peace. When you are in that place within you and I am in that place within me, we are one'."

"That's powerful."

"It is. It's customary to say it before and after each yoga session."

"Why do you say it three times?"

"You say it three times when you're with someone or in a group. Once to yourself—the god or goddess within you—once to your partner or group, and once to your higher power, whoever that may be. For me, He's God Almighty. I respect all religions and borrow philosophies from some."

She liked that they had that in common. "Can we say *Namaste* together again now that I understand its significance?"

"I would be delighted to, *mia dolce*." He took her empty glass and set it next to his.

As they bowed and repeated the sacred word, Tashi felt the warmth of Light and Truth and Peace hover above her heart and soul, but it didn't enter. Perhaps she was too damaged for it to reach that place inside her. The feeling of hopelessness was so intense, she choked up and soon tears sprang from her eyes and flowed down her cheeks.

"Tashi, darling." Adam enveloped her in his arms and she melted into him.

The thought of leaving Adam, of leaving the safest place on earth—his arms—broke Tashi's heart. How was she going to survive without him, especially now that she had no money and no home? No friends in over a year. No one to care about her since her uncle died, no one, until Adam. The desolation of her future overwhelmed her, and she began to sob.

Patient Adam asked no questions, but seemed quite content to hold and soothe her until she was spent. He was the kindest, gentlest human on earth. Finally, he placed his finger under her chin and raised her face to his. His eyes brimmed with tenderness and concern. And questions, but the only one he asked was, "Feel better?" as he pushed her hair from her face and wiped away her lingering tears.

"Adam—" She swallowed, then opened her mouth to tell him everything, but the words were lodged in her throat.

"That too will come naturally, Tashi. In the meantime, I'm here for you. You can cry on my shoulder or on my chest any time you want." He searched her face. "Now, I don't know about you, but I'm famished."

"I am, too." She had no idea that a practice as relaxing as yoga could make one sweat and work up an appetite.

"We can put our clothes back on and return to the house or we can stay here for the rest of the day. The pantry and fridge are stocked with all sorts of goodies, and my garden is blooming," he said, swiping his wrist to the back of the building where a vegetable and herb garden were indeed blooming.

No wonder his dishes always tasted so fresh and flavorsome. "I would like to stay here. But," she added, knowing that he usually spent the latter part of his days, and half of his nights in his home office. "I feel kind of guilty keeping you away from your business."

"You are my business for now, *cara*." He touched his knuckles to her cheek. "Don't feel guilty. I enjoy being with you. You brighten my every waking and sleeping moment. Perhaps after we eat, we can go for a swim and stand under the waterfall. It's quite invigorating to feel the force of that water crashing down on you."

"Isn't it cold?" she asked, glancing at the water gushing over the granite rocks.

"It's temperature controlled."

"Of course." As he led her toward the kitchen and dining area, Tashi realized that Adam would be hurt whether she left tomorrow or next month. He was already too deeply involved with her—a murderer and a fugitive from the law.

Where was that FBI agent? Was he dead or alive? Should she stay and wait for him, or should she leave to protect Adam and everyone he cared about? When she'd agreed to come back to his home, she'd told him that it was temporary.

How long should she allow temporary to go on?

CHAPTER TEN

"Dad, I have everything under control. It's not as if I've completely neglected the company. I've been working from home. I just needed a sabbatical to take care of some personal issues."

"Another sabbatical, Adamo? How many of those do you need a year? I've been running Andreas International since I inherited it from your grandfather thirty years ago, and I've never taken a sabbatical in all those years. Even when I'm on vacation with your mother, I leave room to conduct business. I've been receiving calls from CEOs all over the world complaining that you've been canceling and postponing important meetings for the past two weeks. I called your cousin Massimo to see if he knew what was going on. He hasn't seen you in two weeks."

"In all fairness, Dad," Adam said in his own defense, "Massimo has been busy with his new wife and daughter, and with running Andretti business."

"My point, precisely. Massimo has a family and yet he finds time to run the company his father left in his care. You have no family, Adamo," his father stated, reminding him that he had yet to produce an heir to carry on the Andreas bloodline. "Yet you're neglecting Andreas business. What have you been doing? Are you ill?"

Adam closed his eyes, inhaled and exhaled on a ten-second count as thoughts of Tashi filtered through his brain. Yes, he was ill—burning up with fever for her. He wanted to be with her, make sweet love with her in the worst way, but he had to keep himself in check. He had to wait until she was ready. She had to make the first move and it had to be for the right reasons—even for their first kiss.

"Adamo, are you ill?"

Adam opened his eyes and stared out the row of French doors in his home office. "No, Dad. I'm not ill." He wiped his hand down his face.

"Then you'd better get back to business. I didn't work this hard all these years to watch Andreas International go to ruin. I knew you were too young to handle a company of this magnitude, but your mother assured me you could do it…"

As his father ranted on, Adam put the call on speaker, vacated the chair behind his desk, and paced the floor. He'd grown accustomed to Alessandro's lectures, which were merely his way of convincing himself that even though he was not running Andreas International, he still had some control over his company and his son.

Adam understood why his father would be upset that he'd been shirking his duties as the head of one of the most prosperous hotel and restaurant chains in the world—never mind that Andreas International's profits had quadrupled annually since Adam took control several years ago. If his own son had pulled this number, he'd be questioning him too. He'd want to know why he'd been neglecting his duties, but *sans* the flare and passion his father was wont to exhibit.

That was where the Andreas males differed in personalities. His father was a workaholic who never really took a vacation even when he was on vacation, as his own words just confirmed. He reacted quickly and vociferously to situations, whipped people into shape with an imposing domineering hand, and crushed his enemies with lethal force. Even the heads of organized crime rings were afraid of the formidable Alessandro Andreas, as they'd been equally afraid of Luciano Andretti. They struck in broad daylight and let their enemies know they were coming. Together, those two men had made the world tremble.

Adam was the very opposite. He preferred to observe and analyze quietly and then react calmly and covertly, but just as lethally to situations—just like his mother—a trait his father had always claimed was too effeminate for a boy. It didn't help his father's opinion of him when he decided to stop cutting his hair at age twelve.

Adam smiled as he remembered the family meeting his father had called after he'd missed their third simultaneous haircut appointment. Visiting the barber together had been a father and son affair ever since Adam was a toddler. It was bonding time for the Andreas men. Adam remembered sitting in the big chair and listening to his father boast about his smart son who was already fluent in five languages at age five, and who would become monarch of the Andreas fortune one day. As he got older and became interested in ballet and yoga instead of soccer and hockey, his father began to doubt the masculinity of his only offspring.

"Arabella," his father had said, "who is the biological father of this boy you claim is my son?"

His mother had looked up from the book she'd been reading, and spoke in the soft, calm voice Adam had been addicted to since he was a baby. "Okay, Alessandro, I can't keep the truth from you any longer." She'd flashed Adam a wink. "There was a mix-up in the hospital after our son was born. The nurse brought this beautiful little baby boy into my room and placed him into my arms, but by the time I realized their mistake, I'd already fallen in love with him. I couldn't give him back. I'm sorry, Alessandro, but if you want your son, you'll have to go out and search for him. I'm quite happy with the one I have."

He and his mother had sat quietly, their faces tight with humor as they tried not to burst into laughter while his father had gone off into his habitual lengthy impassioned speech in Italian that included flailing of the hands, shaking of the head, and pacing of the floor. Massimo's name, as usual, had been thrown out a few times—his father's wish that Adam was more like his cousin, even at age twelve. His speech ultimately ended with him standing in front of his wife, out of breath, beads of sweat on his forehead, and his blue eyes flashing.

His mother had calmly raised her head again and flashed her brown eyes at her husband. "Are you quite finished, *caro*?"

His father had grunted and glared down at her.

"Good. Now bend over and kiss me. Apologize for subjecting me to yet another of your insufferable tirades about our darling son whom I know you love with all your heart, and for whom you'd take a bullet without hesitation. You know they bring on my headaches."

"*Vieni, Bella,*" his father had said, gently nudging his wife from the sofa and pulling her into his arms. "*Mi si permetta di prendersi cura di quel mal di testa per voi.*" He'd joined his lips to his wife's in a leisurely kiss.

Accustomed to his parents' open show of affection in front of him, Adam had smiled at his father's offer to cure his mother's headache, and the haste with which they headed out of the room, anxious to begin the 'curing' process.

"Adamo," his mother had said, pausing at the door to smile back at him. "*Ottenere un taglio di capelli, per favore. Rendere felice il tuo paparino.*"

"*Sì, Mama,*" he'd responded to her appeal that he cut his hair to make his father happy. But he never did cut his hair, and eventually his father had come to accept his decision to grow it— yes, like a woman's.

As he'd watched them leave arm in arm—his father's tall muscular stature dwarfing his mother's petite frame—Adam had promised himself that when he grew up, he would have the kind of marriage his parents had.

Adam's mother had explained sex to him when he was nine. He'd approached his father with questions about girls, but the older Andreas had been either too busy or too embarrassed, and had told him to go ask his mother.

His mother had held nothing back. She'd pulled out her copy of *History of Fine Art* and shown him paintings and sculptures of nude men and women by some of the most famous artists who ever lived: Canova, Modigliani, Courbet, and Rodin, and of course, Michelangelo, to name a few. And without going into details, she had simply informed him that she enjoyed lovemaking with his father. She'd explained that the human body was nothing to be ashamed of, and that sex was enjoyable when it was shared between two people who cared for each other, but even more beautiful, spiritual, and magical with one's soul mate.

"You will probably make love with many women, Adamo, but one day, that special woman, your *Anam Cara*, will come into your life, the one you'll pledge your heart, and soul, and life to. There are to be no other women after her. You're to wait for her, *amore mio*," she'd said, brushing his hair from his forehead.

"How will I know when I find her, Mama?" he'd asked, gazing up into her eyes.

A tender smile had graced her lips. "Your heart will know, and it will be the most natural feeling you've ever experienced. You'll feel as if you've arrived—Home. And together you and she will transcend beyond the physical to a spiritual realm where your hearts, your souls, and your spirits become one entity in the light and beauty of your pleasure and your love."

Being raised under his mother's salubrious tutelage about sex and the opposite gender, Adam had developed a deep respect for women and their bodies—no matter the age, color, shape, or size. He saw women as delicate flowers, princesses, and goddesses who should be protected, cherished, and worshipped.

He wanted a woman like his mother—one who was delicate, sweet, warm, who would tolerate his eccentricities, advocate for his children when he was being domineering and unreasonable, and love him even when he was unlovable.

Adam's heart jolted, and warmth spread through him as he thought of the woman with whom he'd just spent two of the most amazing weeks of his life. She was very much like his mother.

It had been four days since Tashi begun her journey into self-discovery and acceptance of her true nature. She'd grown more comfortable with him, taking off her clothes without hesitation and baring her body without blushing in preparation for their daily couples' sessions. He'd spent the last three days coaching her deeper into the world of yoga, teaching her the healing benefits of conscious breathing and meditation, and the heightened intimacy between two people through tantric soul gazing exercises. But even in her voyages into the deepest regions of her inner universe, Adam detected fear and hesitation in her.

Sensing that his presence might be the cause of her inability to face both her fears and her feelings for and about him—feelings he saw in her incredibly beautiful emerald eyes each time she looked at him—he'd suggested that she meditate alone today. He hoped she'd return, ready to confide in him so that they could transition into the next phase of their relationship.

Adam's lips tingled in anticipation of kissing Tashi for the first time, of experiencing the thrill of their passions blending, of the light of their love curling around each other, becoming one. It would be her first kiss and he planned to make it one she would never forget. He closed his eyes and breathed deeply as he recalled the feel of her small warm hands wrapped around him, the tentative, curious manner in which she stroked him, the look of surprise and wonder on her face at realizing the effect her caresses were having on him.

"Do I need to hop the jet to Granite Falls, Adamo? I can be there tomorrow morning. Your mother and I are about to leave for dinner, but I'm sure she'd rather visit with you."

Adam came to a sudden halt and back to reality at his father's threats. "No, Dad. That won't be necessary. I will return to the office on Monday. By the end of next week, I will make up all the canceled and postponed meetings. Andreas International will be rolling again. There is no need for you to come to Granite Falls. No need at all."

"It sounds as if you have something to hide, son."

"I don't, Dad," he responded emphatically. The last thing he wanted was his father pressuring Tashi like he'd done with Claire and Denise. His father had pressured him into proposing to Claire. Denise had had the good sense to run before he'd made a fool of himself again. He was certain now that it was his father's domineering attitude that had scared them both—well that and Claire's claim that he'd never told her he loved her. He was certain he had, at least once, at some point.

After Denise, even though he knew his relationships were temporary, Adam had kept his women away from his father—except Sadie, whom he'd taken to Positano for Christmas last year. Yep, Sadie who was past the age of childbearing was safe from Alessandro's pressures. It was the first time Adam had enjoyed the experience of taking a woman home to meet his father.

"Are you sure?" his father asked, breaking into Adam's thoughts again. "You don't sound too convincing, or perhaps you're trying too hard to convince me that you have nothing to hide."

Damn it. Adam had forgotten how intuitive his father was when it came to his only son. His mother had told him that his father had been in love with him from the moment she'd told him of her pregnancy. When he was younger, Adam had watched videos of his father dancing to music in the middle of the night as he cradled his crying infant son in his arms. Sometimes his mother, awakened by the music, and his crying, would join them in the nursery, and his father would lace one arm around his wife and the other around his son as they danced together into the wee hours of the morning.

All that love and devotion had created a deep bond between them, so deep that as a child, Adam had had difficulty lying to his parents. Sometimes he felt as if they knew his thoughts even before he did. "You'll just get in my way," he said to his father. "When you're here, you question everything I do. You make me anxious. You and I know that I do my best work when I'm left alone. The numbers attest to that fact."

"*Va bene, allora,*" his father stated in a somewhat conciliatory tone. "If you're not back in the office at Hotel Andreas on Monday, I will be in Granite Falls on Tuesday, Adamo."

"*Sì, papà.* If that's all—"

"*Un minuto.* Your mother wishes to speak with you about something. *Ti amo, mio figlio.*"

A smile curved Adam's lips. "*Ti amo, troppo, papà.*"

As he waited for his mother to come online, Adam gazed out

at the distant outlines of the skyscrapers in downtown Granite Falls—Hotel Andreas, Fountain Enterprises and Towers, and Andretti Industries—dwarfing all other buildings. It was a town his ancestors, along with the Andrettis, the LaCrosses, the Forsythes, and more recently, the Fontaines, had shaped into the prosperous little mecca it was today.

As a child, Adam had spent many summers in Como, his mother's native town, and on the Amalfi Coast in the town of Positano from where his great-great-grandfather, Vincenzo Andreas, had boarded a ship for America during the mid-nineteenth century. Although he enjoyed visiting his ancestral homes and learning about his family roots, Adam was always happy to return to Granite Falls, the place where he was born and raised.

Granite Falls was the only place on earth where he wanted his children to call home. He wanted it to be the place that Tashi could call home, too, but his patience and his hopes were waning with each day she kept her past a secret. He'd been in proximity with her for the past two weeks, but now that he had to return to the world beyond Andreas Estates, Adam's fears that she would slip away while his back was turned mounted by the second.

I have to go. Adam closed his eyes. Tashi had been repeating those words since the first day he met her. He'd promised himself that he'd wait for her to open up to him, but he had to come to terms with the fact that she might never share her secrets with him—whether from fear or shame, he didn't know—but what he did know was that with each passing day he sensed her growing anxiety as she fought with the decision of whether to stay or leave.

She was stronger now, both physically and emotionally, and logically she would think that she could survive on her own. That scared Adam. Although a part of him was happy she'd recovered and was glowing with self-confidence, the other part wanted her to remain dependent on him.

Since he was returning to work next week, he hoped Tashi would confide in him once she returned from the garden. And if she didn't, he was prepared to go out and find the answers himself. He had no idea where to begin since she'd been careful not to drop any hints as to where she'd come from, but the Andreas family had its own band of *polizia segreta* who were as inconspicuous as ghosts. It was time he called upon them.

He hadn't yet told Tashi that he'd recovered her money and her cell phone. Granite Falls' Chief of Police, Chief Jordan, had brought them to the mansion in the dead of night just hours after she'd discovered them stolen. Since he had no idea how much money had been stolen, he didn't know how much had been recovered.

Adam shook his head, still unable to believe the amount of cash Tashi had had in her possession. Where had she gotten that kind of money? Had she stolen it from the people who were looking for her? Was she an accomplice, a member of a nefarious criminal gang? And how in heaven's name did a young girl with her kind of upbringing get mixed up with villains?

He had no answers, but deep down Adam knew that Tashi would not have voluntarily associated herself with criminals. It was easy for a naïve girl to be tricked by the masterminds of the criminal world. What had been their plans for her?

He should do the right thing and give her back her money and her phone, but knowing she'd bolt the moment she regained financial independence, he'd opted to do the wrong thing. The thought of Tashi on her own, out there in the world with no one to protect her from the vultures who were hunting her, sent icy fear twisting around Adam's heart.

"Adamo."

"Adam."

Adam whipped around as he heard two versions of his name being called simultaneously by two different women.

"Tashi." Her name spilled out before he could stop it. He hurried over to where she stood at the door in a pair of white shorts and a yellow blouse.

"Adamo, what's going on?" his mother asked through the phone line.

"I'm sorry. I didn't know you were busy," Tashi said.

"It's just my parents."

"Adamo, are you entertaining? Is that a woman's voice I hear? Is there a woman at the house with you?"

Now how should he respond to that question? If he said, "No", Tashi might think she was not important enough to be introduced to his parents. And if he said, "Yes", his mother would insist on hearing more about her. He wasn't ready to share Tashi with his parents, simply because he didn't know what to tell them about her.

"Adamo. Is there a woman there with you?" his mother asked again.

"I—I should go," Tashi whispered, backing up.

"No. You're not going anywhere." He caught her hand, and tugging her along with him, he marched her over to his desk and sat her down in one of the chairs in front of it. "Yes, Mom," he stated, dropping his weight into the chair next to Tashi. "There's a woman here with me." He placed his hand over Tashi's that were clasped tightly together on her lap. "She's the reason I haven't been to the office in two weeks."

"Oh darling, this is so exciting," his mother screamed, clapping her hands. "Put her on satellite. I want to see her. Alessandro! Alessandro, come quickly. Our son is dating again."

"Is that true, Adamo?" his father's voice boomed over the wire. "How serious are you about this woman?"

Yep, get straight to the point.

"Quite serious, I'd say," his mother remarked, thankfully in Italian, which was customary when they were excited about something. "She's obviously important enough for him to put aside business for two weeks. Could she be the one Adam? Is she your *Anam Cara*? The last time we visited, you promised the next woman you presented to us would be the one."

Yes, he'd said that, but it was only to get his father off his case about Sadie's incapability to produce an heir, and he hadn't really presented Tashi to them. It was just a coincidence that she'd walked into his office during their chat.

There are no coincidences in life...

"I'd like to see her. I'd like to see the woman who'll be bearing my grandchildren," his father stated, more command than sentiment in his tone.

"*Mamma, Papà, per favore, voi stessi contengono. Non voglio che lei spaventata.*" As he warned his parents to contain themselves and not to scare Tashi, Adam sent up a silent prayer that she didn't understand a word of the conversation, which was evident in her next question.

"What are they saying?"

"Mom, Dad, give me a second." He reached across his desk and pushed a button on the phone. "They're Italians," he said in response to Tashi's question. "They get excited about everything, especially any woman I date. Ever since I was of marriageable age—twenty-one to my father—he's been harassing me about carrying on the Andreas bloodline."

"But we're not dating."

Aren't we? "I told them that the next woman I presented to them would be—" He cleared his throat. "Would be the one."

"The one what?" Her face contorted in confusion.

"The one I'd marry."

She dropped her gaze and color stole into her cheeks. "But you didn't present me to them. I just happened to walk in on your conversation. I'm not the one, Adam," she said, raising her head to stare at him.

You are. "They don't know that. All they know is that for the past two weeks I've neglected my duties as CEO of Andreas International to be with you. For them, that is serious business, and the fact that you've been living here with me on the family estate—"

"But I'm only here with you because I was sick the first time, and then because my money was stolen and I had nowhere else to go."

"Is that what you want me to tell them?" he asked, guardedly.

She broke her gaze and glanced around the office. "No. I guess not."

"Okay, then we'll pretend we're dating, that you're "the one" just to appease them and hide the truth." *Whatever that was*, he thought to himself. "They want to chat via satellite, though. Are you comfortable with that?" He wasn't, but it was her call.

She seemed thoughtful for a minute, then said, "Yes. I'm okay with it. It would be nice to meet them even though it's only through satellite."

She'd clammed up every time he'd questioned her about her background, but today she seemed relaxed about being interrogated by a couple of total strangers. Was he too close for her comfort, or did she receive some enlightenment about her situation while meditating alone? He hoped for the latter. "My father will grill you for information about your background, but feel free not to answer any of his questions. Don't let him bully you. Okay?"

She squared her shoulders as if she were preparing to do battle and braced herself with a smile. "I'll be fine."

Still not convinced that it was a good idea, Adam picked up the remote from his desk and walked Tashi over to the other side of the office. He seated her beside him on the black leather sofa facing a wall, and then pushed a button on the remote.

His parents were already seated, arm in arm, on a red loveseat, big grins on their faces as they looked out from the huge monitor mounted on the wall. Adam looped an arm across Tashi's shoulders as he felt her shiver beside him. "Mom, Dad, this is Tashi Holland. Tashi, my parents, Alessandro and Arabella Andreas."

"Hello, Tashi," his parents said in unison, waiving all formalities.

"Hello," Tashi responded, smiling into the monitor. "It's nice meeting you, Mr. and Mrs. Andreas."

"The pleasure is ours, my dear," his mother said. "And please call us Alessandro and Arabella. Adam, she's such a lovely delicate creature," she remarked in the next breath. "How did you meet?"

"Was it a formal introduction by a friend or business associate?" his father asked, his blue eyes assessing Tashi from thousands of miles away.

"We bumped into each other at Mountainview Café a couple weeks ago," Adam replied.

"Oh, tell us more," his mother said, pushing her brown hair—sprinkled with slivers of silver—away from her oval-shaped face. "It's always so exciting to hear how lovers meet." She leaned into her husband who tightened his arm around her and kissed the top of her head.

"Oh, we're not—"

"Are you a native of Granite Falls, Tashi?" Tashi's denial of their being lovers was cut short by his father. "I've lived there most of my life and I don't think I know of any Hollands in the area."

Adam held his breath, but he could feel Tashi breathing

deeply and calmly next to him. She was tapping into the power of control he'd taught her.

"No, Mr. An—" She paused and swallowed. "No, Alessandro. I'm not from here. I'm from Ohio."

Blood pounded against Adam's temples. She'd just told his father where she was from within two minutes after meeting them, via satellite, when she'd spent two weeks with Adam in total silence and secrecy.

"Where in Ohio?" His father continued his interrogation.

"I was born in Cleveland. My mother died when I was four. She left me in the care of my uncle. He moved us to Sebring after she died."

Adam tilted his head and gave her an incredulous glance as she divulged the facts methodically and objectively as if she were talking about someone else.

"I'm sorry to hear about the loss of your mother when you were so young, practically still a baby," his mother remarked in a sympathetic tone. "But it seems as if your uncle did quite an excellent job raising you. You're so poised and elegant. He must be very proud of you."

Adam watched a blush flitter across Tashi's cheeks as she said, "Thank you, Arabella. I think he was, up until he died two years ago."

"*Tu cara bambina*," his mother murmured, crossing her arms over her heart.

"Where was your father?" Alessandro enquired, pushing forward in his seat. "Why wasn't he taking care of you? Did he pass away also, or was he just an absentee father?"

"Dad!" Adam said through clenched teeth, as he watched Tashi stiffen as if someone had dealt her a sharp blow.

He glared at his father, knowing exactly what he was thinking. Both Claire and Denise had been emotionally damaged from their abusive relationships, but that didn't matter to his father. They were both from affluent families in the community —good stock for breeding Andreas babies—Alessandro's top priority for marriage. Sometimes Adam wondered if he'd forgotten how he and his mother had met.

"You don't have to answer," he whispered in Tashi's ear.

"Perché lei non dovrebbe rispondere? Lei ha qualcosa da nascondere, Adamo?"

Adam closed his eyes as his father asked if Tashi had something to hide. "I knew this chat was a bad idea. This is the reason I—"

"I don't know who my father is, Mr. Andreas—" Tashi's tear-smothered voice cut him off in midsentence. "My mother was never married, and she died before I was old enough to ask. My uncle didn't know his identity either. He said my mother never told him. I don't know if he's dead or alive, or anything. I don't know. I'm sorry." Tears brimmed her eyes. Her lips trembled, and her hands, clenched tightly on her lap, were shaking uncontrollably.

"Abbastanza! Mamma, papà, non si sa di Tashi è qui, o nelle Granite Falls. Apprezzerei il vostro silenzio. Per favore." Adam pressed Tashi closer to his side as he requested that his parents keep her presence in his home, and in Granite Falls to themselves.

The muscles in his father's jaws tightened. *"Terrò silenziosa per ora, ma—*

"Grazie. Addio." He pushed the end button on the remote, then gathered Tashi into his arms, pressing her tear-soaked face into his chest. "Tashi. I'm sorry. They're very family-oriented. They want to make sure I'm making the right decision, especially after—" He sighed. "I should not have subjected you to their badgering. *Perdonami, cara.*"

"I killed a man. I shot him in the back of his head two times. I just shot him in cold blood. He had a family—little kids. I didn't want to. I didn't want to. He was wearing earphones and listening to his iPod when I shot him. I just shot him and pushed him out of the car."

The choked words staggered out of her mouth like an ominous drum echoing from deep inside a cold empty tomb. She clutched the front of his shirt and began to sob hysterically as if the weight of the entire universe had just come crashing down on her.

CHAPTER ELEVEN

Adam's mouth froze open as the shock of Tashi's confession reverberated through him. Ice slowly seeped through his veins as he floundered in an agonizing maelstrom of anguish and despair.

Tashi had just admitted to committing murder. Cold-blooded murder. Her troubles were far worse than he could have ever imagined. She was a fugitive from the law, and he'd been harboring her. Thank God his parents hadn't witnessed her confession, or his father with his rash temperament would have had the authorities storming the estate already and hauling Tashi off in cuffs.

Adam tightened his arms about her as she cried out her guilt and pain against his heart. *Take stock. Take stock*, he cautioned his mind as it catapulted toward a judgmental zone.

He swallowed the groan that rose in his throat, and forced logic into his thoughts. Knowing what he knew about Tashi so far—what she'd told him about her upbringing and about people looking for her, granted she hadn't lied to him—Adam surmised that she'd had no other choice but to do what she did.

No wonder she'd been jittery that day at the café, and then at the supermarket when she thought he'd been following her. Since then, all the signs had been there: anxiety, paranoia, withdrawal from society, inability to make friends—or decision not to—the tensing each time he'd probed a little, the fear in her eyes each time she looked at him.

The first time she'd ever seemed at ease around him was the day she happened upon him in the garden and had taken off her clothes to join him in yoga. That Tashi—Little Eve, as pure and innocent as a newborn baby—had emerged from her cocoon and had been dancing with him for the past three days, until today when his father's questions exhumed the old Tashi who was tarnished with the ghastly crime of her past.

As the enormity of Tashi's situation registered in his brain, Adam knew without a doubt that the people from whom she was hiding were notoriously dangerous, so dangerous that she'd had to kill one of them in order to escape their clutches. It was a simple case of kill or be killed. What she was feeling, what she was sobbing over now was nothing more than a case of survivor's guilt for killing a man who had a family. Guilt, she'd been carrying around for God knew how long.

Pandora's box had been yanked wide open, and there was no way of stopping the plagues of Tashi's past from permeating his world. If he were to help her, protect her, it was imperative that he knew everything. Every tiny detail leading up to the moment she shot that man, and the ensuing events that led her to Granite Falls and to him.

Since he'd climbed through her bedroom window that night, Adam had known that he would do anything for Tashi—even die for her. It was time he proved it. He could not allow her to continue living in fear.

It was time he found those maggots and made them pay for whatever they'd done to her. Thoughts of murder floated through his brain. He was never one to use violence as a means of solving a problem. In fact, he avoided conflict at all cost. This was one problem he couldn't meditate away. He had to face it head-on. Be the kind of man his father always wished he would be.

Life had kicked him in the ass. He was kicking back.

"I'm a criminal, Adam. A monster. I killed a man, and now I've dragged you into my messed-up life."

Adam tensed as the teary voice. Taking a deep breath, he unclasped her hands from his shirt and held her a little away from him. He cupped her chin and raised her face. Her eyes were red and her lips were puffy and rosy. He so longed to kiss her fears and pain away.

Forcing composure into his voice, Adam said as calmly as he could, "You're not a criminal or a monster, Tashi. You're the sweetest, purest, most innocent soul I've ever met. AndI'm sure there is a good explanation for what you did." There had to be. "Stop these negative thoughts about yourself, okay?"

She nodded.

"Would you like some water?"

"Yes. Please." She wiped her fingers across her eyes.

Adam walked to the mini bar in a corner of his office. He poured two glasses of water from a pitcher and brought them back. He placed one on the coffee table and handed the other to Tashi. He watched her as she drank, then took her half-empty glass and set it next to the other.

He sat back down beside her, bending a knee and turning sideways to face her. Tears dampened her long, dark lashes, and he hoped that these would be the last tears of fear, guilt, and sorrow she would ever shed.

He took her trembling cold hands and held them together on his knee. "You have to tell me everything, Tashi. No holding back. No more secrets between us."

She sniffed and shuddered, but nodded in compliance.

He could simply sit back and ask her to relate the story from beginning to end, but all Adam needed for now were the cold, hard facts. *When* did it happen? *Where* did it happen? *Who* was involved? *How* and *why* were they involved? He would connect the dots on his own later. "Why did you have to shoot this man?" he began in a gentle tone.

She glanced down at her hands enveloped in his and answered in a low raspy voice. "The FBI agent told me to do it. He said if I didn't kill him, he would kill me."

Just as he'd suspected. She'd had no other choice. "What FBI agent?"

"The one who was in the house when I got there."

"Was the house in Sebring?"

A fresh tear rolled off her cheek and landed on the back of his wrist, causing him to quiver inside from the heat of it. "No. It was in New York City."

New York City? He grimaced in confusion. "What were you doing in New York?"

She paused on a deep breath and he felt her tense before she raised her head and looked at him. "I moved there for college. My uncle told me that it was a big dangerous city filled with bad people, but I wanted to go." Her voice cracked. "I was so bored and isolated in Sebring. I just wanted to live, to be a part of the world, to make friends and see things."

She pulled her hands from his to wipe at the river of tears streaming down her face. "And then when Uncle Victor died, I didn't want to go back. There was no reason to go back. I didn't have any other family there or anywhere else. I was all alone in the world. So I just stayed." She buried her face in her hands.

Adam's heart broke for her, but he sucked it all in and waited for her to stop weeping. He dared not offer her any more comfort until he'd heard everything. He wanted her to remain in that dark moment, in that frozen frame of time so that she left nothing out. As far as he was concerned, it would be the first and last time she would ever have to relive her nightmare, or talk about it. Finally, she dropped her hands on her lap and looked up at him.

He breathed calm into his voice. "Okay, Tashi, so you were living in this house where the shooting took place?"

She rubbed her hands as if she were using her tears as a moisturizer. "It was my boyfriend Scottie's house. Or that's what he told me. I went there to meet his parents. Supposedly."

Her boyfriend? Was her boyfriend the person who was supposed to call the cell phone that had been stolen from her? God, was she already in love with and committed to another man? The thought made him tremble inside, but then he recalled Tashi telling him that she'd never been kissed. Surely, if her relationship with this boy was serious, she would have been kissed already. Or maybe the boy was brought up with the same philosophies as Tashi, and they were forbidden to engage in any type of premarital intimacies. Adam was going crazy. He shook the sour thoughts from his head. "Why did the FBI agent go to your boyfriend's house?"

She swallowed. "He—he was already at the house when I got there. Scottie was supposed to be there, but he—the agent told me that Scottie wasn't really my boyfriend, that he was working for these people and—and that they'd sold me to this—this—um—" She stopped and swallowed again. "This Arabian prince and —um—he said the man and the woman who were pretending to be Scottie's parents were going to drug me. The man in the car —the one—I—I, um shot—he was supposed to drive me to the airport. He said I would be in Saudi Arabia the next day if I didn't do what he said..." Her voice faded off into a whisper.

Adam felt a wretchedness of mind he'd never felt before. He was going to track down and kill this Scottie bastard with his bare hands. The thought of Tashi as a sex slave in the palace of some sick prince who'd bought her, and of him offering her to his friends and guests until he was tired of her and either sold her to another prince, or dumped her on the streets of Rubal Khali to live out the remainder of her life as a prostitute in order to stay alive, filled Adam with rage and nausea.

He was cognizant of the daily lives of the sex slaves—both male and female—who were held prisoners in royal palaces and other places around the globe—some way under the age of consent, too young to be even called women and men. Some years ago while visiting a prince he'd met on the French Riviera, Adam had been offered a girl of his choice to warm his bed for a night. The girls looked no older than twelve to sixteen years old. He'd immediately left Dubai and vowed never to conduct business in that region where the government condoned such atrocious behavior and practices.

He'd been so disgusted that he'd gotten involved with The National Center for Missing and Exploited Children and other organization that fought human trafficking. It was an eye-popper for him. Most people around the world still refused to believe the extent to which these people would go to drug and kidnap young boys and girls and turn them into sex slaves. Most of them were tricked with offers of bogus modeling jobs abroad, only to wake up in a palace of horror or a dungeon of filth the next day.

And to think that *his* Tashi had almost fallen victim to the very criminals, rapists, and pedophiles he'd been helping to put away for years. Adam closed his eyes and fisted his hands in an effort to stop the nausea from rising to his throat and the tears from gushing from his eyes. He had to stay strong for Tashi.

He opened his eyes to find a dead, vacant look in Tashi's eyes. She stared through him, past him as if she were transfixed in another place.

"What did the agent tell you to do? How did you escape?" he asked.

"He'd already killed Scottie's pretend parents before I got to the house," she continued in a low, dreary voice. "They were lying on the floor with blood pouring out of holes in their heads. He'd shot them in the head. Their eyes were open wide and they were staring up at the ceiling, but they were dead," she whispered as if she were afraid to disturb the ghosts.

She'd seen too much, witnessed too many painful horrible scenes in her young life. Where did she find the strength to cope? She was strong. He never realized how strong until now.

She pressed her lips together as if to stifle a cry. "And he—he—made me put on a bullet-proof vest and gloves. He said I couldn't leave any fingerprints behind. He gave me a gun and showed me how to shoot it. He said—" She raised her hands in front of her and demonstrated as she spoke. "He said, just—just wrap your hands around the barrel, point at his head, and pull the trigger." She dropped her hands and squeezed her eyes tightly as if she were trying to block out the vision. "I'd—I'd never even seen or touched a gun before, and I was scared, but he said I had to learn to shoot it if I wanted to stay alive." She dropped her head in her hands again as a new wave of sobs overwhelmed her.

Watching her, listening to her weep, seemed surreal to Adam. He felt as if he was watching a movie, or trapped in a nightmare, struggling to wake up, to cry out, but unable to move or speak. He desired to hold her and promise her that no one would hurt her ever again, but he had to wait until she'd told him the entire story.

"What happened next, Tashi?" he urged quietly.

"He—he said after I killed the driver, I should push him out of the car and drive around the block to another car he had left for me. He said he'd left a bag of money inside. He took my cell phone and gave me another one. He said he was going to call me and explain everything, but he never called. And—and now my money and the cell phone are gone, and—and he has no way of getting in touch with me." She flung out her hands in despair.

Now Adam understood her anxiety over the cell phone being left at the apartment the night he'd brought her to his home, and her falling apart three days later when she went back to find it gone, along with her only means of financial support in this world. "How did you end up in Granite Falls, Tashi?" he asked in a tremulous voice. He needed to know what wind had blown her here.

"The agent told me to drive here. He said I couldn't take any public transportation and I couldn't use my driver's license or credit cards or anything that could be traced back to me. He told me to toss the gun into the Hudson before I left the city and ditch the car in the Aiken River once I got here. He said I was a witness and that they would be looking for me. That's why I was living in that dump. I—I couldn't put my name on any lease. I can't even rent a car. I couldn't go to the hospital when I was sick. I can't use my name. I can't do anything. I might as well be dead." She gulped hard as fresh tears slid down her cheeks.

"Do you know why the agent sent you to Granite Falls, Tashi? Did he tell you why he picked this town?"

"He said he had a friend here who would take care of me. He said he was going to call and let him know I was coming, and that he—he was to make me his temporary bride and give me the protection of his family's name until he got here and explained everything."

"What's the name of his friend, Tashi?" Adam asked in a tremulous voice.

"I don't know. He was about to tell me his name when some men came in and starting shooting at us. All I heard was, "His name is *A*—"" and the rest was swallowed up in the gunfire.

A—Adam. Temporary bride. If the situation weren't so grim, Adam would laugh.

"Then more men came in and fired at us," Tashi continued without prompting. "He told me to run out the back door, and so I ran out and shot the driver like he'd told me to. But I didn't hear anything else from inside. It was quiet like death. I don't know if he made it out alive. And—and I've been searching the Internet for information about the shooting, but the only thing out there is about a man shot to death in the driveway."

Adam's gut was tied up in knots but he forced himself to breathe through the pain. There was only one New York FBI Agent he knew who had friends in Granite Falls. "What was the agent's name?"

"I don't know. He just said he was an FBI agent, and that he had come to rescue me from some bad people." She dropped her head and gazed at her twisting hands.

"Can you describe him?"

She licked her lips, then gazed up at him with a face bleak with sorrow. "He's black, and really tall and muscular, and he had—um—a small scar on his right cheek." She touched her cheek. "And now he's probably dead because of me." She dropped her head again.

It was Paul. Tashi's case of survivor's guilt wasn't just about the driver she'd killed. It was about the agent who'd come to save her—a man she didn't even know. "Were there any other agents at the house that night?" he asked.

"No. He was alone."

Why would Paul work alone? Where was his partner? Why would he put his life on the line for a strange girl and then send her to him for protection? *Why?* Adam didn't ask the questions because he was certain that Tashi didn't have the answers. Only one person did. "How long ago did this happen? When did you come to Granite Falls?"

She took a deep, steadying breath. "Umm—about a year and a half ago. Last—um—around the end of March."

The same time that Paul Dawson fell off the grid. Adam remembered Massimo trying to get in touch with Paul last year—around the time he married Shaina. But the agent's phones had just kept ringing, and the agency had simply told him that he was unavailable, which wasn't unusual since Paul did go undercover quite a bit.

But after hearing Tashi's horror story, Adam had to wonder. Was Paul dead? Was that the reason Massimo was unable to reach him? Adam couldn't remember Paul ever being undercover for this long. In his recollection, the longest he'd spend incognito was three to four months. He was a meticulous agent who got in, hit hard and fast, and then got out unscathed.

"I've been waiting all this time for him to call or show up, but I don't think he ever will," Tashi said, cutting into his thoughts. "I was so happy when you told me your name was Adam. I knew it was a long shot that you were that man whose name began with an *A*, but I was holding on to hope." A look of tired sadness passed over her features.

Hope. The last gift to leave Pandora's box after the seven plagues had been unleashed on the world. Adam gathered Tashi into his arms. "I *am* your hope, Tashi. I am the man whose name begins with an *A*. The agent who rescued you is Paul Dawson." Adam refused to think of Paul in the past tense. He had to hope that his friend was alive, but for whatever reason was still unable to contact him.

He cleared the croak from his throat. "Paul is a good friend of mine, and of Bryce, Erik, and Massimo. We met him at a restaurant in Paris a few years ago, and we became instant friends that night. Since then, we've gotten together at least once a year in New York or here in Granite Falls. That's why he sent you to Granite Falls and to me, so that I can protect you."

"Really?" she asked in a hoarse voice. "Are you really the man he sent me to find?" Her arms tightened about him as tears of relief, he supposed, flowed freely from her, seeped through his shirt, and warmed his skin.

"Yes, Tashi. I am *that* man, and you did find me. I won't let anything or anyone hurt you again. I will protect you."

"It just seems too good to be true."

"Sometimes it is, sweetheart. Sometimes, but not this time. This time it's really true."

"I'm glad he picked you, and I'm glad I found you."

"Me, too." And he was so glad that Felicia and Lillian had gone against their sons' advice and bought out that café, or they might never have found each other. *There were no coincidences...*

"You asked me once if I believe in fate. I didn't know the answer then. But I believe in it now. It had to be fate that brought us together in the café. It had to be."

"*Sì cara, era destino.*" Adam closed his eyes as joy flowed copiously through him. She had accepted the fact that fate had placed her in the path of the man the agent had sent her to, fifteen months ago. But had she recognized and embraced her place in his life and his home, and was she ready to take the next step into the secrets of the unknown with him? He needed to know. "Tashi, what decision had you come to in the garden today?"

She burrowed her face deeper into his neck. "I was going to leave. I was going to sneak away once you returned to work because I didn't want to put you in danger. I didn't want to be responsible for someone else's death. Those men are dangerous, Adam. They will kill anyone who stands in their way, just like they killed your friend, and tried to kill me. I might be the only person to ever escape from them. I cost them a lot of money. They won't stop looking for me. That's why your FBI friend told me to stay off the radar. I'm scared for you, Adam." She tightened her arms about him.

"You don't need to be scared." Adam combed his fingers

through her hair, even as his flow of joy ebbed to a trickle. She'd been planning to leave. "And you're not responsible for anyone's death. Agent Dawson knew what he was walking into. He was doing his job. You did what you did to survive. You're not alone anymore. You're where you belong, baby." Reluctantly, he eased her out of his arms and held her at arm's length. "And the only way to keep you safe is to do what Agent Dawson asked."

"Marry you?" She shuddered and looked away.

He brought her face back to his with a gentle nudge of his fingers to her chin. "Yes, marry me."

"But he said it was only temporary until he came to me and explained everything. And so much time had passed. If he's dead, it doesn't matter anymore, and your association with me would just put you in danger."

"It does matter, Tashi," Adam said with an emphatic tremor in his voice. "And I'm not afraid of danger. Paul made the request because he knows I can protect you."

Probably more than anyone else he knew, Adam thought. Paul had heard the story about Adam's grandfather, Demitri, taking on a Rome-based mafia ring after they'd tortured and murdered Alessandro's older brother, Vincenzo—a gambling addict who was unable to pay back a huge amount of money he owed them. Killing Vincenzo wasn't enough for the mob boss who then ordered the kidnapping of Vincenzo's five-year-old son and held him for ransom to pay back the debt. The boy had been rescued alive and well, but it was the biggest and last mistake that mob boss and his organization ever made.

When Demitri was finished, all the members of that mafia organization had been wiped off the face of the earth and their finances had been crippled so drastically that even their extended families had been forced to sell their homes and auction off their possessions. Up to this day, many of the mobsters' descendants were still suffering the consequences of their parents' sins. No

Andreas had had any trouble since then, and it was known across Europe and the rest of the world that messing with an Andreas would bring certain death and destruction for generations to come. Paul knew the Andreas name would provide the type of protection Tashi needed.

Alessandro was just as merciless as his father. He crushed his enemies and stamped out any signs of threats to any family member or to Andreas International long before they took root. He'd even stopped talking to his best friend, Luciano, after learning that it might have been Luciano's affair with his secretary that had caused his sister-in-law's death. He was even more livid now that he'd discovered that a bastard child had been derived from that tragedy. Massimo hadn't forgiven his deceased father for hurting his mother, but he'd accepted his half-brother Galen into his life.

Like Massimo, Alessandro was not a forgiving man, and it was with great pains at his wife's insistence that he'd started talking to Luciano again. Adam knew that his forgiving nature was one of the reasons his father was so disappointed that he was less like him and more like his mother.

But his father was so wrong about him, Adam thought as fury gave flight within him. The Andreas's ruthless trait had been lying dormant inside him because up until now, he'd had no reason to go to war. Nothing and no one had ever been important enough for him to fight for, no wrong severe enough for him not to forgive.

"Agent Dawson trusts me with your life, and I'm asking you to do the same," he told Tashi, even as his mind began to race with more questions concerning Paul's interest and involvement with her.

"I trust you, Adam. But—"

He placed his hands on her shoulders and held her gaze. "I want you to stop being so brave and let me take care of you. We don't know why Agent Dawson singlehandedly risked his life for you, but until we do, we need to do what he asked. If anything happens to you, he will never forgive me. I will never forgive me." He paused as his mind spun into the future. "There's another reason we should get married as soon as possible."

"What?"

"As your husband, I cannot be forced to testify against you in court if it ever came to that. As husband and wife, everything we discuss, everything we share during our marriage is confidential. It falls under marital privilege laws and it extends beyond divorce. So even a temporary marriage falls within the parameters of that law."

"But— we—we aren't married, and I already told you everything."

"Only you and I are aware of that fact. I can have a copy of your birth certificate here by tonight."

Her eyes widened in a panic. "Adam, that's a paper trail. They can follow it here."

He gave her shoulders a reassuring squeeze. "I have ways of being inconspicuous while getting the job done, Tashi. Nobody will know. I promise. We can be married tomorrow, and as far as the rest of the world knows, you disclosed the events of that night after we said our vows. I would perjure myself for you, but I'd rather not go that route."

"No," she said, shaking her head. "I can't let you do that, Adam. And—and your father wouldn't allow it, even if he knew it was temporary. You see how he got when I told him that I was illegitimate and didn't know my father. He cares about family traditions and lineage, and such."

That was precisely what Adam was banking on. As long as Tashi bore the Andreas name, Alessandro wouldn't dare deny her the protection of the family—tainted lineage or not. If there was one thing he knew about his father it was that family loyalty meant everything to him. He would move heaven and hell to ensure the safety of the future mother of his grandchildren. "You're not marrying my father, Tashi. You're marrying me. You can't fight these people alone. Accept that you need me. Do what Agent Dawson asked. It's the best way to keep you safe and alive. Don't you want that?"

She looked thoughtful for a minute, then nodded. "Okay. I'll do it. I'll marry you."

Adam expelled a sigh of relief. "After tomorrow you'll be known simply as Tashi Andreas." He pulled her into his arms again and kissed the top of her head as the faint smell of ginger wafted up his nostrils. She'd had such a lonely childhood, forbidden to associate with her peers, and isolated from society. She'd been taught that the world was a dangerous place and to be suspicious and fearful of everyone, and then her worst fears had come to life one horrible night in a house in New York City.

No wonder she'd been so paranoid and frightened when she'd bumped into him at Mountainview Café and found herself locked in his arms. It was just her schemas of vulnerability, social isolation, and alienation at play. She'd barricaded herself in her apartment, thinking that the multitude of dead bolts on her door would keep her safe. But she'd been proven wrong when her most precious possessions had been stolen.

This most recent and blatant invasion of her privacy was enough to send her into an emotional downspin, but it hadn't. She was a survivor, strong, and determined not to let her circumstances cripple her, and not only that, but she'd challenged the doctrines of her upbringing and sought out and embraced the true nature of her own soul. Adam loved her strength, her tenacity, and her determination to live.

He loved her. Adam's entire body trembled at the knowledge. He'd loved Tashi from the moment she'd gazed up at him from her bed in her apartment—frail and weak—and thanked him for cleaning her up. It had to be love at work for him to dive right in without any concern for his own health or safety.

The word 'love' itself was more than a combination of letters, or a sound to the ear. People threw the word out so frequently and casually that it had lost its meaning and its power. Love wasn't a feeling, either. Love was action. What he'd demonstrated that night, and the way Tashi had responded to his actions was his interpretation of love. His heart had known since the moment he'd bumped into her, even long before he was ready to admit it, to accept the truth.

The fact that he could love someone he knew absolutely nothing about proved that the past of the object of one's desire was immaterial. What was pertinent about Tashi was her smile, her smell, the silky warmth of her body, the flash of her emerald eyes, the sexy sound of her voice and chuckles—though hesitant at times—even her frowns, her uncertainties, and her paranoia moved him deeply. Those were the virtues in which his heart delighted.

Sadie was so right when she'd asked if it was he or his heart that had been in love before. His heart hadn't been involved with what he thought he'd felt for Claire and Denise, especially Claire. Because of the way his mother had raised him, he'd mistaken lust for love, and had further convinced himself that he loved them to get his father off his back. It was his mind at work. Not so with Tashi. Both his mind and his heart loved her deeply, and he wanted so much to tell her, to shout it from the top of Mount Washington.

But he knew if he shared his feelings, she might take it upon herself to leave in order to protect him—just as she'd tried to do after he'd nursed her back to health. Unwilling to risk her life and his happiness, Adam concealed that sweet knowledge in the warm abyss of his heart for now, just until the opportunity to reveal it presented itself—not too far in the future, he hoped.

"Are you hungry, sweetheart?" he enquired when her stomach rumbled against his. "It is after one o'clock, and we haven't had lunch."

"I don't want to eat. I just want to sleep. I'm so tired." She sighed deeply.

"Of course. All that crying, and reliving the horror of that night have drained you emotionally and physically. Do you want me to carry you to bed?"

She snuggled into him like he was a comfy mattress. "No. I just want to stay right here if it's okay."

"It's okay, Tashi. It's okay. You can stay here with me."

She raised her head and looked at him with tired eyes. "What about your parents? They know I'm here. Suppose they—"

"I asked them not to say anything. They wouldn't."

"Thank you."

Stretching out on his back on the sofa, Adam eased Tashi down on him. He laid her jasmine-vanilla-scented cheek into the crook of his neck, and arranged her auburn, ginger-spiced curls across his chest.

He pulled a brown *qiviut* shawl from the back of the sofa and spread it over them. "Just close your eyes and sleep," he said, wrapping his arms about her.

CHAPTER TWELVE

Tashi awoke to the sound of a steady heartbeat beneath her cheek, the rhythm of labored breathing in her ears, the pressure of a hand in the curve of her back, and another on her buttocks. She wasn't scared, but the feel of something hard pressing against the insides of her thigh made her tense, just a little, and brought her fully awake.

She opened her eyes and scanned her surroundings. She was in Adam's office, on his sofa, or more precisely on top of him, where she'd fallen asleep. She glanced out the French doors where the bright light of the sun indicated it was still daylight—probably mid-afternoon—and eventually, the reason she was lying in Adam's arms surfaced to the forefront of Tashi's mind.

She'd told him everything about the worst night of her life... and about the FBI agent, and his request that Adam marry her. Tashi wished she'd known Adam was *that* man before she'd revealed that bit of information. His knowing, and offering to grant his friend's request to marry her and protect her had changed the dynamics of their relationship.

No more was *she* merely a helpless stranger whose life he'd crawled through a window to save, and *he* wasn't just the sweetest, kindest, sexiest man she'd ever met.

She was his charge, a young, inexperienced girl he was supposed to protect.

Would he have treated her differently if he'd known from the beginning who she really was? Would he have taken the liberties he'd been taking with her—encouraging her to undress for him, dance and play with him naked? Would he have protected her from himself and the raw desires she saw in his eyes each time he gazed on her naked body?

That day in the garden, when she'd voluntarily undressed in front of him, she'd been eager to test the limits of her newly discovered passions, but Adam had told her that she wasn't ready. Tashi hadn't understood his reluctance at the time, but in the past three days as she gained deeper insight into and control of her own mindfulness through yoga and meditation and learned to love and accept the uninhibited spirit of her true essence, she'd come to appreciate Adam's wisdom. It seemed as if he knew her better than she knew herself.

During the past few days, Adam had told her that most people went through life being unconscious of so much. He'd stressed the importance of becoming still, of listening to the universe speak to her. He'd taught her to be conscious of her breathing and allowing it to awaken parts of her she hadn't been conscious of before.

After understanding all that, Tashi knew that if she and Adam had made love that day, it would have been a mistake for both of them. She had no doubt that it would have been intense, sweet, and like nothing she'd ever experienced, but the aftermath would have been counterproductive.

The restrictive teachings of her upbringing were still prevalent in her heart and mind, and their power over her would have filled her with doubts and shame and guilt. She was certain that once caught in the moment, she would have enjoyed Adam, but she was just as certain that making love that day with him, or any other man, would have destroyed her perception about the overall sexual experience, perhaps for the rest of her life.

And Adam? Well, he would have been plagued with guilt for taking her innocence, for robbing her of the opportunity and the joys of first accepting and embracing her own sexuality before sharing it with another.

In that respect, he was not only the sexiest man she'd ever met, but also the wisest and most patient of them all. During her years in New York, Tashi had learned a few things about male sexuality, and one of them was that men needed sex on a regular basis, that it was all they thought about, day and night. It had to be killing Adam not to make a move on her, yet he'd promised to wait for her, wait until she knew in her heart and without a doubt that making love with him was what she truly wanted.

Would he look at her differently now that his role in her life had taken on a different meaning? Were their days of naked yoga and meditation a thing of the past? God, she hoped not because even though Adam never touched her in an explicitly sexual way when they were naked—which was more often than not—it was obvious that they shared an intense physical awareness of each other, even when they were fully clothed. The long hours of yoga and meditation with Adam were the moments when she felt most desirable, cherished, like she belonged to something bigger than herself.

As if to eradicate her doubts about him, about them, Adam's hands began to roam slowly across Tashi's back and buttocks. She held her breath and remained still. This touch was different from all the other times he'd touched her. It carried a thread of urgency and expectation. He was touching her for pleasure, not for comfort, healing, or instruction.

As the delightful sensations washed over Tashi, she tucked

her hair behind her ears and lifted her head. Adam was staring at her, his dreamy blue eyes brimming with passion and light and some other warm, drugging, deeply affectionate emotion she'd never detected in him before. Her first instinct was to look away as she'd done when they first met, but harnessing the energy of tantric soul gazing he'd taught her, she locked her gaze with his.

They were both fully awake and aware now—not just physically, but emotionally, spiritually, and sexually. The waiting was over. Their relationship had meaning and purpose now. He was seeing her differently, but not in the way she'd feared.

"Tashi." The husky whisper of her name reverberated throughout Tashi's body as if Adam had shouted it from deep inside her. Her pulse quickened in response and she felt that familiar tingling in her belly and the warm rush of moisture between her thighs.

She gasped aloud when Adam suddenly shifted his body beneath her, and brought their sexes in perfect alignment. The pressure of his hard length pulsing against her softness sent waves of pleasure careening to the core of her being. She trembled and moaned at the first deliberate intimate contact of their sexes. It was shockingly electrifying and intensely titillating, even through the barrier of their clothing.

His hand slid slowly down the dune of her buttocks, and when his fingers skimmed her upper thighs, just below the hem of her shorts, her heart began to hammer in her chest. She licked her lips and moved restlessly against him, unable to control this new form of fierce sensuality that was spreading like slow hot molasses through her veins.

"Adam," she whispered his name.

"What?" he asked. "What do you want, Tashi?"

"I want—" She wished she knew how to ask for what she wanted.

"This?" he asked, drawing his fingers slowly up one leg of

her shorts, as his other hand crawled higher along her back up to her neck, adding pressure, pulling her upper body down toward him.

"Yes," she whispered, as his teasing fingers on her thighs sent shivers rippling through her. Her gaze slid to Adam's sexy mouth and, compelled by her desire to kiss him, her hunger to taste him, she licked her lips as he drew her head slowly toward his lying flat against the cushion of the sofa. Her body felt warm and heavy and flushed. She was floating through space, yet seemed to be standing still as she took in the dreamy glaze in his eyes. Closer and closer, he drew her in until she could smell the heady scent of his masculinity, feel the warm whisper of his breath on her lips...

Then the shrill ring of his office phone pierced the silent air.

They both stiffened as if they'd been caught in a forbidden act. The dream had ended, but the remnants of its effect still lingered in the sound of their heavy breathing and the pulsing of their aroused sexes against each other.

They stared at each other in bated silence, waiting for the phone to stop ringing, but it didn't. Their moment had come and gone. As if to prove her point, Adam swore—something Tashi had never heard him do before. When he turned his head and flung a frustrated glance toward his desk, Tashi took the opportunity to push herself up, and off him. She shot to her feet and stared down at him, still sprawled out on the sofa with his thick mass of hair around his head and shoulders and the outline of his arousal still evident at his groin.

He looked so sexy—this large, beautiful man who would become her husband tomorrow. "I'm sorry," she said.

"About what?"

She had no idea. Was she sorry for involving him in her crime, for making him put his own life on hold, for almost seducing him, or was she sorry that they'd been interrupted?

His gaze skidded down her body before he sat upright, pushed to his feet, and walked across the spacious office. Instead of picking up the receiver, he pushed a button on the base of the phone, then another. He turned, facing her, passion still ablaze in his eyes.

"Adam, are you there?"

Tashi held her breath as Dr. LaCrosse's voice broke the tense silence. Why had Adam put the call on speaker?

Adam paused on a frown before responding. "Yes, Erik. I'm here. Where else would I be? I asked to be alone. You know that."

"Yes. I understand," the doctor responded.

Why were they talking in code? Tashi wondered. Erik knew she was here with Adam.

"Glad to know you're still alive."

That's why, Tashi thought as an unfamiliar voice joined the conversation. Who was that, and how did Adam know Erik wasn't alone? Was he just being cautious or was he psychic?

"Massimo." Adam inadvertently answered her question.

"I'm here, too." Another unfamiliar voice, deepest of the three, spoke.

That had to be Bryce. Tashi clasped her hands together in front of her.

"You told us you wanted to lay low for a couple weeks," Bryce began, "and we were prepared to respect your wishes. It's not like you haven't secluded yourself before, but we can't ignore your parents' request to check up on you. They're worried, and frankly, we are too since learning that you put your household staff on an indefinite leave of absence."

Tashi's mouth opened in surprise. *He did what?* He'd told her he didn't have a housekeeper.

Adam grimaced in obvious frustration. "Where are you guys?"

"On our way to see you," Massimo said.

Tashi's stomach crunched up into tiny little knots. She shook her head and mouthed the word, "No" to Adam. She'd just told him her deepest darkest secret, and he'd agree to marry her and protect her, and although she knew she'd have to meet his friends at some point, this was not a good time. She and Adam had to talk some more about what to tell everybody about her place in his life and his home. They had to get their stories straight.

"I'm fine. There's no need for you to come. I don't need anything." He glanced over at Tashi and the lazy seductive look in his eyes indicated that he had everything he needed in the world already.

Tashi didn't know whether she should rejoice or cry about it. She couldn't be all he needed.

"Tell that to Uncle Alessandro and Aunt Bella. They insisted I visit you today and give them a full report."

They apparently hadn't called Massimo back since the satellite interview, Tashi thought, grateful that Adam's parents had kept their promise to their son. But for how long? Even though she didn't understand Alessandro's last statement just before Adam had cut him off in midsentence, she'd heard the tone of disapproval in the older man's voice. He was upset with the decisions his son had been making lately, as any concerned father should be.

"We're already on Andreas Drive," Bryce said. "Almost at the gatehouse. We'll be there in a few minutes. We're not leaving until you see us."

Tashi clenched and unclenched her hands as Adam picked up a tablet from his desk and proceeded to type rapidly on it as if he were sending an emergency text. In a few seconds it chimed. He read the response, set it back on the table, and pushed a button on the base of the house phone.

What was he doing?

Tashi opened her mouth to call out to him, but he raised his hand to silence her, a crafty smile parting his lips. They waited as the low hum of a car's engine came to a stop, followed by a murmur of male voice exchanges, and then...

"Seriously! You're not letting us through the gate? This is ridiculous. He's gone mad."

"I'm sorry, Mr. Andretti, but your cousin gave me strict orders not to allow anyone on the estate," one of the guards said.

"I'm not *anyone*! I'm his family!"

"Are you sure he's not being held hostage in his own home? Have you seen him, spoken to him?" Bryce asked in a more conciliatory tone, but edged with a touch of concern nonetheless. "His restrictions definitely don't apply to us. Why don't you call and check with him?"

"I'm sorry, gentlemen, but he said no one is allowed in," the guard responded in an apologetic tone. "Mr. Andreas is not receiving today."

"Receiving? Not receiving? What the hell is that? How can he not receive family?"

A smile spread across Tashi's face as Adam began to laugh so hard, he fell back against the edge of his desk. His laughter was deep and rich and warm. It was the first time she'd seen him so amused.

Deprived of the luxury of expressing her own glee, Tashi clasped her hand over her mouth to stifle her chuckles. It had been so long since she'd laughed, had had reason to laugh. Already, she was feeling like a different person. The dark shadow over her heart had been lifted. Adam knew the horrible secret of her past and he hadn't judged her nor condemned her.

"You think this is funny?" Massimo asked.

"Adam, you've had your fun. Let us in," Bryce demanded.

Adam sent her a conspiratorial wink. "I'm sorry guys, but I really can't see you. I'm already engaged for the rest of the day."

"Doing what?"

"And with whom?"

"I can't say. But I promise to show up for Little Erik's birthday party tomorrow afternoon. Five o'clock, right, Erik?"

"Right. Our families are meeting an hour before the other guests arrive, just to catch up. We don't get a lot of time to do that anymore."

"Okay. I'll be there," Adam said, then mouthed "we" to Tashi.

Tashi's nerves tensed immediately at the prospect of meeting Adam's friends, especially Bryce and his wife—the couple she'd seen at the outlets just hours before she ran into Adam. Would they know her, recognize her as the girl they thought was very beautiful?

"And Adam, just so you know, I called your cell to warn you that we were coming by," Erik said with a note of caution in his voice.

"Thanks, buddy. I appreciate it. I left my cell in the bedroom while I took a nap in my office."

"Napping in the middle of the day? What's this? Do you have a girl up there with you? Is that why you're being so secretive?" Massimo demanded.

Tashi bit back a gasp.

Adam held her gaze from across the room. "I assure you, cousin. I do not have a girl up here with me."

Now, he was lying for her.

There was a brief silence, then Bryce spoke. "Okay, Adam. We'll give you one more day. But if you don't show up tomorrow, we're coming back whether or not you're 'receiving'. We'll drive right through this gate if we have to."

"See you tomorrow. Give my love to the wives and kids." He hit the intercom button, ending the conversation."

Tashi walked over to him. "Thank you. I know it wasn't easy

blowing off your friends like that, and especially lying to them about not having a girl up here."

He bunched his hair in his hands and tucked it behind his ears. "You've been interrogated enough for today. Let's leave some drama for tomorrow when you meet them. As my wife." His eyes and voice softened on the last three words. "I didn't lie to them. You're a woman, Tashi, not a girl."

His elucidation brought Tashi a giddy sense of awareness. She was a girl when she first came here, but she'd evolved into a woman. "They care about you, and they're worried," she said, deciding not to follow through on his perception of her.

"As they should. It's what friends do. They look out for each other's best interests."

Friends. She and Adam had been colliding strangers in a café, wary strangers on the street, intimate strangers on an estate, and now she could honestly say that over the course of the past two weeks, their relationship had evolved into a trusting, genuine friendship. And tomorrow, he would become her husband at the request of a friend.

Agent Dawson was his friend. *Agent Dawson*. Tashi repeated the name in her head. It was so nice to have a name to put with the face—a face she might never see again, but one she could never forget. What was so special about her that two men—total strangers to her—were so willing to lay down their lives to protect her? She might never know Agent Dawson's reason, but she could understand Adam's sense of duty to grant his friend's request.

Their marriage might be temporary, but based on what just almost happened on the sofa, Tashi knew that it didn't interfere with their desire to be together. It was pointless to try to recapture the moment right now. They'd just have to wait until another came around again, and make certain there were no interruptions when it did.

And speaking of interruptions... Tashi folded her arms and frowned up at him. "Adam, you told me you didn't have a housekeeper. I should have known you couldn't maintain the upkeep of this mansion by yourself. Just how many people did you put out of work?"

He dipped his head and smiled sheepishly. "They're not out of work, just on a paid vacation. And I don't have *a* housekeeper. I have six, along with eight gardeners, two butlers, four kitchen staff, and a driver. The only staff members I kept are the four, armed guards at the gatehouse. And it's a good thing I kept them around, or we'd be entertaining three inquisitive men right now. Would you have been able to handle the pressure?"

She shook her head. "No. It would have been too soon."

"We need time to digest all that has happened today and prepare for what's coming tomorrow and the days following."

Guilt raised its ugly head in Tashi's mind. "Adam, I'm sorry. I'm sorry that you have to put your life on hold and place yourself in danger for me." Tears choked her.

He clasped his hand under her chin and raised her face to his. "What are you talking about, sweetie? My life isn't on hold. It's exactly where it should be. These two weeks I've spent secluded with you have been the most amazing of my life. I've had time to reflect on my past mistakes, my desires, my dreams. I know what I want, and it's you, Tashi. I want you in my life. So stop apologizing. Promise me that you will. Promise," he reiterated, his electric blues piercing through to her heart, warming her.

"Okay," she finally said. "I'll stop apologizing."

His eyes pierced her for a few tense seconds, then he dropped his hands to his side. "However, *I* have to apologize to you for something."

"What could you ever possibly do to upset me, Adam?"

"That remains to be seen." He picked up the pad he'd used

to send the text to the guards and while typing on it, he strolled to the other side of his office where a built-in door swung open from the wall. He reached inside and pulled out something, then turned around. "I was able to retrieve this the day after it was stolen. I don't know how much—"

"You found my money?" Tashi screamed as she raced across the room. She grabbed the bag from him and hugged it to her chest like it was a long lost child coming home. Tears of joy raced down her face as she dropped into the nearest chair. She set the bag on her lap and opened it.

"The thief swore he hadn't spent any of it. Since I don't know how much you had, I don't know if he told the truth."

Tashi dumped the contents of the bag on the floor, then got down on her knees and began counting out the stacks of hundred dollar bills. "It seems to be all here," she said, gazing up at Adam. "Who stole it?"

"Your landlord," he said, his voice laced with barely controlled bitterness.

"Mr. Yoder?" Shock and rage surged through Tashi. Mr. Yoder had seemed so nice, always smiling at her when he came by for the rent or to fix something in the building. He'd even stayed and had a cup of coffee with her one frigid winter morning when he'd come around to plow snow. She was the only tenant in the building who was home, and she'd just wanted to thank him for agreeing to their arrangement. Her uncle was right again. People couldn't be trusted. "How did he know I had money?"

Adam dropped to his knees and helped her stuff the cash back into the bag. "Well, you were paying your rent with cash. You didn't have a job. You'd bought nice furniture, a top-of-the-line laptop and camera. You wore nice clothes—not extravagant, but nice. He figured you had to have money stashed away somewhere. He was just waiting for the right time to get inside your apartment and look for it. I'm just happy that you weren't home when he decided he'd waited long enough. It gives me chills to think of what he might have done to you if you'd walked in on him trying to steal from you, or worse, if he'd broken in while you were sleeping and you'd awakened to find him in your bedroom.

Adam's last sentences sent panic rioting inside Tashi. Her fingers shook as she zippered up the duffel bag. "Where—where's he now?"

"In jail, where he belongs."

"He knows my name, Adam," she said as her mind began to race again. "All he has to do is tell somebody, the police—suppose they want to question me about where I got the money. What do I tell them?"

He placed a finger on her lips. "Shh. I took care of it. I warned him to keep your name out of it. I told the police that he stole the bag from my car while it was parked near Mountainview Café. I go there all the time, so..." He shrugged and pushed to his feet, taking the bag with him.

Mountainview Café, where the story of her and Adam's lives began. "What about my cell phone?" she asked, taking the hand Adam held out to help her up.

He reached into the vault again. "It's here. It's locked, so he couldn't sell it or use it since it's code-protected. It's fully charged."

Tashi snatched it from his hand and turned it on, her heart pounding in her chest as she waited for it to go through the loading process. She typed in her security code and scanned the 'Message' and 'Phone' icons. Her shoulders slumped in despair. There were no messages, no missed calls. Agent Dawson hadn't tried to contact her. Her river of hope of ever hearing from him dwindled into a tiny trickle.

"Are you upset?" Adam asked. "I realize now what the phone

means to you, but I didn't tell you about the money because I was afraid you would leave. I'm sorry. I should have been honest with you."

Tashi threw her head back and stared up at him. "Are you kidding me? Really? How shallow do you think I am, Adam? I just told you that I committed murder. You didn't judge me," she began, counting off on her fingers. "You didn't condemn me. You didn't call the cops. You didn't throw me out. And on top of that you promised to marry me." She flailed her hands in the air, irritated that she even had to point out the obvious to him. "How can I be mad at you for protecting me from myself? If you'd given me the money, I would have been long gone. In fact," she continued, her voice dropping in volume and fervor, "I'd decided to leave Granite Falls the day you took me back to my apartment."

"I figured as much, but why?"

"Because you wouldn't have left me alone and I was starting to like you, and I didn't want to like you."

His eyes grew openly amused. "Was I that bad?"

She pursed her lips and smiled at him. "You were that good, Adam, and I knew your association with me would put you in danger. But once again, fate took the decision out of my hands. Leaving Granite Falls would have been the absolute worst thing I could do because I wouldn't have gotten to know you, and I'm exactly where I'm supposed to be—where Agent Dawson sent me. If you'd given me the money yesterday, I would have left. So in that regard, you did the right thing in keeping the fact that you'd found it from me."

His chest rose and fell on a deep sigh. "Then all's well." He held up the duffel bag. "What do you want to do with this? I can return it to the vault and give you the combination, or you can keep it in your bedroom. It will be as safe there as anywhere in this house."

Tashi stared at him, affection for him swelling full and deep inside her at his trust in her. Was there anything wrong with this man who was so compelling, whose magnetism was so potent? Did he have any flaws she could point out and use as a reason not to like him? "You can hold on to it." *Until it's time for me to go.* "I'll keep the phone in case Agent Dawson calls." She pushed the small device into the front pocket of her shorts as she held on to her last glimmer of hope.

"He will. We have to hope." He returned the bag to the vault and closed it. "Now," he said, placing his hand on her shoulder as he walked her toward the door. "Let's talk about when and where we'll tie the knot tomorrow while I prepare us a late lunch to hold us over until dinner. Then after lunch, I do have to spend some time setting up meetings and conferences for next week, so I'm afraid you'll be on your own for a few hours. I can't have my father showing up on my doorstep unannounced, especially not immediately following our marriage."

"No, we can't have that," Tashi agreed on a tremor.

As they walked along the corridor toward the kitchen, Tashi had to remember that their marriage was temporary, and that whether or not they found Agent Dawson alive, it would still come to an end. Even during their most intimate moments when they danced over the waves of passion together, she would have to remember that Adam had married her out of a sense of duty, not love.

Fantasizing about him as a lover was one thing, but as a permanent husband and father of her children was a far cry from reality. Her heart ached within her. She didn't want to be alone in the world again. She wanted to belong to somebody.

She wanted to be loved.

Was that asking too much of fate?

CHAPTER THIRTEEN

While Adam took a shower, Tashi measured out the portions of polenta, butter, chopped garlic, freshly ground black pepper, fresh sage leaves, prosciutto, grated Gruyère and crumbled *torta di Dolcelatte* cheese, as she reflected on the past few hours since they'd agreed to get married.

During lunch, Adam had suggested that they exchange their vows in the garden, but Tashi, feeling that it was too intimate and meaningful for a temporary arrangement, opted for the first floor parlor.

Reverend Reuben Kelly, the pastor of Granite Falls Community Church, where Adam worshipped, would officiate the ceremony. He and his wife, Dr. Samantha Kelly, would make up the wedding party. There would be no music or flowers, or bridal walk. They would merely stand in front of the minister and pledge themselves to each other.

That was the way Tashi wanted it. Her wedding ceremony to Adam wasn't an event she wished to remember with warmth and happiness in the years to come. It would just be too heart-wrenching. She had to remember it for what it was—a temporary arrangement.

Satisfied that she had all the ingredients Adam had asked her to prepare, Tashi sidestepped to the stove and opened the lid to the pot of water she'd put on earlier.

"Good, the ingredients are ready."

Tashi looked up as Adam walked into the kitchen. "Well, it wasn't that difficult," she said. "I was good at math in school."

He chuckled. "I bet you were good at a lot of things." He moved behind her and placed the metal handle of a whisk in her hand.

Tashi's breath caught in her throat and heat instantly and rapidly spread throughout her body—heat she knew had nothing to do with the steam rising from the pot of boiling water on the stove. The sparks that had been triggered when she'd awakened in his arms hours ago were beginning to glow between them again.

"Ready for the next stage?" he asked.

"Yeah, I guess."

"You're going to whisk gently as I pour the polenta into the water. Okay? And you'll continue whisking until it begins to thicken." His voice, low and steady and spiced with seduction, sent a lurch of excitement through her.

As he reached for the cup of raw polenta on the countertop, his bare knees brushed against the backs of her thighs, just below the hem of the dress. The nimble caress, coupled with the faint scent of sandalwood exuding from his recently showered body alerted her senses, making her acutely aware of his proximity, more so than she had been for the past weeks. He was brushing against her on purpose, deliberately, yet subtly trying to arouse her.

"Hold the handle of the pot with your other hand so it doesn't topple off the stove."

Rendered speechless, Tashi followed his instructions and began to whisk as he poured the polenta into the water in a slow steady stream. *Polenta Elisa* was a simple dish, and one of his favorites when he was a child he'd told her while he'd helped her collect the ingredients from around the kitchen. It came in second to *saffron risotto alla milanese*, which he would have loved to cook for her, but he was fresh out of *carnaroli* rice. He was out of a lot of things, seeing he hadn't left the estate for two weeks.

"Easy. Not so hard," he cautioned. "You don't want the polenta to thicken prematurely."

Her heart fluttered wildly. Why did it sound like they were making love, and he was giving her instructions on how to please him? Her mind immediately rewound to their first day in the garden and how she'd been fascinated by the way Adam's penis had thickened and lengthened before her eyes. She could still feel the heat and strength of it pulsing in her hand as they'd stood in the shade of the willow tree. She tightened her grip on the whisk and kept her gaze riveted on the pot as the flutters in her heart turned into a heavy thumping against her chest.

"Slow down, Tashi."

She swallowed a gasp as Adam set the empty measuring cup on the countertop and reaching around her, placed his hands over both of hers. "Relax your grip," he murmured, edging closer to her. "Gently, like this," he instructed in a husky voice as he began to guide her motions into a gentler, slower pace.

Tight knots formed in Tashi's stomach as she felt the pressure of Adam's flexing muscles and the heat from his skin burning through the barrier of their clothes to fuse with hers. If she'd known that cooking with him could be even more intimate than sharing a meal, or engaging in naked couples' yoga, she might have asked to help him before. *No*, she argued the thought away. Even though she'd been thinking about it, she knew she hadn't been ready to go all the way with Adam until today—until she'd told him about her past.

Tashi had a feeling that if Adam's friends hadn't called when they did, they wouldn't be in his kitchen making *Polenta Elisa*. They would still be in his office or across the hall in his big white bed, making love.

Somehow, Tashi found the strength to bring her focus back to the polenta and her whisking until the motion of her hand and the depths of her strokes were in perfect rhythm with Adam's. Even that innocent chore seemed like foreplay, a prelude to lovemaking.

"*Sì, meglio.* You've got it, *bella.*" He released her hands and stepped back.

Tashi's body yearned for the return of his, but she breathed a sigh of relief, nonetheless. It was getting too hot in the kitchen. It probably wasn't a good idea to be caught up in erotic visions of Adam and her together while she was standing in front of an open flame.

"How long do I have to keep whisking?" she asked, as Adam opened up a cupboard and took out a large saucepan.

"Until it's thick enough so it doesn't settle back on the bottom of the pot when you stop whisking. A few more minutes perhaps." He moved to the left of her and placed the saucepan on the front burner of the eight-burner stove.

"Then what?"

"Then you'll turn the heat down to low, cover it, and let it cook for about fifteen minutes. Are you having fun?" he asked, pouring milk and water into the saucepan.

She actually was. "Yes. I've never cooked anything this complicated before. It's usually simple stuff, like baked chicken, boxed macaroni and cheese—those kinds of things, and sometimes I mess them up." She chuckled. "My uncle used to grill hamburgers and hot dogs on the back porch in the summers, and when we ate out—which was a lot—it was mostly fast food."

"Well, there's nothing quick and fast in my kitchen. Stick with me kiddo, and I'll teach you the benefits of enjoying your own slowly cooked meals. Before long, you'll be making *Polenta Elisa* better than my mother, which isn't an easy feat. She makes the best in all of Como," he said, smiling with obvious pleasant memories. "I can teach you a lot about the joys of cooking."

He could teach her the joys of lots of things, Tashi thought. Since her self-discovery and sexual awakening, she'd been spending a lot of time in the library with some of Adam's books about Tantric and Taoist secrets of lovemaking. Tashi had been shocked at the numerous erotic positions of couples making love in the sultry pages of the Kama Sutra and other similar books.

She'd had no idea that different and specific positions could increase and prolong the level and depth of one's passion, and that a woman could have multiple orgasms that went on for minutes. She'd been sensuously amused at the Taoist terms for sexual organs. She had to say that *Hidden and Celestial Palace*, *Valley of Solitude*, *Jade Terrace*, *Precious Pearls*, *Yin Bean* for the female, and *Jade Stalk*, *Ambassador*, *Yang Peak*, and *Dragon Pearls* for the male sounded a lot more sensual and erotic than vagina, clitoris, penis, cock, and the other terms Westerners used to describe private parts of the anatomy.

Tashi had even fantasized about Adam's ambassador forging its way inside her hidden palace. Back there on the sofa in his office, she'd been close to asking if he'd do her the honor of breaching the walls of her celestial palace, and plant his jade stalk deep inside her valley of solitude. Would he have been shocked or amused at her lascivious request? Perhaps both. An unexpected giggle burst from her.

"What's so amusing?"

Tashi sobered up at Adam's question. She'd been so caught up in her fantasies, she'd almost forgotten he was standing right next to her. She cleared her throat. "Nothing."

"Doesn't seem like 'nothing' to me. What made you laugh, Tashi?" he asked softly.

"I was just thinking."

"About?"

She quivered when his hand cupped her chin and he forced her to look at him. "Jade stalks and celestial palaces."

"What do you know about jade stalks and celestial palaces, *cara*?" His voice was dangerously low and husky. "You've been reading my books."

"Studying them, actually." She wanted him to know that she was curious about sex, and anxious to learn about what men and women did to each other in private. She wanted him to know she was ready to explore that aspect of their relationship.

His gaze slid to her lips, and lingered there as if he were surveying them, contemplating the texture and sweetness of them, and then just as she started to feel prickly all over, he dropped his hand. "You think you'll be okay alone for a bit? I have to make one last call for the day."

"Yeah—I'll—I'll be fine." Tashi licked her lips.

"Just remember the instructions I gave you."

With her mind in utter turmoil, Tashi blinked in confusion.

"About the polenta."

"Oh yes, yes, the polenta," she responded in an unsteady voice. "When thick enough so it doesn't stick to the pot, cover, cook on low for fifteen minutes."

"*Perfetto.*"

As Tashi watched Adam stroll away, she took some deep breaths to steady her pulse and heart rate that had accelerated during those tense moments. Cooking with Adam was dangerously sensuous. She'd been surprised when he'd asked her to help him prepare dinner. She'd been reluctant at first since she was vastly lacking in culinary skills. Adam had assured her that she would do great, and had teasingly added that since they were to be married tomorrow, she should learn to appease all her husband's passions, including the one he had for food.

Left alone to her own thoughts, Tashi wondered if Adam invited any of his former lovers into his kitchen and played games of seduction as he taught them how to cook his favorite meals. Had he referred to their private parts as *precious pearls* and *hidden palaces*?

To Tashi's surprise, she felt something she'd never felt before. *Jealousy*. A thick stream of green gooey envy made its way slowly through her veins. It was more painful because she knew that her marriage to Adam had an end, and that when that end came, she would have to step aside and watch him fall in love with, and marry another woman.

From the way he'd been treating her, catering to all her needs, exhibiting extreme patience and understanding, Tashi knew that he would make the quintessential husband one day. Even his parents seemed to be on a perpetual honeymoon. During the few minutes of satellite exchange with them, she'd sensed the love between them as they sat arm in arm—the love Adam told her had begun the moment they'd met. No wonder Adam was such a warm, loving human being. He'd come from love, had grown up in it, had lived it all his life.

'Children became what they lived' was a profound axiom. Adam was love and patience. She was isolation and paranoia. Her uncle had kept her in isolation because he'd been paranoid of something terrible happening to her.

The show of concern from Adam's parents—especially his mother's sympathy—had broken through the wall of silence and solitude Tashi had been living behind for most of her life. The horror, the pain, and the guilt that had been simmering inside her for fifteen months had reached the boiling point. She'd felt that she'd detonate from the inside out if she didn't tell somebody. She was so grateful that Adam was her *somebody*.

"I think it might be thick enough."

Tashi jumped at the sound of Adam's voice. She glanced up to find him standing at the archway leading into the kitchen, and like ice cream melting on a hot summer's sidewalk, all her cares seemed to melt away. His presence calmed her fears and filled her with peace.

How long had he been standing there watching her? And exactly what had been on his mind as he observed her? Was he having doubts, regrets, or second thoughts about agreeing to marry her? Or had his honor and duty to his friend replaced the desire and affection he'd had for her? Is that why he ran out of the kitchen a few moments ago when she'd brought up hidden palaces and jade stalks?

Stop it! Stop the paranoia and feelings of insecurity, she told herself. *You've moved beyond that. They're just thoughts, not reality, anymore. You're safe with Adam.*

"Tashi, you can stop whisking."

Tashi took a deep breath of composure as Adam walked back into the kitchen. Remembering the instructions he'd given her, she placed the whisk on a cast iron holder between the burners, turned the flame to low, covered the pot, and set the timer to fifteen minutes.

"*Perfetto*," he said, turning on the burner under the saucepan he'd placed on the stove before he left to make his call.

He'd been leaving her alone in the kitchen an awful lot, Tashi thought, as she stepped to the side, away from him. Maybe he was just trying to get her accustomed to taking command of cooking meals. "Would you like me to do anything else?" she asked, glancing at the ingredients she'd measured out. They hadn't even been mixed together, yet it smelled delicious in the kitchen already.

"No. I think we're set. I just have to make the milk sauce to add to the polenta once it's cooked." He picked up a wooden spoon from the countertop.

From beneath her lashes, Tashi peeked at Adam's long fingers curled around the spoon as he stirred the milk sauce. She felt herself growing warm as she watched the muscles in his arm flex, and imagined the coating of hair brushing against her skin as he caressed her. She didn't even know that merely watching a man's hands and fingers at work could stir desire in her, make her think about things she shouldn't be thinking about—like making love and making babies.

Babies? Tashi had never thought of herself as a mother, especially since she never had one to learn from. She hadn't even thought of herself as a woman, much less a desirable one in over a year. It seemed as if exposing the darkest secrets of her heart had freed up space for other dreams to materialize. And since Adam was the man she'd confided in and the man she was to marry, even though temporarily, she supposed it was only natural that her new dreams would involve him—dreams she knew would never come true with him.

Her lips and brows puckered. "How come some lucky woman hasn't snatched you up yet?' she asked. "You said your father thought you were ready for marriage at twenty-one. Are the women in Granite Falls and the rest of the world simply blind and stupid?"

He turned his head and glanced at her, a flash of some indescribable emotion in his eyes.

Had she said the wrong thing? Tashi wondered, as he pressed his lips together and his jaws flexed visibly. The air around them immediately became charged with something Tashi couldn't quite fathom. Why would such a simple question bring on such tension? She felt as if she were standing smack in the middle of a magnetic field. Her mind told her to put physical distance between them, but her legs had morphed into rubber.

"Well, it's not for lack of trying," he said, finally. "I've had two serious relationships. I was even engaged once. Several years ago."

So that was his 'especially after'. "What happened?"

"She left me standing at the altar."

I'm sorry came to her mind, but Tashi wasn't sorry. She was glad *that* woman, for whatever reason, had left him, because if she hadn't, the past nineteen days of her life would never have happened, and she would not be marrying him tomorrow. Tashi was grateful for the time she'd already spent with Adam and looked forward to more before the inevitable end of their relationship. He'd taught her so much. He'd taught her how to trust and love. And for that she appreciated him, adored him. *Loved him.*

Tashi pressed a hand to her chest as the knowledge spread, like warm honey flowing slowly through a tiny spout, into every cell of her being. It settled in her erratically beating heart. *She loved Adam.* Her heart leaped with excitement as she accepted and embraced the breathtaking knowledge.

What was there about this man not to love? *Nothing.* Apart from duty—in her case—he didn't strike her as the kind of man who would ask a woman to marry him unless he meant it, so he must have loved this woman deeply. Perhaps that was his flaw. He'd made a mistake with one or both of his previous serious relationships. He'd been rejected and humiliated, and was now damaged, perhaps incapable of commitment.

Tashi understood Adam's logic. She'd thought she loved Scottie, too, and had told him so. But he'd never said it back. She hadn't understood why until the night of the shoot-out. He didn't, couldn't love her. She was merchandise. He hadn't even kissed her like a boy should kiss his girlfriend. He'd given her pecks on the cheek, and when she'd tried to kiss him on the lips, he'd said that he respected her and wanted to wait until after she met his parents. It was all a big load of crap. He was probably forbidden from touching the merchandise—especially the virgin ones.

Tashi sighed inwardly. She was as damaged as Adam when it came to relationships. She'd felt rejected when Scottie hadn't shared her declaration of love, and she'd been humiliated when she'd found out why he'd pretended to like her in the first place.

Adam had no problems with marrying her because he knew it was just granting his friend's request. His commitment was temporary. "She must be a very foolish woman," Tashi murmured with a tinge of bitterness toward the woman for breaking Adam's heart and probably scarring him for life.

"Or, I'm a very lucky man."

Okay… Not the response she expected. "Didn't you love her?"

"I thought I did back then, but now I know I was wrong."

"How do you know?"

He inclined his head and gazed at her, and within that intense moment of time, Tashi felt their inner universes colliding as surely as their bodies had collided the day they'd met. She tried to steady her breathing as that magnetic energy surging between them pulled her into the center of that "open heart" space where their past and their future simply melted away, leaving them transfixed in their *now*, their *present* where they were one.

Namaste! The word and its meaning resonated inside Tashi over and over again, and she expelled a ragged breath as she felt her heart and soul unlock and open in complete surrender to Adam.

His body tensed for a split second as if he'd felt it too, as if he'd reached that place of Light, Truth, and Peace in him at the same moment she'd reached that place in herself. He inhaled sharply as his eyes raked boldly over her. It was a look of unmistakable passion—a distinctive brazen look that was void of all vacillations, and full of purpose and promises Tashi had been afraid of acknowledging before—but no more.

Her body responded to the potential fulfillment in that look. It grew full and heavy with yearning. Her breasts swelled and her nipples hardened and tingled beneath her dress. She felt a heavy thudding between her thighs and a rush of moisture in her panties as her body prepared itself to be overrun by passion's storm.

There was no masking it, no denying it. They were going to make love. And it was going to start right here in his kitchen with uncooked *Polenta Elisa* on the stove, portions of ingredients laid out on the countertop, and the smell of garlic and sage, and pepper and prosciutto scenting the air.

Where it would end, was anyone's guess.

As he shut off the burners and the timer, Tashi remembered his words to her in the garden three days ago: *When the time comes, we'll both know, and we'll strip ourselves of everything foreign to us, everything that's not us, so our union will be pure and sweet and wholesome.*

As if in a trance, Tashi watched Adam's fingers reach for his shirttail, just as hers clutched the cotton material of her dress. She pulled it over her head at the same time he rid himself of his shirt. The items of clothing slithered to the floor on top of each other. A few seconds later, his khaki shorts, her bra, and her panties completed the pile on the kitchen floor. He wore no briefs.

An impatient need rumbled through Tashi as her gaze drifted down Adam's body to the place at his groin where his shaft pulsed against his stomach. Nineteen days of yearning was packed inside him and ready to explode—deep inside her. The walls of her vagina contracted in anticipation of his long-awaited invasion.

She was not a little girl anymore. She was not afraid, not

ashamed, and she felt no guilt over the wanton indulgences she was about to embrace.

He stood in front of her, his blue eyes blazing into her emerald ones like crackling streaks of lightning directing heat and current through a summer storm. "I know." He stepped closer still, trapping her between his body and the counter. Reaching behind her, he loosened her ponytail and threaded his fingers in her hair as it fell around her shoulders. He cupped her face in his hands, and bending down, he tipped his head to the side.

Every atom in Tashi's body sprang to life when Adam's mouth settled on hers as if it belonged there. His lips were sweet, moist, soft, and warm—just as she'd imagined—but his kiss was hard and demanding. Harsh groans erupted from inside him as he immediately began to suck her lips hungrily into his mouth as if he'd been starving for her for centuries.

She quivered from the initial reckless savagery in his kiss and the pulsing of his erection trapped between them. He wrapped her in his arms and thrust his hips into her belly, arousing her, daring her to stand still while the tune of passion's song played out around them. An unreserved hunger to devour him and to be devoured by him engulfed Tashi. It was as if she'd given birth to some lust-crazed nymph who was demanding to be fed. She had no idea she was capable of such yearning, or that a kiss could produce such rhapsody in a woman, in her.

As Adam's mouth moved possessively over hers, Tashi rose up on to her toes, threw her arms around his neck, and tangled her fingers into his hair. She pulled him down and closer, undulating her hips against him, opening her mouth under his, inviting him inside to ravish, plunder, and taste of her spoils that had been guarded for far too long.

Another sharp groan broke from Adam as their tongues collided in a titillating game of tags chasing each other in and out of the hot wet caverns of their mouths. They suckled each other until the ferocity of their passionate exchange turned Tashi's lips into pulsing orbs of flesh.

As ecstasy hummed through her, Tashi breathed Adam into her veins—his sandalwood scent, his hunger, his need, and his passion—she took them and made them hers.

His hands skidded down her body, leaving a fiery trail of desire in their wake. He'd touched her before—every inch of her —but not for pleasure. Before, his hands had moved upon her body to bathe her, to nurse her back to health, to teach her self-discovery and trust. Today, she welcomed the scorching heat of those very same hands as they moved intimately upon her.

He caressed her back and the small circle of her waistline. "Sweet, so sweet," he murmured into her mouth as his hands meandered between their bodies. Tashi gasped as her aching breasts and hard nipples made contact with the smooth warmth of his palms. He squeezed her and molded her as he sucked on her tongue, sending tingling sensations down into the pit of her stomach, causing her to tremble and shiver. Then his hands were moving down and around to the firm hills of her buttocks. He cupped her and drew her deeper into his embrace. She melted into him, became one with him.

Eager to pleasure him as he pleasured her, Tashi ran her hands across his back, shoulders, his stomach, and moaned her triumph as the hard muscles tightened under her soft caress. Working her way up to his chest, she curled her fingers into his silky mat of hair with a sigh of bliss, then slowly, daringly, her hands trailed down between them and her heart lurched when her fingers encountered the moist tip of his shaft nestled tightly between them.

His body stiffened on a long groan, and without interrupting their kiss, he picked her up off the floor and settled her moist heat on the hard ridge of his shaft. It was raw flesh against raw flesh, and the flicker of passion that sizzled at their first intimate *knowing* touch was so sweet, so intense, they gasped their pleasure into each other's mouths.

Tashi began to shake as the pressure of his shaft on her clitoris sent shock wave after shock wave through her. Deep in her belly, she felt the tingles of an approaching orgasm. It had to be an orgasm—her first. Her arms and legs tightened around Adam.

As if sensing her approaching climax, Adam lifted her away from his body and eased the pressure of his mouth on hers. Tashi groaned in protest as her body struggled to hold on to those tingling sensations, but they were gone, dissolved in the feathery kisses Adam was administering on her lips, her cheeks, and her eyes.

Finally, he lifted his head. His eyes were a dark and dusky indigo blue, his lips red and swollen from passion.

"Why'd you do that?" she asked on a frown of frustration.

He smiled. "I wasn't ready for you to come."

"So you decide when I come?"

"I decide everything."

"Oh really?" She rolled her eyes at him. "We shall see about that."

He chuckled, and brushed her hair away from her face. "How was your first kiss?"

"Amazing. It exceeded my imagination," Tashi said, licking her lips that felt as if they'd been dragged through fire.

"It was amazing for me, too. You're very sweet." She whimpered when he traced the soft pads of his thumbs over her swollen lips. He drew back his fingers immediately and his eyes brimmed with apology. "I'm sorry for being so rough. It's just that I've been waiting so long for this, for you. I got carried away. Did I hurt you, *cara*?"

Tashi threaded her fingers though his hair. "I love the fury of your passion. It's a side of you I've never seen before. You're always so gentle and patient with me."

"That's because you're precious to me. I will never do anything to hurt you."

"I know."

He slid her down his body and joined their sexes again.

Tashi gasped as her body contracted in a swift and violent reaction to him. She began to shake.

"Easy," he murmured. "You must learn to control your passion, Tashi. I must teach you how."

With their gazes locked, he trailed his fingertips down her back, across her buttocks and over her thighs, sending more heat rushing to the surface of her skin. He untangled her legs from around his body, and one at a time, he slowly raised them upward, and placed them flat against his chest with her feet sticking out at the sides of his head.

Tashi had seen this position in one of his sex books. It afforded deep penetration and intimacy. Holding on to his shoulders, she glanced down to where auburn and black hair meshed like a colorful bale of silk threads. Even more arousing was the broad head of his shaft peeping up at her while the pressure of its ridge was jammed tightly against her moistness. Although it all seemed erotic and pleasurable, Tashi didn't think she was ready for such a vulnerable position. One deft move and Adam could be inside her. What if he got carried away? "Adam," she called in a moment of fear.

"Shh. I won't enter you. I just want to watch you bathe in your first orgasm before I get too lost in my own passion to enjoy it. This position helps me keep control. Do you trust me?" His voice was warm and heavy in her ears.

Tashi nodded. She did trust him. The position was awkward, but she felt no pain. She was fit and flexible, thanks to yoga, and time spent in his gym.

"You don't have to give anything. Just relax and receive." He pressed his arms against her back and, clasping his hands over her shoulders, he immobilized her against him, and began to simulate the act of copulation, grinding the column of his male hardness into the wet, slick cleft of her woman's flesh, over and over again.

Up and down and side to side, he rocked against her until a fire began to burn in the deepest parts of Tashi's belly and spread upward and outward. Electricity arced through her, and her body jerked spasmodically as the fire grew in temperature and speed, blazing through her like a violent storm as it careered toward that tiny knob of flesh at the center of her womanhood. Her heart hammered in her ears. Her chest heaved, and she began to pant in a frightening combination of pleasure and fear —fear of burning up from the inside out. "Adam. Adam," she whispered.

"Breathe, Tashi. Control your pleasure. Hold on to that pulsating energy of passion and weave it into every corner of your inner universe. Revel in it. Master it, *cara*. Compel it to transcend beyond the physical into the spiritual, massage the aches deep inside you, fan and feed your own desires, become one with *you*, and when your ecstasy becomes too intense, too intolerable to bear, let it explode inside you, my love… Breathe…"

The deep baritone of Adam's voice and the erotic instructions of his words flowed slowly and magically through Tashi, calming her, soothing her, bringing her down from that physical pinnacle of sensations where she teetered precariously out of control. As ecstasy hummed through her body, she breathed deeply and slowly, directing her focus inward toward that twirling liquid orb of fire and directed it away from the inferno between her thighs, and up into her lower belly—her *chi* —the center of her energy and physical universes, spewing fire and heat and light into her heart, her lungs, her limbs, to every cell, every crevice of her being until she felt as if her body had morphed into one colossal ache of pleasure, and she was floating in an eternal *now* of blinding light, tingling sensations, and divine ecstasy. Her fire massaged and caressed and fanned and fed, filling her to completion.

She began to tremble, and her stomach heaved and rumbled out of control. Her breasts grew fuller and tighter, her pebbled nipples crushed against Adam's chest were excruciatingly sensitive. Her skin, melded with Adam's, felt hot and prickly. Her toes curled, painfully, and she felt weak, and powerful, and sensational all at the same time.

"*Sì. Sì. Vieni, mia cara. Mi si bagnano nel tuoi amore dolce succhi.* Come, and bathe me in your sweet love juices."

Deep sobs erupted from Tashi and tears flooded her eyes, as she clung to Adam, digging her nails into the muscles of his shoulders. He rocked against her with rapid speed as his hands rushed up and down her back. She was a bundle of nerves, jittering out of control as the fire leaped through her, scorching her flesh, separating, yet melding her physical and spiritual worlds together. She had become her own orgasm. Her eyes rolled back into their sockets and her lids fluttered shut.

"No. No. *Apri gli ochi*." Adam commanded. "I want to look at you. I want to look inside you as you surrender to the power of your passions, and to me."

Tashi opened her eyes, and the smoldering flames she saw ablaze in Adam's pushed her over the edge. Her heart thundered. Her pulse pounded against her temples as she felt herself spinning through space, racing toward that pinnacle of pleasure's ultimate delight, packed with flaming explosives, and falling aimlessly. Her entire body tightened as that orb of passion exploded deep inside her like a ton of rockets detonating on a Fourth of July night.

Energy burst forth from every pore of Tashi's body, and headed straight toward the gate of her jade terrace, now transformed into a blazing inferno between her legs. She was pulled helplessly down into the watery, fiery current. Unable to do anything else in her immobilized state, Tashi threw her head back and scream her orgasm into the garden below. Torrents of hot fluids gushed from inside her and pooled around their sexes, some escaping to stream across her buttocks and down Adam's thighs in a warm sticky mess.

"*Squisita. Bella. Proprio squisita.* Mmm… Mmm..."

As Tashi shivered and moaned in the throes of her climax, she felt Adam's hot mouth on the damp skin at her throat. He kissed her gently and slowly, and spoke to her softy in Italian, soothing her, helping her back into herself. It seemed to take forever for her pulse to quiet down and her heart to beat steadily again.

When she finally relaxed in his arms, Adam lifted his head and gazed into her eyes. "That, my darling, was the most beautiful orgasm I've ever witnessed. I will remember that look of sweet rapture and complete surrender on you gorgeous face for the rest of my life. It will be the last thing I remember when I draw my last breath. You are amazing."

"It *was* amazing. Totally gratifying," Tashi said, smiling with the utmost fulfillment. "I didn't know that height of passion was attainable, even possible. It's the breathing, isn't it? You've been training me to control my emotions through breathing so I could tap into it when we make love."

He gave a wickedly handsome smile. "Partly. An orgasm is not about releasing. It's about holding, controlling, reveling in the continual sensational flames of desire for as long as you can. It's about feeling with your heart and not your mind. That way, every breath you take is an ultimate exchange with your partner. Just imagine what it will be like with me deep inside you, holding with you, exchanging with you." His voice was tight and slurred with unleashed passion.

"I can't wait," Tashi said as the beast of her yearning began to stir again.

"You're sweet. The sweetest thing I've ever tasted. Simply delectable, and I mean to taste every inch of you before the night is out. It's going to be a very long one." He joined their lips as he eased her legs off his shoulders and wrapped them around his waist again, keeping their sexes snugly joined.

With their mouths and tongues tangled in another breathtaking kiss, he began to make his way out of the kitchen. They were skipping dinner and she wasn't even hungry—well not for food anyway—seeing that they'd finished off a small antipasto plate just before they'd begun cooking. And from the way he was munching on her mouth, Tashi knew that she was the only thing Adam hungered. And that was just fine.

As he made his way across the hall, and into the direction of the master suite, the motion of his movements caused his shaft to bounce against her slick flesh, and by the time he reached the bedroom door, Tashi was experiencing her second orgasm, albeit a small one like a petite aftershock to the rocket that had fired inside her in the kitchen.

Adam kissed her through it, swallowing her sighs, until she released her hold on him and opened her eyes to find him smiling at her. "Why's the door closed?" she asked, her voice mellow in her ears. The last time she was in the bedroom, which was to shower and change after lunch, she'd left the door open.

"Close your eyes," he said with that devilish smile again. And keep them closed until I say "Now". Got it?"

Tashi pouted. "Oh, now you want me to close my eyes?"

"Just for a few seconds, and when I tell you to, I want you to hold your breath, as well."

"Wha—"

"Just do as I ask. I promise you won't be disappointed.

"Okay, fine," she relented, wondering what he was up to, but deciding to close her eyes and wait for his command to hold her breath.

He reached behind her. "Hold your breath," he said, opening the door and taking a few steps forward. "Now."

CHAPTER FOURTEEN

Tashi released her breath and opened her eyes.

"Oh my gosh, Adam!" Her hand flew to her mouth as her eyes darted around. This was definitely not the same room she'd left hours ago. It had been transformed into a sensual chamber of love. The drapes had been drawn against the fading evening light, and soft music floated out from the built-in surround sound system. Huge crystal vases with red and white roses were placed in each corner, and giant pillars of glowing candles lining the perimeter of the bed, provided the only light in the room while scenting the air with a pleasing aroma of jasmine, vanilla, and ginger.

The bed had been remade with white silk sheets and pillowcases that were embroidered around the edges, but what brought tears to Tashi's eyes were the red rose pedals arranged in the middle of the bed that spelled out *Adam and Tashi*.

"When did you do all this?" she asked.

"While you were cooking." He wiped at her tears with his fingers. "Don't you like it?"

Tashi sniffled and slapped him playfully on his arm. "It's perfect, you idiot."

He chuckled. "Well that's a name no one has ever called me before."

"So that's why you asked me to help you cook dinner, and then kept disappearing."

"Guilty." He grinned shamelessly.

"You did it yourself?"

"No. I called an interior decorator after what almost happened in my office earlier. I'm so happy my friends interrupted us, by the way," he added after a short pause.

"You are?"

"Yes." He kissed her lips. "I knew this waiting game we were playing was coming to an end and I wanted your first time to be special. I hoped it would be tonight so I could finally show you how I feel about you. When I left you alone in the kitchen the last time, it was to tell them to scram. This was all they could manage working quietly and secretively, and within a short space of time."

How *did* he feel about her? Tashi wondered as she stared into his eyes. She wanted so much to believe that his feelings for her had transcended the physical like hers had for him. Being on his estate had been the safest place on earth for her. And now being in his arms was the sweetest. She wanted to share the secret in her heart with him, but that might scare him and cause him to feel guilty for taking the virginity of a foolish girl who thought she was in love with him, especially since he was aware of her strict upbringing.

Adam wasn't the kind of man who would hurt anyone intentionally, especially where the emotions and psyche were involved. This *knowing* they'd spoken about was all about sharing themselves physically and maybe even emotionally and spiritually with each other. It didn't involve a lifetime of loving each other until death did them part. They would make that promise aloud to each other and in front of witnesses tomorrow, but in their hearts, they would both know the truth. Tashi didn't want temporary to end, but she knew it would, because that was the nature of Adam's relationships. Agent Dawson had requested that he make her his temporary bride. He was just following his friend's order to protect her, and his own sexual nature to possess her. She need not read more into the situation than there was.

He was hers for tonight, and only God knew how many more after this one, so she would enjoy him, and this romantic little nest he'd thoughtfully created for them. Tashi wrapped her arms around his neck and hugged him tightly. "Thank you, Adam. This is the most beautiful thing anyone has ever done for me." She kissed his cheeks and then his lips, softly and gently, while she graciously cloaked the truth in her heart.

"And it won't be the last time. As my wife, you will be treated like a queen, Tashi, so get used to it. Prepare to be pampered, and adored, and cherished."

His promises wrapped around her like a warm blanket, and even though he never promised she'd be loved, Tashi pretended that Adam was hers forever as he began to move toward the bed where she'd slept alone for the past eleven days. She would not be sleeping alone tonight. She might not sleep at all, Tashi thought, as he placed her in the middle of the mattress on top of the rose petals that spelled out their names.

Her heart hammered in her chest as she gazed up at the man standing over her with his black hair flowing freely down his perfectly chiseled olive-toned body—a body that made Michelangelo's David look like a wimp. His shaft was beginning to lengthen and thicken again, and the passion in his blue eyes assured her that he was as anxious to be with her as she was to be with him.

Everything they'd said to each other, done *with* and *for* each other since the day they met—the bathing, the nurturing, the physical and emotional healing, the preparing and sharing of meals, the shedding of clothes, the self-discovery, the yoga, the meditation, the unraveling of secrets, the tears, the comfort, and the promise to protect—had brought them to this moment where all inhibitions, all distractions, and all fears had melted into nothingness around them.

Tashi couldn't have asked for a more beautiful setting in which to become a complete woman. Only the two of them existed in this special place where soft music floated around them, where flickering candles scented the air, and bouquets of red and white roses created the perfect atmosphere for lovemaking.

"I want you, Adam," she said, as her body began to crave more of the ecstasy it had experienced in the kitchen. "I want to make love with you, tonight," she added just in case he had lingering doubts about the teachings of her upbringing, or that he was overstepping his bounds as her protector. "I want you to teach me."

"Such a sweet invitation," he said, stepping closer to the bed.

Tashi opened her arms as he came down over her, stationing his arms on the mattress on either side of her head to support his upper body. The weight of his hair fell on her chest and her nipples immediately hardened at the tantalizing caress. But when he settled his hips between her parted thighs, fitting their sexes together, Tashi jerked away, pressing her buttocks into the mattress at the same time her hands went to his chest.

"There's no need for you to be afraid, Tashi," he said, giving her a reassuring smile. "We'll take this very slowly. There's no rush to get anywhere."

"I'm not afraid, but I know it will hurt since it's my first time, and—" She looked away, suddenly feeling like the scared little girl who'd first arrived at his home and not the passionate woman she thought she'd evolved into over the past two weeks.

"And what?" He cupped her face, and caressed her cheeks with the pads of his thumbs.

"You're—you're so big, Adam. It's just hard to believe that you can ever fit inside me. That day—our first day in the garden, I couldn't even wrap my hand around you—around it. Is—is that a normal size for men? Are they all as big as you?"

His unexpected chuckles sent Tashi's mind racing, as an even more humiliating realization washed over her. What if she couldn't satisfy Adam, reciprocate the kind of pleasure that he'd already given her, would give her more of tonight? She had to admit that for a twenty-two-year-old woman, she sounded like a naïve little girl who was clueless about the carnal indulgences between men and women.

And face it, she was.

Studying erotic pictures in books didn't make her an expert. Adam was the first naked man she'd seen, the first man she'd kissed, and it wasn't like she had experienced girlfriends to discuss these kinds of things with. In her desire not to disappoint her uncle, she'd avoided conversations where girls talked about their sexual escapades, even in college. Now, she wished she hadn't been such a good girl back then. She wished she'd at least peeked. Even though her questions were natural, she nevertheless felt foolish. "You're laughing at me. You think I'm a child," she said, closing her eyes against his amusement.

"No, *bella*." He immediately sobered up and began to drop soft kisses on her lids until they fluttered open. His eyes reflected gentleness and a hint of apology. "First, if I thought you were a child, you wouldn't be lying naked under me. And second, I laughed because you're so innocent and sweet, and I can't believe that I'm this blessed to have you in my life, in my bed. And lastly, without even knowing it, you've just spoken the very words every man on this planet wishes to hear from the woman he's about to make love to."

Tashi frowned. "Which ones exactly?"

"*You're so big.*" His eyes brimmed with mischief as he mimicked the higher pitched voice of a woman.

Tashi relaxed and smiled as some of her humiliation evaporated. "No woman has ever told you that you're big?"

"Oh, they have."

She looked across the room, feeling even greener.

He gently drew her back. "And to answer your question, yes, I'm bigger than most men. Most women like that," he added in a voice void of modesty.

"They do?"

"Yes, Tashi, they do," he replied with quiet patience. "But it's not the size of a man's jade stalk that matters," he added on a note of experience as if he were explaining an intricate philosophy to a child. "It's how he uses it to pleasure his partner. And you will learn to love the feel of my enormous jade stalk strolling leisurely through the terrace of your celestial palace. But before we get to that stage, I intend to bring you pleasure in so many other ways before I release your passions inside you."

Tashi felt heat rise to the surface of her skin and all her insecurities vanished, but... "Adam?" she called.

"Yes, Tashi?"

Protection. The word came at Tashi like a blast from the past—her mother's past, actually. What if she got pregnant? Would Adam make their arrangement permanent? It's what she would want, but he might not. He might see a child as a burden, and her as a trap, and he might resent her for placing that burden on his shoulders, or more precisely on his lap.

But Lord, she would love so much to take away a part of Adam with her—something more tangible than his smile and his kindness. Something she could actually hold in her arms, and love, and watch grow. She had enough money to make a decent life for herself and her child. It wouldn't be anything close to what Adam and the Andreas family could provide, but her child wouldn't starve, and once she got her photography career going.... Her own mother had done it. Since she didn't have a sibling or any other family to name as guardian for the child, she would make plans for Adam to be notified in case something should happen to her.

Tashi realized that her reasoning was selfish and unfair, but she didn't care, didn't want to care. She'd been good all her life. She'd followed rules and obeyed orders without question. She wanted to do something original, and natural, and having Adam's baby felt like the most natural thing in the world to Tashi.

Besides, *he* knew where babies came from. He knew she had her period exactly two weeks ago, and *he* hadn't brought up the matter of protection, either, she thought, watching the strained look of desire in his eyes as he waited for her. He'd been waiting for her, for *this* for almost three weeks. Maybe, just maybe, he wanted the same things she did, but was afraid to voice his feelings after being hurt and humiliated by women he'd thought he loved.

They were so different on so many levels, yet so much alike on others. She didn't know if he loved her, would ever love her, but she loved him enough to abandon her upbringing and give herself to him outside the bonds of marriage. She was done being a good girl, and if making love with Adam was bad, then tonight she would be bad. So bad, she thought as the pressure of Adam's shaft pressed against her heat stirred a quivering deep inside her womb.

"Yes, Tashi. What is it?" he asked again.

"I'm happy," Tashi said, smiling up at him. "I'm happy that I waited for you." And that was the honest truth dragged from the depth of her heart.

"Me too, love. Me, too." And with that, Adam bent his head

and captured her mouth as if to shut her up, and when he thought he'd cleared all questions from her mind, he raised his head and gazed down at her. "Tell me, what do you want, Tashi? What do you want me to do to you?" he asked in a voice thick with passion.

Tashi swallowed as he pressed his hips into hers. "I—I don't know. Make love to me."

His eyes shimmered like blue shard of light. "Be specific. Making love is a lot more than intercourse. It's an endless foray of caressing, licking, even blowing… So tell me, where exactly on your tantalizing little body do you want me to place my hands? Where do you want me to caress, lick, blow you?"

Tashi licked her lips at the sultry questions. She fidgeted under him and swallowed again. "I want you to kiss my neck and —and my—my breasts. I guess."

"Is that it? That's all you want me to kiss?"

Tashi's mind was suddenly ablaze with the images from the *Kama Sutra* and other sexually related books in Adam's library— images of men with their heads between the open thighs of their partners, and women kneeling before men with their mouths clasped around their shafts. The rapturous looks on their faces must have been the same one she'd had while Adam was bringing her to her very first orgasm in the kitchen. As she recalled that moment, Tashi felt her heart pounding in her chest and the familiar tingles return to her belly.

Adam let out a long sigh and suddenly he was off her, rolling over to the side of the bed, and switching on a bedside lamp. Puzzled, Tashi watched him walk toward the bathroom, and in less than a minute he returned holding a small leopard print pouch in his hand.

"What's that?" she asked, rising up on her elbows as he climbed back onto the bed and sat back on his haunches.

"We're going to play a little game," he said, opening the

pouch and dumping a stopwatch and two ivory dice with words etched in black onto the mattress. He held his hand out to her. "Sit up."

Her perplexity swiftly turning to curiosity, Tashi took Adam's hand and sat up in the bed, facing him. "What kind of game is this?" she asked, tucking her hair behind her ears.

"A sex game." He picked up the dice.

"A sex game? I guess we know who's gonna win this one," she said on a skittish giggle.

"There are no winners or losers, or perhaps there are only winners. Anyway, hopefully by the time it's over, you, my dear, will know exactly what you want me to do to you, and you'll not be shy about asking for it."

Well in that case, Tashi felt she would like this game. "Have you played it before?" She knew she sounded like a jealous schoolgirl, but she didn't care. He was so experienced, she wanted to share something new with him, something he'd never shared with any other woman, something more intimate than being the only visitor to his garden.

He smiled. "No, Tashi. I've never played this game with anyone before. I've been saving it."

Tashi bit back her cry of joy. "For what?"

"Whom. I've been saving it for you, for my wife."

"I'm not your wife, yet."

His eyes swept over her face, then swiftly scanned her body. "We can wait until tomorrow if that's what you want," he said, reaching behind him for the pouch.

Tashi watched him guardedly, trying to figure out if he was bluffing. It would be just like Lady Fate to throw a curve ball at her, and send Agent Dawson knocking on his door tomorrow, then temporary would be over before it even begun. She didn't think she could go on living the rest of her life without the experience of making love with Adam. "No. I don't want to wait."

"I was hoping you'd say that," he said, his smile turning into a full grin. "Now here are the rules. One die has action words, and the other nouns—body parts. The person who throws puts the words together to form a command, a task that the other person has to perform for thirty seconds—no more, no less. The timer allows both the giver and the receiver to concentrate on their pleasures. But once it goes off, we move on. Any questions?"

"Yeah, when does it end? When do we know the game is over?"

His eyebrows arched upward. "Excellent question. The game ends when either party cries, "Game" and the other responds, "Game Over" so they know they're in agreement."

Tashi's body was already tightening in anticipation. She felt like a giddy schoolgirl playing with her best friend after school. The only difference was that this was a very naughty, grown-up game. "Okay," she said, catching her lower lip between her teeth.

"Okay. There's a question mark on the 'noun' die." He held it up so she could see. "If it turns up, just fill in the blank with a body part of your choice. Oh, and we're not allowed to use our hands, unless it's part of the command."

"What happens if we do?"

He tossed her a look of mock impatience. "Then that partner forfeits the game."

"Then what?"

"We get dressed, and go back to the kitchen and finish making dinner."

"Yeah, right." Tashi rubbed her hands against her thighs in a slow seductive manner.

He smiled suggestively. "It's all about control, Tashi, being able to control your sensations to build tumescence in order to acquire ultimate gratification, like you did in the kitchen."

That was awesome, Tashi thought on a tremor. Never would she have imagined that these types of games existed. She'd always thought that sex was a serious ordeal, that it wasn't a time for humor—just moans and groans as partners expressed their feelings. But now, she was so eager to learn how to prolong those feelings of arousal for both herself and for Adam. "What are the action words?" she asked.

"You'll see." His smile was almost boyish, suggesting that he was having as much fun as she. "Do you want me to go first?"

"No, I'll go first," Tashi said, feeling a jolt of wickedness and valor infuse her blood. It would be fun to camouflage her primitive longings in the rules of a game.

"Your wish is my command, *bella*." He handed her the dice.

Having no idea what to expect, Tashi took a deep breath and threw her hand. She got 'lick' and 'above waist'.

"Good start. All you have to do is tell me where specifically above your waist you want me to lick."

Tashi's nipples tingled as if screaming "Me first, me first" like little kindergarten kids, anxious to please their teacher. "My nipples, I guess," she said, as her heart began to thump.

"Any preference?" His voice was low as he leaned toward her.

Tashi swallowed. "Um—the left?"

"You're not sure?" He stopped to gaze up at her, his eyes like azure stones, the sides of his mouth quirking mischievously. "You can request that I lick both. I'll try to split the time equally between them."

She trembled as the tips of his hair brushed across her thighs, tickling her sensuously. "Um—just the left one. Start with the left." That seemed to be the nipple that was aching most.

"The left nipple it is, then." He set the timer.

Tashi sucked in a harsh breath as Adam's wet warm tongue made initial contact with her pebbled nipple—a nipple that had never felt the warmth of a mouth on it before. The sensations were sweet and wispy, not intense like those at her groin when their sexes were joined.

"Like that?" he asked, retreating his tongue and coming back to lick her again as he stared into her eyes.

"Yes." Tiny shivers ran up and down Tashi's spine as Adam flicked his tongue against her, being careful to remain within the brown area of her areola and her nipple, even though she could feel her breast grow full and thrust forward as if begging for some attention. In fact, a number of other erogenous zones in Tashi's body were on high alert now, jealous of her left nipple and buzzing with impatience for their turn.

Then the time went off and Adam sat back, leaving her nipple in a tingling wet mess.

"Did you like that?" he asked, his lips moist, his eyes bright with delight.

"Yes, oh yes. It was delicious. Your turn," she said on a shaky eager breath.

CHAPTER FIFTEEN

Adam smiled as he picked up the dice and rolled them around in his hand. His tongue was on fire from those too few seconds of daubing at her nipple. He'd been tempted, so tempted to suck more of her breast into his mouth and listen to her moan with pleasure, but rules were rules, and he was the master of obeying them.

He recalled the night Erik and Bryce had talked him into attending a sex toy show at one of Michelle's friend's home. He was between lovers at the time, and he'd known they were trying to set him up with one of the single ladies who were in attendance, but it was a no-go. He'd enjoyed the evening, nonetheless, watching the host and hostess, and various other couples examine the games.

Even Bryce and Kaya, newlyweds at the time, had joined in the fun. To support the independent consultant, he'd purchased a few games—none of which he'd ever used, perhaps because he kept them here on the estate and not at his penthouse suite at Hotel Andreas where he entertained—*used to entertain his women* —he immediately corrected his thoughts.

This initiation game was perfect for an inexperienced woman

like Tashi, and he hoped that before long she'd grow into the more advanced ones that involved pleasure toys, restraints, blindfolds, melted wax, role play, and much more. Oh, yeah, he was going to enjoy teaching his temporary bride all about the tricks and joys of lovemaking, and he prayed she'd love it so much, she'd never want to leave *la camera dell'amore* he planned to create for them.

Adam's heart pounded against his chest as he gazed at the delicate face of the woman who would be his wife tomorrow—a face that had been invading his dreams for the past nineteen days, and one he knew he'd dream about for the rest of his days. Passion and pride mounted inside him as he studied her young seductive body kneeling in the middle of his bed with her auburn curls and smooth chestnut skin glowing in the candlelight. She was the epitome of loveliness. He'd undressed her, bathed her, and held her naked in his arms so many times before, but he'd never really had the joy of admiring her, openly lusting after her like a man lusted after a woman he desired—not even when she'd voluntarily taken her clothes off for him in the garden. His patience and control had never been tested as much as they'd been tested in the past two weeks.

The warmth of Tashi's presence—her ginger-jasmine-vanilla fragrance that lingered on his towels and his sheets, his shirts when she hugged him, on the wind as she passed by, the fleeting brush of her silky hair against his arms, the shimmer in her innocent eyes, the outline of her sweet plump lips—had kept him in a state of satisfied hunger, until now.

A fire burned in the pit of Adam's belly as he gazed upon Tashi's nymph-like beauty, seeing her for the first time as a lover. She was no longer a woman in need. She was a woman he needed. And soon he would feast on the fruits of her delights and drink from the fountains of her desires.

A few moments ago when she'd called his name, Adam had

prayed she didn't bring up the topic of birth control, because if she had, he would have had to respect her wishes. It wasn't just about getting her pregnant as much as it was about the experience of feeling her tight hot flesh wrapped about him. This was her first time—their first time together—and he didn't want to use a condom with her. But if she'd asked…

"Come on, Adam," she said, her thumb on the timer button at the ready.

Adam chuckled at her impatience. Seems she was as anxious as he was to continue their lovefest that would last throughout the night. "Eager little thing, aren't you?" he said on a deep chuckle.

"Well, yeah. I want more of what I had in the kitchen."

"Then who am I to deprive you, my sweet?" He tossed the dice. He got 'suck' and 'lips', a bit disappointing he thought—or not—he reconsidered as he felt the pressure of Tashi's hot mouth on his.

He stationed his hands on the mattress to keep from falling backward as she began to suckle and nibble on his lips and run her tongue over them as if they were a ripe peach and she was hell bent on extracting the last drops of juices from him. Adam groaned his appreciation as his heart began to race and his groin tightened, then just as he was getting into the rhythm of her kiss, the timer went off, and Tashi reluctantly disengaged her mouth from his, leaving him hungry and frustrated. He was beginning not to like this game, at all.

"That was hot," Tashi said, licking her lips to capture the string of saliva that stretched between their mouths.

"Yes, that *was* hot." Adam grinned. "You're liking this?"

"I'm loving it." Tashi picked up the dice and threw them. 'Suck' and '?' was her command. Her nipples and breasts wanted more of his tongue, his lips, and his mouth. She swallowed and pointed to her right breast.

"Ah, your bells of love," he said, and in the next instant, his lips were brushing against her nipple, tantalizingly, softly, his breath warm and moist against her skin.

Tashi sighed at the tender caress that sent tiny shivers rushing through her body. The sensations were a little more intense than when he'd merely licked at the nipple of her left breast, but his command was to... "Suck me," she whispered. "Suck my bell of love."

On her command, he opened his mouth, clamped his lips around her aching mound, and began to suck her. A series of electrical shock waves zinged up and down Tashi's spine, and she arched her chest forward and moaned aloud. Her nipple hardened in his mouth and he flicked his tongue against the hard bulb as his teeth grazed her swollen globe.

That was it for Tashi. Thirty seconds would not be enough this time. "Game," she moaned in weak surrender, as her hands came up to the sides of Adam's head and her fingers tangled in his hair, holding him in place.

"Yes, game over," Adam acquiesced against her breast, then suddenly his hands were around her waist, and he was picking her up and placing her across his lap. Their sexes burned and sizzled at being joined together again.

Wrapping her legs around Adam's waist, and her arms around his neck, Tashi pulled his face into her bosom. When his hands began to explore the hollow of her back, pressing her deeper into his tight hard body, a sense of urgency drove her, and she began to ride the ridge of his shaft with little circular motions as pleasure mounted between her thighs.

"Oh yes, ride me baby," Adam whispered. His hand roamed intimately over her other breast—each caress a command. He sucked her so ravenously and deeply, her hardened nipple hit against his throat, heightening her desire.

As their commingled moans of delight filled the room, Adam

cupped her buttocks with one hand, and pulled her snugly against his male muscle, and soon the thrusts of his hips were matching the tempo of the suction of his mouth on her right breast, and the kneading of his palm on her left. Pleasure pounded in her brain, spread to her heart and spilled into every cell of her body, setting her ablaze.

"Adam… Adam," she panted as she felt the simultaneous throbbing of her breasts and the walls of her sex grow into an unbearable ache. With no command to hold it this time, Tashi let it explode deep inside her. Her body tightened into a numb shock of delight, then she screamed as a torrent of fiery sensations washed over her. She clung to Adam, drenched in pleasure and sweat.

"Lovely, lovely," Adam crooned against her breast.

While she was still caught in the wave of her orgasm, he switched his mouth and hand on her breasts and repeated his sensual assault, sucking, kneading, and thrusting, tentatively at first, then deeper and harder as her passion escalated to a new and sensational height, until she was drowning in another orgasmic wave, and she threw her head back and cried out his name.

"*Sì, così caldo. Così caldo e selvaggio. Vieni per me, mia dolce piccola Tashi. Vieni per me. Vieni!* So hot, so hot and wild, come for me, my sweet, little Tashi."

While Tashi recovered from the onslaught of her third and fourth climaxes, Adam's mouth made a wet hot trail to the pulsing hollow of her neck, up her chin, to her lips where he kissed her gently as a butterfly sipping nectar from a petal. As her tremors ceased, Tashi's heart swelled with her love for him.

She felt him cradling her, and then he was moving, shifting his weight on the mattress, reaching out to turn off the bed lamp, inviting back the flickering shadows of the candles, and then she was lying on her back and he was crouched over her, supporting his upper body on his arms with his lower half joined to hers as they were before they'd begun their game. They'd come full circle. She opened her eyes and smiled at him, the expression on his face promising her that they hadn't even begun yet.

"Playing that game really loosened you up, didn't it?" he asked, smiling down at her.

"Yes, it did." She tucked his hair behind his ears and brushed her knuckles against his cheek where a five o'clock shadow was making its appearance. He'd given her so much pleasure already, and yet he'd taken none for himself. He was as patient in bed as he was in every other area of his life. She, on the other hand was anxious to experience the ultimate act of lovemaking—to indulge in the carnal debauchery her teachers had warned her against.

"I long for you, Adam. I burn for you." As she gazed into his beautiful blues, shimmering brilliantly in the candlelight, Tashi couldn't hold back the tears that seeped from the corners of her eyes. Maybe she was too weak to contain them, or maybe her love was too strong to be contained.

"Oh, Tashi. I burn for you." He sipped her tears and brushed her temples with his fingers. "I promised to kiss every inch of you before the night was out. But there is one special place I'd love to kiss before I make you mine. Can you guess where that place is?"

Tashi felt warm and feminine. "You want to kiss the gates of my celestial palace?"

"Not just the gates, *cara*. I mean to sweep my tongue inside you and lick the walls, the ceiling, and the floor of your valley of delight until they collapse in my mouth." He thrust his hips forward as he spoke, pushing a new wave of desire through her. "Yes, like that," he whispered when she began to tremble under him. "I want to feel you falling to pieces in my mouth, and then I want to feel you fall to pieces again while I'm buried deep inside you, my Little Eve."

"Show me." Tashi clasped her hands on the sides of his head

and buried her fingers in his hair as he began to kiss and caress his way down her body. He brushed his lips against her brows, her eyes, her cheeks, her nose, then his mouth closed over hers briefly in a sweet kiss before moving to the hollow of her throat, where he licked her sensitive skin. He kissed the sides of her bells of love, and gently, soothingly, his lips skimmed across her stiff nipples as if he knew they were too sensitive for a deeper, more meaningful caress.

His tenderness and thoughtfulness shook Tashi to the core and she felt herself floating on a cloud of fiery titillation as Adam worshipped her with his mouth and hands. He kissed her stomach, drawing skin and flesh gingerly into his mouth, nibbling with his teeth, massaging with his tongue, arousing her senses as her admiration and love mounted into unadulterated lust.

He emitted a deep groan, then his fingers stroked her quivering stomach as he plunged his tongue into the shallow groove of her belly button, cautiously at first, then more fastidiously as if he were trying to lick the last drop of his favorite gelato from the bottom of a chocolate cone.

Tashi closed her eyes and curled her fingers into Adam's hair at the delirious stimulations that the combination of feathery caresses and steady thrusts were generating in her. Never would she have imagined that her belly button was such an erogenous zone. She was learning so much about the thrills of lovemaking —so much, she thought as her whole being seemed to awaken and respond to the lascivious call to mate.

As she teetered on the edge of ecstasy, Adam trailed his tongue along the thin dark line extending from her belly button to her pubic area, then his fingers were twirling into her thatch of hair, and he was tugging, gently stirring the underlying elements of her *mons* and deepening her sexual arousal and fantasies.

He raised his head and smiled at her. "You know one of the

things I love most about you?" he asked in a thick hoarse voice, his eyes like blue diamonds flickering in the candlelight.

He loved something about her? Was that a figure of speech or did he just admit that he loved her? "What?" Tashi asked on a breathless whisper.

"That you're not bald down here, that you just shave around the borders and trim the edges into a flat, silky mat. It's very natural, very sexy, like you."

As Tashi reveled in the sweet compliment, Adam nudged her legs apart and settled himself between them. He flipped his hair over his shoulders out of his way then dipped his head, hovering above the most private part of her being, the place where he had cared for when she was too sick to do it herself.

Tashi was certain now that she'd fallen in love with Adam the night he'd crawled through her bedroom window to rescue her. He didn't even know her then, had only talked to her for a few minutes three days prior, yet he'd come to her aid when she'd called, and not only that, but he'd picked her up and held her in his arms without hesitation, even though she was covered in filth.

As she'd gazed into his eyes and thanked him for cleaning her up, she'd felt something pierce through her heart, then a burst of energy, euphoria, warmth, and awareness of him as a man had washed over her. It must have been love. Unrecognized at the time, because she'd never experienced it before. But she knew it now—oh did she know it—she thought with bliss as Adam's breath, slow and deep fanned the mat of hair on her Venus mound.

He dipped his head and took a deep long inhale as if he were trying to become familiar with the true essence of her femininity, of all she had to offer as a woman. "*L'odore è inebriante.* Your scent is intoxicating. I'm drunk with you. Tell me what you want, *cara*," he whispered, placing a hand on her belly and pressing the heel into the area just above her groin as if testing the exterior regions of her feminine landscape. "What do you want me to do for you?"

Fire raced through Tashi's blood at the thought of Adam's mouth fused to the most intimate part of her body, his tongue swirling inside her as it had swirled in her mouth, then later to experience the ecstasy of his jade stalk thrusting deep inside her. She didn't bear his name yet, but in her heart, her mind, and soul, Tashi had already claimed Adam Andreas as her own, had already pledged her life and her body to him forever, so giving herself to him felt like the most natural thing in the world. She knew in her heart that as long as she lived, she would never share her body with another man. *Temporary* couldn't break that bond, nor change her fate.

"*Cara...*"

"I want—" She licked her dry lips. "I want you to kiss my cinnabar cave, Adam. I want you to open the folds of my hidden palace, lick my precious pearl, thrust your tongue inside me, graze upon the path of my yin, and make me come. I want to fall to pieces in your mouth, Adam."

"*Dio! Sono ubriaco con la vostra essenza, annegando nel tuo amore, tesoro mio. Dolore per il sapore delizioso di voi sulla mia lingua.* I'm drunk with your essence, drowning in your love, my darling. I ache for the delightful tastes of you on my tongue," he translated for her as his lips brushed her red thatch, and his breath melted into her skin.

The naughty, erotic Italian words and the sexy sound of Adam's accent made Tashi's senses spin. She shuddered as his fingers caressed the outer regions of her slick folds, parting her, holding her open as the tip of his tongue made contact with the naked flesh inside. She gasped and groaned from the tantalizing sensations as he traced his tongue along the perimeter of her clitoris in steady circular motions, and then he flicked her sensitive knob, licking at it for a few heart-stopping seconds before resuming his mind-blowing tracing designs.

She was a canvas, his tongue a brush, and he was painting the picture of his passion inside her.

Over and over again, he alternated his teasing, pushing her along passion's fiery trail, and as she felt herself drowning in a sea of liquid fire, Adam pressed the tip of his tongue against the hot tight entrance of her womanhood. Her cinnabar cave began to throb at the unexpected, yet delicious attempt to breech its velvety walls.

"Oh God." Tashi grabbed a handful of the silk sheets as Adam's mouth closed completely over her throbbing heat, and he began to eat her, drawing her into his mouth and sucking on her woman's heat like a lascivious rascal who'd been on a hunger strike for months.

"*Squisoto, semplicemente squisito,*" he groaned, draping her thighs over his shoulder, sliding his hands under her buttocks, lifting her off the mattress, and holding her suspended in the air. His tongue was a buzz of activity as he alternated between licking and flicking at her clitoris, and probing the entrance of her quivering body, pushing deeper and deeper into her virgin flesh, stroking her, strumming her, lapping up the juices flowing copiously from inside her.

The fusion of sensations sent Tashi's heart racing, her mind whirling and her body bucking and twisting like a live wire as Adam devoured her with his mouth. Under his masterful lovemaking strategies, Tashi became a swift flowing river, rushing downstream to where the current was wildest and hottest, where the waves coiled and wrapped around her pulling her down until her body tensed, then snapped, and she yielded. Just before she fell apart, Adam shoved his tongue deep inside her and kept it there sending sharp shards of purely pleasurable explosions ricocheting throughout every pore of her being.

"I'm coming. Adam!"

"Sì, *cara. Vieni per me.*"

Tashi's thighs tightened around Adam's head in a killer grip and her heels beat against his back as he continued to suck and slurp her female nectar from her body. Then she began shrieking, thrusting violently against Adam's mouth until her passion became physically unbearable. Her body tensed and jerked. She heard a harsh groan or perhaps it was a chuckle from Adam as she was hurled into that sweet abyss where ecstasy engulfed her in a pit of mindless, senseless bliss, then spat her out in a quaking ball of listless flesh.

Tashi moaned and struggled to suck precious air into her constricted lungs as Adam lapped at her flood of hot love juices, while he whispered softly against her quivering sex, soothing her with his tongue and words. And then he lowered her to the mattress and untangled her legs from around his neck. He pulled her thighs wide and knelt between them.

Tashi opened her eyes and gazed at him, her chest still heaving from the aftershocks of her orgasm. His cobalt eyes were blazing with desire and his mouth resembled a glazed donut, glittering with her juices. She wanted to lick his lips, find out just what it was about her taste and her scent that had driven him to such licentious lengths.

As if a window had opened from her soul to his, he came down over her, supporting his weight on his elbows and knees, his silky hair falling across her chest and face. "Go ahead," he whispered, his mouth inches from hers. "Taste your love on my face."

Tashi didn't need a second invitation. She pushed Adam's hair out of the way and clasping his head in her hands, she pulled him down and began licking his face like a mother cat cleaning her kitten. Then she wrapped her lips around his and kissed him deeply and passionately. He surrendered on a groan and a chuckle, kissing her back with equal fervor, thrusting his tongue into her mouth as if he were painting the roof with the juices he'd sucked from inside her. Tashi reveled in the rudimentary eroticism, and when she was certain there was no trace of her left in Adam's mouth, she let him go.

"Wow," he said, lifting his head and staring down at her. "You're a quick study, my little, virgin, temporary bride."

Tashi's heart swelled with love and warmth. He'd called her his bride even though they hadn't yet exchanged their vows.

"I want to please you," she said, rushing her hands up and down his back, loving the feel of his muscles bunching under her palm. "I want to give you some of what you've given me." To show him how serious she was, Tashi reached down between them, her fingers searching him out.

"Tashi." He jerked when her fingers brushed against his hard smooth shaft, and as they curled around it, he sucked air into his lungs.

His mouth opened on a silent gasp and his eyes rolled back in their sockets as she squeezed him, hesitantly at first, then feeling a bolt of power at her ability to make him groan, Tashi began to pump him. She ran her hand up and down his jade stalk, feeling it lengthen and thicken and pulse furiously as if it had a heartbeat of its own.

"Tashi," he hissed again, dropping his head on the pillow beside her head as she caressed the sensitive tip that was coated with his juices.

Tashi lubricated her palm with those juices and, circling him once more, she began to pump him as he trembled above her. "I want to taste you, Adam. I want to lick you and suck you into my mouth as you did to me. I want to blow you."

"*Mio Dio.*" His body tightened. He let out a long growl and dropped his full weight on to her, crushing her breasts beneath his hairy chest, trapping her hands between their heaving stomachs, ending her ability to stroke him, though she could still feel him flexing in her palm.

He stayed like that, trembling for a few tense moments, before raising his head. "Not now. Not tonight," he said gazing into her eyes, his speech slurred and dense as if he had trouble forming the words. "I promise you can take me into your mouth later, but right now I need to be inside you or I'll go raving mad. I've wanted you ever since I met you, and I can't wait another minute to love you, my sweet Little Eve?"

A quiver surged through Tashi's veins and her heart overflowed with love and desire. She squeezed him as she felt an empty craving inside her woman's heat, like something was missing and needed to be filled. "Fill me up, Adam," she murmured, as that craving grew stronger and tighter between her legs.

A deep ache grew in Adam's throat as he gazed down at Tashi spread out beneath him with red rose petals garnishing her auburn hair. God, she was the sweetest, most angelic, sexiest, desirable woman to ever walk the face of the earth, and he loved her. She was a garland of light, a love-gift that had come to him in the shadowy hallways of night to perfume and brighten the pristine corners of his life. He loved her so deeply, so honestly, so purely that his love had become a physical pain in his gut, his heart, his entire being.

Adam lifted his lower body from hers, and reaching between them, he unclasped her hand from around him. "Drape your arms around my neck and wrap your her legs around mine." His cock twitched, missing the tight warm grasp of her hand. *Don't despair. You're gonna love what's coming next even more*, he silently promised as he took it in his hand. "We'll take this slowly," he said, his throat tight with passion as he felt her legs tremble around his.

She swallowed and her pupils grew large and luminous, but

her desire never dimmed as he settled the ridge of his shaft on her moist heat. A few minutes had gone by since her last orgasm and he needed to build up her passion again, make sure she was caught up in another when he finally entered her. "Don't be afraid, Tashi. I will try to make this as painless as possible for you. Just relax, baby."

A nervous shudder ripped through Adam's gut. He'd never been with a virgin before, so in that respect, he was as much a virgin as she was. He, however, refrained from sharing that bit of news with his little bride-to-be. In her eyes, he was the experienced lover, the master of seduction, and that's exactly what he had to deliver.

Adam cupped her face in his hands and as his mouth closed over hers, he began a series of tantalizing rotations of his hips and buttocks, allowing only the ridge to graze the rim of her slick entrance and the sides of her sweet little yin bean. He teased her, over and over again, reveling in the delirious feel of her hot juices coating his smooth skin. And soon she was whimpering and twitching beneath him, raising her hips upward for a more solid contact, whispering his name as her fingers sent tingling sensations rushing up and down his back.

In response to her silent pleas, Adam reached down and, clasping his cock in his hand, he dragged the head up and down her slippery slope from the top of her clit to the base, studiously avoiding the entrance to her body. This deeper level of teasing sent her into a wild frenzy, and he released her mouth to gaze down at her, to witness her passion. Her eyes closed and her head began to thrash about on the mattress, her red curls flipped back and forth on the white sheets, and her body trembled decadently.

The erotic vision proved too much for Adam. His cock was on fire pulsing in his hand as the tip sought out the hot tight entrance to her body. And then it found it. And nestled against it.

They both shuddered involuntarily. Her eyes flew open to

stare up at him, wild, and misted in the deepest shades of green, but he detected her fear, which he realized was only natural.

"It's going to hurt," she said, then closed her eyes to hide her pain from him, even as her fingers dug into his arms.

"Just for a little bit." Adam bent over her. Her hot breath bathed his face. "Open your eyes, Tashi," he rasped. "Yes," he said when her lids fluttered up. "Keep looking at me, okay? I feel your pain, darling. I feel your pain, but your passion as well. Don't be afraid."

Tashi stared bravely into his ardent eyes. She'd been dreaming about this moment ever since she'd come upon him in the garden. That day, she'd abandoned everything she'd been taught about her sexuality. She'd dropped the shame of her own nakedness, buried the guilt of her cravings. And that night as she'd lain in this very same bed, she'd dared to draw back the soft folds of her womanhood and touch herself for the very first time. Shrouded in the darkness of night, she'd fantasized that it was Adam's strong fingers, and not her trembling, clumsy ones that were exploring the vestal terrain that lay beneath them.

She needn't fantasize any longer. She had the real thing lodged between her thighs, knocking at the gate of her celestial palace, asking permission, waiting for an invitation to come inside. If Adam could bring her to such heart-stopping orgasms so many times with his fingers and his mouth, Tashi could only imagine what it would be like to have that orb of fire explode in her being while Adam was buried to the hilt inside her. "I'm not afraid, Adam. I want it. I want you."

"Then you shall have me, darling." He pulled back and thrust forward again. "You are so hot, so tight. Like wet silk and hot velvet." He thrust again, and the head gained entrance. She shivered and quivered beneath him, and her body tightened as if refusing him entrance.

He held himself still just a fraction of an inch inside her and captured her mouth and kissed her passionately until she sighed in ardent submission. As her passion resurfaced, he reached between them, tangled his fingers in her damp thatch and toyed with her yin bean, until he felt the muscles just inside the entrance to her jade terrace relax around the head of his stalk.

Only then did he begin to thrust against her again, cautiously, and ardently, edging deeper and deeper into her moist heat, feeling her virgin walls give way to his hard intrusion, coating him with its hot love juices, cheering him, daring him inside to taste her delight.

He raised his head and gazed down at her, watching the passion in her eyes, listening to the moans of pleasure coming from her throat, mingling with his, filling the room with melodies of love.

Deeper and deeper he plunged, until the tip of his shaft hit that delicate barrier inside her that proved he was the first man to tread upon the sacred ground of her valley of solitude. An amazing rush of testosterone and adrenaline swept through Adam's veins at the knowledge, and the animal lust in him overwhelmed everything else, just for a fraction of a second. He pulled back and thrust forward, breaking through Tashi's maidenhead and planting his ambassador inside her, claiming her as his own.

She stiffened beneath him, her eyes wide liquid emerald pools of pain and passion. And when her mouth opened, he leaned over, gathered her tightly into his arms, and swallowed her scream in his mouth, absorbing her pain deep into his own soul. She lay quivering and whimpering, trying desperately to withdraw her body from his.

"It's over, Tashi. The worst is over, *cara*." He soothed her with his words as he dropped soft kisses all over her face, sipping the tears seeping from the corners of her eyes.

She moaned and trembled, and the soft quivering walls of

her vagina tightened around him like a thirsty leech, and he thought he would die from the delicious sensations she aroused in him. He lay still, buried halfway inside her, giving her time and space to adjust to his invasion. He'd claimed his Little Eve. She was his, now and forever.

"Look at me," he whispered when she finally grew still and quiet.

Her lids opened slowly, and her beautiful emerald eyes locked to his. She was so worth the wait, he thought as he found himself drowning in her eyes—her sparkling emerald eyes, once shy, frightened, and subdued, now glowing with life, and light, and trust, and yes—desire. So much desire…

"How do you feel?"

Her lids squeezed shut for a second. "Ur—full, stretched, and stinking a little."

"I'm sorry, but the worst is over, and you did beautifully. There will be nothing but pleasure between us from now on, *cara*."

She nodded and bit into her bottom lip.

"I have to start moving again and it might hurt a little bit more, but I promise the pleasure will come and it will be hotter and stronger than any you've experienced so far. Okay?"

"Okay. It doesn't hurt so much anymore." She gave him a tremulous smile.

That smile sent a hot tide of passion rippling through Adam, and he began to move with love and patience inside her. Back and forth he thrust, each stroke going deeper and deeper. He reveled in the play of emotions in her teary eyes, and soon her painful whimpers turned into sweet moans of ecstasy as the fire mounted in her anew.

His thrusts built in speed and force and soon she wrapped her legs around his hips moving beneath him, matching his rhythm as together they danced the intimate, primitive dance of love.

She arched her back and trembled beneath his possessive invasion. The shocking heat soared to Adam's heart. He watched with delightful satisfaction as the sensual emotions and waves of ecstasy rippled through her honeycombed body. He cherished the changes in the pupils of her large green eyes—the dilating, the hazing, the glazing. He wrapped his arms around her and clasped her buttocks in his palms holding her securely as he loved her.

Tashi felt heat, raw and pulsing, rising in her like the hottest fire. Her body vibrated with the force from the leaping flames. She whimpered against Adam's ears as the solid impact of his deep thrusts ricocheted through her. Instinctively, her legs tightened about his waist, her heels dug into his buttocks, and she raised her hips and drew him deeper into her hot body.

Her act of complete submission seemed to heighten his lust. His hips had a mind of their own and began thrusting wildly into her slick softness. He rode her hard and fast as if she were a tenacious mare he'd trapped in a corner of the coral, and needed to bring under subjugation.

Tashi shrieked as wave after wave of an oncoming orgasm began to crash through her body. Her heart was on fire. The walls of her passion cave throbbed and contracted so ferociously around Adam's jade stalk, she could feel every pulsing vein in him as he pulled the heat, the passion, the hunger out of her, feasted on them, then gave them right back.

And as the flames from the battering friction of raw flesh against raw flesh engulfed her, Tashi let out a ragged sound, somewhere between a sob, a moan, a scream. Her body tensed, and then she exploded as spurt after spurt of fire cannonballed though her. Adam rode her right through the exquisite typhoon and soon she felt another building, even before the previous one had passed.

"How does it feel now, Tashi?" he moaned as he drove deeply and solidly into her.

"Sweet. Hot. Full. Like I'm dying," she cried.

"Yes, my love. Hot and sweet. Let's die together."

Adam pulled his hands from beneath Tashi, and clasping hers, he entwined their fingers and spread their arms above her head, flat against the mattress. He bent over her and as she twisted and bucked beneath him, Adam thrust himself into her, each stroke lifting her hips off the bed, only to slam her back into the softness of the mattress.

All his nerve endings, all his senses were riveting between his legs as she moaned, matching his quick stabbing thrusts with her own jerky moves. Adam held those sensations in check, sending them to every crevice of his being until he was a throbbing machine of desire, driving him and Tashi through the sacred spaces of their intimacy where divine winds danced between them, binding their souls together on an ever pulsating sea of love.

Drenched in sweat, Adam felt the familiar tingling along his spine, and the heavy rush of semen bubbling in his groin and speeding toward the tip of his cock.

His lungs started closing up and he knew it was over for him. Adam's back stiffened as a tsunami of lightning bolts churned in his groin and ripped through his pumping body. He tightened his hold on Tashi's hands and pressed them harder into the mattress. He bared his teeth, trying to capture the electrifying moment, fighting the flames that threatened to consume him as Tashi locked her body to his, sealing their wet skins together while the hot velvety walls of her vagina tautened and quaked around his aching shaft as she teetered on the realm of yet another orgasm.

The sweetness of her love, the heat of her wantonness, the friction of her desire was too much for Adam to handle. He reared up over Tashi and held her legs wide apart as he plunged into her fast and deep. Her breasts jiggled and bounced, making him hotter and harder, driving him toward his own release. And soon his face was twisting in exquisite pain as he ground his hips against hers in the last desperate thrusts. He came down hard, crushing her tender breasts beneath his chest while his hair spread out like a veil across her face, some mingling with her red curls. He buried his face in the soft pulsing hollow of her throat, and a harsh animal sound rumbled through the air as the liquid dam of fire broke, plunging him into the consuming heat.

"Tashi!" He cried out in a wild voice as he felt himself being swept along with her into the sizzling vortex of sweet surrender. His cries mingled with the shrill screams that ripped from her throat. His body shook with tremendous force and he erupted inside Tashi, spilling his hot seed deep into the receptive softness of her open waiting womb. Her muscles sucked him, forcing the last drop of semen from his shaft and the final tremors from his body.

As he lay trembling on the succulent woman beneath him, and gulping desperate air into his constricted lungs, for the first time in his life Adam Andreas experienced what the French call, '*La petite mort*', and the Italians, '*La piccolo morte*'.

In the early pre-dawn light, Adam held a sleeping Tashi close to his heart and basked in the humble pleasure of finally lying naked with her without having to curtail his desire as he'd done a few weeks ago. Three times last night he'd delighted himself in her, emptied himself into her fertile womb before hunger and fatigue had overtaken them both.

Since they'd skipped dinner, they'd awakened totally famished, and he'd ordered up a five-course meal from Ristorante Andreas to satisfy their hunger for food. After eating, they'd shared a bath, and while washing each other's bodies, their appetite for each other had returned with robust force. Adam had taken Tashi in the warm bubbly water of the hot tub before they eventually moved back to the bedroom where they'd loved their brains out until they both slipped into a state of gratified unconsciousness with their lifeless limbs twisted about each other.

Even though they weren't married yet, there was something distinctly holy about falling asleep in Tashi's womanly arms after making love. It felt like a primitive rite, like their bodies were in love with each other, just as surely as their hearts and souls were.

Never in the eleven years since his first sexual experience did Adam feel such a sense of oneness and completeness with a woman as he did with Tashi. And judging from her insatiable appetite for him, her violent reaction to his lovemaking, her cries of abandoned ecstasy, and the indescribable expressions of bliss on her face when she climaxed, Adam was sure Tashi had also felt complete in her love from him, and for him.

It had to be the mutual, yet unspoken love between them. Nothing but love could have synched their bodies so perfectly and sacredly, and transported them to that pinnacle of divine delight where each died, only to be reborn in the other.

It was a height Adam had never attained with any of his former lovers—all of whom were experienced and who'd come to him with their individual bags of tricks. They'd attained physical gratification together, but as he lay in the aftermath of lovemaking, Adam had always felt like something was missing. He'd found that *something*, last night.

Last night, he and Tashi had bathed in the pools of each other's light, soared to passion's highest mount on each other's sighs, tumbled together into desire's whirlwind, over and over again, until they'd spun themselves into dizziness and danced themselves beyond the horizons of earthly boundaries.

Tashi had come to him, untouched, inexperienced, with no tricks up her sleeve, and yet she'd satisfied him beyond his wildest imagination. His heart was in love for the first time. He was certain of that now as it pounded wildly against his chest at the knowledge that he'd found his *Anam Cara*, the woman his mother had promised would bring him the most natural feeling in the world—the feeling of coming home.

Adam knew he'd come home from the moment he'd met Tashi, from that first touch, that first glance. The three days he'd lusted after her, longed for her was just as natural as what he'd done for her when he'd climbed through her bedroom window that night. Their two and a half weeks of living together was natural. And last night, it had felt natural when he'd shut the door on the world, and within the existence of her love become nonexistent.

Adam tightened his arms around Tashi and kissed the top of her head. Instinctively, she moaned in her sleep and snuggled her delicate little derriere into his groin. His body trembled and his cock pulsed once in response to her nudge, then it pulsed again with blissful memories of being sheathed inside her tight hot woman's flesh.

Adam hungered for her again, but he'd promised to let her sleep. She'd earned her right to her beauty nap for their impending nuptials. In a few hours, they would be standing in the parlor in front of Pastor Kelly and Dr. Samantha and promise to love, cherish, and protect each other for the rest of their lives. They would exchange their vows knowing that their marriage was temporary—a pack of lies to anyone who was aware of the truth.

For Adam, those vows would be the most significant, meaningful, and truthful he would ever make to himself or any other human. Tashi was his life now, his reason for living, the air he breathed and soon, he hoped, opening his palm over the flat expanse of her stomach, he would make a vow of protection to another little human—his child. The next generation of Andreases. It had been two weeks since Tashi's last period, so he knew she was possibly in the ovulating stage of her cycle. He was so relieved that she hadn't asked him to use protection yesterday.

Adam closed his eyes and breathed in Tashi's intoxicating scent mingled with the musky odor of recent lovemaking. A baby, he knew, would keep her grounded. He didn't think she would want her child to grow up without knowing its father, as she had.

Yesterday, they'd talked about everything, but that. He'd waited for her to bring up the subject of her father, but she hadn't, and realizing that it might be too painful and or embarrassing for her, he hadn't broached the subject either. He was sure that when she was ready, she would talk about what it was like not knowing him, not having him in her life—something he could never relate to.

In the meantime, Adam would show Tashi how much she was loved. He would be her husband, her friend, and her lover. Whether or not they found Paul alive, Tashi was no temporary bride. She was his. Forever.

Adam frowned into the predawn darkness. When she'd related the details of that night in New York City, Tashi had mentioned that Paul had said that he would explain everything to her when he arrived in Granite Falls. Could 'everything' be about her father?

Adam's body tensed as a worrisome thought fired inside his brain.

Dear God, could it be?

CHAPTER SIXTEEN

On Monday morning, Adam stepped into the foyer of his fourteenth floor penthouse office suite at Hotel Andreas, and almost ran over his personal assistant who was waiting for him at the elevator.

"Good morning, Mr. Andreas," she said, handing him a stack of papers.

"Good morning, Ms. Jenkins."

"Welcome back. It's good to have you back," she added, hurrying along beside him as he made his way to his office on the far side of the building that overlooked Crystal Lake and the Presidential Range of the White Mountains. He had his own private elevator, but to save time, he'd used the one closest to Noelle's office so they could talk on the way to his.

He glanced down at the top sheet of paper on the pile—a response from the owner of a vineyard in California he'd set his eyes on. Andreas International owned several wineries in Italy, France, and Australia, but none here at home. His grandfather had never been interested—in fact he didn't think that California's soil, topography, and climate could compare to the steep-terraced vineyards of Piedmont, Puglia, and Sardinia where the bulk of Andreas wine was produced. Adam was out to test his theory.

"Well, it's not as if I really left, Ms. Jenkins," he said, giving his attention back to his assistant. "You and I have been in constant communication for the past two weeks."

"Yes, Mr. Andreas, but it's nice to have you here in the flesh. Everything runs a lot smoother when you're around."

They turned a corner and headed down a commodious corridor that served as a waiting area with comfy leather sofas, chairs and tables, along with coffee, espresso, juice, and water machines. The corridor ended at a one-way mirrored wall that separated and protected his office from the waiting area. "Are you suggesting that my staff slacks off when I'm absent?"

"Definitely not, sir. I'm just saying that it's nicer when you're around. People miss you. Your smile, actually, I've heard them say. Word is that you're very different from your father. Not that he wasn't liked, but—" She shrugged. "I'm sure you understand what I'm trying to say."

Adam gave the attractive brunette a placating smile. Noelle Jenkins was fresh out of Princeton when he hired her four years ago to replace his father's middle-aged assistant who was more like a seasoned butler whose main goal in life was to kiss Alessandro's ass. Adam did not need an ass-kisser. He kissed his own ass. Noelle came with stellar recommendations. She was intelligent, candid, and spoke several languages, including Italian. But what really earned her the position as his assistant were the facts that she wasn't intimidated by him, and she didn't hint at the possibility of a future sexual liaison between them, like some of her feminine counterparts had done.

"I understand, Ms. Jenkins," he said, opening the glass door to his office and walking inside. "It's nice to know I'm missed, and liked." Adam dropped the pile of papers and his briefcase on his desk and dropped his weight into his chair. "Speaking of which, how is Ms. Marshall doing in the boutique?"

"Mindy is doing well, sir. H.R. is helping her with enrollment into Evergreen State College. She should begin classes in the fall."

"Good." Adam folded his arms and gazed up at Noelle as she slid into her chair on the other side of his desk with her tablet at the ready for his day's instructions. Although he would like to keep his change in marital status a secret, for now, he felt she needed to know, just in case his wife ever called asking for him. Tashi had his private numbers, but providing her another avenue through which to reach him, could not hurt. "Ms. Jenkins, I'm about to share something with you—something I will ask that you not publicize. You cannot tell anyone. Do you understand?"

She straightened her shoulders and gave him her customary professional nod.

"I'm no longer a bachelor. I'm married."

Her hand flew to her chest. "You're married? Is that where you were, on your honeymoon, sir?"

A quiver ripped through Adam's gut. Yep. He'd been honeymooning all weekend. After exchanging their vows, he and Tashi had returned to the bedroom to consummate their marriage. They'd remained locked away in each other's arms until it was time to get ready for Little Erik's birthday party. They'd arrived at the LaCrosse Estate where Erik and Michelle now lived—an hour ahead of the other guests—just enough time for him to introduce the gang to his new bride, tell them how they met and the fact that they'd been living together for the past couple weeks, but not enough to bring them up to date on her past and the reason he'd married her. Well, not the real one, but the one he was prepared to tell.

They'd all been shocked, but given the circumstances under which each one of them had gotten married, they were in no position to judge his rash rush to the altar. They'd congratulated them, and welcomed Tashi into the family, as he'd expected they would. Then Bryce and Kaya had mentioned seeing Tashi at the shopping mall outlets the same day he and Tashi met, and that Kaya had thought she was beautiful and would be perfect for Adam.

Adam's heart had skipped a beat at the knowledge that he was not alone in thinking that Tashi was perfect for him. Finally, he could understand what his friends had felt when they met their wives. Like him, they'd each found their *Anam Cara*—their soul friend, their soul mate for life. His search was over.

He and Tashi had left the party early to hurry back home to do what newlyweds did in the privacy of their bedroom, the bathroom, the kitchen, the terrace... They'd taken advantage of having the house to themselves before his staff returned, and so for the rest of Saturday and all day Sunday, they'd walked around naked and made love wherever and whenever the desire arose—which was often—very often, he thought on heated memories. Trouble was ahead of them, and Adam wanted Tashi to enjoy her time with him before it came raining down on them.

"Mr. Andreas." Noelle's enthusiastic voice pulled him into the present.

Adam shook his head to clear his thoughts. He could not contain the big grin that splashed across his face.

"Congratulations, sir. This is the best-kept secret of the century. I wish you and your bride a long and happy life together."

"Thank you, Ms. Jenkins." His eyes followed hers to his ring-less finger. He'd opted not to wear his wedding band in public to keep curious minds at bay. However, there was no reason for Tashi not to wear hers since no one but Pastor and Mrs. Kelly, and his three friends knew who she was, and to whom she was married.

Noelle's brows furrowed. "Do I know her, sir?"

"Um—no. She's not from around here, but when the time is right, you will meet her." And that was all he was prepared to say about his wife. It wasn't just the threat from New York he had to worry about. Tashi had made an appointment to see Samantha this morning, then she was having lunch in public with the other wives. He didn't want the local paparazzi harassing her, chasing her around Granite Falls and taking pictures of her to be plastered around the world. He had four more days before he had to officially file their marriage certificate, after which he would have no control over who knew what. He wanted those four days to be as pleasant and stress-free as possible for Tashi.

"Remember, not a word to anyone. But if my wife calls for me, you are to put her through immediately. Also, if anyone else calls, or shows up with information or questions about her, you are to buzz me directly."

"Yes, sir."

Adam proceeded to give Noelle a list of duties he needed performed immediately, which included arranging meetings—both in person and via satellite, organizing travel arrangements, and preparing correspondence to various heads of Andreas International departments, both domestic and abroad, and further researching the Neighborhood Winery in California. He was just about finished with his instructions when the elevator that led directly from the underground garage to his office chimed, indicating that his first meeting for the day was on the way up.

"That will be all, Ms. Jenkins. I think you have enough to keep you busy for the rest of the day. And, I'm not to be disturbed for the next hour or so."

"Yes, Mr. Andreas. I will see that you're not, and I will get going on these right away." She pointed to her tablet as she stood to her feet. Knowing better than to question him about his unmentioned appointment, she immediately left, closing the door behind her.

Adam stood and stepped to the elevator, reaching it at the moment it stopped. Three men, dressed in dark business suits, filed off the elevator, each greeting him with a hug and a slap on the back and another round of congratulations on his recent marriage.

"So why this early meeting?" Massimo asked with a grin. "Has your bride flown the coop? Is she a fugitive, already?"

If his cousin's questions didn't elucidate the reason for the meeting so accurately, Adam would join the laughter.

"Is she reluctant, buddy?" Bryce gave his shoulder a commiserative squeeze.

"Well, we know she isn't a secret." Erik punched his arm, playfully.

"Ha-ha," Adam said in mock humor.

"All joking aside, Tashi seems very sweet," Bryce said. "I'm happy for you, brother."

"Me, too," Erik added. "I'm glad you have a wife so you can stop using your goddaughter to pick up women. You think Michelle and I don't know what you've been doing with our sweet little angel?"

Adam chuckled. "Using!" he declared in an affronted tone. "I love Tiff as if she were my own daughter. I enjoy spending time with her."

"You've always wanted children," Massimo stated. "So perhaps you and Tashi should start a family right away. It would make Uncle Alessandro happy, and besides, Aria needs a little cousin to play with."

Adam smiled as he recalled the fond memories of himself and Mass playing together, and fighting each other as children. "I would love nothing more than to be holding my son or my daughter in my arms, nine months from now," he said, his heart jolting at the thought. "But I have to keep my wife safe and alive before I can enjoy that blessing."

"What?" The men looked at him with puzzled frowns.

"Is Tashi in some kind of trouble, Adam?" Massimo asked. "You know I had my share of problems with Eddie's threats against Shaina and Cameron. What's going on, and how can we help?"

"Yeah, buddy. I can only imagine the gravity of the situation since Tashi was afraid to go to the hospital when she became ill."

"When was Tashi sick?" Bryce gave Erik a black look. "Wait a minute, you knew about Tashi all along?"

Adam exchanged a confederate glance with Erik. "Yes, Erik knew. I called him. Tashi needed a doctor, and he was the only one I could trust."

All eyes turned on Erik. "That's why you tried to talk us out of visiting him last Friday," Massimo stated in exasperation. "Why didn't you just tell us the truth? We would have understood."

"He couldn't." Adam spoke up in defense of his friend. "I had sworn him to secrecy."

"Against us? I thought we were a team and that we shared everything." Massimo's blue eyes pierced Adam's. "I guess I was mistaken."

"Come on, guys." Erik glanced from one to the other. "Why don't you just hear Adam out? You should be more concerned about why he kept Tashi a secret rather than the fact that he did." He shrugged impatiently. "I don't even know why. He never shared his reason with me."

"Erik's right. We've all kept secrets from each other for various reasons, but we do share when we're ready." Massimo gave Adam a twisted smile of apology.

"Especially you, Mass," Bryce stated. "You only recently told us how you and Shaina really met." He turned to Adam. "If you're ready to talk, buddy, we're here to listen."

Adam expelled a heavy breath, thankful for his friends' concern, but piqued that he had to repeat the details of that night. He'd convinced Tashi that it was best the gang knew about New York, so that they could all look out for her until the threat to her life—their lives—had been eliminated.

"I think we need to sit for this." The men followed him across the office to a cluster of chairs near the glass wall that overlooked Crystal Lake. "Coffee or espresso for anyone?" he asked, glancing at the bar that separated the chairs from a long conference table with more chairs arranged around it.

"No, we're good," Bryce responded for all. "Just tell us what's going on, Adam."

Adam waited until they were seated. "You already know how I met Tashi at Mountainview Café," he said diving right in. "But what you don't know is that three days later, I got a panicked call from her at two thirty in the morning. She'd been sick for three days with salmonella poisoning. When I got to her apartment, she was too weak to go to the door and let me in. I had to climb through her bedroom window to rescue her."

"So why didn't she go to the hospital?" Bryce repeated the question he'd asked a few minutes ago, in a tone laced with concern and curiosity rather than agitation.

"Didn't she have any friends or family, a neighbor who could have helped her, at least given her a ride to the emergency room?" Massimo brushed his fingers through his shoulder-length hair.

A chill rushed through Adam as the image of Tashi on the bed flashed across his mind. Never will she ever be in that condition again, he vowed. "No," he said blandly. "Tashi has—had no one." She had him now, and hopefully, his friends as well after he brought them up to date. "Tashi couldn't go to the hospital because she's on the lam."

"From whom, the authorities?" Bryce asked.

"Possibly," Adam replied on a nod of his head. "But other people are also looking for her. Bad people. who want to kill her, and who would probably kill anyone who stood between her and them."

Adam shuddered at the look of horror on his friends' faces as their bodies jerked forward in the chairs. It got so quiet in the room, he swore he could hear Noelle typing away on her keyboard on the other side of the building.

Finally, Massimo asked the questions, no one else wanted to. "Are our wives in danger for hanging out with yours, Adam?"

"Possibly," he said on another nod.

"But they're supposed to have lunch together today." Bryce reached for his phone. "Perhaps I should call Kaya—"

"I should call Michelle." Erik reached for his.

"There's no need, guys." Adam stopped them with a swipe of his hand when his cousin reached into his pocket. If he were in their places, he would be doing the same damn thing. What good was a husband, a father, if he didn't worry about his family's safety and protection? "They're all safe for today. I've hired a team of armed bodyguards, eight ex-marines to follow Tashi around. She met them this morning, and knows she's being followed, and that she will always be within sight of at least two of them, although they are to remain totally inconspicuous to everyone else. I've cautioned her not to alert your wives. I think the fewer people who know what's going on, the better."

Massimo nodded. "I agree. No need to cause them undue stress. But, who are these people, Adam?"

"And why do they want Tashi dead? What did she do to them?" Erik picked up.

And so, as calmly and precisely as he could, Adam repeated

the story Tashi had relayed to him three days ago. Beginning with her conversation with his parents, he gave them everything except for one tiny little detail—well two.

"*Dio!*" Massimo exclaimed, slapping his hand against his forehead. "This makes Shaina's problems look like a Sunday afternoon picnic."

"No wonder the poor girl was afraid to seek medical attention," Erik said.

"How can you protect her from such evil?" Bryce leaned forward in his seat again.

Adam's eyes darted from one to the other as he anticipated their reaction to what he was about to reveal—the details he'd previously omitted. "The thing is, I never gave you the name of the FBI agent who helped Tashi escape, and I never told you how and why she ended up in Granite Falls." He paused on a deep breath. "It was Paul. Paul Dawson. He sent Tashi here to us, to me. He asked that I marry her, make her my temporary bride and give her the protection of the Andreas name."

Their mouths dropped open and their eyes bulged in their sockets.

"Are you saying that Paul is dead?" Mass shot to his feet and began to pace.

"I hope not." Adam followed him up. "But this—this thing happened last year around the same time you were trying to reach him, Mass."

"*Dio, mio!*" They told me he was unavailable. Not that he was dead."

"Did he say anything to you that could indicate what was going on in his life before he disappeared?" Adam stood in front of his cousin, forcing him to cease his pacing.

Massimo narrowed his eyes. "Well, when we spoke, he said he was working on a top-priority case. He said it was personal, and serious, I think. He'd promised to clue me in later, but as we know, later never came."

"Did he say anything else? Drop any other clue about this case?" Adam asked, his heart hammering in his chest.

Massimo placed his hands on Adam's shoulders. "I'm sorry, cousin, but that's all I have."

"Isn't it obvious?" Erik asked, coming to stand beside them, Bryce following in his wake. "You want Massimo to confirm what you already suspect."

Massimo stared at Erik. "And what's that?"

Erik spread his hands. "Tashi might be Paul's daughter."

Adam closed his eyes as the words sank into his gut. He'd suspected it. Had felt it, ever since Tashi had told him about the sacrifice Paul had made for her. Very few men would go to such lengths to protect another person, unless it was a loved one. Adam just hadn't wanted to believe it, and so he'd allowed his desire for Tashi to overwhelm his logic, the honor and trust Paul had put in him to keep his daughter safe and probably still intact.

"You must have suspected, Adam," Bryce said, pulling him out of his trance. "I mean, Tashi's biracial, like Kaya. Is her mother white?"

Adam nodded. "She inherited her mother's auburn hair and emerald eyes."

"Then her father must be black or of some other non-Caucasian ethnicity. Paul is black. And he risked his life for her. His actions supersede those of an FBI agent doing his job. That's the behavior of a father or a husband. I would have done the same for Kaya and any of my five children."

"He must not have known about Tashi," Erik offered his opinion. "Or else he would have told us about her. Paul's not the kind of man who would walk away from his responsibilities. He would not have walked away from his child."

"He'd probably just found out about her when we spoke last

year. God, I can't imagine discovering that I had a kid twenty-odd years ago, and then lost her before I had the chance to get to know her. He obviously didn't get a chance to tell her that he was her father before that night. He was probably just working up to it." Massimo paused and his lips twisted in thought. "Are you guys forgetting that Paul had a younger brother?"

"Yeah," Bryce replied. "He was a New York City fireman. He died in the Twin Towers. Tashi could be George's daughter, which would make her Paul's niece."

"It's possible," Erik concurred.

"Paul and George did not get along. They hadn't spoken in years," Adam said. "Even up to the day he died—something Paul told me he would always regret. So if Tashi is his niece, I could understand why he would put his life in danger for her. She's family."

A long brittle silence ensued as the men tried to absorb the information and deal with the fact that one of their best friends might be dead. Adam didn't know which possibility he would welcome more: the fact that Tashi was Paul's daughter or his niece.

"Anyone up for an espresso?" Massimo broke the silence and walked over to the bar.

"I'd love a couple shots of tequila, after what I just heard," Bryce said, "but I have meetings all day."

"I have surgery in two hours," Erik said as they all joined Mass at the bar.

"Then espresso for everyone." Mass busied himself at the machine.

"I knew it," Adam said, dropping his weight on a bar stool as he watched his cousin make the first cup. "I just didn't want to believe it."

"You did what Paul asked." Erik tossed Adam a smile. "You brought Tashi under the protection of the Andreas name by marrying her. You were attracted to each other long before you knew who she was. I saw the way you looked at her the night you took her to the mansion. Your temporary marriage just happens to come with benefits."

Bryce chuckled. "I don't think there's anything temporary about Adam's bride or his marriage. You heard him hoping for a baby in nine months. They haven't been using protection. Are those the actions of a man who intends to end his marriage?"

"From the moment I met Tashi, I knew I couldn't live without her. I just knew. It was as if we were old souls who'd parted in a past life and had spent centuries searching for each other again. I've never felt that way about any one. Ever! I have no intention of ever letting her go, not even for Paul," Adam declared with an emphatic shake of his head.

"Finally, cousin, you do understand the power of serendipitous love. The gut-wrenching, heart-stopping knowing when it's right. We've all experienced it." Massimo plunked down four cups of espresso on the counter. "We're all so very blessed to have such amazing, hot, sexy, brilliant women in our lives. I'd like to propose a toast to Adam and Tashi."

Adam's heart flooded with warmth and indescribable love for his wife, as they all stood to their feet, picked up their cups, and held them high in the air, huge grins on each of their faces.

Bryce took the initiative. "To Adam and Tashi. May they be as happy and fulfilled in their marriage as we are in ours."

They sipped espresso, very carefully, then Erik said, "We haven't made our club's toast for a while, not since Aria was born."

The others agreed and raised their cups again. "To God, to Life, to Love, to Family, to Friends, to Prosperity," Adam recited the Billionaire Club's fifteen-year-old mantra, along with his dearest, most trusted friends. It was a toast they'd written and pledged to recite when anything monumental happened in any of their lives—personal or professional. These occasions included marriages, births, and professional accomplishments. They also included deaths to celebrate the life of the deceased. They'd toasted four deaths since the inception: Cassie, Pilar, and Michael and Lauren. He hoped to God it would be decades before they had to lay a friend or family member to rest again.

Adam waited until they were all seated again before voicing his thoughts. "I don't know about the rest of you, but I don't think Paul is dead. He's too damned good at what he does. I think he might have infiltrated that organization and is just waiting for his chance to blow them apart from the inside out. He's one of the best field ops in the FBI."

"I agree." Erik held his espresso halfway to his lips. "There has to be a good reason he hasn't contacted us."

"He's probably waiting for us to contact him," Bryce said. "We have to do it discretely so we don't tip off the wrong people and lead them back to Granite Falls."

"Until we want them tipped off." Adam was ready for this fiasco to be over, so he and Tashi could begin living in peace and harmony. He longed for balance.

"I know just the man for the job." Massimo pulled his cell from his pocket.

"Your own personal New York City bitch," Adam said with a wide grin.

All four men burst into laughter as Mass dialed the number and handed Adam his phone.

※

Tashi felt a thousand pounds lighter when she walked out of Dr. Samantha Kelly's office and headed in the direction of the elevator in the mill building that lined the Aiken Riverfront.

Adam had suggested that she speak with the therapist to help with her healing process. Not only had the doctor addressed Tashi's guilt over possibly causing Agent Dawson's death, but she'd also identified schemas of exclusion, vulnerability, paranoia, and perfectionism she said Tashi possessed.

Dr. Kelly had described these schemas as mental concepts based on the situations and experiences of her childhood, and that her feelings of abandonment, anxiety, and mistrust were direct by-products of these schemas. She'd added that her schemas had been richly magnified by the way her uncle had raised her. No wonder she'd never been able to form lasting friendships. *And abandonment?* Tashi hadn't even realized that she'd felt abandoned as a result of her mother dying when she was so young, and the hard fact that she didn't know the identity of her father. *Unknown.*

Tashi shook the word from her head as she pushed the down arrow for the elevator. Dr. Kelly had stated that the best way to rid herself of these negative schemas was to do something extremely different from what she was accustomed to. Break her habits. If she weren't the wife of the minister who'd married them, Tashi would have told her that she'd already broken one habit. She'd made love outside the bonds of marriage, didn't feel guilty, had enjoyed it immensely, and had even hoped to procure a child from that sweet illicit union.

Yes, talking with Dr. Kelly was very therapeutic. Between her, yoga, and meditation, Tashi knew that she was well on her way to a total emotional overhaul.

When the elevator stopped, Tashi boarded it and turned her back on the two other occupants riding down with her. Three weeks ago, she would have been too paranoid to be cornered in an elevator with two strange muscular men, and would have waited for the next elevator. But the fact that Daisy, one of her two bodyguards for the day, stepped on behind her, gave her a measure of security. Her schema of paranoia wouldn't go away so easily. Her involvement with the shooting in New York and the whereabouts of Agent Paul Dawson had to be resolved before she would feel totally safe and be able to move forward with her life, wherever or with whomever it might be.

Adam had introduced her to the security team of five men and three women this morning. She was to be under constant covert surveillance every second she was off the Andreas estate. They were not to make eye contact with her, or approach her unless there was a direct attempt on her life. She was to act as if they didn't even exist. When Tashi had suggested that she would be safer if she were chauffeured around instead of driving herself, Adam's response was that she would draw less attention to herself and to whom she was married if her bodyguards were incognito.

Even though the plan had recharged the anxieties that had begun to dissipate while she was secluded on the estate, Tashi had given her consent for its implementation. What else could she do? She was safer with Adam in plain sight of danger than out on her own cloaked in obscurity. If Agent Dawson trusted Adam, then she should too. And so with that thought in mind, she had put her faith and her life in her husband's hands.

Her husband. Tashi's breath caught in her throat. She was a married woman, and one who was head-over-heels in love with her husband. She quivered as wanton images of her and Adam tangled up together on the bed, in the shower, and the Jacuzzi, surged to the forefront of her mind. Her steps were wobbly when she left the elevator and strolled toward the automatic doors—the two men and Daisy bringing up the rear.

It was only a few hours ago that Tashi had been writhing in pleasure under her husband yet her body craved the touch of his hands and his mouth, the carnal desires he aroused in her. If it weren't for the fact that Adam had told her he would be in meetings all day, Tashi would have canceled her lunch date with

Michelle, Kaya, and Shaina, gotten into her stylish sports car and driven to the northeast corner of town to Andreas International headquarters to pay her husband a surprise visit.

She had to be sensible. Adam had cut back on his duties as CEO of Andreas International for two and a half weeks to take care of her. She would be a responsible, understanding wife and give him time and space to devote to the professional part of his life. She didn't want to come off as needy and suffocating even though Dr. Kelly had said that apart from being a new bride, her constant desire to be in Adam's presence was a result of the fact that he was the first person since her horrifying ordeal who'd been kind and honest with her. He was the only person she trusted, for now. It was natural that she would want to maintain and strengthen that bond.

Tashi exited the building, donned her sunglasses, and strolled leisurely across the esplanade that ran along the banks of the river. It was Monday midday and even this early in the day and week, the residents and visitors of Granite Falls were out enjoying the beautiful weather, the discounts, and the delicious food from the myriad of boutiques, restaurants, and cafés.

Children and adults danced—most, comically off rhythm—to the live music of a local band that had set up shop in the gazebo situated in the center of the esplanade. Tashi didn't blame them. This was New England and in a few months, this colorful pandemonium of people, chairs, tables, umbrellas, and live music would be gone, and the esplanade would be cold and deserted. It made sense to dance and play while the sun was shining.

Tashi felt happy, alive for the first time in her life. Her second winter in Granite Falls would be a far cry from her first. And as she anticipated her lunch date with Michelle, Kaya, and Shaina, she realized that she was about to alter another of her schemas:

opening her heart to making new friends, and hopefully growing to trust them.

She'd taken an instant liking to the ladies on Saturday, at Little Erik's birthday party. She was especially fond of Shaina since they were cousins, by law, and their children would be cousins by blood one day. They were all successful, amazing, sophisticated women and Tashi wanted her relationship with them to be as tight as her husband's was with theirs. Adam had told her that she had completed the circle of the Billionaires Brides club. *Trust*, he'd said, was the glue that kept them together. She had to learn to trust.

Tashi pulled her phone from her purse and checked the time. The women would be here soon. She glanced around, trying to find an empty table closest to the riverfront. She spotted an elderly couple vacating one under a big white umbrella with the words "Blue Diamond Bistro" in bold blue letters printed on it. Blue Diamond was a favorite of all the ladies, and so they'd planned to eat lunch there. Besides, it was close to Dr. Kelly's office, and Andretti Industries, whose private underground garage was theirs to use on a crowded day like today. Tashi hurried over to the table and waited quietly while the busboy cleaned it off.

She was about to sit when her cell phone began to play the ringtone she'd assigned to Adam. Her heart began to hammer as she pressed the 'accept' button and raised the phone to her ears.

"*Ciao, bella.*"

"*Ciao.*" Tashi felt as if her throat would close up on her. God, just the sound of his voice made her quiver inside. She fell into the nearest chair at the table and took deep breaths to steady her thumping heart.

"I just wanted to hear your voice," he said. "I miss you."

"I miss you, too. I can come by after my lunch date with the girls."

He growled in frustration. "I would love to see you, *cara*, but—"

"I know... You have to work."

"I'll be tied up in business meetings all day." He uttered a deep sigh of frustration. "Where are you?"

"At the esplanade. I just left Dr. Kelly's office."

"How did your first session go?"

"Really well. I learned a lot about myself. I'll tell you about it later." She hung her purse over the back of her chair and laid one arm across the glass surface of the table.

"Hmm. You alone?"

"Yes, for now. I'm waiting for the girls. I just sat down at a table." She squinted at the noonday sun, shimmering on the river.

"You were delicious this morning," he said, his voice deepening with passion. "I can still taste you in my mouth and smell you on my breath."

The walls of Tashi's vagina began to contract violently at her husband's erotic words. "Adam," she whispered, and glanced around wondering if her neighbors could guess the subject of their conversation.

"Close your eyes."

"What?" Tashi's mouth trembled.

"Close your eyes and think of me."

Tashi took a deep breath and did as he asked. It wasn't like anyone would know her eyes were closed since they were hidden behind her sunglasses, and she was facing the river. Turning her back on a crowd was something she would not have done three weeks ago. Plus, even though she couldn't see them, she knew her bodyguards were keeping a watchful eye on her. "Okay," she said, relaxing into the cushion of the chair. "I'm thinking of you."

"Tell me your sexual fantasy. What do you see?"

Tashi inhaled sharply at the indecent request. Not what she expected, but… "I see me lying naked on the bed—no, no, on the floor of your yoga sanctuary."

"*Our* yoga sanctuary, *cara*."

"Our yoga sanctuary. Our bodies are bathed in moonlight and you—you're bending over me, your long hair fanned out over my chest like a silky mist."

"And?" he prompted, hoarsely.

Caught up in the enthusiasm, Tashi continued in a low sultry voice, "You're thrusting deep inside me, and I can feel every inch of your huge pulsing cock…"

CHAPTER SEVENTEEN

Oh my God. She'd said cock. Tashi squeezed her legs together to combat the earthquake and the torrent of fluids gushing from inside her. She felt wicked and sinful engaging in phone sex with her husband in broad daylight in the midst of a bustling crowd, and whispering words like *cock*. When did she become such a strumpet, the proverbial preacher's daughter gone wild? She felt like the lead role in *The Awakening of Tashi Holland*.

"What's my huge, pulsing cock doing to you, baby? How is it making you feel?"

The sound of Adam's unsteady breaths and his sexy baritone voice squeezed a soft erotic moan out of her. She crossed her legs and locked her knees together. Her toes curled in her fashionable sandals as she fought to control her arousal.

"Excuse me, Miss. My name is Gina and I'm your attendant today. Can I start you off with something to drink?"

"Huh?" Tashi's eyes flew open and she stared into the questioning ones of a young, pretty girl. She hastily pulled herself together and sat up straight. The inner walls of her vagina were still pulsating and her panties were soaked through, but there was nothing she could do about them at the moment.

"Just a second," she said to the girl. "I have to go," she whispered to Adam.

"I don't want you to go. I want you to come. For me."

"Adam, the waitress is standing right here. I promise I'll do that later." Wanton frustrations edged through her at being interrupted just when her phone sex was getting good, and the young waitress was too untrained to take a walk and let her finish her conversation.

But Adam was not one to let it go. "Say it. Say you'll come for me later. Over and over again while I'm thrusting deep inside you."

Oh, God. This raunchy side of her husband was one Tashi never expected, and it was making her horny and dizzy. She cupped her hand over her mouth and said in a low voice, "Okay, Adam. I'll come for you later, over and over again while you're thrusting deep inside me."

"*Vedo l'ora, mia cara.* Have a great lunch, and enjoy your time with the girls, Mrs. Andreas." And with that he was gone.

Mrs. Andreas. That's who she was. Tashi kept the phone glued to her ears for a few seconds while she tried to bring herself down from that unexpected sexual high. When she thought she could speak without stuttering, she placed it into her purse and gazed up at the waitress. "I'm sorry."

"That's okay. Did you have a chance to check the drink menu?" She pointed to the two-sided laminated menu stuck between the salt and pepper shakers on the table.

"No. Um—I'll just have—um a bottle of sparkling water with a glass of ice." She was stuttering anyway. "And I'm waiting for some friends. There will be four of us."

When the waitress left, Tashi turned sideways in her chair and cased the crowd, looking for her friends who were now fifteen minutes late. She supposed being tardy was excusable when one had children to attend to, especially for Kaya who had five and Michelle who had three. Seeing the women and children in action at the LaCrosse mansion was an eye-popping experience for Tashi. Even though they had nannies, those women were totally devoted to their children and paid attention to their little grumblings as well as their cries of laughter.

Tashi rubbed her left hand over her belly as a warm smile parted her lips. If she were lucky, she would have her own baby in nine months. The morning after she and Adam first made love and hours before their wedding, Tashi had pointed out the fact that they hadn't used protection. Adam had asked if she regretted it and if she wanted to start some method of birth-control, and when she'd responded negatively, he'd said neither did he. Adam hadn't come right out and said it, but a pregnancy, Tashi knew, would make their temporary marriage permanent, and her husband very happy to have his own child to love, even if he didn't love its mother. *Yet.*

Tashi's smile widened as she recalled the tenderness in Adam's expression as he'd cradled Massimo and Shaina's daughter, Aria, in his arms, spoke to her tenderly in Italian, and then how enthusiastically he'd played with Bryce and Kaya's twins, Eli and Elyse, making funny faces and garbling sounds as they squealed with excitement. The kids seemed to love their Uncle Adam, especially Alyssa, Anastasia, and Tiffany who followed him around ceaselessly. He was definitely a big hit with the girls. Adam had told her it was his hair they loved. True. They were always grabbing it, tugging on it, playing with it like a kitten plays with its tail. And Alyssa had pinned a couple of barrettes in it that Adam had worn proudly around.

Tashi had gotten a glimpse into her future as she'd watched Adam and the other husbands romping on the floor with all the kids. Even Jason and Precious who she would think were too old for romping, had been drawn into the fun. This magnificent circle of friends and family really loved each other, and…

"Are you Adam's wife?"

Tashi's body stiffened in alarm, but remembering who she was—an Andreas—where she was in a public place, and who was watching her, she took a deep breath and turned her head in the direction of the voice. An attractive medium-height, athletic-looking brunette in casual attire was standing on the other side of the table. Tashi frowned as mild curiosity replaced her initial unease. "Who are you?"

"I'm sorry." The woman extended a hand. "I'm Claire Forsythe. I'm an old friend of Adam's. We go way back to childhood."

Well that didn't explain how she knew her, Tashi thought shaking her hand. Adam hadn't made their marriage public knowledge. Only his close friends knew. Out of old habit, she made no attempt to give up her name or any other personal information.

Tashi watched as Claire pulled out a chair on the other side of the table and quite presumptuously sat down. "My sister was at Little Erik's birthday party on Saturday. She has a son his age. She told me she saw Adam with a strange woman who was wearing a wedding ring, even though he wasn't wearing one." Claire Forsythe's eyes zeroed in on Tashi's ring finger still resting on her stomach.

Strange! Really?

"She accidently captured you in the background of one of the pictures she took of the kids," Claire said.

Since she and Adam had left the party shortly after the other guests began to arrive, Tashi was sure it was a calculated move, and that Claire's sister had taken more than one picture of her. Instinctively, her right hand came up to finger the rings—a platinum wedding band and an enormous diamond engagement ring both studded with emeralds and aquamarine stones. The engagement ring belonged to Adam's maternal grandmother. He'd had it sized for her the day they'd decided to get married.

Her husband had done a lot of things that day when she was otherwise occupied: ordering a new wardrobe—complete with shoes and handbags—from Joanne's Boutique, an exclusive store on Main Street Tashi had passed by many times, and having it delivered on Saturday. He'd ordered a Bugatti Veyron Super Sport car from France that was delivered to the estate this morning. He'd also contacted the DMV about a driver's license with her new name: Tashi Andreas, which she'd picked up before dropping Adam off at Hotel Andreas and heading across town to see Dr. Kelly.

"So it's true. You're his wife." Claire's jarring voice cut into her reverie.

Tashi took off her sunglasses and stared the woman down. Her gut told her that Claire Forsythe was not here to congratulate her, and that she had some ulterior motive in mind when she'd decided to approach her. She knew she was on her own. Even though Claire was blatantly rude, she wasn't a threat. Her bodyguards would not intervene unless the woman made an attempt to bodily harm her. Besides, she felt calm and balanced due to both her yoga and meditation sessions with Adam and her talk with Dr. Kelly this morning. She wasn't going to let this insignificant gnat that had flittered into her air space fluster her. "I guess you and my husband aren't that close, or he would have informed you of our marriage."

"Oh, you're a catty little thing," Clare hissed, her brown eyes darkening with resentment. "Maybe Adam hasn't made your marriage public because it's a farce, or maybe he's ashamed of you. Ha! He isn't even wearing a ring."

Those words cut Tashi to the core, but she pressed her lips together as the waitress approached them. She forced a smile as the girl placed a tray with her bottle of water, her glass of ice, and four menus on the table.

"I see one of your friends has arrived," she said, opening the bottle and pouring some water into the glass. "What can I get for you?" she asked Claire.

"She's not my friend, and she isn't staying," Tashi said in a cold and exact tone.

"Oh, I'm sorry. I just assumed because she's sitting here."

"Thanks, Gina."

The poor girl took off, wheeling through the cluster of tables like she was dodging bullets.

"Tell me, Mrs. Andreas, has your husband told you that he loves you?" Claire resumed her attack.

"I don't see how that's any of your business." Which one of Adam's past serious relationships was she? Tashi wondered, even as her stomach churned at the reality in Claire's question. She took a sip of her water and welcomed the cool bubbly liquid splashing against her throat.

Claire flashed an evil grin. "He hasn't, has he? So, it wasn't for love. What's the real reason he married a mousy little thing like you? What do you have on him? Did you get pregnant on purpose? Is that how you landed him?"

"Oh my God, Claire. You had your chance and blew it. Stop making a fool of yourself."

At the sound of Michelle's calm and collected voice behind her, Tashi let out the breath she'd been holding. She turned as her friends filed into rank around the table like guardian angels to the rescue. They were sophisticatedly dressed in body-hugging designer dresses, sandals, and carrying purses she was certain were as expensive as the one she'd chosen to use today instead of her backpack.

Her backpack days were over, she supposed. She was an Andreas, and she had to present herself as one. Refraining from emotional outbursts in public when approached by venom like Claire Forsythe was expected. Her friends knew the rules, and kept their calm even though she could feel the rage and the disdain simmering behind their eyes.

"Adam is done with you," Kaya said, coming to stand on one side of Claire. "It's been ten years. Get over it. Get over him, already."

Shaina stood on the other side, glaring down on her as if she wanted to punch a hole in her throat. "If that huge rock on my cousin's finger doesn't shout, 'I've moved on', I don't know what does."

Warmth crept into Tashi's cheeks at being called someone's cousin, even though it was only by law. She not only had friends. She had family.

"That's still to be determined," Claire spat, her gaze bouncing from one woman to the next. "Adam isn't even wearing a wedding band. That should tell you a lot."

"You're in my seat," Michelle said through clenched teeth, her black eyes flashing murder. "No one invited you to sit at this table, and no one wants you to stay. So do us all a favor and go project your demons somewhere else."

"We're attracting attention." Tashi nudged her head in the direction of the tables to their left and right. She didn't want attention. She didn't want her bodyguards thinking they needed to intervene.

Shaina and Kaya stepped back, giving their uninvited guest hardly enough space to squeeze past them.

Claire stood up and flipped her glossy long hair over her shoulders. "Good luck, Mrs. Andreas. You'll need it when Adam tires of you. Don't say I didn't warn you." She glared at the ladies and walked away as indecorously as she'd arrived.

The ladies exchanged hugs and kisses as if Claire was never even there, and then Shaina and Michelle settled into the seats on the opposite side of the table while Kaya sat next to Tashi, who was bubbling inside. It was nice to have friends to look out for her—someone besides paid bodyguards to watch her back. She could have handled Claire on her own, and she was just about to tell her to go take a dive into the river when the ladies showed up. This was an honor she never had before. She was quickly learning the benefits of girlfriend bonding. If she'd had this kind of support in New York, she wouldn't have gotten mixed up in Scottie's sick game, but then, she wouldn't have had to flee to Granite Falls, and she wouldn't have met Adam.

"Who was she?" Tashi asked the ladies as they looped their bags over the backs of their chairs. It was good to know who her enemies were, especially the ones who filled her with misgivings about her marriage and her husband's feelings for her. "She said she was Adam's friend. That they'd been friends since childhood."

"She's not his friend. She's his ex. His nosy, pathetic ex." Shaina picked up her menu and flipped through it absentmindedly.

"The one who left him at the altar?"

Kaya did a double take. "Adam told you about her?"

With her finger, Tashi made little circles in the condensation on the side of her glass. "Just that he was left standing at the altar. He didn't mention her name."

Michelle combed her red-tipped fingers through her short crop of black hair. "That's because her name is not worth mentioning. But yes, that was her."

"You must tell Adam that she approached you," Kaya said, her face clouding with uneasiness. "You don't want her to become another Victoria."

The looks the women exchanged sent disturbing quakes rumbling through Tashi. "Who's Victoria?" she asked Kaya.

"A woman from Bryce's past," she answered in a dismal

voice. She placed a hand on Tashi's arm. "I don't want to spoil our appetites by talking about her. Just promise you'll let Adam know about your encounter with Claire."

"Okay. I'll tell him," Tashi promised even though her mind was congested with confusion and questions.

"How did Claire know who you were, anyway?" Shaina asked. "As far as I know the news of your marriage hasn't hit the local media yet."

"She heard it from her sister who was at Little Erik's birthday party on Saturday."

"Remind me to cross Penelope Forsythe off my list of invitees," Michelle said. "Why did she approach you? What did she want?"

"She wanted to know if Adam has told me that he loves me." Tashi's voice dropped in volume and so did her gaze as three pairs of eyes pierced her. "A weird question, I know."

"Has he?" Kaya's tone was rife with interest.

"No. It's not that kind of marriage." Tashi felt as if she could be truthful with these women. It was part of learning to make herself vulnerable to people she felt cared about her. They'd earned her trust after the way they just chased off Claire, her new nemesis. She would take a thousand Claires over one vicious mobster any day.

"And what is *that* kind of marriage?" Shaina, who was sitting directly across from Tashi, placed her elbows on the table and made a bridge with her hands to support her chin.

Tashi shrugged. "We didn't marry for love. He married me to—" Tashi stopped in midsentence. She'd given Adam permission to talk to the men about New York and Agent Dawson, but he'd warned her not to say anything to the ladies about that night or about her bodyguards. The less they knew, the safer they would all be. She shrugged again. "It's a temporary marriage. He's helping me with something. That's why he isn't wearing a wedding ring." Her last statement was a half-truth.

The women laughed and high-fived each other like high school girls at a lunch table.

"Why is it so funny?" Tashi frowned at them.

Kaya threw her arm around her shoulders. "We're not laughing at you, Tashi, but ever since we met you, we were wondering what adjective bride you were."

"Adjective bride? What do you mean?"

Michelle reached over and picked up Tashi's glass. "May I?"

"Go ahead."

Michelle took a few sips, passed it to Shania for her sips, who passed it to Kaya for hers, who placed it back in front of Tashi. Tashi took the last sip, then refilled the glass, emptying the bottle. She loved having friends to share things with, even simple things like a glass of sparkling water.

"It's like this," Michelle said, finally. "None of our husbands married us for love."

"Well, that's what they thought." Shaina stroked her long black hair and tucked some strands behind her ears.

"No, it's what they told us," Kaya corrected her.

Michelle cleared her throat. "I was Erik's Secret Bride."

"Bryce's Reluctant Bride." Kaya raised her hand.

"Massimo's Fugitive Bride," Shaina finished with an animated grin. "We'll explain the adjectives later," she added as if reading Tashi's next question.

"Then I guess I'm Adam's Temporary Bride." Tashi chuckled along with the ladies, finally comprehending the source of their humor.

From the corners of her eyes, Tashi noticed the family of four on her right vacating their table, and just as quickly as she'd grabbed this one, two women who looked to be in their mid-thirties slid into the chairs while the busboy cleaned it off. One of the women gave her a flash of white teeth—somewhere between a fake smile and a leer.

"I would go out on a limb and guess that these ladies are your friends." Gina's voice drew Tashi's attention back to her table. "I mean, you guys are laughing and everything, not like the one who left."

She glanced up at the girl. "Yes, Gina. These ladies are my friends, and they're staying."

"Oh, thank God. Gina pulled her pad from her apron pocket. "Have you had a chance to look at the menus yet?"

"We're regulars," Kaya informed her.

"And unfortunately, I'm new. This is my third day."

"You're doing fine," Michelle assured her. "We'll make it easy for you since we already know what we want. We'll start out with sparkling water like our *friend*." She gave Tashi a wide grin of camaraderie.

They made their orders and as soon as the waitress left, Kaya said, "There's nothing temporary about your marriage to Adam, Tashi. If he didn't love you, he wouldn't have married you."

"But he hasn't told me. It's like Claire said." Tashi kept her voice low, hoping her neighbors didn't hear her statement over the music.

Shaina reached across the table and patted Tashi's hand. "As *we* said, none of our husbands married us for love. They're unconventional men, who marry unconventional women for unconventional reasons. But deep down inside, they know it's for love and they know it's forever when they're exchanging their vows."

"He was about to exchange vows with Claire, ten years ago. He apparently loved her. The fact that she's the one who called it off suggests that he didn't think marrying her at the time was a mistake."

Tashi had to think logically, now that her friends had shed

light on her husband's possible state of mind when he entered this temporary marriage with her. He'd told Tashi that he felt lucky Claire had jilted him, but what if she wanted him back? Is that why Kaya had given her that morbid warning? Had Victoria tried to steal Bryce back from her? With worrying about people trying to kill her, the last thing Tashi needed was Adam's jealous ex breathing down her neck. Kaya was right to suggest that she let Adam know about Claire. But what if he thought she was the jealous one who couldn't deal with the women from his past?

Gina brought out three bottles of sparkling water and glasses of ice. She promised that their orders would be out shortly, before she moved on to the neighboring table. Tashi felt uneasy about the women, but since they seemed to be ignoring her, she pushed her misgivings aside. She'd been living in paranoia way too long. *I'm safe with Adam*, she told herself.

"From what Massimo told me, it was Uncle Alessandro who was pressuring Adam back then." Shaina resumed the conversation. "He wanted grandchildren. He didn't care if his son was miserable. Adam was young and malleable ten years ago, and he was willing to sacrifice his happiness to make his father happy. Believe me, if he loved Claire, she would be sitting where you're sitting right now."

"And what a catastrophe that would have been." Kaya wrinkled her nose and shook her head, causing her long brown curls to sweep back and forth across her bare shoulders.

"Can you imagine us suffering through lunch, and playtime, and our once-a-month get-together with her?" Shaina shivered as if she'd walked into a blast of frigid air.

One thing that was explicitly clear to Tashi was that these women did not like Claire.

"She would not have lasted that long." Michelle spoke with dazzling firmness as she smiled at Tashi. "Bottom line is, if

Adam didn't love you and intend to make your marriage permanent, you wouldn't be sitting here with us."

"She's right," Shaina concurred. "So, please put Claire Forsythe, and *temporary* out of your mind, cousin. You're here to stay."

Shaina's words perked up Tashi's spirit. "Okay," she said. "I'll forget about Claire. On a different note, I propose a toast to new friends and family."

They picked up their glasses, and Michelle said, "To friendship, and love, and children. Speaking of which—" She ruffled her lips. "I'm pregnant again."

"Michelle! Both Shaina and Kaya screamed. Shaina threw her arms about her, and Kaya rushed around the table to hug her.

Tashi felt a deep pang in the core of her womb. Thankfully, her moan was lost in the joyful screams. "How far along are you?" she asked Michelle, wondering if their babies would be born around the same time. She had no proof, yet, but deep in her heart and her soul, she just knew she was pregnant with Adam's baby.

"Just a month. I promised Erik seven children, and he means to pull every one of them out of me." She chuckled. "Actually, I love it. I love being pregnant. I love the thought of a new life growing inside me. And pregnant sex is so awesome, especially in the last trimester."

"I know, girl. It's like your body comes alive at the slightest touch, and you become this quivering ball of nerves." Kaya's eyes turned a deeper shade of brown as she obviously reminisced about making love with her husband.

"It's not just that." Shaina's eyes sparkled with intimate memories. "When I was pregnant with Aria, Massimo's lovemaking became so intense that it scared me at times. It was as if he was trying to touch his child inside me. My God, it was so thrilling. And I swear, since we got the okay to start making love again, it's been better than before. But," she added, "I'm not ready to have another baby. Mass and I want to devote quality time to Aria before she has to share us with a sibling. Maybe in a couple years."

"Same here. My twins are only seventeen months, and between them and my nephew and nieces, it will be a couple years before Bryce and I even think about making another baby." Kaya turned to Tashi. "What about you and Adam? Are you guys planning on starting a family anytime soon?"

Tashi felt a fluttering in her belly, but she fought the urge to rub it. "Well, Adam and I just got married, and we haven't discussed children." Which wasn't really a lie. They'd discussed birth control, but not children.

"Are you using protection?" Michelle asked, quite bluntly.

"No."

"Then you've discussed it. You might be pregnant already. You know they have tests that will tell you as early as a week after conception."

"They do? I thought you had to wait to miss your period."

"No, girl. How early will you know?"

Tashi puckered her lips. "Well, I had my period about two weeks ago, and we made love on Friday for the first time, so maybe by the end of this week. Friday or Saturday, I guess."

"I'll give you Dr. Walsh's contact info. She's Erik's partner. She's great. She delivered Kaya's twins, and Aria. You'll love her," Shaina promised.

"Okay, thank you." Tashi's heart beat with anticipation as she pictured the look on Adam's face when she told him she was going to have his baby. She hoped it would be a look of pure joy, and not disdain. *Did you trap him by getting pregnant?* Claire's insolent question rang in her head, but she forced it away. Adam had already admitted that he didn't regret them not using protection before their marriage, and he hadn't suggested that they start after it. *So there.*

"Wouldn't it be awesome if we could all get pregnant at the same time and drive our husbands crazy when they have to deal with our mood swings and our bizarre cravings?" Kaya asked.

Shaina laughed. "They wouldn't have each other to complain to because they'd all be going through the same crap at the same time."

"I like that," Michelle said. "It's definitely something we should aim for in a few years. "I'll probably be on baby number four by then."

They agreed, and toasted their plan, and then their orders arrived. As they ate their gourmet salads and grilled seafood and pasta dishes, Tashi learned a lot more about her new family and friends. Bryce and Kaya had recently moved into their new estate on Mount Reservoir, just a few acres away from the Andreas Estate. In fact, they were all living on the mountain now, while Erik and Bryce's parents had, respectively, taken up residence in the lake houses their children had vacated.

She also learned about the stories behind each bride's 'adjectives'. Shaina's, she thought, was downright hilarious, especially because of Massimo's past reputation with women. Tashi felt even closer to Shaina when she learned they'd both lived in New York around the same time.

She also learned about Michelle's career as a *New York Times* bestselling author, her charity—Children of the Future Foundation—a home that took in disadvantaged children and that had recently opened up in the neighboring town of Evergreen. Michelle managed the organization of her foundation. Kaya, an interior decorator, had designed the interior. Also a gourmet cook, she managed the kitchen staff that prepared three free meals a day. Shaina, a math teacher, facilitated a free tutoring service to anyone who came through the doors. Upon hearing that Tashi studied photography, they asked for her assistance with photos for local, national, and international media.

When they asked about her past and how she ended up in Granite Falls, she told them half the truth: that she was from Ohio, had gone to study photography in New York and that she'd come to Granite Falls on the suggestions of a friend to photograph the beautiful landscapes since nature was her focus in college. She told them how she and Adam met at Mountainview Café, and the night he crept through her bedroom window to rescue her, then took her back to Andreas Estate to take care of her. And now that she had Adam, and new friends, she had reasons to stay.

As soon as she was finished relaying the truncated story of her most recent past, Tashi noticed the women at the table on her right leaving. She breathed a sigh of relief.

Then somehow the topic of conversation moved to Dr. Kelly after Tashi mentioned that she'd seen her earlier in the day to help her deal with the loss of her mother at an early age and issues about the way she was raised.

"Well, you're in good hands with Samantha," Kaya said. "She helped the kids deal with the loss of their parents, and she counseled Bryce and me about being substitute parents, and even how to strengthen and deepen our marriage. We still see her from time to time, as a family, just to talk. No marriage, no partnership is trouble-free. But as long as you stay on course, stay focused, you'll reach your goals, whatever they are."

"I know Mass sees her, even though he's too macho to admit it." Shaina held her spoon on her plate and, using her fork, she picked up some linguini and twirled it into the spoon like a true Italian wife. "He's still dealing with the pain his father caused his mother. He thought he was over it, but they resurfaced when he decided to connect with Galen."

Tashi had met Galen at the party on Saturday. He was a handsome young man, with curly dark hair, hazel eyes, and a killer smile like his older brother. The nannies and single moms had been vying for his attention, but somehow she felt that he wasn't interested. She wondered if he had a girlfriend already, and if he did, why she wasn't with him.

"Don't get me wrong," Shaina was saying. "I know Mass loves Galen and he's been a wonderful big brother to him this past year, but knowing that his mother and sister are dead because of his father's liaison with Galen's mother isn't something he can forget or even forgive. But at least he isn't blaming Galen anymore."

"Deep wounds are hard to heal," Michelle said, placing her fork on her plate. "I may as well confess that I see Samantha, too." She turned to Tashi. "You don't know this, but it was my father who killed Erik's first wife."

"Precious' mother?" Tashi's eyes bulged.

"Yes. Well, he raised my brother and me, but he wasn't our biological father." She paused. "It's a long story and I will tell you about it another time. The point is, I finally told Precious about the man who killed her mother. I just thought she should hear the truth from me and not someone else."

"How did she take it?"

Michelle sat back in her chair and looked off for a second. "She was shocked, mad, and didn't talk to me for days, wouldn't even look at me. She was upset at her father for marrying me, too. I was scared that I'd ruined our friendship. In the initial stage of our relationship, I kept secrets from Erik that he found out from someone else. It took him a long time to get over that betrayal. We almost didn't make it back to each other."

"That was Bridget Ashley's fault," Kaya interjected.

"Who's Bridget Ashley?" Tashi asked, chewing on a mouthful of lobster tail.

"Michelle's Claire Forsythe. She tried to keep Michelle and Erik apart." Shaina popped a grilled scallop into her mouth. "But Michelle beat the crap out of her, put her in her place."

Tashi almost choked on her lobster tail. "You fought her?"

Michelle crossed her eyes at Shaina. "No."

Shaina waved her hand dismissively. "I would have. I dare any woman to make a play for my husband. I'll rip her braids, her weave, or her blond hair from her scalp, and then I'll shoot Massimo right through the heart for hurting me."

Kaya chuckled. "You're crazy, Shaina. You know Massimo would never betray you."

Shaina tapped her mouth with her blue napkin. "Seriously, though, if Massimo's mother had been a fighter, she and her daughter might still be alive today. I wouldn't allow any woman to back me into a corner, humiliate me, and make me scared of my husband."

"I hear you, girl. I had to fight Bryce's deceased wife's ghost. He was still in love with her when we got married. I guess first love is hard to get over."

"Well, he got over her," Michelle said, before taking a sip of sparkling water. "Just like Erik got over Cassie."

"Only after I told him that he couldn't have us both, that he had to choose. I kicked him out and told him not to come home until he'd made a decision—whatever it was."

Tashi smiled, happy to know that her marriage wasn't the only eccentric one, and the fact that these women knew how to have innocuous fun with each other. "I guess Bryce chose you." She bumped her shoulder to Kaya's.

Kaya shrugged. "Well, it's not like he can make love to a ghost, and we know how important sex is to them."

They had a hearty laugh and then Tashi turned to Michelle. "So what really happened with Bridget Ashley?"

"Well, Erik's and my problems weren't really Bridget's fault.

By the time we separated, I was tired of fighting for everything in my life." She shook her head, regret livid in her eyes. "And Erik, well, he had no idea how to fight for anything. He'd never had to. Nobody had taught him how. So he didn't fight for me. Bridget saw an opportunity and she took it, but Erik did not succumb to her attempts to seduce him. Even though we were apart and we had no idea if we'd get back together, he remained faithful to me, as I was to him."

"I guess that's true love," Tashi murmured, awed at the kindness of this woman's heart.

"I wasn't about to make the same mistake with Precious," Michelle continued. "I love that little girl like she was my own child. I would jump in front of a speeding train for her just as quickly as I would for Little Erik or Tiffany. Erik suggested that we see Samantha, and in no time, we were back on track. Precious and I are closer than we've ever been. You have to forgive even when it's hard, but especially when it's least expected."

Tashi's heart warmed to the group of remarkable women God had placed in her life. They could teach her so much about life and relationships and love. She didn't feel so naïve when she learned that both Kaya and Shaina had been virgin brides like her, and that Michelle had only been with one other man before Erik. It was nice to have sisters with whom to share such intimate details and still walk away feeling dignified and sophisticated.

Before they parted, they made plans to shop for the perfect dresses at Joanne's Boutique the next day. Bryce's parents were celebrating their forty-fifth wedding anniversary at Hotel Andreas the day after. According to the girls, it would be a night to remember.

CHAPTER EIGHTEEN

A few hours after her lunch with the girls, and after stopping at the hotel boutiques to say a quick hello to Mindy, Tashi walked into the room that used to be Adam's home office before he moved to the more spacious one across the hall. Glancing around, she bit into her lower lip as she tried to visualize the photography equipment, furniture and other decorative pieces Kaya had promised to help pick out to beautify the now empty spaces.

During breakfast with Adam this morning, she'd mentioned her desire to advance her photography career. She needed something to occupy her days while he was at Andreas International Headquarters in downtown Granite Falls. Adam had suggested this room as her home office, the place where Tashi Holland Photography would come to life. He'd also pointed out the added benefit of merely crossing the hall to indulge in her sweetness on days he worked at home.

Tashi's cheeks flushed with memories and promises, but knowing they would leave her in a state of frustration, she pushed the thoughts aside, and gave the room a sweeping glance.

It wasn't even half the size of Adam's, but it was still a lot more than she needed. Heck, it was bigger than the apartment she had in New York, and even in that cramped space, she'd still been able to carve out a nice little corner for her photography apparatus.

She'd left so much personal stuff in her apartment in New York—stuff she wondered if she'd ever see again. Agent Dawson had promised to pack it up and keep it safe. Had he been able to, or had her landlord auctioned off her belongings to pay for the rest of her lease? She had no idea, and no way to find out without revealing her whereabouts to the wrong people.

Sighing deeply, Tashi walked to the glass wall and stared down at the gardeners in the courtyard, trimming the shrubbery and mowing the green lawn that had been neglected for two weeks. She looked beyond the domestic scene to the still green tree line, the majestic mountains, and a gray sky in the background—the calm before the storm, much like her mood. When she'd spoken to Adam this afternoon, he'd told her that he'd already commissioned someone in New York to find Agent Dawson. That bit of news had brought a bittersweet taste to Tashi's mouth.

She wanted him to be found alive and well for a multitude of reasons—first because he deserved to be. She would thank him for saving her from a life of degradation and imminent death, and then in advance for testifying on her behalf to help exonerate her for killing that driver. But it would also mean that her temporary marriage to Adam would come to an end. She would no longer need his protection. But if he weren't found alive, how long would she have to keep living in limbo with bodyguards following her everywhere?

And then there were Adam's feelings to take into consideration. Tashi never missed the flashes of dread that swept across his face each time they spoke about Agent Dawson who was as close to him as his three billionaire friends. It would crush him to find out that his friend was dead.

Tashi had only spent a few minutes with the agent, and yet it brought her pain each time she remembered the mixture of sadness and anxiety in his gentle brown eyes when he'd told her to run. He'd risked his life to save her and she might never know why.

"Mrs. Andreas."

The sound of the voice, rather than the utterance of her name made Tashi turn her head toward the door. She had to get used to being called Mrs. Andreas. A plump woman, whom Adam had told her had been head of the kitchen staff since he was a child, stood just inside the door. She was wearing a red skirt and a white top with a black apron tied around her waist—the official Andreas household employee attire.

When Adam had introduced her to his household staff, Tashi had given them permission to call her Tashi. None had acknowledged her request, but had insisted she addressed them by their first names. Tashi didn't understand this blurred line of formality and informality between employer and staff, but according to Adam that was the way it had been for as long as he could remember. If the servants didn't mind, she supposed she shouldn't. One thing the staff all had in common was their determination to make her feel at ease.

Tashi had returned home to a household bustling with activity. Window washing, dusting, floor polishing, gardeners gardening, cabana boys pooling... It would take her a while to get used to people hurrying about the house after the tranquil two weeks she and Adam had just shared.

"Mrs. Andreas."

Tashi harnessed her wandering thoughts and smiled at the woman. "Yes, Prudence."

"The garden is prepared and everything you requested for dinner has been delivered and stored in the refrigerator. Everything, that is, except the oysters."

"You couldn't find any oysters?" Tashi asked, walking toward her.

"Oh, no. I'm just waiting until it's closer to the time when Mr. Andreas arrives. He likes his oysters freshly shucked."

Tashi felt a tweak of embarrassment that this woman knew her husband much better than she did. Upon her return to the mansion, Prudence had approached her about dinner choices and arrangements. Tashi had been at a loss. Since he'd brought her to his home, Adam had been in charge of the meals—both choosing and preparing them. She had no idea which appetizers or wine complemented which main dishes, and which dessert completed the meal.

She had so much to learn about the etiquette of the rich and famous. But to save herself from seeming like a fool in front of her staff, she had announced that she and her husband would have a moonlight picnic in the garden. The girls had told her that men loved surprises—sexy ones—and that she had to be creative in keeping Adam interested and their passion alive. Recalling Claire's threats, Tashi had decided to give her husband a sexy surprise tonight. She didn't want him thinking that he was missing anything.

"What time does Mr. Andreas usually get home?" she asked Prudence.

"It depends, Mrs. Andreas, but usually between six and seven o'clock. And sometime he doesn't—"

She caught herself and stopped, dropping her gaze to her white slippers—the only type of footwear allowed on the second and third floors.

Tashi knew exactly what she was going to say. It was no secret that Adam had spent many nights at his penthouse suite with his former lovers. Claire Forsythe was one of those lovers, she thought, as her insecurity raised its ugly head. Even though the ladies had told her to forget Claire, Tashi couldn't forget the woman's questions about Adam's love or lack of love for her. But 'had' and 'former' were the operative words here, and the fact that Adam never made love with Claire or any of the others in the bed they'd shared gave her a hint of hope that she was different, a little more special than any of the women in his past. She didn't have to fight any images of Adam and any other woman in his bedroom. The only memories he would have of making love in his huge white bed were with her. He was coming home to her tonight and every night as long as they were married.

Home. The word filled her with ecstasy. She shared a home with Adam. A home, where hopefully, they'd welcome a baby soon. Her hand automatically went to her stomach. Was this the way her mother felt when she'd found out she was pregnant with her? Tashi wondered. Was she excited even though she wasn't married, and didn't know the identity of the father of her baby? Shaking off the shattering reality that she might never know her father, Tashi jutted her chin and straightened her shoulders with dignity. "Seven o'clock, you said? That's kind of late."

Prudence smiled as if asking for forgiveness for her near implied insult. "If you would call Mr. Andreas to confirm his estimated time of arrival, I would have a better idea of when to shuck the oysters and have them delivered, Mrs. Andreas."

"Thank you, Prudence. I will do just that and get back to you."

Prudence curtsied as if to a queen and backed away.

I'm never going to get used to all this bowing and reverence, Tashi thought as she left the empty room and walked across the hall into Adam's office.

Adam rocked to Robin Thicke's "Blurred Lines" blasting through his car stereo as he sped west on Route 80 toward Mount Reservoir. A huge grin was splattered on his face as he thought of his 'good girl' wife who'd turned nasty on him. He chuckled, still unable to believe she'd actually said the word "cock" in their way-too-brief phone sex conversation this morning.

His sweet little innocent virgin Tashi had evolved overnight into a wanton hussy. He loved it, and so did his cock, he thought as it stirred against the restriction of his trousers. He couldn't believe how excited he was about going home after a long day's work to someone he cared about, someone in whose arms he longed to spend himself, and then fall asleep. But as he turned off Route 80 on to Mount Reservoir Way, and passed the road that led to the Forsythes' home, Adam's excitement ground to a halt.

He glanced at his dashboard clock. He had just enough time to make a quick stop before arriving home at the appointed time he'd promised his wife he'd be there. Adam applied his brakes and pulled to the side of the road. He waited for several cars to pass by before making a clean U-turn. This wouldn't take long. Not at all.

Five minutes later, he was knocking on the front door of the Forsythe mansion, and a few seconds later their prim-faced butler opened it. "Good day, Mr. Andreas," he said, bowing to Adam.

"Good day, Jimmy. I'm here to see Ms. Claire. Is she in?"

"She is, sir." Jimmy stood aside and ushered him inside. "I believe she's reclining at the outdoor pool, sir. Is she expecting you? Should I announce you?"

"That won't be necessary, Jimmy. Thank you."

Adam walked through the house that he'd frequented ten years ago when he and Claire were seeing each other, and it was as stuffy and boring as it was back then. He couldn't believe that he'd even considered becoming a member of this snobbish family. He turned right at a long hallway, paying no attention to the two maids who were busy dusting off paintings on the walls. He was grateful that Claire's parents were out of town, sparing him the trouble of suffering through meaningless pleasantries with them.

He'd seethed with rage earlier today when Daisy had informed him that Claire had approached Tashi at the esplanade. Luckily for him, Daisy read lips, so she was able to tell him exactly what Claire had said to his wife. No way was he going to let this slide. Tashi would not become another Pilar. No way in hell.

"Adam!" Claire rose from her lounge chair as he took the few steps from the patio to the poolside. "This is an unexpected surprise, darling."

Adam swallowed his repulsion as she ran forward, scantily clad in a navy blue bikini that covered very little of her ashen white body. What did he ever see in her? Adam took a backward step as she attempted to embrace him.

"What's the matter, darling? Not even a hug for old times' sake?" Her lips ruffled and her eyes narrowed with mock confusion as if she didn't know why he'd darkened the doorway of her family's home for the first time since she'd left him at the altar.

"This is not a social call, Claire, as you well know," he said, staring at her painted face. She wore far too much makeup. "I'm here to warn you, in person, to stay away from my wife."

She waved her hand dismissively. "I was just toying with the little thing, Adam. She obviously can't take the heat of competition. She ran straight to you whining like the insecure little girl she is."

Competition? She actually believed that she and Tashi were in some kind of competition for his affection? Had she taken a good look at his new bride? And how could she be so mean and insensitive when she herself had once been the victim of abuse and ridicule? Adam felt pity for her more than anything else, but he would be damned if he'd let her demons inflict pain on his wife, or him for that matter. Perhaps he should have been blunt when she'd come begging him for another chance. There was no reason for him to be cruel back then, but now…

He cleared his throat. "I never told you before, Claire, because I didn't want to hurt you, but perhaps I should have, if for nothing else, to spare us this futile conversation ten years after our near fiasco. So here it is: I never loved you. Not even for a minute, and that's why—as you've mentioned in the past—you never heard those words from me. However, I love my father, and I was willing to marry you to make him happy, give him the grandchildren he wanted. You spared our families a lifetime of misery by unceremoniously dumping me at the altar. It was the best thing you ever did for me. Looking at you now, it would have been the worst mistake of my life to breed with you."

She clasped her hands to her flushed cheeks. "Adam, you don't mean that." Tears formed in her eyes, but Adam wasn't moved. "You've never said anything unkind to me before, not even after I left you at the altar, for which I have apologized profusely. You've changed."

Yes! Love changes you.

"Look at what this girl has turned you into. She's definitely not of our social status. What hole did you dig her out of, Adam? She must have tricked you into marrying her, but I can save you, darling." She reached a hand toward his face.

Adam jumped back again, knocked his heel against the bottom step, and almost lost his balance. He quickly straightened himself up. The woman was delusional, and quite frankly, it scared him a little. "Claire," he said in a lethal cold voice, "I'm warning you. Stay away from my wife. If you even look at her, much less approach her again to engage her in conversation, I swear I'll—"

"What Adam? What will you do?" She stared, challenging him.

Adam fisted his hands at his sides. He swore to God he could strangle her with his bare hands and feel nothing as he watched the life drain out of her. His stomach churned with disgust at the thought that he'd once been intimate with her.

"You don't want to find out, Claire." Adam turned a deaf ear to her gasps, and his back on her appalled face. He retraced his steps through the house and made his way to the front door, slamming it behind him.

※

Twenty minutes later, Adam walked into his master suite to find a note from his wife: *Adam, join me in the garden for dinner. We're spending the night. Tashi.*

After a quick shower, and instructions to his staff not to disturb him, even if the sky was falling down around them, Adam left his cell phone behind and set out to join his wife.

His heart was beating a mile a minute as he passed the flagpole with the white flag flying at full staff. He tried to remember ever being this nervous about going to meet a woman, and he couldn't think of one single occasion. When it came to women, he was always in control, especially of his emotions. Tashi Holland Andreas had stripped him of that power.

Since the night he'd rescued her, today was the first day they'd been separated, and he'd missed her something awful.

He'd been experiencing moments of breathlessness every time he thought of her. Yep, he'd been suffering from Tashi Withdrawal. He was hooked, addicted to her.

The rushing sound of the waterfall alerted Adam that he was nearing the garden. His steps quickened as his mind wandered back to the first time he'd brought Tashi to his home. That night while Tashi's specific reason and her benefit for meeting him had been as clear as day, he'd wondered about his reason and benefit for meeting her.

The answer was simple: Love. Just by *being*, Tashi had shown him what it meant to love someone so genuinely and unconditionally that without her existence, he had none. Love was his benefit, not just love for Tashi, but love for himself, because loving Tashi meant loving Adam—something he hadn't done for years, because he hadn't really liked the person he'd become—the temporary man who'd been hesitant or afraid to commit. Well, he was committed now.

He liked that Tashi was taking the initiative in planning intimate moments for them only days after her first sexual experience. She was still somewhat shy when it came to matters of lovemaking, but she was quickly learning about what he liked in bed, as he was learning about her needs, which were infinite and insatiable.

It was the first time they would spend the night in the garden and he suspected that it was the suddenly crowded mansion that had prompted her to plan their night of seclusion. After two weeks of solitude and quiet with her, the return of his household staff wasn't something he'd been looking forward to. He wanted more alone time with her—private time and space, without thoughts of, or intrusion from the outside world. The garden would provide that, for now.

Adam rounded the bend that brought his sacred sanctuary into view. He was half-expecting a naked Tashi to be standing on the platform waiting for him. His disappointment quickly melted into anticipation, excitement, and curiosity, at the thought of her laid out on the bed in the bedroom.

Adam ran across the lawn and up the steps. He stopped at the foyer to catch his breath and shrug out of his clothes, dropping them in the basket on top of Tashi's. Soft music and floral fragrances twirled around him, and he noticed a few oversized pillows scattered about the platform indicating that Tashi had engaged in a session of yoga and meditation.

He stepped up onto the platform and took the three steps leading down to the bedroom. Without knocking, he slowly opened the door. The room was empty, but a fire was glowing behind the encased hearth of the granite fireplace. Perhaps she was in the bathroom, preparing to make an enticing entrance. "Tashi."

"Out here, Adam, by the pool."

Adam retraced his steps and walked over to the poolside area. He stopped in his tracks. A tent-like cabana made from metal posts staked into the ground, with white netting for the roof and walls, and a pole-to-pole red rug had been erected on the lawn. Cushions of varying sizes were strewn about the romantic little lair.

But the thing that made Adam's heart stop, then begin to thunder loudly in his chest was the sight of his wife, reclined on an oversize white chaise lounge, with her flaming red hair fanned out above her head. One leg was draped over the cushioned back while the other hung off the side with her foot resting on the rug. Her alluring posture allowed Adam a full frontal view of her lotus flower blossoming and glittering beneath the patch of red hair at the apex of her thighs, in which, dear God, was nestled a red cherry.

And if that wasn't enough to take Adam's breath away and send hot aches of lust pumping to his throat and into his cock, the brown sexy body of his young inexperienced wife was covered in whipped cream and slices of fruit—strawberries, kiwi, peaches, pears, bananas, pineapples, melon, and pomegranate seeds, and a piece of chocolate was lodged in her mouth. Tendrils of red hair spilled ardently over her swelling breasts rising like twin hills of love from her chest.

Adam swallowed and his pulsing jade stalk slapped against his belly with impatience as his eyes feasted on the hypnotizing vision his wife presented. She was a goddess, a nymph—far more bewitching than Aphrodite, Venus, Himeros, Inanna, Nanaya, or any of the other deities of love gracing his garden. She was love, lust, eroticism, sensuality and fertility personified. She was sweet fragrance, softness, moisture, and heat all wrapped up into one tantalizing package.

However did he get this lucky?

Adam forced life into his legs and descended the steps, slowly, his eyes locked to Tashi's as he walked the short distance across the granite floor of the poolside and on to the lawn. He parted the silky netting of the cabana, and stood gazing down at his wife. He swallowed the saliva collecting in his mouth. "I guess I don't need to ask what's for dinner."

She attempted to smile and the chocolate fell from her lips, rolled down her chin and nestled into a squirt of whipped cream on her right breast, right next to her nipple hiding under a slice of strawberry.

"I'm sorry. You were supposed to pluck that from my lips." She reached for it.

"Hmm. Sexy." He brushed her hand and her hair away, knelt on the carpet between her opened thighs, and being careful not to disturb her erotic buffet, he lowered his head to her breast. "Hmm," he groaned, as the heat from her body scorched his skin, and her fruity fragrance made his stomach growl with hunger—not for food—but for her.

Adam opened his mouth over her breast and slurped up the strawberry, whipped cream, and chocolate bar. Cradling them securely in his mouth, he licked his way up her chest, to the hollow of her delicate throat, up over her chin, and then he covered her lips and dropped the contents of his mouth into hers. "Ladies first," he whispered.

He closed his eyes and reveled in the erotic sensation of her mouth moving under his, the motion of her rolling tongue as she chewed the bit of morsel. He kissed her deeply and sensuously, sweeping his tongue into her mouth, strumming the roof and the sides of her cheeks until the strawberry and chocolate were gone and she was whimpering against his lips and rubbing herself against his thigh, the moisture and heat from her womanhood coating his flesh, setting him on fire. They gave and took, to and from each other, with sighs and moans of delight until the tart-sweet taste was obliterated.

Adam raised his head and smiled down at her and the passion in her emerald eyes sent spasms of lust through him. "I guess that was my antipasto." He traced his finger around her lips all wet and swollen from their kiss.

"Did you enjoy it?" she asked with a smile laced with shyness and lingering fervor.

"*Moltissimo, grazie, signora.*"

Her smile deepened. "Are you hungry?"

"Only for you, my love." Adam allowed his eyes to graze her slender form and the spread of fruit and cream in which the tips of his mane were now tangled. His cock was pressed hard and tight against his belly and hovered over the entrance of her hidden palace, which wasn't so hidden seeing that her thighs were spread nice and wide. "I've already taken your cherry, you know," he said, glancing at the lone red fruit resting on the red scrub.

"I thought you might like to take it again."

She was nasty, and he loved it, but he did not need an invitation to enjoy his wife. His gaze wandered to a table in the corner of the cabana. It was romantically set for two with a white cloth, a bouquet of red roses and burning votive candles. A bottle of wine and a bottle of sparkling cider were chilling on a smaller nearby table, and a bowl of sliced fruit and a can of whipped cream lay on the carpet next to the lounge. On the other side of the netting, a covered silver, serving platter was warming over burners on the granite countertop of the outdoor kitchen.

Adam couldn't believe what he was about to say when his bride had gone to so much trouble to create this mood for ultimate eroticism, but his gut told him that Tashi's encounter with Claire today had caused her to feel insecure. He could tell her that he'd taken care of the situation, but he wanted her to trust him, to know that she could come to him with her problems, no matter how grave or insignificant she thought they might be.

He didn't want her keeping things from him like Pilar had kept from Bryce. Pilar's tragic death was the very reason they'd started the Billionaire Brides club, to which Tashi was the newest and last member. Daisy had told him that the wives had intervened and sent Claire packing with her tail between her legs. He hoped their defensive move and his warning would be enough to scare Claire. He didn't want to have to deal with her, but he would if she came near his wife again.

"Tashi, why did you do all this?" he asked, bringing his gaze back to her face.

She pouted her lips and her eyes darkened. "You don't like it?"

"I do, but just being in your presence is enticement enough."

"I just want to keep it interesting."

"Tashi," he said with gentle patience, "this is something a spouse would do later on in a marriage when there's trouble or when passion wanes because of the pressures of life and the obligations of raising a family, et al. We just got married two days ago, baby. We're nowhere close to needing this." He swiped his hand around the tent.

Doubt clouded her eyes and she turned her head and gazed out at the cascading waterfalls. "You're used to experienced women and I don't want to bore you. I don't want you to get tired of me."

Adam placed a finger under her chin and turned her face back to him. "Who told you that you would bore me, that I would get tired of you?"

Her lashes crash-landed on her cheeks for a few silent seconds, then she raised them again. "I wasn't going to say anything because I don't want you to think that I'm jealous or insecure, but then Kaya said I should tell you."

"Tell me what?" He had to remember to thank Kaya.

Her chest trembled on a shudder and the slice of strawberry on her left nipple rolled down the side to nestle between the valley of her breasts. "Tell me what?" Adam asked again as he dropped his head and began nibbling on that slice of strawberry.

She trembled and moaned. "I—I—I ran into your—your ex today."

"Which one?" he asked, lapping at the cream on the side of her breast and taking a slice of banana and melon into his mouth. Her heart was beating so ferociously, it gave pulse to his lips as they skipped across the silky heated surface of her skin.

"Cla—Uh—Claire..."

"It's a small town. Where?" He licked at her nipples in turn, rolling his tongue around them before feasting on the slices of kiwi and pineapple on her breasts.

Her fingers burrowed into his hair. "At—at the esplanade when I was—um—wait— Ahh," she screamed when he pulled one of her breasts into his mouth and began to suck her earnestly. She grabbed handfuls of his hair, and her lower body jerked upward bringing their sexes into heated contact. Her leg that had been draped over the back of the chaise lounge crash-landed on his shoulder in a trembling heap.

Adam seized the opportunity to ease her down the lounge so that her sweet little behind was on the edge. He spread her wide, and holding her open with a hand on each of her thighs, he settled between them. "Continue," he said, bending to lick his way over to her other breast. He flicked at her nipple, loving the feel of it hardening against his tongue, and welcoming the sighs of pleasure escaping from her throat. To fan her desire, he pressed his hips into her and began sliding the ridge of his cock along the slickness of her femininity. He felt the pitted cherry pop between them, splaying warm, sticky juices into the hairs at their groins. "Go on, Tashi. I want you to hear exactly what Claire said to you. Tell me everything." His voice was thick and slurred with constrained passion, and a little bit of pain from her tugging on his mane. He licked his way down her breasts, leaving no traces of fruit or cream behind.

"She—um—she asked me if I got pregnant to trap you into marrying me."

"Well, we both know that's not the case." His lips trailed south to her torso. He took his time eating every bit of fruit she'd placed there before he licked her quivering stomach clean of the whipped cream. "What did you say to her?" He used his tongue to pluck the red grape from inside her belly button, and as the sweet juice burst into his mouth, he proceeding to lick the remnants of the whipped cream out of the hollow.

Tashi was trembling now, and her hands were beating out an erratic rhythm on his shoulders, his back, and his head. "I—I didn't re—respond."

"Do you think you're pregnant?" He dropped feathery kisses all over her stomach as he rocked his hips against her.

"I don't—don't know. I feel I might be. Michelle says I could find out by the end of the we—week."

"Hmm..." Adam disconnected their sexes and trailed one hand along her silky thigh toward her moist heat. He parted her and slipped a finger inside her—knuckle deep. Her muscles clamped around him, hot and wet and so tight he had to exert effort to move his finger back and forth.

"Adam," she moaned, trying to squeeze her thighs together to combat the pleasure of his finger moving back and forth inside her. "Oh...Yeah... Oh yes." She began to gyrate her hips, trying to match the rhythm.

With a wicked smile, Adam traced his tongue from her belly button to the outline of her furry groin. He nibbled at the remnants of the crushed cherry, licking her bush clean of the sweet tartness. As usual, her scent thrilled him, and he headed south. He flicked the tip of his tongue against her little swollen yin bean, her musky taste making his cock dribble on his stomach. She gasped and jerked into his mouth. "What else did Claire say?" He traced his tongue along the insides of her folds as he fondled her breast with his other hand, lightly pinching the nipples between his fingers.

"Oh, God, that feels so—so good." She began to buck into his face as her breath came out in sharp short gasps. "Eat me. Yes, eat me."

"Is that what she said?" he asked in mock humor.

"No. No."

Adam glanced up to see her head rolling from side to side on the chaise as her breathing became heavier and more labored. "I want to know what else Claire said, Tashi." He licked up and down her moist heat from her clit to her opening time and time again as little mewling sounds escaped her throat. He loved those wild sounds of nature she made—sounds he'd only heard from the big cats in the jungles of Africa. No other woman had mewled for him. Longing for more, Adam opened his mouth over her naked flesh and began to eat her, and suck her like she was a piece of succulent fruit—only sweeter, so much sweeter and hotter, he thought as his finger delved deeper and faster into her.

She began to ride against his face and press on his head to keep it between her legs. She needn't have worried. He wasn't planning on going anywhere. "Tell me, Tashi. What else did Claire say to you?" He let his hand slide off her breast to her heaving stomach. He opened his palm and pressed the heel to the area just above her groin to heighten her desire.

"Oh, God, I'm gonna… Adam…" She arched upward to meet his hand and his mouth.

"Is that what she said?" he asked easing his pressure, forcing her back from that chasm of ecstasy she was about to topple into.

"No, no," she wailed in frustration. "She—she asked… Oh God…Hmmm… She asked if you—you told me you loved me."

He strummed her clit with his tongue.

"Ummph!"

"What was your response?"

"I um— Oh… God…"

He dragged his tongue down the length of her pleasure trough, moving it left and right so as not to miss one sizzling inch of her, then pulling his finger away, he replaced it with his tongue, pushing it deep inside her, as deep as it would go while his thumb moved up to play with her engorged yin bean. As she called out his name, Adam mixed it up, alternating between his tongue and his finger, easing, then intensifying the pressure until Tashi's whimpers, moans, and unintelligible garble indicated that she had no idea whether she was coming or going.

"Adam, please," she begged in a broken whisper, pulling on his hair as her body twisted like a whirlwind on the lounge.

"Please what?" he asked against her raw flesh. "What do you want, Tashi?"

"Come. I want to come... Let me come...."

"After you tell me how you answered Claire." Adam was done playing with her. He pushed his finger back inside her, and locking his lips over her clit, he feathered it with his tongue as his finger burrowed deeper and faster within her. She was quivering and her teeth were chattering if she was lying naked on a bed of snow. Her thighs clamped around his head in a killer grip as her fingers tightened around his mane, causing him a bit of worry that she would rip handfuls of hair from his scalp. "What did you tell her?" he demanded on a deep groan brimming with a mixture of pleasure and pain.

"I told her— Oh God! Adam. Eat me! Adam... I'm— I'm cooo—ming... I'm coming..."

"Perfect answer, *mon chéri*." Adam chuckled with wicked intentions as he tightened his tongue and jabbed it deep inside her. Her muscles clenched around him like a vise. Her stomach heaved more violently. She uttered a moan that turned into a long mewling cat-like sound. Her body tightened taut as a banjo string, and her breathing stopped for a few seconds before she released her passion on a vigorous tremor and collapsed on the edge of the lounge. He waited, and sighed with satisfaction when a deluge of warm sticky moisture splashed into his mouth. Adam replaced his tongue with his finger and lapped up her delicious woman's juices, all of it while she shuddered under his face and the velvety walls of her vagina contracted around his finger like a wet ring of fire.

When she finally lay still, but still panting, he kissed the insides of her trembling thighs as he slowly and reluctantly pulled his finger from inside her. As he pushed to his feet, he clasped her hips and pulled her buttocks closer to the edge of the lounge, stationing her feet on the cushion. He knelt between her spread thighs and gazed down at her.

Her body was coated with perspiration, her hair a tangled mess above her head. Her eyes were closed, her mouth slightly parted, exhibiting the expression of a woman who'd just been thoroughly satisfied—dreamy and hazy. God, he couldn't wait to be inside her, to feel her slick heat clutching at his thrusting cock like it had clutched at his finger. She'd promised to come for him over and over again tonight, and he wasn't about to let her renege on her promise. Adam's cock twitched against his stomach as if telling him that it was its turn to be inside her. To temporarily oblige it, he reached between Tashi's legs, curled his hand around the aching muscle and stroked it a few times as he crawled up the lounge. Supporting his weight on his elbows and his knees, he bent his head and covered Tashi's mouth with his.

Her eyes popped opened. Her pupils were so large, so wide, Adam felt as if he was free-falling into her enchanting, innocent soul—the soul on whose walls he was determined to hang a plethora of enjoyable, beautiful memories to replace the unpleasant ones she'd had up until now. She opened her mouth to welcome his tongue coated with her juices and the musky smell of her womanhood while her hands caressed his back, lovingly, tenderly as if thanking him for the pleasure he'd brought her. That show of tenderness was just what Adam wanted from her, and as they kissed softly and affectionately, Adam reached between them and, grasping his cock, he blindly aimed the tip toward the entrance of her garden of delight. It hit home on the first thrust.

Tashi stiffened, her nails dug into his back, and her eyes popped open as the head gained entrance and nestled just inside her sweetness. Adam sighed into her mouth as the electrifying sensations of entering a wet furnace washed over him. He lay still for a moment, breathing control into his system. Finally, he raised his head and gazed down at her. "Now for the main course," he said with a heated smile.

She chuckled and he slid a little farther in, conjuring a little "Oohh," out of her.

He thrust again, grazing her tender walls with the rigid head of his shaft, coaxing sweet moans out of her. She licked her lips as she tried to adjust to his size. They'd made love so many times in the past three days, yet each time he entered her, Adam was amazed at the tightness of her body. As she'd mentioned, it was like taking her cherry all over again.

He swallowed the ache of passion in his throat. "You asked me a question three days ago in the kitchen, to which I gave no response," he said. "Do you remember?"

Her forehead crinkled and she shook her head. "No."

"You asked me how I know I didn't love Claire."

She licked her lips again and lowered her lashes.

"Look at me," he commanded softly, as he drew his hips back and thrust, pushing more of his cock into her slippery warmth.

Her lids fluttered open even as her muscles contracted around him, clinging to him, inviting him to go deeper inside her warm feminine abode. "I know I never loved her," he said between a gasp of sheer pleasure, "because—because I didn't feel for her, or any other living soul, what I feel for you. Her leaving me at the altar is the second best thing to ever happen to me."

"What—what's the first?" Her legs tangled around his thighs as she raised her buttocks to meet his downward plunge.

He lay halfway inside her, fighting the need to bury himself and begin some serious thrusting in and out, but he wanted to make sure that she heard every word he was about to utter. He cradled her face in his hands and stared into her eyes. "You, *cara*. You are the utmost best God has ever—will ever bestow on me, and I'm smart enough to know that I need to cherish you, protect you, and honor you with every beat of my heart, every fiber of my being. I swear as I kneel over you, half buried inside you that I am yours now and forever. When I promised to protect you, it wasn't just from the threat in New York. It was from everyone on this planet, including Claire or any of my other exes who might foolishly think they still have a chance with me. They don't. We're not temporary, baby. We're permanent."

Tears gathered in her eyes. "Are you saying—"

"I'm saying... Dear God," Adam hissed as her muscles squeezed him. "I'm saying that I love you, Tashi Evelyn Holland Andreas. I love you." He pulled way out and sank into her, feeling her velvet walls spread with a bit of resistance that only increased the friction between them.

"Oh, Adam, I love you, too. I love you so much." Her arms tightened around his neck and her legs around his waist.

"Then let's seal our love, darling," he whispered, easing back, leaving only the head nestled in her moist heat. "Tell me you love me again. Pledge yourself to me forever," he whispered.

"I love you, Adamo Alessandro Andreas." Tashi moaned as he sank partially into her and stayed there. Her muscles clutched at him.

"And?"

Tashi choked on a soft sob. "And I will never feel insecure again."

"*Sei amato*. Say, '*Sono amata*'! I'm loved." He still didn't move.

"*Sono amata. Sono amata, Adamo,*" she said with an ultra sensuality that rocked Adam's heart and soul and mind to the core.

Her hypnotic emerald eyes sparkled, and as she gazed up at him with and love and surrender, Adam pushed through her tight heat until he felt the tip of his cock hit bottom. He stayed there for a moment, savoring the feel of being sheathed in hot honey. But she wasn't having it. She squeezed her legs against his sides tightening her muscles and increasing the fiery friction as she began to move beneath him, raising her hips, pulling him in, daring him to hold back, and as her tight muscles began to work their lustful magic on him, she pulled his head down and thrust her tongue inside his mouth.

Adam knew he wouldn't last long. He grabbed her hands from around his neck and pressed them into the lounge.

He began to thrust wildly, his buttocks tightening, his hips bucking as their damp bodies slapped together, and their tongues matched the thrusting tempo of their hips. Her velvet muscles gripped him fiercely, trapping him inside her, forbidding his to leave her snug channel as he retreated, but as he pushed forward again, she parted and welcomed him, welcomed the vigor and strength and pleasure of his thrusts.

He was out of control. Lost. With one course in mind. Release. No other woman had ever done that to him. He had always been the one in control. The fiery feel of her was driving him mad with lust, and love and passion. His back stiffened as a distinct bolt of lightning ripped through his pumping body and churned in his groin. He tightened his hold on Tashi's hands and pressed them harder into the cushion of the lounge. His lungs constricted. He clenched his teeth, trying to capture the electrifying moment, fighting the flames that threatened to incinerate him.

"No... No..." he groaned in a continual sensual protest, even as he hammered fiercely into her, even as his tears wet her throat, even as the sweet agony threatened to rip him apart.

"Yes..." Tashi demanded against his ears, opening wider, arching higher to meet each of his powerful downward strokes. He had driven her to the edge of passion's uttermost summit. But she wanted him to surrender to her, first. Her hands were still captured above her head, but Tashi locked her lower body to his, sealing their wet skins together, and tightened all her muscles securely around the hardness of him. "*Scopami di brutto, Adamo! Scopami!*"

On that lubricious command, a harsh sound rumbled through the air as the liquid dam of fire broke, plunging Adam into the consuming heat. Three more deep thrusts, and he erupted into Tashi's womb.

With a triumphant moan, Tashi followed him into the blazing pit of ecstasy.

For long moments, their harsh groans and the heavy sounds of labored breathing could be heard above the gushing waterfalls. It was a long while before their heartbeats returned to a steady pace, before their bodies were quiet again. Tashi's knees were slightly bent, her feet resting on his legs. And Adam lay exhausted and helpless within the cradle of her thighs.

Tashi had a satisfied smile on her face as she stroked his slick back and felt the tense muscles slowly relax under her fingers. She relished the feel of his weight, and the final pulsing of his semi-hard ambassador inside her. He never ever went completely limp after a climax. It brought her a sense of power. She was still smiling when Adam eventually lifted his head from her throat and looked directly into her eyes.

"You are a wicked woman, Tashi Andreas. A real nymphet," he said in a slurred, rough voice. His azure eyes were glazed with lingering passion. He brushed her damp hair back from her face then kissed her lips tenderly and sweetly. "Where did you learn that Italian phrase?"

She chuckled, making her muscles tighten around him. "Shania taught it to me."

"I'm having a word with my cousin about his wife corrupting mine. And I don't think I want you playing with those bad wives again."

Tashi felt a distinct feminine glow light her heart as she held his hair back from his face. "Why, because I made you lose control? Now you know what it feels like." She chuckled mischievously. "What happened to all that talk about breathing and holding and controlling?"

"The night isn't over yet," he threatened.

"I would hope not. You wouldn't want to ruin your infamous reputation for keeping control."

Adam's lips ruffled temptingly as his fingers brushed the curls at her hairline. "I think I lost control the day I met you, *cara*. I just didn't like admitting it."

His eyes probed intimately into hers, and Tashi felt a new warmth circulating in her lower stomach. That fierce explosion had left her hungry for more. She had asserted all her energies to giving him pleasure, to making him yield to her. And it felt wonderful to know that she had the power to break him, even though her inner and outer muscles ached from his rough demands.

But the feminine side of her longed for a different kind of pleasure. One that was slow, and sweet and drugging. She needed that, too. She stirred restlessly beneath him.

"I'm too heavy for you," he grumbled.

Tashi winced as Adam slid out and off her.

He lay on his side, resting his head on his arm.

"Are you hungry?" she asked, stroking her fingers up and down his arms.

"I had a heavy luncheon meeting. Maybe later." He trailed his fingertips across her stomach, lightly and intimately.

"Me, too, with the girls. But I have freshly shucked oysters."

"Your shucked oyster is the only kind I'm sucking juices from tonight." His warm hypnotic gaze probed her deeply.

Tashi flushed and trembled from the intensity of his gaze and the evening air cooling her damp skin.

"Are you cold?" he asked.

"It's a little chilly now that the sun has gone down."

"Let's head inside. I need room for what I'm going to do to you next, anyway." He scooped her up in one fluid motion and carried her up the steps of the podium and into the bedroom. He placed her gently on the bed and came down beside her. "You promised to come for me, over and over again tonight, and I'm holding you to that promise."

She delivered.

CHAPTER NINETEEN

Jake Fletcher tightened his jaw as he walked briskly down East 39th Street in Upper Manhattan. He was being tailed—for the second day—and the idiot following him either wanted him to know, or he was an amateur on his first surveillance job. A five-year-old would have made this guy in ten minutes. Jake doubted it was one of Boris' men. They were too well trained to be this obvious.

Or perhaps Boris was messing with his head, letting him know that he was watching him, especially when they were a week away from making their first shipment of girls after several months of inactivity. After that shoot-out a year and a half ago on the upper end of the island, Boris, a wannabe Russian mobster had been forced to halt his family-run human trafficking operation.

Boris was back in business, and seeking revenge for the money and the crew he'd lost—two brothers, an aunt and an uncle, three nephews, and a cousin—manpower Jake and a few other newbies had replaced. Boris had been searching for the man responsible for their deaths, but most diligently for the girl he blamed for all his troubles. Jake knew it was only a matter of time before he found her. Boris had plans for her—personal sadistic plans, before he shipped her off to the worst whorehouse in Russia.

She would have been better off in Sheikh Armad's palace harem.

Hastening his steps, Jake took a left on to Lexington Avenue. Half a block down, he ducked into a familiar bagel shop and headed for the restrooms. The breakfast rush was over and it was too early for lunch, so the place was deserted. He tried the door to the one marked 'Women' and finding it unlocked and unoccupied, he stepped inside and left the door a fraction opened. He peeped into the semi-dark hallway and just as he'd expected, a few seconds later, his tail passed by and went into the men's room.

In a flash, Jake was out of the ladies' room, and in the men's. He grabbed the man from behind, slammed his face into the wall and patted him down. Satisfied that he was unarmed, he wrestled his hands behind his back with one hand, and pressed the barrel of his Glock into his neck with the other.

"Who are you, and why are you following me?" he growled, putting pressure on his lock. The man was about six feet, a couple inches shorter than Jake, and muscular to boot, but Jake was confident that he could hold him.

"It's not what you think," the man said. "I have a message for you. Someone you know asked me to deliver it."

"Who?" Jake barked, not easing his hold.

"I can't say his name, man. The walls have ears."

Jake stiffened. Could someone in the agency be trying to warn him about impending trouble or changes? Boris' business was small and still in its early stages of operation—which worked well in Jake's favor. The FBI was determined to purge it before it festered to inflict more pain and damage on innocent victims. To that end, Jake had gone deep undercover after that fatal night a year and a half ago—the night Paul Dawson died.

"Listen man, I'm not here to hurt you."

Jake scoffed. "Like you could."

"If you look in my left back pocket, you'll find an envelope addressed to you. It was delivered to my place of business two days ago."

"What kind of business is that? What kind?" he demanded, when the man hesitated.

"Check-cashing! I run a check-cashing business."

"Is it legit?"

"Yes. I swear."

Jake smirked as he felt the man tremble under his hold. His decision whether or not to investigate the claim that his business was legitimate would be determined by the nature of the message he delivered.

"If you twitch as much as a muscle, I'll put a hole in your neck." Jake released the man's hands and pulled a white envelope from his left back pocket. He ripped it open with his teeth and fingers. A return envelope and a note were inside. Jake read: *Package arrived in mint condition. Have taken action to make permanent. Are flies buzzing?*

Jake grunted. "Okay, you're good." He pulled his weapon from the man's neck and holstered it.

"Is—is it bad news?" The man turned around, his hands in the air.

"Depends on how you look at it. Put your hands down." He scratched his heavily bearded face. He'd been itching a lot lately. He didn't know if it was a psychological premonition or just a physical irritation, perhaps a little of both. "You friends with the sender?"

The man shrugged. "Not really, but when he and his buddies say dig, I ask how deep."

Jake leaned against the wall, chuckling. "They do have a way with people. How did you find me?"

"They gave me a name and told me to find you."

Yeah, they would know how to find him discreetly. Paul had shared a lot with them. Maybe too much.

"I staked out your apartment and began following you yesterday."

"I knew the second you began following me. You're not good."

"Oh, I am," the man said with a touch of pride and dignity. "But they told me to be sloppy and not to approach you, but to wait for you to go on the defense and only to talk with you in private."

They would make excellent FBI and CIA spies. "Do you know what's in the note?" Jake narrowed his eye, rubbing at his beard again.

"No. It was sealed when it was delivered."

"Good. I'm happy I don't have to kill you. Jake pulled a pen from his pocket, and turning his back, he ripped off the blank bottom part from his note, scribbled something on it, sealed it in the unaddressed return envelope, and turned to the man. "Now, you deliver this. Make sure it gets out today." He wasn't about to ask how it would happen because the less he knew, the better off all involved were.

The man folded the envelope and pushed it into his pocket, then just stood there and stared at Jake with uncertainty in his eyes.

"What you waiting for?" Jake barked, wondering which one of the men held the leash around this dog's neck. "Well, go on. Get out of here. I don't know you. You don't know me. We never met."

As the man scampered out, Jake ripped the note into shreds, balled the pieces in his fist and held his hand under the faucet.

Once the pieces became a ball of pulp, he flushed it down the nearest bowl and left the bathroom.

So the girl was safe and still off the radar, he thought as he walked up to the bar and ordered a bagel and an ice coffee to go. She was tough to have survived, and clever to have found her ally all on her own. Jake couldn't help but smile. Paul would have been proud of her.

Taking Boris down and out was the only way to ensure her continued safety, but the problem was that he had no idea who Boris was. He was a shadow, a disguised voice, and a name, that probably wasn't even real. It was a difficult mission, but not impossible. Sooner or later, Boris' hatred for the girl would cause him to make a mistake. Revenge was indeed a bitch. And she was going to take a huge bite out of Boris Sokolov's Russian ass.

❧

Adam flipped through the photos on the retractable projector screen suspended from the ceiling in his office at A.I. The renovations for turning an old Japanese hotel into a new Hotel Andreas were temporarily halted due to an electrical fire that damaged the main and first floors, setting him back a few months. He probably would have suffered a much greater loss if it weren't for the fact that the hotel was situated in the vicinity of the Imperial Palace, which inadvertently sent the fire department into a panic to control the flames. Luckily, the fire happened at night when the workers had already left or he would have been looking at a much bigger problem.

Shutting off the projector, he pushed to his feet and crossed over to the bar. He poured himself a scotch and walked to the wall overlooking Crystal Lake, the mountains, and gray skies that fit his mood perfectly. A concerned CEO would have been on the first jet to Tokyo after receiving the news, but for the present,

Adam was more of a concerned husband than a CEO. He'd had to explain his reason for not leaving the country and Granite Falls—for that matter—to his father.

Adam raised his glass to his lips. His father had predictably gone into a long tirade about why he wasn't informed about, and present at his only son's marriage ceremony. Adam hadn't held anything back, and as he'd expected, his father had understood, and furthermore offered to travel to Tokyo to take care of the situation. Knowing that his mother would be on his doorstep the moment she heard the news of his marriage, Adam had asked his father not to share it with her, yet. Her presence in Granite Falls would just complicate the problem. He didn't know who these people were and didn't want to make another Andreas accessible for any ruthless plans they might be cooking up. The only person he wanted to worry about keeping safe right now was Tashi.

At the knock on his door, Adam walked back to his desk and set down his scotch. He glanced through the one-way mirror at his assistant. She'd just left him half an hour ago. He'd already signed away his life for the day. Why was she back? He hit a button on his desk. "Yes, Ms. Jenkins," he said, as she stepped inside.

"A messenger just delivered this, Mr. Andreas." She held out a large brown envelope.

Adam took it, his heart rocking in his chest when he noticed that it wasn't addressed. He was about to rip it open and stopped, staring at the curious expression on his assistant's face.

"Is it anything I need to be aware of, Mr. Andreas?"

"No. It's personal. Thank you, Ms. Jenkins. That'll be all."

"I'll be leaving in a few minutes, sir. You know how to reach me if you need me." She gave him a professional smile and a nod and left him alone.

Adam dropped his weight into the chair behind his desk. He closed his eyes and took some deep steady breaths to slow his racing heart. When he thought he was prepared to take whatever the news was, he opened the envelope, and then the smaller one inside that he'd included in his outgoing message. *Keep secured. Trust no one. Won't be long. Cease contact.*

Adam dropped the note into the shredder beside his desk and, leaning back against his chair, he gazed off into space. He still had no idea if Paul was dead or alive. Didn't Jake, the partner Paul had told them to contact if he ever fell off the grid, understand his question about the buzzing flies? Last year when Massimo had been trying to reach Paul, he hadn't bothered to contact Jake because his situation wasn't that dire, and he'd already decided to marry Shaina anyway. Perhaps they should have been a lot more worried about their friend.

Adam pushed to his feet and began pacing. In two days, Pastor Kelly would have to officially file his and Tashi's marriage certificate, making it a public record that anyone with good or ill intent could access. Adam bunched his mane in his hands and tugged on the strands. He'd never felt more helpless in his life. He couldn't fight since he didn't know what or whom he was fighting. His actions were limited to maintaining a semblance of serenity and balance in his and Tashi's lives while they waited for the roof to cave. The fact that Jake was on the case didn't ease his anxieties, but it was nice to know he wasn't alone.

To help him with his mission to keep his and Tashi's marriage from the public, Bryce had suggested moving his parents' anniversary party from Hotel Andreas to Mountainview Café. Trusted members from each of their household staff would manage the serving of the five-course meal that would be catered in from Ristorante Andreas. Galen, who had some experience as a DJ, would take charge of the music and entertainment, and instead of nannies, the grandparents, and older kids would help look after the little ones.

Bryce had also suggested that since Mountainview Café was

where Adam and Tashi had met, it would be the perfect venue for their first formal evening out together. Adam had agreed. Tonight, they would all be able to share each other's happiness in splendor and elegance without worrying about the local press and prying strangers snapping pictures of Tashi. He and his friends had vowed to make this a night their wives would never forget.

There was no reason not to start the fun early, Adam thought on a smile. He pulled his jacket from the closet and walked to his private elevator.

※

Tashi stepped through the door of Mountainview Café as one of the guards on duty opened it for her.

"There you are!" Kaya said, switching Elyse from one hip to the other. "Girl, look at you. Told you you'd be stunning in that dress."

"Wow. You guys look lovely, too." Tashi grinned at the three women hovering in the small foyer. Like her, they were dressed to kill in Zac Posen floor-sweeping evening gowns of silk and chiffon that were studded with precious gems: Michelle in a low-cut, spaghetti strap, thigh-high split warm gold, Kaya in a sleeveless V-neck champagne, Shaina in a red hot, short sleeved scoop neck, and Tashi in a strapless, backless, diamond-studded V-neckline emerald chiffon that Adam said enhanced the color of her eyes. Except for Michelle, who wore a sleek short haircut, they all wore updo hairstyles with curly tendrils brushing the sides of their faces and down their necks. Sparkling diamonds and pearl earrings, necklaces, and bracelets, along with high stiletto heels topped off their attire.

Even little Elyse in a cute pink dress made from satin and French netting looked sophisticated. Anyone seeing them would think they'd walked off a Paris runway and were en route to some ball of the century. And they smelled amazing. When they'd been shopping together yesterday at Joanne's Boutique, Tashi had learned that sometimes these ladies took pride in dressing up, just for their husbands' pleasures, and their families' admiration. This was one of those times, and they'd all decided to wear Zac Posen dresses. Joanne was grinning from ear to ear when they'd left her boutique.

"Why are you so late?" Michelle asked, leaning in to hug Tashi when Kaya stepped back.

"Do you really have to ask?" Shaina, who was holding baby Aria in her arms, brought up the rear. "They're newlyweds. Did you forget what it was like in your first few days of marriage?" She tossed Tashi a knowing wink, making her blush.

"Girl, try after a few years," Michelle said with a chuckle, patting her flat belly they all knew would be rising into a little baby bump soon. "Where's Adam?" She stared out into the empty parking lot which would have been overflowing if the café hadn't been closed in order to prepare for tonight.

"He had to take a call from his father." Tashi had an uncanny feeling that the call Adam had received just before he dropped her off wasn't from his father. He'd looked worried, almost terrified as he'd listened to the speaker on the other end.

"Well, with Uncle Alessandro, he might be a while," Shaina said.

"Yeah." Tashi tried to shake off her misgivings with a smile. She tucked her clutch under her arm and kissed Aria on the cheek. "She's such a gorgeous baby, Shaina," she said of the curly black-haired, brown-eyed baby girl, wearing a pink satin ruffled dress with a matching band around her head. "I think she looks like you," she told Shaina.

"Me, too. But don't let Massimo hear you say that. He swears she looks like him."

"Well, she can't lose either way." Michelle ruffled the baby's hair, which caused her to whimper and clutch the front of her mother's dress.

"She's a little cranky tonight," Shaina explained, soothing her baby. "Had her shots today."

"Hmm. I remember those days. Only mine were double the trouble and sleepless nights."

"Aaahah!" Elyse exclaimed, flashing her black button eyes and a four-tooth grin as if agreeing with her mother. As they all laughed, she reached out her little arms for Tashi.

"Aha, indeed," Tashi said, hugging her tightly and smoothing her straight dark hair. She was starting to love the feel of babies in her arms. They were so helpless and trusting, and impish, she thought as Elyse made a grab for her hair. No wonder all the little ones loved Adam. He let them pull his hair like a kitten pulls its mother's tail.

Come to think of it, he allowed her to pull his hair when she was caught up in the throes of passion. When he'd complained that his head hurt, she'd told him that he should think about cutting his hair, to which he'd responded that she sounded like his father.

"Come, let's introduce you to everyone else while we wait for Adam." Kaya placed her arm around Tashi, her voice and touch bringing her back to the present.

"Who's everyone?" Trying to control the blush creeping up her neck to her face, Tashi followed the women into the front dining area of the café.

"Well there's my brother, Robert," Michelle began…

Tashi's heart jolted as she passed the place where she'd bumped into Adam almost a month ago, and where the spark had started between them—a spark that had blazed into a fiery, inextinguishable furnace.

She and Adam were late for Bryce's parents' anniversary

party because they'd been making love all afternoon. It had begun in her studio when Adam walked in, still wearing the suit he'd worn to the office, and without saying a word, picked her up from her chair and began kissing her passionately.

He'd taken her the first time against the wall of the studio while they were still fully clothed. He'd just hiked up her skirt, pulled her thong aside, unzipped his trousers and shoved himself deeply and firmly into her. Tashi shivered as she remembered the hot ache in her throat and belly at that initial conquering thrust.

The fact that the door was wide open and that any of the servants could have walked in on them had only amplified the thrill of their erotic coupling. It hadn't lasted long. A few more deep powerful thrusts and Adam was coming, groaning loudly as he emptied himself inside her. He'd instantly pulled out and as his hot seed dripped down her thighs, he'd zipped up his fly and carried her down the hall to the master suite and stripped them both naked.

There were still no words between them as they'd made slow love to each other. Their eyes and hands and mouths and sighs and moans had said what needed to be said: *I want you. I need you. I desire you. I worship you. I love you,* until the silent words themselves had materialized into tiny floating matter between them, growing, thickening, lengthening, wrapping around them like sweltering mist, melting them down, then bonding them together into one rolling, heaving liquid globe of flesh.

"And then there's Cameron and—"

"Did somebody call my name?"

Tashi snapped out of her daydream and turned to see a handsome young man in a tux, and an attractive young lady in an orange gown approaching them. The girl was giggling and leaning against the young man's shoulder.

So this was Shaina's brother and his girlfriend, Monica. Shaina had told her that they'd been away visiting Monica's family on the island of Dulcina in the Caribbean. They just returned yesterday and were spending some time with her and Mass before they left for MIT in Boston to begin their second year of college. They were both pursuing engineering degrees.

"What have you two been up to? Why did you leave the party?" Shaina asked, frowning at the young couple. "What were you doing in that dark empty room?"

"We're both over eighteen. We don't need your permission for anything," Cameron retorted, his hand on his hip.

Monica giggled, flipped her hair over her shoulder, and burrowed closer to him.

Shaina crossed her eyes at them. "Cameron, don't think you're too old for me to ground. As for you, Miss Hamilton, in your culture, you're not an adult until you turn twenty-one. Do I need to call your father?"

Cameron flashed a boyish grin that made his gray eyes sparkle. "Oh come on, sis. You know I'm just messing with you." He gave Shaina a peck on her cheek, and then pinched Aria's cheeks and tried to pry her away from her mother. "Give Uncle Cam some sugar."

Aria whined and, yanking the band from around her head, she threw it at him, her bright brown eyes flashing under her long eyelashes.

He stepped aside and, just before it landed in Monica's face, she caught it and swung it around her forefinger. "Look, Cameron, I caught the garter. You know what that means," she said, her brown eyes flashing impishly at him.

"Teenagers. Teenagers in love." Shaina growled and snatched the headband from Monica. She turned to Tashi. "I guess you figured out that this is my pain-in-the-butt younger brother."

"Oh, yeah, you must be Uncle Adam's new bride," Cameron said, smiling at Tashi.

"Yes, I'm Tashi. It's nice to meet you, Cameron, and you Monica." She offered her hand to them.

"Hmm, hmm, hmm. Uncle Adam is one lucky devil. You are hot!" The next instant Cameron was groaning and dropping Tashi's hand as Monica's fist went flying into his chest. "Girl, you trying to break my ribs? Football season is around the corner. What's wrong with you?"

"That's what you get for ogling another man's wife, especially when you have a lovely, intelligent girlfriend of your own."

Tashi took a deep breath, trying to conquer her spontaneous reaction to Adam, as his well-muscled body, clad in a black tuxedo, moved with easy grace toward them.

"Thanks, Uncle Adam." Monica poked her tongue out at Cameron.

"Cameron's right. All you ladies look stunning. Even you, little sweetie," Adam added, kissing Elyse on the cheeks.

Elyse hung on to Tashi as if to tell him that she preferred his wife tonight, but the other little lady in their presence reached out for him.

"Hmm...hmm. I see how it is. She likes her white uncle better than her black uncle." Cameron scowled.

"Well, her white uncle doesn't pester her like you do." Shaina glared at her brother.

"Come on, Moni. When our brown little babies shun their white uncles in favor of Uncle Bryce and the black part of Uncle Erik, let's see how that goes down with them."

They laughed when Monica made the crazy person gesture with her finger and allowed him to drag her toward the room from where music, laughter, chatter, and the delicious smell of gourmet food made Tashi happy that she'd come to Granite Falls.

"We'd better get back inside before Mom and Dad think we

ditched them for a better party," Kaya said, taking Elyse from Tashi.

"We'll just be a minute," Tashi said.

"Don't be too long." Shaina took her daughter from Adam and followed Michelle and Kaya down the hallway, their long dresses making swooshing sounds as they hurried.

"Adam, what's going on?" Tashi asked, as soon as they were alone. "Was that phone call really from your father?"

He averted his eyes for a few seconds. "No. I lied because I didn't want to upset you." He placed warm comforting hands on her shoulders. "I just want you, *us*, to have a good time tonight."

"Who was it from?"

"Someone I'm working with in New York." He began leading her down the hallway. "A man has been asking questions about you. He's been questioning your former neighbors and students at your university."

"Well, we know people are looking for me, so—"

"No, this man was asking questions those people would already have the answers to."

"You think it could be Agent Dawson?" she asked on a glimmer of optimism.

"Paul wouldn't be asking questions about you. He'd call you on the phone he gave you."

Tashi halted and stared up at him. "There's another threat I have to be worried about?" *When was it going to end?*

Adam wrapped her in his arms. "No, *cara*. No one is going to hurt you. I promise. I've already given orders for the man to be picked up by some associates in the city. I will get to the bottom of this." He eased her away to gaze into her eyes. "You are safe. Say it."

Tashi swallowed the lump that had formed in her throat. "I—I'm safe."

"Now put it all out of your pretty little head. Just have fun tonight, for me. I need to see you having fun. Especially when you look so sexy and hot."

His irresistible grin snapped the burdensome chains of Tashi's paranoia and fear. She'd lived for a year and a half by herself with danger looming over her. She was now married to one of the most powerful men in the world, and into a family that would pull out all the stops to ensure her safety. The least she could do was make her husband happy tonight. "Okay. I'll have a good time tonight," she said on a vivid, ecstatic smile.

"That's my girl." He kissed her lips and walked her to the door of the party room that had suddenly become very quiet.

CHAPTER TWENTY

"Congratulations, Adam and Tashi!"

Tashi gasped at the loud cheer as she and Adam made their entrance. Before they had time to recover from the surprise, Monica took her clutch and placed a glass of sparkling cider in her hand while Massimo handed Adam a drink.

"It's your night, too," he said, giving them both hugs, before stepping back to stand beside his wife, along with Michelle and Erik, and Bryce and Kaya who'd formed a small circle, nearby.

Tashi took a quick glance around the room that was romantically decorated with flowers, balloons, red and white heart-shaped garlands, and two aesthetically set dining tables—one for the adults and one for the children.

But more importantly were the three generations of family and friends, dressed in elegant evening gowns and tuxedoes, holding glasses of wine, mixed drinks, sparkling cider, and milk, and chanting, "Adam, Tashi." Even Eli, the smallest male present, was clapping his little hands and shaking his head from the safety of his father's arms.

Tears stung Tashi's eyes as she felt Adam's warm hand in the small of her back. Never had she felt so wanted, and appreciated.

These people didn't even know her, and yet they were welcoming her into their family and close-knit circle, simply because she was Adam's wife.

"Everyone, let's get ready to toast the newlyweds," Galen said, from a temporary stage on the far side of the room.

Tashi waved at him. He looked debonair in a beige tux, with his curly dark hair brushing the white collar of his shirt.

He winked at her and raised his glass. "To Adam and Tashi."

The chinking of glasses filled the room, followed by another round of cheers and well wishes while Luther Vandross' "There's Nothing Better Than Love", a song that was so appropriate for all the couples present, floated from the speakers.

Then one kid screamed, "Mommy", and another "Daddy," and her friends were rushing to the back of the room to take care of their children.

Adam hoisted two pieces of crostini topped with chopped clams sautéed with garlic from the tray of a passing waiter. "Try this," he said, popping one into Tashi's mouth.

"Hmm, that's good," she said as the flavor burst inside her mouth. She was starved, and she knew Adam was too, since they'd both worked up hearty appetites in their bedrooms. She was about to grab a bruschetta topped with tomatoes, when Philippe and Felicia—Erik's parents—and Henry and Lillian, flocked around them, giving them hugs and kisses.

The men looked sharp—both sporting goatees that matched their full heads of hair—Philippe's a rich gold, and Henry's black, both seasoned with silvery strands. And their wives were gorgeous. Felicia—a Diahann Carroll look-alike—in a black, off-the-shoulder sequined dress, and Lillian—dark-eyed and smiling—showing off her curves in a white satin gown. Tashi hoped she looked that good when she reached their age.

"You ladies look amazing." Adam voiced her thoughts as he

caressed her shoulders. "These young women have nothing on you."

"I thought this was supposed to be your night," Tashi said to Lillian and Henry.

"It is, but we don't mind sharing the spotlight," Lillian replied.

"We're just happy that Adam found love, the love of his life," Henry added.

"So he can stop using my granddaughter as bait for chicks." Philippe punched Adam on the arm.

"No! He didn't." Tashi gave her husband a look of disapproval.

"Think about it, *cara*. If it weren't for Tiffany, you wouldn't have trusted me, would you?" The warmth and veracity of his voice echoed in his azure eyes.

It was Tiffany's presence that had calmed her anxiety about him, made her trust him enough to tell him her name. Her gaze wandered across the room where the moon-faced, brown-eyed little girl in a red dress played with Anastasia—an equally beautiful hazel-eyed darling in a yellow dress. "You're right," she said, smiling up at Adam. "It was because of Tiffany that I trusted you."

"And now that I'm pledged to you, you're the only chick I want to pick up for the rest of my life."

"As it should be," Felicia said. "Enjoy the evening."

"You, too," Tashi said as the older couples wandered into the middle of the room and began to sway to "That's What Love is All About" by Michael Bolton. Their love and adoration for each other after so many years was something to strive for. Feeling inspired, Tashi wrapped her arms about her husband and gave him a lingering kiss as they too began to sway.

"You guys need a room? There are children in our midst, you know."

Massimo's voice broke them apart and Tashi turned to see him approaching them, with Aria clinging to him.

"I'm in with the owners at this grand place called Hotel Andreas. I can get you a discount," Massimo said.

"Actually, they told me that you and your wife come around every once in a while to use their facility, and leave without paying. Think I can get the same deal?" Adam retorted with a grin.

Massimo lifted an eggplant fritter from a passing tray. "Tashi, if you have any trouble with my cousin, I'm just a few acres across the mountain." He placed the appetizer into his mouth and licked his finger.

"And what will you do?" Adam asked.

"We'll set Cameron on him." Shaina appeared and laced her arms around her husband's waist. "He made a punching bag out of Mass's face two seconds after meeting him."

"Why?" Tashi asked.

"For having me arrested, among other things."

"Oh." Tashi giggled, remembering how Shaina became Massimo's fugitive bride.

Mass rubbed his jaw as if it still hurt. "You don't want to meet his fists. They're lethal," he said on a chuckle.

"My poor baby was in pain for days." Shania reached up on tiptoe to kiss her husband—a kiss that was interrupted by a screaming Aria, pulling on the bodice of her mother's dress. "Feeding time, I guess." Shaina took Aria and made her way to the back of the room, and into a smaller one.

"She probably needs help." Massimo winked and followed his wife into the room and closed the door behind him.

"Aria isn't the only one who will be nursing back there," Adam said with a chuckle, as he steered Tashi toward a table where Michelle and Kaya were filling plates, before taking them over to the highchairs, three of which were occupied by

Anastasia, Tiffany, and Elyse—all banging on their trays with impatience.

"Take a good look." Bryce, still carrying Eli, fell into step beside them. "That's your future. And don't even try to sneak a quickie in the morning. Before you get halfway to first base, they're bouncing on you. I suggest you enjoy each other as much as possible before that happens."

It may already be too late, Tashi thought, fighting the urge to hug her stomach as she watched Michelle and Kaya place the plates on the children's trays. Their banging and whining immediately ceased as they began stuffing food into their mouths with their hands.

"Kaya and I didn't have the luxury with our ready-made family."

"Seems like you managed to get a few shots in, anyway," Adam said, tickling Eli's tummy and making him squeal.

Bryce laughed. "Even though we're now living on the estate, and our master suite is on the third floor and half a mile away from their second-floor bedrooms, they still manage to sneak into our bed at the most inappropriate times, sometimes all five at once. Locked doors mean nothing to them. They just keep banging until we open."

"It was a wise decision to keep his penthouse suite at your hotel, Adam," Kaya said as she joined them. "And we're headed there tonight after we leave here." Her brown eyes sparkled as she gazed lovingly up at her husband who was grinning shamelessly down at her, leaving no doubt in anyone's mind what they would be doing later.

Tashi jumped when Eli suddenly threw himself at her and, grabbing her cheeks, he dove in and glued his mouth to hers.

"Hey, that's *my* wife. Take your grubby little hands and your drooling, toothless mouth off her." Adam tried to pry the toddler off Tashi.

"That's my boy. Knows a beautiful girl when he sees one, and goes right after her." Bryce chuckled heartily as he cradled his son again who was still drooling and eyeing Tashi as if he wanted seconds.

Tashi's lips burned from his sharp little teeth gnawing her.

"You okay, sweetie?" Adam wiped the last remnants of baby drool from her chin.

"Mama," Eli said, springing into his mother's arms and locking his arms about her neck.

"Now you know how she feels when the little girls give you kisses and play with your hair." A grinning Erik, with his arms about Michelle, made his way toward them. He gave Tashi a peck on the cheek. "You're glowing tonight, light years away from the first time I saw you."

"Thank you for taking care of me, Erik. You saved my life. You and Adam."

Michelle laid her cheek on Erik's chest and touched his face lovingly. "It's always good to have a doctor in the house. I love to play doctor with him."

"I guess we know why you're pregnant again," Adam remarked.

"I—" Tashi startled when, "Uncle Robert! Uncle Robert!" rang through the air. She watched as Jason, Precious, Alyssa, and Little Erik raced toward the door and threw themselves at a tall, dark, handsome man.

Luckily for him, a sofa broke his fall or he would have been on the floor with four rambunctious kids tackling him. He didn't seem to mind the attention, though.

Tashi glanced curiously at the slender, attractive young woman of average height, dressed in a colorful African outfit, complete with a matching, intricately tied head cloth looking on as if she didn't know whether to join the frolicking group or run in the other direction.

"That's enough." Michelle pulled the kids off Robert. She helped him to his feet, hugging him in the process. "Go play," she said, chasing them off. She brought the couple over. "Tashi, this is my big brother, Robert, and my best friend, Yasmine Reynolds." She glanced from one to the other. "Are you guys together, or not, on this trip? They have this on-again, off-again thing," she explained to Tashi as she rolled her eyes at them in open frustration. "Yasmine, the ball's in your court."

"That's right. Just air my business, Best Friend Mitch." Yasmine turned her back on Michelle and shook Tashi's hand. "Nice meeting you, Tashi," she said with a genuinely warm smile. "And congratulations."

"It's nice meeting you, too, Yasmine," Tashi replied. "I love your outfit."

"You look like an African queen, Yasmine." Adam gave her a hug.

As Robert kissed the back of Tashi's hand, and congratulated her and Adam, Tashi wondered what was keeping him and Yasmine from taking the love plunge. It seemed as if Michelle blamed Yasmine for whatever it was. At least they still thought of each other as best friends.

In the midst of her musing, Galen announced that dinner was served. And as Whitney Houston sang, "I Will Always Love You", the adults and children claimed their assigned seats at their respective tables.

For the next two hours, the room was aglow with music, chatter, laughter, giggles, clinks of glasses and silverware, and a few outbursts of toddlers screaming, as the blended families and friends enjoyed each other's company and the delicious meal.

As Tashi glanced from one end of the table to the other, her heart was filled with gladness like she'd never known before, or even thought possible. This was just the beginning of many more affairs like this, Adam had told her.

She was blessed. She was truly blessed.

"Can we borrow your wife for a little while, Adam?" Michelle, seated to Tashi's left, rested her hand on her wrist.

"Of course," Adam said, cutting short his conversation with Bryce who was seated directly in front of him on the other side of the table. "Just bring her back in one piece."

Michelle tossed him a pretty smile and nudged Tashi to her feet as Shaina and Kaya, seated across from them, gathered their dresses together in preparation to stand.

The men hustled to their feet to help the ladies. In fact, all the men at the long table stood in respect as the women stepped away from their chairs.

"What are they up to now?" Adam drawled as they disappear into the room where Shaina had nursed Aria earlier.

Bryce shrugged. "I have no idea. But as you'll soon find out, they are full of surprises."

"Nice surprises," Massimo said, rubbing his thumb across his lips. "Cousin, you remember last year in the limousine en route to Kennedy Airport when we talked about how amorous they became after being together?"

"Yeah." Adam remembered it quite well. "I'm already understanding what you meant. That day they had lunch at the esplanade—"

"That was a night to remember," Erik said, brushing his fingers through Tiffany's hair.

"Oh, yes." Adam choked back a groan as visions of Tashi's naked body covered in whipped cream and fruit crashed over him. God, how could he be hungry for her again after making love to her all afternoon? He had never, ever craved a woman—anything—the way he craved Tashi.

"Can I have your attention please?"

The chatter died down eventually and everyone turned to Galen who'd returned to the stage.

Adam's eyes narrowed as the brides filed back into the room with Michelle taking the lead and Tashi bringing up the rear. They stood below the stage, facing the tables.

"Would Erik, Bryce, Massimo, and Adam, please stand?" Galen asked.

Adam glanced at his friends who looked just as puzzled as he was.

Philippe reached across the table. "Come to Grandpa, darling," he said, taking Tiffany from his son.

Once the men were standing, Galen ducked down out of sight behind the ladies.

The wives each called out their husband's names, and with Train singing, "Marry Me" in the background, they began to read from slips of paper, indicating that they'd planned their speech.

"We love you with everything inside of us, and we know that you love us. We mean, look at us. How could you not love us?" They shrugged their shoulders and wiggled their waists causing laughter to erupt. "However," they continued, "none of you ever got down on your knees and asked any of us to be your wife. We think we deserve that honor."

"You definitely do," Henry shouted from his seat. "Shame on them."

"Ahah! *Same!*" Elyse agreed from her grandfather's lap, which made everyone chuckle.

"And so—" They held up their left hands and displayed their bare ring fingers. "We would be honored if you'd get on your knees and propose to us in front of our families and dearest, closest friends."

Rendered totally speechless, the men began to walk briskly toward their wives.

"Wait." Michelle raised a hand to stop them.

"Mommy, I gotta go potty." Little Erik ran toward Michelle.

"Me, too, Mommy," Alyssa said, racing for Kaya.

"A mother's job is never done," Michelle said, as she and Kaya shook their heads in resignation.

Two staff members led the children away, and soon the amusement died down.

The ladies continued. "Furthermore. None of us got married at church."

"One of them got married in jail." Adam just couldn't resist.

"I'm really going to sic Cameron on you," Massimo retorted.

"In the short time we've known each other, we've grown to love, respect, and trust each other, just as you, our husbands have since high school, and some of you, even since birth. To strengthen our bonds with each other and with you, we have decided to renew our vows standing side by side. And so, we have asked Pastor Kelly if he would officiate our wedding at Granite Falls Community Church where we'll all say, "I do", together."

They held out their palms, and the room was ablaze as four enormous diamond rings and wedding bands studded with smaller gems coruscated in the chandelier lights.

As the four men knelt in front of their wives and asked for their hands in marriage while slipping their rings back on to their fingers, a hush fell over the room and tears were streaming down the faces of everyone who understood what was going on. When they stood up and pulled their wives into their arms, cheers and clapping erupted around them.

"I love you, Tashi," Adam said, his tears mingling with Tashi's as he kissed her passionately. "I'll get down on my knees and propose to you every single day if that is your desire. I love you with all of me."

"I love you with all of me, Adam." Her arms tightened around his neck, and Adam found himself lost, lost, lost in her love, her grace.

Galen cleared his throat—twice to get the men's attention.

They reluctantly released their wives, and as the couples stood, still embraced in each other's arms, Galen spoke. "Ladies, your husbands also have surprises for you. They have chosen songs to which each would love to dance with his wife."

Adam watched as the women exchanged glances and smiles.

"Since Adam and Tashi are newlyweds," Galen continued, "they will have the first dance." He handed the mike to Adam. "Gentlemen, keep it short and sweet."

Adam cleared his throat as he smiled at Tashi. She was the most beautiful thing he'd ever seen. He took her hand and gazed into her eyes. "Tashi, my love, from the second I met you, my heart was captivated by the splendor of your innocence, your purity, your grace. I knew that I would always choose you above everyone and everything in this world." His voice shook as he watched her lips tremble and new tears pool in her eyes. "And so, I ask that you grant me the honor of dancing with you to "I Choose You" by Sarah Bareilles." With unsteady hands, he handed the mike to Erik.

Erik took Michelle's hand. "Michelle, our love has been tested to the max, but if there's one thing we know, it's that it's endless. Thank you for coming into my life, for forgiving my follies, and for being an exceptional mother to my daughter, to all our children. No matter what trouble comes our way, our love will remain true and strong. Dance with me to "Endless Love" by Diana Ross and Lionel Ritchie, my love." Erik passed the mike to Bryce.

"All Of Me", by John Legend," Bryce said, clasping his wife's small hand in his. "Kaya, there was a time when I kept part of my heart from you. A part that was dark and broken, but your love mended it. You healed me, and taught me the true meaning of happiness and the sweet rewards of loving you with all of me. I'm yours, forever and ever."

Massimo took the mike, and Shaina's hand. "Shaina, I loved

you before I even knew you, and I thank God for keeping you for me during the years I searched for you. Your love has changed me in ways I thought impossible. You have shown me that it's okay to let myself be loved. Please dance with me to "The One He Kept For Me" by Maurette Brown Clark."

Adam looked around. More tears were streaming down the adults' faces, and the children were looking on in awe as if they knew something significant was happening.

Then someone shouted, "Okay. Let's get this party going."

Others shouted, "Woohoo," and some, "Come on Adam and Tashi. You're up first."

Adam's knees were weak and his heartbeat was out of control as he took his wife's delicate hand in his and led her to the center of the room. He pulled her gently into his arms and opened his palm over the warm silky skin of her back. "We've danced naked before," he whispered in her ears. "Let's see how it feels to dance fully clothed."

She quivered as she curved her soft sexy body into his and rested her cheek on his chest—right where it belonged and where his heart beat only for her—and wrapped her arms about him, holding him tightly. As their bodies moved as one to the rhythm of the song he'd chosen for his bride, Adam knew that the only reason for his life was simply to lose it to Tashi, to disappear completely into the light and shadow of her beautiful soul. She was the shining star in his inner universe, forever guiding him toward the perfect beginning and perfect end of every perfect day.

༶

Much later that night when Tashi was asleep, Adam eased his satiated, naked body from her arms and the bed. With a smile on his lips, he kissed her cheek and pulled the covers up about her shoulders. Turning, he picked up his cell phone from the nightstand and frowned when he noticed that he'd missed a call.

Damn! His DND had kicked in automatically. With his cell in hand, Adam left the bedroom and walked down the hall to his office. Not caring that it was three o'clock in the morning, he picked up his private line and dialed a number.

"Somebody better be dead," a groggy voice said.

"Mr. Wallace."

"Who's that calling at this hour, baby?" Adam heard a female voice ask.

"Go back to sleep, Sandy. It's business." Pause. "Sorry about that, Mr. Andreas," Eddie said.

"I apologize for calling at this hour, but due to the nature and urgency of the matter, I'm sure you understand."

"Yes, I do. I called earlier, but it went straight to voicemail. I didn't leave a message for obvious reasons."

"So, were you able to question this private investigator who's been asking questions about my wife?"

A deep sigh echoed through the line. "I'm sorry, Mr. Andreas, but when I got to his office, he was dead."

As the blood drained from his body, Adam dropped down onto the edge of his desk. "Dead?"

"Yes, sir. Somebody put a bullet in his head."

"Well, were you able to retrieve the file or any other information he had about my wife."

"No, sir. There was nothing about her lying around." Pause. "I have a friend on the force. You want me to—"

"No. No one is to know you're involved with this man." No one!" he ordered.

"I understand. If I hear anything else, I will call you immediately."

"Thank you, Mr. Wallace. You've been most helpful." Adam hung up the phone and dropped his head in his hands.

Why the hell was that private investigator asking about Tashi? Adam asked himself for the millionth time since Eddie first called him. Could it be about the trust fund Tashi had told him she hadn't touched since she fled New York? Could it be about an insurance policy her uncle had left for her? It was a year and a half since she disappeared from New York without a trace. And naturally, people would want to know what happened to her. But she had no family or friends in the city. And if the private investigator was legitimate, why was he killed, and by whom? Did his death have anything to do with Tashi? Or was it related to some other case, and it was just a fluke that he happened to be the one investigating her?

The only person who might have the answers to the questions swirling around in Adam's head was Jake Fletcher. *Keep secured. Trust no one. Won't be long. Cease contact.*

Jake, where the hell are you? What's happening in New York City?

Pushing off the desk, he left the office and made his way back to his bedroom. Tashi was still fast asleep with moonlight kissing her face. He eased back into bed and spooned her.

She snuggled against him and sighed.

Adam tightened his arms about her. The one thing he could do, was keep her safe.

&

One week after he'd received that cryptic message, Jake was exiting the underground garage where he'd just briefed his allies about the shipment of girls later that night when his cell phone began to ring. He picked it up from the passenger's seat and checked the ID. The identity of the caller was blocked.

He raised it to his ear as he made a right turn on to Centre Street. "Jake here."

"The boss wants to see you," the voice said before the line went dead.

Jake's gut crunched tightly. There were only two reasons Boris would summon one of his men to his den. He had a job he thought no one but that particular man could do, or he was about to take him out. Four months ago, Jake had replaced a man Boris had no more use for. To say that he wasn't scared brainless would be a lie. He was scared. He'd been careful when he met with his allies, but Boris was a smart son-of-a-bitch whose identity was still unknown to Jake.

On a sigh and a prayer, Jake crossed the Manhattan Bridge and drove to the prearranged location where Boris's men would meet him. If they blindfolded him, he'd live. If they didn't, well...

※

"I can't believe you're actually married to Adam Andreas. A month ago, he wasn't even your boyfriend, Tashi."

Tashi and Mindy shared a booth and a large veggie pie at Big Boy's Pizza shop, the place from where Tashi had ordered takeout on a weekly basis last winter. Even though they hadn't been close when they lived next door to each other, Tashi had developed a liking for Mindy, and she did adore her children.

But things were different now. She didn't have to be scared of letting people into her heart. Mindy was harmless. She'd proven that she could be trusted since she hadn't told one living soul about Tashi's stolen money. When she'd stopped to see her at the hotel boutique over a week ago, they'd promised to get together soon. Mindy had the weekend off, and Tashi was free for the morning, so here they were having pizza way before noon. Even though Tashi only had toast and coffee for breakfast, she still wasn't hungry. Mindy had eaten most of the pie.

"So how long have you been married?" Mindy asked, as she bit into her fourth slice.

Tashi did a quick mental calculation. "Actually, today would make two weeks."

"Are you pregnant? Is that why you guys got hitched?"

Tashi tried to maintain her composure. It wasn't the reason, but it was probable. "No," she told Mindy. She took a sip of her bottled water. Her period was due yesterday. It hadn't arrived, and although she had no other symptoms to indicate she was pregnant, she'd made an afternoon appointment with Dr. Walsh. She couldn't go another day without knowing.

"So what's up with you?" she asked, to steer the conversation away from herself. There were still a lot of things about her past she had to keep to herself, things that the other wives still weren't aware of.

Mindy dropped her pizza on her paper plate and grabbed Tashi's hand. "Oh, my God? I'm so glad you asked."

"What?" Tashi stared at her, puzzled to the bone.

Mindy wiped her mouth with her paper napkin, then glanced around to make sure the two men in the next booth weren't listening.

They probably were, Tashi thought, since they were her bodyguards who'd come into the joint ahead of her to scope out the place. Adam had them stationed within arm's length of her since the night of the party.

Mindy leaned closer to Tashi. "I met someone."

Tashi's eyebrows raised a fraction, not because Mindy had met someone, but because of the secretive way she was acting. For heaven's sake, the girl had been in love once and had two children. "Who?"

Mindy sat back and placed her hand over her heart. "I don't know if I should tell you."

Tashi shrugged, and picking up the half eaten slice of pizza from her plate, she took a small bite. She tossed Mindy a skeptical look. She was the one who'd brought it up.

"It's Galen Carmichael. Massimo Andretti's half-brother. Your in-law."

Tashi coughed out the mouthful of pizza. She took a long sip of water. "Did you say Galen Carmichael?" she asked, once she could speak again.

Mindy nodded as she stared at Tashi.

"Where did you two meet?"

"At the boutique. He came in one morning to buy a gift for some friend back in London. Then he came back in like two hours later and asked for my number."

"Did you give it to him?"

"Hell no. I mean, from the way he dressed, spoke, and carried himself, I could tell he came from money. I actually told him that rich boys like him didn't faze me. I told him I wasn't some cheap toy he can play with for one night and then toss aside."

"Good for you."

"But girl, while I was lying my mouth off, I was quivering inside, melting. No man ever made me feel like that. And then when I heard that he was an Andretti, there was no way in hell I was going to let my heart get broken. Those men have bad reputations when it comes to women."

Tashi chuckled. "Well, they can be tamed," she said, thinking of the love and admiration she'd seen in Massimo's eyes when he'd danced with Shaina that night a week and a half ago.

"Well—" Mindy halted as her phone made a choo-choo train sound. She pulled it out of her bag. "It's my mom," she said. "She's watching the kids. I'll be right back." She got up and walked out of the diner.

Tashi smiled as her mind wandered back to that glorious night. In fact, all the men had had that same look of utter wonder, passion, and adoration as they'd danced with their wives. She hadn't seen much of any of them after that night, except Kaya who'd helped her turn her studio into a stylish work area.

Since the staff returned to the mansion, she and Adam had been spending a lot of time at the garden. The acre of charm and serenity had become their own little world. They meditated, did yoga, swam in the pool, ate, made love under the moonlight and sometimes they'd fall asleep on the podium only to wake and make love again in the sunrise. Sometimes they would lie on a blanket on the grass and watch the sunset, and then gaze at the stars popping out and the moon gliding across the sky. At those times, they didn't even talk at all.

While he was at the office, Tashi worked on her photography, trying hard to create a collage that Adam said she could enter at Granite Falls' upcoming annual Photography Premier Exhibit night. He said it was a time when a lot of new local talent was discovered. And once Adam got home, they would escape to the garden.

Tashi knew he was deliberately avoiding taking her out in public because of the phone call he'd received the night of the party. And the few times she did leave the estate, he'd doubled up on her bodyguards. Now, there were four following her instead of two. Tashi wasn't complaining. She loved having him to herself. They didn't even take their phones to the garden with them.

Last night, Adam had unwrapped another sex game. This time, instead of words, the dice had erotic sex positions etched on them. Tashi squeezed her thighs together at the memories of her buttocks perched on a folded towel on the edge of the bathroom counter, her legs draped over Adam's shoulders as he stood in front of her, and deep inside her. It was super erotic to watch multiple images of his jade stalk thrusting in and out of her in the mirrored walls. *God, that was so good.*

This morning, she'd awakened and reached for Adam,

forgetting that he had an early morning trans-Atlantic satellite conference. He'd left a note and a white rose from his garden on the pillow. *Darling, it was with regret and reluctance that I left your arms. I'll call you when my meeting is over. Sei amato, Tashi! Adam.* She was loved!

"Is everything okay?" Tashi asked, as Mindy came back to the booth.

"My mom has to go somewhere, so we have to cut this short. You don't mind, do you?"

"No." Tashi was planning on visiting the camera shop a block over before she made her doctor's appointment anyway. "But you have to tell me more about Galen."

That made Mindy's eyes light up. "I really like him, and he asked me out, but I'm worried about what his family would think about me."

"They're not like that," Tashi assured her. "The only thing that matters to them is loyalty and honesty. They are good people."

"I told him right up front that I had two kids, the first when I was seventeen. He told me that he's illegitimate, so that didn't bother him." She gave Tashi an animated smile. "I miss having you around. I wish we'd gotten closer when you lived next door."

Tashi touched Mindy's hand. "That was my fault. I'm sorry, but we still have time to get to know each other." She'd cleaned up well, Tashi had to admit. And she'd told her that she was starting classes at Evergreen State College in the fall in pursuit of her accounting degree. Andreas International was paying for it, just as Adam had promised.

Mindy nodded. "We have to get together again when I get my next weekend off. You can visit me at my new apartment. It's in the nice side of town, and you can see what I did with your furniture."

"I'd love that," Tashi said as the women left the pizza shop, with her bodyguards covertly bringing up the rear, reminding her of the imminent danger to her life. In the parking lot, she and Mindy hugged, and then went their separate ways. As she got into her car, Tashi watched her four bodyguards get into their two Hummers.

She couldn't wait for this phase of her life to be over.

୬.

Adam ignored the buzzer for as long as he could. He didn't worry that it might be Tashi since she was to call his private number in an emergency. When the ringing began to break his concentration, he apologized to the three gentlemen in Munich with whom he'd been conducting a satellite conference and, vacating his chair at the conference table, he walked to the other side of his office.

Instead of pressing the button as he usually did, he picked up the receiver. "Ms. Jenkins, I'm in the middle of a meeting. I asked not to be disturbed," he said, with as much patience as he could muster.

"I'm sorry, Mr. Andreas, but there's a man in my office who insists on seeing you."

"Did you mistakenly book him an appointment this morning?"

"No, sir."

"Then I don't understand the problem. Have him make an appointment."

"I tried, sir, but he says it's urgent he sees you immediately."

Adam raked his hand through his hair and glanced back at the monitor. He was not visible to the men, but they were to him, and he could see the looks of exasperation on their faces. "Ms. Jenkins—"

"He says it has something to do with your wife."

A paralyzing chill zipped down Adam's spine. His body dropped like lead on to his desk. He grabbed his chest as his ribcage tightened around his heart.

"Mr. Andreas?"

"What—what did you tell him about—about her?" He forced the words through his constricted lungs.

"Nothing, sir."

Trust no one. "Did—did he give you his—"

"Sir. No." Pause. "Sir—you— you can't—sir—"

"Adam?"

A roller coaster of emotions careened through Adam: shock, relief, confusion, joy. His hand holding the receiver was shaking so hard, he had to use his other to steady it.

"Paul?"

CHAPTER TWENTY-ONE

"Yes, it's me, buddy. We need to talk, so stop whatever you're doing. I'm on my way to your office."

Adam took a few seconds to recover after the line went dead. He scampered to his feet, and recalling where he was, he forced composure into his system and walked in an unhurried yet confident gait back to the conference table. "Gentlemen," he said, "I'm sorry, but I have to cut this meeting short. A family emergency has arisen."

"Again, Andreas? Come on. This is the second time," Herr Schneider, the owner of a sinking German hotel chain who'd offered Adam the first option of a buyout said in a voice ripe with contempt. The others voiced their opinions about his unprofessional behavior and about seeking out other revenue.

Adam understood their frustrations. He'd canceled their first *vis-à-vis* meeting a month ago to take care of Tashi, and here he was blowing them off again for her. "Herr Schneider, I realize you may have other investors in mind, and if that's the way you think you should go, then do what you think is best for your company. My assistant will be in touch with you shortly, and if you're still interested in doing business with Andreas

International, we will renegotiate the financial aspect, in your favor, the next time we meet. *Guten Tag, meine Herren.*" Adam ended the meeting.

He walked over to the door and watched the six-foot, two-inch, muscular figure of a man dressed in tan slacks and a striped chambray shirt, and carrying a Mountainview Café coffee cup in his hand, limp—though slightly—toward his office. Adam's eyes narrowed. *Limping.* Paul never used to have a limp, but after the tale Tashi had told him about that night, Adam surmised it must be a result of the shootout. It was the only thing that was different about him, he thought, surveying the clean-shaven dark face, wide forehead, and identifying scar on the right cheek, as he got closer. There was no doubt that the man he was about to entertain was Paul Dawson.

Adam yanked the door open just as Paul raised his hand to knock. In the next second, they were hugging and thumping each other's back with lots of enthusiasm.

"Paul, you have no idea how good it is to see you," he said, stepping back.

"Nor I you," Paul responded with a deep chuckle. He followed Adam into the office and closed the door.

Adam looked him over, from his short crop of salt-and-pepper hair, to his brown Cole Haan shoes. "We thought you were dead," he said, in a voice mixed with underlying accusation.

Paul flashed him a broad white smile and his brown eyes almost disappeared completely between the deep cleft of his sockets and the heavy bags beneath them. "Not yet, my friend. I don't die easily. Almost did in the gunfire that night. Took a couple in the thigh and one in the shoulder." He tapped his right thigh and shoulder, respectively. "I lost a lot of blood, and my memory for a short while. Was unconscious, then in a wheelchair for months, but I was determined to make a complete recovery. Kept the limp for posterity."

"So that's why Tashi never heard from you," Adam said, pointing toward the sitting area. There was no need to beat around the bush. He followed Paul, and once they were facing each other across the coffee table, he continued. "She's been going crazy with guilt about your presumed death." He glanced at the coffee cup, and warm memories of his first meeting with Tashi and that glorious night of dancing a week ago surged through him. "She was a mess, Paul, scared and suspicious of everyone." His voice cracked. "She didn't know the identity of the man you'd sent her to."

Deep wrinkles appeared in Paul's forehead. "The fact that she might not have heard your name over the gunfire had been haunting me, Adam. I knew she'd made it here when the marked bills I gave her began to circulate. But I thought it best not to contact either of you to keep her whereabouts hidden."

Adam crossed his left leg over his right knee. His mind was swimming with a surplus of questions for this man and there was no order to how he would post them. "Why wasn't there any news about the incident, except for the man she shot?"

Paul passed his hand over his short crop of hair. "I promise I'll answer all your questions Adam, but right now I'd like to know how she is. How's Tashi?" he asked, his eyes softening as he said her name.

"She's well," Adam responded with an eager smile. "Safe and well."

Paul reached over and placed a hand on Adam's knee. "Thank you, buddy. I knew you could protect her. I knew that as long as she had the Andreas name, she would be safe."

Adam dropped his left hand over the back of his chair, as if hiding his wedding band from Paul's view could erase the events of the past two weeks, and most profoundly of last night. "She's not just a job is she, Paul? She's special to you."

Paul's eyes pierced his, and his voice trembled as though

touched by some raw emotion. "Yes, she's very special to me," he replied, catching his lower lip between his teeth, just like Tashi.

Adam blinked. *Dear God*. How could he not have picked up on that telling trait? "As in niece or daughter?"

Paul's chest heaved on a deep sigh. "Tashi is my daughter, Adam, and since you ordered a copy of her birth certificate, you're aware that she doesn't know who her father is."

Adam unfolded his leg, and leaning forward, he planted his elbows on his knees, causing the diamonds on his wedding band to sparkle in the morning light. "You're not the kind of man who'd turn his back on his child, Paul. So why are you recorded as *Unknown*?"

Paul closed his eyes and pressed his lips together for a brief instant. "I didn't know about Tashi until a month before that awful night." A faraway look settled in his eyes as he stroked the scar on his cheek with his thumb. "And again, that's something we'll discuss later."

Fair enough. "Our marriage is not in name, only, Paul." He might as well get it out in the open. "Tashi and I—"

Paul shut him up with a swipe of his hand. "Is she happy?"

Adam's heart jumped. He sat back abruptly. "Yes. We both are. It's only been a few weeks, and you may think it's crazy, but we love each other very deeply. I would die for her." Adam held his father-in-law's inquisitive gaze.

Paul's lips ruffled on a smile of approval. "Those are the words every father wants to hear from the man who married his daughter. Your patience, gentleness, and deep sense of spirituality are exactly what Tashi needs. I've always admired those qualities in you. If it were up to me to choose a husband for her, you'd be it, Adam." He took a sip of coffee.

Adam smiled with relief and respect. "Well you did choose me when you asked me to marry her—temporarily."

"I was giving you a way out," Paul said, with a glint of humor in his eyes.

"There was no need. I fell for Tashi the moment I laid eyes on her. To be truthful, I was a bit scared you'd think I took advantage of her."

Paul chuckled. "If it was Massimo, I'd probably be bashing his face in right now. I love that rascal, but I wouldn't have left a bird in his care. He would have swallowed Tashi alive."

Adam laughed. He'd harbored the same thoughts about his cousin. "He's married you know, and has a baby girl."

"Yeah, I know. He made an honest woman of the virgin schoolteacher from Brooklyn he had me investigate last year."

Adam's eyebrows raised in surprise. He hadn't known Shaina was a virgin. Good for her. Now he could tease Massimo about really not deserving her. "You should be happy to know that your daughter was also—untouched, Paul." He refrained from telling him that she wasn't at the actual time they exchanged their vows. "She's a good girl."

A proud smile lit Paul's face. "When and how did you and Tashi meet?"

Adam's face broke into a huge grin. "A month ago at Mountainview Café." He inclined his head toward the cup at Paul's lips.

The older man chuckled and lowered the cup. "Hmm, best coffee shop in town."

Adam went on to give him a short version of the events from that first collision to the day he and Tashi got married—well, not everything, especially not the garden scenes.

"That poor kid," Paul said, wiping tears from his cheeks when Adam was finished with his story. "She's been through hell for the past year and a half. All I want to do is hold her in my arms, tell her I'm her daddy, that I love her, would have been there for her if I'd known."

"Well you were, Paul. You were there when she needed you most. I suppose that's why you're here. Jake gave you my message."

"Yeah, I got that message. Whose bowwow is that anyway?"

"He belongs to Massimo." Adam ginned. "He's not bad. He found Jake."

Paul expelled a sarcastic chuckle. "I'm Jake Fletcher, Adam."

Adam jumped back, his eyes popping wide. "You're Jake? You told us he was your partner."

Paul caught his bottom lip between his teeth again. "He's one of my doubles. Paul dies when they are in play. Jake is my current. I even grew a beard for him. Thinking of Paul as dead is the best way to fully assume my undercover identities."

Adam rushed his hand through his hair as he tried to absorb the news, but then wariness crept along his spine as the words, *Won't be long*, flashed across his mind. Could it be that it was over, that Paul had caught the people who were after Tashi? "So, you're in Granite Falls because…."

Paul pushed out of the chair and taking his coffee with him, he moved over to the wall overlooking the town.

Adam followed him. "Paul, tell me you have this son of bitch. That Tashi is safe."

Paul rubbed at his right shoulder blade. "I wish, Adam. I wanted to take him down before he found out where she is."

Adam swallowed as a knot lodged in his throat. "Are you saying he's here in Granite Falls?"

"No, but his men are. Got here around midnight last night."

"Oh dear Lord." Adam reached into his pocket for his phone. "Tashi is out having brunch with a friend. I have to alert her guards to secure her immediately."

"No need to call her. She's still relatively safe since I'm one of the two men sent to kidnap her and hand her over to Boris Sokolov."

"Boris Sokolov." Adam said the name once and vowed never to repeat it again as both men dropped down on the window seat.

"He's a man without a face," Paul said. "Nobody, but his most trusted guards knows who he is. He wants Tashi badly enough to come get her himself. She cost him a lot of money, plus a lot of manpower. I took out eight of his relatives that night. He had to cease his operation for a year and a half. He's smart. He stays small and deals only in high-end human trafficking. He has a ritual, though. After the girls are drugged, and just before they're placed on the private jets supplied by his clients, he has them taken to this hotel near Kennedy airport, just so they could see his face and know he's the one who sold them. The sick bastard!" Jake spat out the last words with a vehement shake of his head.

"Was the FBI staking out his organization? Is that how you found out that Tashi was involved?"

Paul glanced out the window for a long time before facing Adam again. "When I found out that Tashi was my daughter, I began watching her, trying to figure out the best way to approach her, when this kid—"

"Scottie." Adam said his name with the utmost contempt.

"Yeah. He began showing an interest in her." He shrugged. "I thought it was cute that she had a boyfriend. Of course I ran a background check on him. I wouldn't be a good father if I hadn't. He was a struggling photographer like Tashi, trying to make his way in the world." He shook his head solemnly. "But there was something about him that just didn't sit right with me."

"It's your training."

"I guess. Anyway, one day after he dropped Tashi off at her apartment, I followed him." He shivered visibly. "I couldn't believe my eyes when the kid drove up to this mansion in upper Manhattan. Then two limos of shady looking characters carrying barely concealed weapons drove up after him and went into the house. I took some pictures and ran facial recognition on some of the men. Needless to say, most were criminals and ex-cons. A couple had done time for various crimes, including sexual assault."

"Oh my God." Adam's hands tightened into fists.

"I waited until the others left, then I nabbed that little jerk and beat the truth out of him. Just in time since they were shipping out Tashi and three other girls that same night." He swallowed. "There was no time to involve the agency. I had to go rogue to ensure her escape and survival. In my haste to save her, I forgot to secure Scottie and he alerted Boris's men. Well, you know the rest."

Adam dropped his head in his hands as he fought back the nausea. Paul's voice was a distant hum in his ears as a thousand different ways that scene could have played out flashed across his mind. Tashi could have been hurt, badly. Killed.

"Boris was forced to halt his operation until he built back up his manpower, finances, and acquired more clients. His first shipment of girls since that night was scheduled to take place last night. The agency was set to raid all his secret locations and the hotel—the one place they were certain to get him. But because of your ex, here we are planning, instead of celebrating," Paul stated in an acerbic tone.

Adam's head snapped upward. "My ex?" He pushed his hair from his face and tucked loose strands behind his ears.

Paul took a sip of coffee. "The one who left you at the altar."

"Claire?" Rage coiled inside Adam.

Paul fixed his eyes on Adam. "Some P.I. she hired was flashing Tashi's picture around her old college campus and neighborhood. Scottie recognized her and told the boss. The boss got all the info he could out of the man and then had him killed. Wish I'd killed that little jerk the second I found out what he'd planned for my child."

"I know about the P.I." Adam said. He told Paul about his conversation with Eddie. "I warned Claire to stay out of my affairs. She got an innocent man killed. When I'm done with her, she'll wish she'd never met me," Adam ground out between clenched teeth. He shot to his feet and began to pace. "What is it about exes? When it's over, it's over. Move on. Get a life. They keep hanging around like bad breath stinking up your space."

"You're not going to have her killed, are you?"

"She deserves something far worse than death. She has too much time and money on her hands. What are this devil's plans for my wife?" Adam came to a halt in front of Paul.

Paul cringed and shook outwardly. "Never ask me that again, Andreas. It's not something any father wants to think about, much less discuss, in relation to his daughter. We have to talk strategy for securing Tashi's safety, permanently. I don't ever want to have to deal with this devil again. I'm sending him and his minions straight back to hell in a blast of smoke."

Being an Andreas, who left no spiders when sweeping the web, Adam understood fully. "Is the agency with you on this?"

Paul shook his head. "They know nothing about Tashi. I kept her a secret because I didn't want her identity or whereabouts compromised. Thank goodness, Boris was in the habit of creating false identities for the girls he shipped off. If possible, I would still like to keep Tashi out of it. I don't want her name associated with this operation. So no, I had to go rogue again on this trip. They don't know where I am." He paused. "And to answer your question about why there was no coverage of the shootout, well, the house, thank God, was completely soundproofed. No one on the outside heard anything. I managed to crawl out of there before Boris sent in his cleaners. He didn't want his clients knowing he'd been raided. Not good for future business. The man in the driveway became a drug deal gone wrong, and since his name happened to be on the deed to the house, it was easy to pull it off."

"You made Tashi wear gloves, so there were no fingerprints," Adam murmured.

"And the gun is untraceable. As far as the agency knows, I shot him with his own gun and drove his car away from the scene—a car that I'd already smeared with my blood. Got my ass chewed out, but I pacified them by promising to go back in to bring down the bastard. They'll probably kick me out this time, which wouldn't be bad since Tashi and I have a lot of catching up to do."

Adam stared in awe at the strength, tenacity, and wit of his father-in-law. "You said there were two of you. Where's the other man?"

Paul rubbed his chin. "I gave Leon some of the drugs I'm supposed to administer to Tashi to keep her malleable. He's sleeping in his motel room. I obviously couldn't have him tagging along when I came to see you this morning." He sighed deeply. "I bugged his phone, and just as I suspected, I overheard Boris's plan to off me once I handed Tashi over to him." He glanced at his watch. "I have to get back to the hotel before he wakes up. It's just you and me and the local police if you still have clout with them," Paul said, standing.

"Yes, what do you need?" Adam headed back to his desk.

"We need a decoy. A Tashi look-alike. We'll stage a kidnapping. I'll have Leon call Boris for the meeting location. Unknown to him, I'll be listening in. The feds would be taking down the rest of Boris's gang. And this is probably the time to call your guards and have them take Tashi to the Andreas estate. She's to remain there until this is all over."

"Definitely." Adam pulled his cell from his pocket. His hands were shaking so hard, he dropped it on a pile of papers on his desk.

Paul placed his hands over Adam's. "It's gonna be okay, Andreas. I'm not gonna let anything happen to my little girl. You already know I would die for her, just like you." He paused on a deep breath. "We obviously cannot meet again until Boris is terminated. So you're on your own getting the decoy as quickly as possible. I'm hoping to have this over by tomorrow. I need to see my daughter, start a relationship with her," he said in a tremulous voice.

Adam nodded. "I understand."

"Does Tashi still have that phone I gave her?"

Adam smiled. "You kidding me? She guards that thing like a baby."

Paul tipped his head to the side. "Funny. I called it several times last night and there was no answer."

Adam dropped his gaze and his lips twisted in a secretive smile. "We spent the night in the garden. We've been spending a lot of time there. We don't take our phones—"

"Hey, say no more," Paul said with a knowing grin. "You're newlyweds." He slapped him on the shoulder. "Once you get the decoy and the details of the kidnapping set up, use that phone to call me." He pulled a piece of paper with a number written on it from his pocket and handed it to Adam. "Both are clean. Don't' attempt to communicate with me by any other means."

They hugged, wished each other luck, and after walking Paul to his private elevator, Adam called Tashi's bodyguard. "Hank, take Mrs. Andreas to the estate immediately. She's to remain there indefinitely."

"On it, Mr. Andreas."

Adam buzzed his assistant. "Ms. Jenkins, have the accounting department begin the preliminary procedures on buying out Forsythe Jewelers. I don't care what it costs."

"Yes, Mr. Andreas. Right away."

Adam pushed another button on his phone.

"Granite Falls Police Department. Office Mike Jordan speaking."

"Mike, it's Adam Andreas."

"Hey, Adam. How are you? What can I do for you?"

"Well, that depends…"

"On?"

"I need a huge favor. Can we meet?"

"Absolutely. I'll be over in fifteen."

"See you then."

꙳

When she walked out of Dr. Walsh's office, flanked by two of her female bodyguards, and noticing two male ones waiting at the door, Tashi knew something was wrong.

"Come with us, Mrs. Andreas," the one named Hank said, as he escorted her toward his Hummer. "Mr. Andreas has asked us to take you home."

"Where's my car?" she asked, staring at the empty space where she'd parked it before she went in to see the doctor.

"Doris drove it back to the estate," Hank said, as he helped her into the backseat of his vehicle and closed the door.

Tashi's heart fluttered inside her chest. This could only mean one thing: her enemies had caught up to her, and they were in town. She swallowed back the lump in her throat and as the Hummer took off, she pulled her phone from her purse and called Adam. "Adam, what's going on?" she asked, trying to keep the panic from her voice.

"Sweetheart, where are you, now?"

"I'm in Hank's car. He's taking me home. Are they here, Adam?" Tears stung her eyes.

He sighed. "It's just a precaution. Something came up and I think it'd be best if you remained on the estate. Inside the mansion. No going to the garden. Okay?"

"You're scaring me, Adam." Tears flowed down Tashi's cheeks. "What about you, are you safe?"

"I'm fine, darling. I'm fine. I'll be home as soon as I can. Okay?"

Tashi sniffled. What if those people were holding him to get to her? She knew he'd die for her, just like Agent Dawson. She couldn't deal with the possibility. She wouldn't survive without him. "Are you sure you're not being held prisoner, Adam? Tell me the truth."

He chuckled. "I'm sure, baby. I'm not being held prisoner. I'm in my office. Hold on," he said after a short pause.

"Mrs. Andreas," a male voice greeted her ears. "This is Officer Jordan from G.F.P.D. Your husband is with me. He's fine, but if you need verification, call the station."

"See?" Adam said. "You'll be holding me in your arms soon. And promise me you won't spend the afternoon worrying. No unpleasant thoughts."

Tashi bit into her lower lip. "Okay, I'm convinced. I'll stay home. I'll remain in the mansion. But I will worry until you get home. I love you."

"I love you, too, *cara. Sei amato,* Eve."

Tashi smiled. "*Tu sei amato, troppo, Adamo.*"

"*Che è la mia ragazza. A presto.*"

After ending her call, Tashi took a deep breath and folded her arms across her stomach as she reflected on her meeting with Dr. Walsh. She still didn't know if she was pregnant, but Dr. Walsh had taken some blood for testing. She'd also pointed out some symptoms that Tashi wasn't even aware of: like tenderness in her breasts, which she'd thought was a result of Adam's constant sucking and kneading them, and the fact that her appetite was reduced. That had surprised Tashi. She thought it was suppose to increase with pregnancy, but Dr. Wash had explained that sometimes it decreased in the beginning of the first trimester as a woman's hormone levels adjusted.

If she wasn't certain of the fact that she was pregnant, Tashi would have demanded that the guards take her to her husband. But it would be foolish of her to place her unborn child in danger. If anything happened to their baby, Adam would never forgive her. She would never forgive herself.

Tashi glanced out the window as the vehicle crossed the Aiken River Bridge. And for the first time in a long time, she thought about the car she'd pushed in there sixteen months ago. Was it still where she'd pushed it over, or had it drifted downstream? Would it ever be found and her crime made public? Would they send her to jail if Agent Dawson wasn't alive to testify on her behalf? Her heart began to race with the questions, and soon Tashi felt as if her throat would explode.

"Stop—stop the car!" she shouted, gripping the door handle.

Hank pulled over immediately.

Tashi was barely able to open the door and lean over the side before she began to retch in the mixture of gravel and dirt along the side of the highway. It was minutes before she realized that her seatbelt was still in place and that Caleb, the other guard was standing beside her and holding back her hair from her face. When she was certain that there was nothing else in her stomach, Tashi pulled herself back into the Hummer and slumped back against the cool leather seat.

"Feeling better, Mrs. Andreas?"

"Yes, thank you," she whispered on a ragged breath. "I'm sorry," she gazed up at him, referring to the specks of vomit she'd seen on his shoes.

"No problem, ma'am. It beats getting it in the car which my wife has done on more than one occasion."

"There are some bottles of water in a cooler on the door," Hank said, passing her a box of tissues from the front seat.

"Thank you."

"Here you go, Mrs. Andreas."

"Goodness." Tashi took the bottle of water Caleb had retrieved and uncapped for her. She took a long sip, happy to get rid of the taste of bile in her mouth. "You guys are the best."

"Just following orders, ma'am," Caleb said with a grin. "Mr. Andreas instructed us to treat you like a queen. Always."

Tashi chuckled. "I'll be sure to tell him you've surpassed his expectations, and I'll insist he give you both raises."

"You're the queen, ma'am." Hank's dark face sported an energetic grin. "Are you ready to go home?"

"Yes, thank you. And please don't report this incident to Mr. Andreas. I'll tell him myself," she added, knowing that they reported everything to him. Adam had finally admitted that Daisy had told him about Claire approaching her. He'd promised her it would not happen again.

"Not a word." Caleb closed the door and retuned to the front seat.

Tashi settled down and closed her eyes as the vehicle pulled carefully back onto the road and headed west on Route 80. She didn't need the results of that blood test to tell her that she was carrying the next generation of Andreas in her belly. Except for the time she had salmonella poisoning, she'd never been sick a day in her life, had never even thrown up.

For the rest of the ride home, Tashi speculated about how she was going to tell Adam he was going to be a father.

CHAPTER TWENTY-TWO

Adam awoke to the clicking sounds and flashing lights of a camera. He blinked and covered his face with his hands. Through his fingers, he peeked up at Tashi standing beside the bed wearing a red satin thigh-high nightgown, while he, he realized, taking a quick glance down at his morning erection, was stark naked with no covering. A long-stemmed rose was lying on his groin area. Thank goodness, she'd removed the thorns. "What are you doing?"

"Making memories."

"I'm in the buff, you know."

"You do everything else buck naked. Why not this? I need memories to lay on my pillow the next time you lie to me. You said you'd be home soon. That was two days ago, mister. Then you sneak in here at one in the morning."

"I thought I apologized for that, over and over again. And I remember you accepting my apologies, quite enthusiastically, I may add."

Her sweet lips puckered. "Want to apologize again?" she asked, placing the camera on the nightstand. "I love the way you say you're sorry."

Chuckling, Adam tossed the rose aside, caught her hand, and pulled her down on top of him. Clasping the back of her head, he drew her face to his and kissed her deeply while his other hand caressed her body through the silky material of her gown. The musky, intoxicating odor of morning-after- sex was pungent on her skin.

She moaned in pleasure and kissed him back, but when she began to rock against him, teasing him through her nightgown, he lifted her head from his, and in one fluid movement, he flipped her over on her back and settled himself on top of her. He pushed her hair away from her face and admired her early morning beauty. "Do you realize that when we're together all we do is make love?" he asked. "I think I've made love more times in the past two weeks than I've done in an entire year of my life."

"Is that bad?" She held his hair away from his face.

He traced the outline of her arched brows with his thumbs, and gazed into her eyes that sparkled like green, polished jade. "No. It's very good."

"Then why are you complaining?" She wiggled beneath him, sending fire shooting through his already burning jade stalk.

"I'm not complaining. It's just that the way I feel about you scares me sometimes. I would do anything for you. *Anything*. I would commit murder and treason, demolish companies, and disown my family for you."

"I hope you never have to do any of those things, Adam," she said with a faint tremor.

Already committed one. Maybe two. He still couldn't believe that Claire has sent her girlfriends to occupy the table next to Tashi and the girls just to eavesdrop on their conversation that day at the esplanade. Armed with a photo, the information that Tashi was born in Cleveland, and that she had attended college in New York, Claire had set out to dig up dirt on her, just so she could humiliate her. Adam cringed inside to think of the danger Claire had placed Tashi in, and what could have transpired if Paul hadn't been the one Boris had sent to Granite Falls to kidnap her. He could really strangle that woman with his bare hands.

"Sometimes I get scared of my feelings for you, too." Tashi's voice cooled his thoughts. "But I'm even more scared of losing you. You didn't come home for two days, even though you did call. Where were you?"

Adam averted his eyes by glancing out the row of French doors that led to the balcony. It was going to be a gloriously sunny day, for so many people.

"Adam." She gently turned his face back to her, and tenderly caressed the stubble on his chin and the sides of his face with her delicate little fingers.

"I was planning a surprise for you. A huge one."

"What kind of surprise planning would take you away for two days?"

"Can't tell you. And you're not allowed to ask me anything about it."

"Am I going to like it?"

"I hope so. I hope you love it."

"When can I have it?"

"How quickly can you get dressed?" What he really wanted to do was spread her wide and love her, but there were other important matters to take care of this morning. Once those were squared away, he would love her for the rest of the day. He kissed her lips and attempted to roll off her.

"Wait." She grabbed his arms. "I have a surprise for you, too. I'm pregnant. Dr. Walsh called me to confirm it yesterday. I'm two weeks along. I'm going to have your baby, our first baby, Adam." Her emerald eyes shimmered.

Adam's heart stopped beating for a split second. He'd suspected it, been expecting it, but to hear it uttered aloud filled him with the sweetest joy. "Oh, baby, that's not really a surprise. I knew there was a ninety-nine percent chance the first time we made love." He kissed her deeply, and thoroughly, their tears blending into a river of joy and excitement before he trailed his lips down her body. He pushed her gown up above her waist and dropped a series of warm kisses on her flat belly. "Hi there, little guy. This is your daddy. Welcome to our little family."

Tashi chuckled. "Could be a girl."

He rested his chin on her belly and captured her gaze. "I know it's a boy because I saw him the instant I first gazed into your hypnotic eyes. He has dark curly hair and emerald eyes like his mom."

"Oh, Adam," she said in a breathless whisper.

"And we're not circumcising him, nor cutting his hair," he continued. "He'll be all natural, just like his *papà*."

She giggled as he tickled her tummy. "Natural is good."

"Very good." He crawled back up to lay beside her, but kept his palm open on her belly. "Why the sad face?" he asked, noting the faraway look in her eyes.

She sighed. "I was just thinking about my mom and if she was as happy when she found out she was pregnant with me."

"I'm sure she was, sweetheart. The way you talk about your memories of her, it's clear she loved you very much."

"Then why didn't she tell my father about me? Why is he listed as *Unknown* on my birth certificate? Didn't he want me?" She paused. "Maybe she had multiple partners and really didn't know which one of them fathered me."

Adam's heart broke for her. He wished he could tell her that Agent Dawson was alive, that he was her father, and that he wanted her. But that secret was not his to reveal. That gift, not his to deliver. That was Paul's gift to his child. Paul had already given him a gift by creating that child with Evelyn Holland, twenty-two years ago. He cleared his throat. "I'm sure your father would have wanted you if he'd known about you, Tashi."

A hopeful smile played at the corners of her mouth. "You think so? You think he didn't know about me?"

Paul had filled Adam in about his relationship with Evelyn Holland and the reason she might not have told him she was pregnant. It was so sad. Adam couldn't tell Tashi that story, but he could tell her the truth. "There's no other reason your father wouldn't have been there for you, *cara*. If he knew you existed, he would have been in your life." He kissed her forehead.

"It's not just not knowing my father that makes me sad," Tashi continued in a dismal voice. "My mother's death was ruled a suicide, but my uncle told me that she would never have killed herself and left me alone in the world." A fresh batch of tears gathered in her eyes. "I wish I could find out what happened to her. I wish I could find out who my father is so he could explain why he wasn't in our lives. I can't tell my children about their ancestry. There are so many things I don't know, and I can't— I can't do anything about them until the people who want me dead are caught. And then there's Agent Dawson. I might never know what happened to him either."

Adam's gut was ripping apart. This was wrong, so wrong. Hearts got broken and lives got ruined when people didn't talk to each other, when they we're honest about what and how they truly felt. "Tashi, darling." He gathered her and held her tightly in his arms. It was all he could do for now.

She trembled on a sigh and locked her arms around him as if he was all she had in this great big world. "I'm glad our children will never have to live with the pain of not knowing their father. I'll learn what a good father is all about by watching you with them. Thank you, Adam. Thank you for rescuing me, and helping me find myself, and teaching me about love."

"No, thank *you*, Tashi," he said, untangling her arms from around him and gazing lovingly into her eyes. "Thank you for coming into my life, for loving me, and changing me. And I promise that all your questions will be answered in time."

"You're the only family I have, you and our unborn child." She rested her hand on his that was still on her stomach, and entwined their fingers. "I know we made love last night, but can you love me, Adam? Our baby and I want to connect with you."

As he gazed at her, Adam lost sight of himself in the sacred holiness of her love. "You never have to ask for my love, sweeting. It's yours for the taking. Always." He knelt beside her, tugged her gently to a sitting position, eased her gown over her head, and dropped it behind him on the mattress. He settled her back against the pillows, and the sight of her curly red hair strewn across the white pillowcase fanned the eternal flame in Adam's heart.

"Now," he said, raising her arms above her head and curling her hands over the cushioned headboard, "this is my gift to you. Do nothing, but receive."

Tashi quivered at the tenderness in Adam's blue eyes. They spoke to her wordlessly, spilling the secret desire of his heart to worship her. Her lips parted on a smile, because she knew that by her merely embracing his worship of her body, his would be worshipped in turn as he reached across the space that separated them as two and touched her skin—the doorway to her body—and made them one. Even though they'd made love so many times already, she knew she would never tire of this man, never reach the point in her life when she would not yearn to be joined with him.

She held her breath as Adam drifted over her like a warm encircling shadow. She moaned softly when his thick hair fell on her belly and breasts, glittering like a black threads of silk against her brown skin, grazing her lightly, tantalizingly, stirring familiar desires in her. She moaned aloud when his mouth settled gently on hers and he worked his tongue inside and danced a slow erotic silent tune around hers until she sighed her surrender into his mouth.

Then his hands were soft and gentle on her body. His touch divine ecstasy. His throaty moans a euphoric song. She shivered as he hovered above her and slowly swayed his head from side to side, brushing his silky strands across her sensitive flesh, bathing her in a sea of tingling sensations, heightening her awareness and deepening her desire for him.

His mouth followed in the wake of his hands and hair as he made his way down her body, kissing her lovingly. Her breath quickened, and her heart beat rapidly. Her body tightened and the fine hairs on her skin rose up like miniature antennas, sending sensual signals to him, begging, wanting all of him to touch all of her.

Tashi's hands dropped to the mattress when Adam lifted her legs, brought her feet to his mouth, and began to kiss and lick her soles. Tingling shivers sizzled up her legs and thighs and headed straight to her throbbing sex when his tongue connected with the underside of her toes and tickled her mercilessly, groaning out his own pleasure as he sucked each into his hot mouth.

Exquisite flickers of wanting hummed through her with sated sluggishness, and as her body shook in the throes of passion, Tashi fisted her hands around the sheets and curled her toes inside Adam's mouth. She whispered his name and squeezed her pelvis, trying to hold the orgasm as her breath came hot and soft, and her mind careened. But God, the pleasure was too hot, too intense to be contained. Tashi felt the explosion deep inside her womb, and as her body arced and quivered, liquid love poured from her, ran down her thighs, and dripped on to Adam.

As she writhed in heavenly bliss, Adam spread her wide and stretched himself out on her. "Do you feel loved, Tashi?" he asked hoarsely, as his big warm hands wrapped about hers on the mattress.

"Yes," Tashi whispered in a daze, feeding on the sensuousness of his dreamy eyes. "I feel loved, Adam. But I'm greedy and I want more. All of you."

"As you wish, sweetheart." Adam supported himself on his elbows and knees and took her right hand and guided it to himself. He sucked in his breath when her delicate fingers clasped around him. He looked deep into her eyes and said, "I want you to put me inside you and take all the love you want from me."

Tashi shuddered from the feel of the long thick shaft pulsing hotly in her hand. She pushed back the thin smooth foreskin and guided the tip to her quivering heat. She gasped when the hard column of flesh grazed her slick softness. She gazed up at Adam hovering rigidly above her. Understanding what he wanted, Tashi gave her hand back to him and began to thrust up and down, pushing her hips into his, riding him from below, taking more of him deeper and deeper into the wet quivering interior of her valley of love and solitude and soon the delightful friction of his jade stalk grazing her slickness was too overwhelming and Tashi began to sob from the sheer splendor of him and gave herself completely over to the sweetness of loving him.

As Tashi's sobs crashed over him and her hypnotic green eyes locked into his, Adam began moving with deliberate slowness inside her, each delicious stroke going deeper and deeper as her body melted into his, filling his world with her loveliness. He rocked backwards and forward, side to side, grazed every crevice of her hot wet cave, coaxing their bodies into an exquisite harmony, one with the other until passion's fury churned and soared within them both.

"*Ti amo. Ti amo, Tashi.*" Tears ran down his cheeks and blended with hers as he watched her shriek, her head thrashing uncontrollably on the mattress and her fingers curled tightly around his as wave after wave of contained orgasms coiled through their bodies. And when her eyes rolled back in their sockets, and her lips trembled, and her mouth opened, and her body quivered beneath him, tightened and arced upward like an evening rainbow, Adam died a thousand deaths in the sunset of her passion, only to be reborn in the glorious sunrise of her love, as they came together, over and over again.

A long while after, when they lay exhausted and sated, Adam glanced at the clock on the nightstand. He wanted to stay where he was, cradled in the sweet haven of Tashi's arms, but…

He sighed deeply and kissed her lips. His heart swelled with an amalgam of indescribable emotions when she opened her eyes. "Perhaps we should get dressed and have breakfast," he said. "You have a new life growing inside of you. You have to stay strong and healthy for him. And if he's anything like his daddy, he loves to eat directly from his mommy's body."

Her efficacious laughter was a hallowed symphony in Adam's soul.

"Why aren't we having breakfast on the master suite balcony as we always do?" Tashi asked as she descended the winding staircase to the first-floor.

"It's part of your surprise," he said squeezing her hand.

"What kind of surprise could there be in the formal dining room? I hope you didn't change the furniture or anything, 'cause I love the house just as it is."

"Well, there is one addition, actually," Adam responded as they turned at the foot of the stairs and walked down a long marble corridor decorated with sculpted full figure statues and busts of great men and women of old.

"Is it another statue?"

"Hmm. Kind of."

"What if I don't like it?"

He pulled her against his side and kissed the top of her head. "You'll love it. I promise." They stepped through the curved archway that led into the dining room.

When Tashi saw the man standing at the row of French doors that overlooked the courtyard below, her hand flew to her mouth. His back was turned to her, but his salt-and-pepper hair, his height, the curve of his wide shoulders and broad back were very familiar to her. She'd briefly studied that back when he'd pushed her behind him to shield her from the first round of gunfire.

He turned on her gasp, and that smile, that big, wide, white smile, made her throat tighten. "Agent Dawson?"

"Hello, Tashi."

The next instant, Tashi was flying across the room to meet him halfway. She was clasped tightly in his strong arms as she gave in to the joyful sobs.

"Goodness, nobody has ever been this happy to see me." His voice thundered in her ears. "And I don't think I've ever been this happy to see anyone. Well, maybe one other," he said, stroking his hand down her hair.

Finally, Tashi lifted her head and gazed up at him. His eyes were red and there were tears running down his cheeks. She stared into his kind brown eyes and took in the image of his roughened dark skin. She reached up and touched the scare on his cheek. He trembled violently.

"I thought you were dead. But I'm so thankful and happy that you're not. Thank you for saving my life." She closed her arms about him again, and laid her cheek on his chest, delighted, grateful to hear the thumping of his heart beneath her ears. He was alive. "You walk with a limp. You didn't have one that night."

He placed his hands under her chin and caressed her cheeks,

gazing down at her with affection and tenderness. "I was badly wounded, my child. I didn't remember anything for a while." He swallowed. "That's why you didn't hear from me, and by the time I could put all the pieces together, I thought it best if I didn't contact you or Adam."

He turned briefly and smiled at Adam who was standing at the side bar where a continental breakfast was set up. He was holding an espresso cup in his hand, and nibbling on something in the other. Even though she knew she should, Tashi was too excited to eat.

"I'm sorry you had to spend all that time wondering about me, and living on your own." Paul's voice drew her back to him.

"The money helped," she said with a bland smile. "It's all in the past. I'm just happy you survived." A shiver ran down her spine. "What about those men? Did you catch them?"

"Yes, dearest. The FBI raided them last night. Most were killed in a shootout, including Scottie and the head of the organization."

He exchanged a brief glance with Adam, and Tashi knew that Adam had been with Agent Dawson for the past two days. He hadn't told her what he was doing because he didn't want her to worry about his safety. She loved him so much.

"The few who survived will spend the rest of their lives in prison," Paul continued. "They pose no more threats to you. You don't have to testify. I took the blame for shooting that man. Nobody knows you were ever involved and that's the way we need to keep it for your safety, and that of your new family."

Tashi took a moment to let it all sink in. She'd never thought about how she would feel about the news, when and if she ever got it. But now that she had it, all she felt was relief. She was free. She could live a normal life. "Oh," she said, looking quizzically at him. "I know this is trivial, but all my stuff I left in my apartment—"

"I had it boxed up and stored in mine. I'm making arrangements to have it transported here."

"Thank you, Agent Dawson. I will find a way to repay you." She hugged him again then, holding his hand, she took him over to Adam and held his hand.

"You two," she said looking from one to the other, "are the most wonderful men in the world. Except for my uncle, nobody has ever been this kind to me." She looked at Paul. "Thank you for sending me to Granite Falls. Because of you, I met this man." She smiled up at Adam. "I fell in love with him and I know he loves me unconditionally and completely."

Tashi was sandwiched in a group hug, then Adam said, "Tashi, Paul has something he needs to discuss with you. I'll leave you alone." Before Tashi could protest, Adam was out the door with his croissant and his espresso.

All of a sudden the room was quiet, and filled with tension. Tashi folded her arms across her stomach.

"Let's sit," Paul said, walking her over to a love seat near the French doors.

They sat at opposite ends and turned toward each other. Tashi didn't understand why she felt awkward, but she did.

"Well," they both said together, and simultaneously caught their bottom lips between their teeth.

"You do that, too," Paul said with a chuckle, tiny lines appearing at the sides of his eyes.

As Tashi continued to stare at him, a cold knot formed in her stomach. She might look like her mother, but the shape of this man's nose, his lips, his eyes... Strange and disquieting thoughts raced through her mind along with the critical question that had been bothering her for a year and a half. Her hands twisted nervously on her lap. "Why did you rescue me that night, Agent Dawson?" she asked, her heart thumping because her gut told her she already knew the answer.

His chest rose and fell on a deep sigh and Tashi glanced at the wet stain on his light blue shirt left by her tears. "Tashi," he began, looking directly into her eyes. "I rescued you because you're my daughter. I'm your father."

Tashi's mouth dropped open. Shock rippled through her. She sprang to her feet and stepped behind the love seat putting distance between them. The information ripped her insides apart. For twenty-two years she had longed to know the identity of the man who had fathered her. *Unknown* was what had been written on her birth certificate in the space where the name Paul Dawson should have been. That pain had been locked deep within her heart all these years. And now this man whom she was just beginning to trust and admire was telling her that he was her father. He wasn't a criminal, or a drunk. He was decent, kind, and loving. So why was it such a big secret all these years?

"If you are my father, where were you when I was growing up?" She threw the words at him. "Where were you when my mother died? When I was a little girl, all I ever dreamed about was that someday, some strange man would knock on our door and I would open it. And he would smile down at me, and say, "Hey, baby-girl, I'm your daddy, and I'm home to stay." Why didn't you want me? Why did you abandon me and my mother?"

Paul passed his hands across his face. This was exactly what he was afraid of, what he had been dreading—his own child's repugnance toward him. The pain of betrayal and desertion evident in her liquid green eyes and her teary voice were killing him all over again. He got up and walked over to her. "I wanted you, Tashi," he said in a broken voice. "But I didn't know about you until just before that night. I'd been watching you and Scottie—"

She shot him a withering glance. "You were following me?"

"Yes, trying to figure out the right time and way to approach you. But then my gut told me that Scottie was bad news, so I began investigating him. I learned about his plans for you just hours before you were to be shipped out. I raced to the house to stop you from being drugged. I couldn't tell you who I was because I needed you to have only one thought in your head: *survive*."

Her mouth tightened and she looked out the French windows thoughtfully before catching his gaze again. "So how did you find out I was your daughter?" she asked in a disillusioned voice.

"After your uncle died, I received a video your mother had made for me before she died. In it, she told me about you. There were clippings of the two of you together, playing in the sandbox in your backyard, eating ice cream, of you swimming at the club, your birthday parties with you blowing out your candles, and making wishes." Paul sniffled. "Was that one of your wishes, baby? Were you wishing for me?" He wanted so much to feel her arms about him again, not as an FBI agent who'd rescued her, but as her father who loved her and would die for her. "I swear to you, Tashi, if I had known about you, I would have been there. I would have turned in my badge twenty-two years ago to be the kind of father you deserve."

"Why weren't you there?" She shrugged her shoulders. "Didn't you love my mother? Is that why you weren't together?"

"No. I loved your mother, Tashi. She's still the only woman I have ever truly loved."

"Then why didn't she tell you about me?" She stomped her foot, and her voice raised several decibels.

"Sit, Tashi, and I'll tell you," Jake said quietly, as his leg began to hurt.

She reluctantly returned to her end of the love seat and he dropped down on the other. "When I met your mother," he began, "I was a cop in Washington, D.C. and she was studying pharmacology at Georgetown University. She worked part-time at a coffee shop, and that's where we met."

"Adam and I met at a coffee shop. History repeating itself," she said with a slight smile.

"Yes." He so loved her smile. "You look so much like your mother, and you smell like her."

Her smile deepened and he knew her anger was dissipating.

"We fell in love. We talked about our future—she becoming a pharmacist and me joining the FBI, and then one day, she asked me how I felt about kids. I told her that I didn't want any until my career was established." Paul closed his eyes briefly as the pain of that conversation hit him like a ton of bricks. He wished he'd added, *but I'd give up everything if I unexpectedly became a father.*

His lids popped open when he felt Tashi's small warm hands on his knee. "It's okay," she said.

Her smile was comforting, encouraging. "We were walking down a dark street one night, when four members of a local gang jumped us and held guns to our heads. One of them recognized me as the cop who'd sent his father to prison for drug trafficking and illegal gambling. They wanted payback. I told them I'd go quietly with them if they let your mother go. I told them she was an escort and meant nothing to me. To prove it, they gave her a knife and made her cut my face."

Tashi sucked in her breath, and her hand flew to her mouth as she gaped at the scar on his right cheek.

Paul's body shook on a ragged breath. "As I stood there bleeding, she backed away with her hands pressed against her stomach and tears in her eyes. Once she was out of sight, I took down the thugs, but my heart died that night, Tashi. Evelyn dropped out of school and moved back to Cleveland. Two weeks later, I got a postcard from her saying that it was over and not to come after her. I wrote to her, called her and left messages until she changed her number. I flew to Cleveland to see her. She refused to see me, and went as far as to take out a restraining order against me." He shook his head somberly. "I guess she never trusted my love and commitment to her. If she'd only talked to me, told me she was pregnant, I would have turned in my badge and married her. I just thought she'd stopped loving me." He wiped at a tear.

"I'm sorry." She reached up and caressed his scar with trembling fingers.

Paul caught her hand and dropped wet kisses into her palm. "I've missed your mother every day since that night. I feel so cheated."

"We were both cheated. I guess Mommy didn't know how much you really loved her."

He glanced away for a second. "It eased my pain to know that she named you after my grandmother. Her name was also *Tashi*."

"I have roots," Tashi said, happy bubbles forming in her soul. She wrapped her arms about him, buried her face in his neck, and inhaled his natural male scent and the light odor of his cologne. *He was her father.* He wasn't there because he hadn't known about her. But as soon as he learned of her existence, he'd ironically put his career, and his life on the line for her. She couldn't ask for a better dad.

"Just one last thing, Tashi," Paul said, running his hand up and down her back before easing her reluctantly away. "Your mother didn't kill herself. After I got the video, I began looking into her death. Some rich kids befriended her and forced her to steal narcotic from the pharmacy where she worked. When she threatened to expose them, they made it look like she overdosed and drowned in one of their pools. The people responsible for her death will be brought to justice. If it's the last thing I do, I will make them pay."

Relief flooded Tashi's heart. "Uncle Victor always told me that my mother would never have left me alone in the world. He raised me to be suspicious of everybody. If I'd listened to him,

Scottie wouldn't have gotten close to me. I was so naïve and stupid."

"No you weren't, baby. You were being a young woman, doing what young people do, looking for love. I'm just glad I got that video in time, and that I got to you in time."

"I cringe when I think of how different my life could have been if you hadn't found me in time—" Her face puckered. "Now I don't even know what to call you. I can't keep calling you Agent Dawson."

"Paul is fine."

She shook her head. "No, I've always wanted a father, and now here you are. I'm calling you, *Daddy*. Daddy." Her bright smile matched his.

With his heart overflowing with love and joy, Paul kissed her forehead then he pulled an envelope from his jeans pocket and handed it to her.

"What's this?" Tashi asked.

"A belated wedding present."

"You didn't have—"

"Just open it."

Catching her lip between her teeth, Tashi opened the envelope then stared wordlessly at the form inside it. It was a brand new copy of her birth certificate. Her maiden name had been hyphenated to Holland-Dawson. And in the column where *Unknown* used to be, the name *Paul Christopher Dawson* was printed in strong bold letters. Tashi began to giggle uncontrollably as she hugged him. It was the best gift ever. "Thank you, Daddy."

"Daddy's home to stay, baby-girl. I retired from the agency and I'm moving to Granite Falls. I'm spending the rest of my life getting to know you, and hopefully, my grandchildren."

Tashi looked toward the door as she heard a commotion outside the dining room. "Tashi, *dove sei mia figlia*? Tashi..."

"Arabella is asking 'Where's my daughter'?" Paul translated for her.

"I didn't know you spoke Italian."

"Had to learn it, and French and Spanish, too, in order to keep up with these four billionaires. Just started on Russian," he said, rising and pulling her with him as Arabella came into the room, followed by Adam and Alessandro.

"Tashi." Arabella hugged her so tightly, Tashi had trouble breathing, and just when she thought she could take a breath, she was wrapped in Alessandro's arms. And then they were spinning her around, talking excitedly in Italian, touching her hair, her face, kissing her cheeks. She loved having a family and people fussing over her. She never had that growing up. Her uncle loved her, but he was not overly affectionate. Adam's parents, and her newfound father had no qualms about showing her how much they loved her. Her children would be so spoiled.

"Okay, Mom and Dad," Adam said with a big grin on his face. "I think Tashi feels very welcomed to the family."

"I do." Tashi grinned at her in-laws as she looped her arms around her husband's waist. Arabella looked stylish in a white designer linen suit that fitted her slender petite form perfectly. Her brown, gray-streaked hair fell loosely around her beautiful oval face, and Alessandro, a few inches shorter than his son, looked very relaxed in jeans and a yellow sport shirt. Gratefully, she noted that his black and silver hairline had not receded. But... she thought, glancing at his slightly emerging potbelly...

"Too much pasta and wine," Adam whispered in her ears as Alessandro and Arabella turned their attention to Paul. "You don't ever have to worry about me growing one of those."

Tashi giggled. "Have respect for your father," she said, feeling a sense of pride that her father spoke Italian like a native. And now that he was moving to Granite Falls, he could help her with lessons while Adam was at work.

"Tashi." Alessandro came back to her. "I apologize for my behavior the day we spoke via satellite. I was out of line."

"It's okay, Alessandro—"

"No, *cara*. We are Mom and Dad," Arabella said, her brown eyes twinkling with happiness.

"Two new dads and one new mom in one day. What more can a girl ask for?" Tashi said, handing her birth certificate to Alessandro. "I have a father. You can query him about my ancestry to see if I'm good enough for your son." She shared a big smile with her dad.

Without even glancing at the certificate, Alessandro placed it on the dining table, and clasped both hands to Tashi's cheeks. "*Sei la cosa migliore mai accadere a mio figlio. E non mi interessa se vi erano di legno intagliato e Geppetto è tuo padre. Ti amo, figlia.*" He kissed her full on the lips.

Tashi had no idea what he said, except that he loved her. That was all she needed. "*Ama anche tu, papà.*" She kissed him back.

"Hmm, a quick study," Arabella murmured, smiling at Tashi.

"In everything, Mom," Adam said, winking at his mother. He pulled Tashi into his arms and bending down he covered her mouth in a long sweet, shameless kiss while the family cheered them on.

Then Prudence came in to inform them that breakfast was ready, followed by a maid, carrying a pair of Tashi's sandals, which she helped her slip on. It was a beautiful Sunday morning so they were *mangiare fuori* on the terrace.

"You ladies go ahead. We men need a moment," Alessandro said.

Arabella placed her arm around Tashi's shoulder. "Come on, *cara*, we have a lot of catching up to do and vacations to plan."

. . .

As soon as the ladies were out of earshot, Alessandro fished two photos from his pocket and handed them to Adam. "These were the photos Sheikh Armad had of your wife. I spoke to his father. You'll have no problems from him."

Adam's hands trembled as he gazed at the first photo of Tashi in white shorts and a blue blouse, standing on the steps of the MET in New York City. The second photo was a headshot. She stared back at him through smiling, innocent eyes. Under different circumstance, Adam's heart would have skipped a beat as he gazed at her. But thoughts of where those photos had been, and the reasons they'd been taken filled him with disgust. He fisted them in his palm, and tossed them into the unlit fireplace. "Thanks, Dad. Sheikh Armad was next on my list."

"I've saved you the trouble."

"And we're working on getting the girls that were abducted and sold to him back home," Paul told Alessandro. "The FBI, and several other organizations are launching a global campaigned to stop this heinous crime against women and children. It's a never-ending war."

"But we'll never give up," Alessandro said, as they began to follow the ladies down the corridor at a leisurely and safe distance. He turned to Adam. "It seems we've expanded into the jewelry business, hmm."

"Not for long, Dad. Not for long. I'm dismantling the company. In good faith and out of respect, I've offered Mr. and Mrs. Forsythe a substantial retirement with strict stipulations in place. It will become null and void if they extend as much as a penny to their daughter, whom I've instructed them, has to move out of the family home. She'll either have to marry into money, or work for a living like the rest of us. As for the employees, I'm making arrangements for them to find work elsewhere."

"What will you do with the empty lot?"

Adam smiled. "I know of an emerging computer company

that could use the space. McCall & Co. Computer Services. I hope you're not too disappointed that this buy-out is a total loss."

"Well, you win some and you lose some. All for a good cause." Alessandro squeezed Adam's shoulders. "You are truly my son. I'm proud of you, Adamo. Now, when will I be bouncing my first grandchild on my knees?"

"Our first grandchild," Paul corrected from Adam's other side.

"In eight and a half months, my wife just informed me," Adam said, his heart racing and his flesh warming as he looked at his mother and his wife—the two most important women in his life—walking arm in arm in front of him.

The grandfathers-to-be slapped Adam on the back. "Congratulations, son," they said in unison.

"And I hear there's a grand wedding in our future. Four brides for four grooms," Alessandro continued.

"Yes, sir," Paul relied. "And I cannot wait to give my daughter away to my dearest, most trusted friend." He squeezed Adam's shoulder.

"It's an honor and a blessing to have her, Paul. Thank you for creating her, and for sending her to me." Adam threw his arm around Paul's shoulder. He really loved this man.

"Have you told your wife why your mother and I are in Granite Falls?" Alessandro asked as the butler opened the door that led to the porch.

Adam smiled. "Later, Dad, I'll tell her of your generous gift to take over the company for a whole month while we honeymoon on *L'isola di Andreas* in the Mediterranean."

Satisfied, Alessandro turned his enquiries to Paul as they descended the steps to the terrace. "Paul, I heard on the news that Boris Sokolov and his accomplice, a Leon Tidwell, were fatally shot while trying to escape arrest from the local police, last evening."

"That's exactly what I heard, too," Paul replied, matter-of-factly.

"Hmm. And where will the rest of that organization be vacationing after their trials?"

"As soon as I get the word, I'll let you know, Alessandro."

EPILOGUE

One year later on a rainy night...

From the door of the nursery, Adam watched his infant son nursing at his mother's left breast, his little pink mouth clamped tight, and a smile of sheer joy was spread across his ruddy little face. Adam knew exactly how he felt, the pleasure he was getting from sucking at her breast.

Adamo Alessandro Christopher Andreas, The Third—Alex —for short, was a beautiful healthy boy with dark curly hair and his mother's gorgeous, emerald eyes—exactly as he'd seen him in Tashi's eyes. "Didn't I predict our firstborn would be a boy?" he asked, walking over to tower over his little family.

"Yes," Tashi said, smiling up at him. "And now Mom and I have to redo the nursery," she added, glancing around the room with silk wallpaper with little ballerinas in tutus floating in midair. "Michelle and I should switch nurseries."

"You ladies tried to prove me wrong. Perhaps you'll believe that our second bundle of joy will be a gorgeous baby girl with red hair and blue eyes." Adam knelt down on the other side of the nursing chair. He leaned over and kissed his son's cheek as he removed his chubby little hand from his mother's right breast and clasped it in his own.

Adam swore the boy winked at him as he slipped the forefinger of his other hand beneath the strap of Tashi's white cotton gown. They'd played this game of "suckling from the fountain of love" many times before, and they would be playing it for many more months in the future. It was a game they all enjoyed.

Adam held Tashi's gaze as he eased the strap down her shoulder until her rosy nipple and full delectable breast, bursting with nourishment, was in full view. His mouth watered as he felt the familiar stirring in his groin. "Hmm," he said, dipping his head to close his mouth over her juicy bell of love.

"Oh, God," Tashi moaned as a series of shocking waves ripped through her abdomen and settled into the core of her womanhood. She tightened one arm around her son and the other around her husband and gave herself over to the pleasure of feeding them her love...

THE END

TRANSLATION PAGE

Italian	English
A presto.	See you soon
Abbastanza!	Enough
Allettante	Tempting
Andiamo, cara	Come on, cara
Apri gli ochi	No, no. Open your eyes
Bella	Beautiful
Dio. Sono ubriaco con la vostra essenza, annegando nel tuo amore, mia cara. Dolore per il sapore delizioso di voi sulla mia lingua	God. I'm drunk with your essence, drowning in your love, my darling. I ache for the delightful taste of you on my tongue
Dove sei mia figlia	Where are you my daughter?
L'odore è inebriante.	Your smell is intoxicating
La camera dell'amore	Room of love
Lei era la spezia e il sapore al suo stufato	She was the spice and the flavor to his stew
Mamma, papà, non si sa di Tashi è qui, o nelle Granite Falls. Apprezzerei il vostro silenzio	Mom, Dad, no one knows Tashi is here, or in Granite Falls. I'd appreciate your silence
Okay, terrò silenziosa per ora, ma—	Okay, I'll keep silent for now, but—
Mamma, papà, per favore, voi stessi contengono. Non voglio che lei spaventata	Mom, dad, contain yourselves, please. I don't want her scared

Mia dolce	My sweet
Moltissimo, grazie signora.	Very much, thank you ma'am
Non ti preoccupare, cara	Don't worry, darling
Ottenere un taglio di capelli, per favore. Rendere felice il tuo paparino.	Get a haircut, please. Make your father happy
Perché lei non dovrebbe rispondere? Lei ha qualcosa da nascondere, Adamo?	Why shouldn't she respond? Does she have something to hide, Adamo?
Addio	Goodbye
Perdonami	Forgive me
Perdonami, cara	Forgive me cara
Perfetto	Perfect
Polizia Segreta	Secret Police
Sei amato	You are loved
Sei la cosa migliore mai accadere a mio figlio. E non mi interessa se vi erano di legno intagliato e Geppetto è tuo padre. Ti amo, figlia	You are the best thing to ever happen to my son. And I don't care if you were carved out of wood and Geppetto is your father. I love you, daughter
Sì cara, era destino	Yes, darling, it was fate
Sì, così caldo, così caldo e selvaggio. Vieni per me, mia dolce piccola Tashi. Vieni per me. Vieni!	Yes, so hot, so hot and wild. Come for me, my sweet little Tashi. Come!
Sì, meglio	Yes, better
Sì. Sì. Vieni, mia cara. Mi si bagnano nel tuoi amore succhi	Yes... Yes... Come, my darling. Bathe me in your love juices

Squisita, bella, proprio bella	Exquisite, beautiful, just lovely
Squisoto, semplicemente squisito	Exquisite, simply exquisite
Tesora, ciò che è sbagliato	Darling, what's wrong?
Ti amo, mio figlio	I love you, my son
Ti amo, troppo, Papà	I love you, too, Dad
Tre volte è il fascino, mio caro ragazzo	Three time's the charm, my darling boy
Tu cara bambina	You poor baby
Tu sei amato, troppo, Adam	You are loved too, Adam
Che è la mia ragazza	That's my girl
Va bene, allora	All right, then
Vedo l'ora, mia cara.	I look forward to it, my darling
Vieni, Bella. Mi si permetta di prendersi cura di quel mal di testa per voi	Come, Bella. Allow me to take care of that headache for you

NOTE FROM THE AUTHOR

Dear Reader,

I hope you enjoyed following Adamo and Tashi on their journey to love and *Happily Ever After*. My wish is that you find your very own Adamo to cater to all your needs—the good, the bad, and the ugly.

Blessings,
    Ana

ABOUT THE AUTHOR

Inspired by the strong heroines and flawed alpha heroes in the stories she read as a young girl, *New York Times* and *USA Today* Bestselling Author, Ana E Ross writes steamy and sophisticated, multicultural contemporary romance novels. Her drama-filled stories feature charming, powerful, larger-than-life billionaires and strong, independent women who fight and love with equal passion.

Born and raised in Nevis, Ana now lives in the Northeast, U.S., and loves traveling, tennis, yoga, meditation, everything Italian, and spending time with her daughter.

www.anaeross.com
ana@anaeross.com

Made in the USA
Coppell, TX
27 August 2023